Conversationally he said, 'Tomorrow you are moving to a different city.'

'Where?' she asked dully.

'It doesn't matter,' he answered. 'It's a different country.' He smiled at her. 'A nice country.'

She took this into her drugged mind and then asked anxiously, 'Will you be coming with me?'

He shook his head. 'No, my job is done now.'

Anxiety registered in her mind. She pointed at the syringe. 'What about that?'

He smiled again. 'Don't worry about that. Someone will be there to give it to you.'

She tried to think through the haze of her brain. 'Will I have to do those things before they give it to me?'

'Yes,' he said nonchalantly. 'But as time passes you won't mind so much.'

She turned away, knowing that she was now a slave.

A. J. Quinnell is the pseudonym of the author of seven previous novels including *Man on Fire*, *In the Name of the Father* and *The Perfect Kill*. He lives on an island in the Mediterranean.

ALSO BY A. J. QUINNELL

THE
BLUE RING

A. J. Quinnell

ORION

An Orion paperback
First published in Great Britain by Chapmans Publishers in 1993
This paperback edition published in 1994 by Orion Books Ltd,
Orion House, 5 Upper St Martin's Lane, London WC2H 9EA

A CIP catalogue record for this book is available from the
British Library.

ISBN: 1 85797 419 0

Printed in England by Clays Ltd, St Ives plc

For Agnes Kwok Sheung Wah
who helped restart my brain

PROLOGUE

Hanne Andersen opened her eyes not knowing where she was. Very quickly she became aware of things: the dull ache in the centre of her head, the dry sour taste in her mouth, the fact that she could not move her arms or legs, the cracked, dirty ceiling above her. Painfully she turned her head, first to one side, then to the other. She was in a small box-like room with no windows, just a grey heavy metal door. Her wrists and ankles were tied to the four corners of the bed. She was clad in the same flame-red dress that she had put on the night before. Cold terror paralysed her as she tried to remember what had happened.

She recalled Philippe picking her up from her hotel, the noisy restaurant and the myriad drinks, starting with wine and moving on to tequila-slams. It became vague after that, a couple of bars and then a very sleazy nightclub in the Rue Saint Sans. She remembered laughing a lot and Philippe also laughing as they watched the sex-show which both nauseated her and aroused her. After that everything was a blank.

An hour passed before she heard the turning of the lock in the metal door. Philippe came in and stood by the bed, looking down at her. He was dressed in the same dark blue suit, white silk shirt and maroon tie that he had worn the night before, but the suit was rumpled and the knot of the tie pulled down. His sharply handsome face was covered in black stubble.

Her voice came out as a croak. 'Where am I, Philippe? What happened?'

His eyes no longer held the spark of laughter, his smile no longer lit his face; it was a sneer. His gaze travelled down her body and he reached down and pulled up the red dress. She wore the wispiest of

7

white lace knickers. He looked at them, muttered something in French and although she had only been learning the language for two months she understood the words.

'A pity ... a great pity ... but orders are orders.' He sneered again. 'But a little something will not hurt.'

He reached down and slid a hand under the waistband of her knickers and onto her crotch. She tried to close her legs but they were bound tightly apart. She screamed.

He said, 'Make all the noise you want. No one can hear you.'

As he tried to push a finger inside her she gave an involuntary spasm and her bladder gave out. With an expression of disgust he pulled his hand away, straightened up and left the room. He returned in five minutes carrying a small metal tray. On it was a syringe, some cotton wool and a bottle containing a colourless liquid. He put the tray down beside her head and sat down next to her. Quickly he pulled up the sleeve of her dress, opened the bottle and put some of the liquid onto the cotton wool. He rubbed the cotton wool vigorously against the inside of her arm, then he held up the syringe.

'Look at this,' he said in a coarse whisper. 'This is your friend. It will make you feel good ... very good. It will take away your fear and your headache. Your friend will visit you many times in the coming days.'

Her body jerked as the needle entered her vein. She screamed again. He sneered again. Within minutes her body and mind began to glow. Her headache and her fear disappeared. She heard his voice as if it was floating near the ceiling.

'Soon a woman will come and clean you up. She will bring you some hot soup. Later I will come again ... with your friend.'

Jens Jensen's office was also very small, without windows, and in need of a coat of paint. As a young detective in the Missing Persons Bureau of the Copenhagen police force he did not merit anything grander. Short, florid of face and somewhat plump, he looked more like a banker than a policeman. He was dressed in a conservative grey suit, a cream shirt and blue tie and black alligator-skin shoes. He sighed in exasperation as he finished reading the report which had arrived that morning from the Marseille police. Then a wave of anger swept over him. He closed the folder, stood up, went out of his office and marched down the corridor.

Chief Superintendent Lars Pedersen's office was spacious, carpeted, and had wonderful views over the Tivoli Gardens. He was thin with grey hair, sharp-faced and looked very much like a policeman. He looked up as Jens Jensen swept into the room and noted the expression on his subordinate's face.

'What now?' he asked.

Without a word, Jensen laid the folder in front of him and then walked away and gazed out over the view.

Pedersen had recently taken a course in speed-reading and it only took him four minutes to get the guts of the detailed report. 'So?' he asked.

Jensen turned to face him. Harshly he said, 'So she's the fourth this year. Two in Spain, one on the French Riviera and one in Rome. And it's still only mid-May. The Swedes have lost three and the Norwegians two ... all in southern Mediterranean holiday countries ... not one found.' His voice was tight with anger. 'It follows the same pattern: single Scandinavian girls, either on holiday or studying in those countries.' He pointed at the folder. 'Hanne Andersen, nineteen years old, very attractive, studying French at a private institute in Marseille. Last seen leaving her small hotel at ten p.m. on the fourth of September and getting into a black Renault driven by a young man who looked French, whatever that means. That's all we know.'

Pedersen mused. 'And all the others were attractive or beautiful, including the Swedes and Norwegians?'

'They were,' Jensen affirmed. 'You've seen my report and the photographs ... and you've also read my recommendations.'

Pedersen sighed and pushed the folder away from him as if to dismiss it. 'Yes, yes. You want to set up a special unit. You have this theory of an organised ring engaged in a modern white slave trade.'

Jens Jensen was thirty-five years old. Were it not for the short fuse of his temper and his inability to show unbridled respect to his seniors he might well have progressed further in the force. He consoled himself with the love of exotic beers and a fascination for sea ferries. But now his anger erupted.

'Theory!' he snarled. 'I've spent four years in Missing Persons. I've liaised with Stockholm and Oslo. I've travelled to Paris, Rome and Madrid on a lousy fucking expense account.' He moved around in front of the Chief Superintendent's desk as his anger mounted. 'I'm the poor bastard who has to tell the parents of these girls that there's fuck all we can do.' He slammed the side of his hand onto the folder. 'This afternoon Mr and Mrs Andersen are coming to my lousy little office to sit in front of my lousy, fifty-year-old desk and listen to me tell them that their daughter has disappeared and by now is probably a forced junkie and selling her body for the benefit of some spic pimps.'

Pedersen sighed again, and in a patient voice said, 'Jens, you know the problem. It comes right down to money. We have over four hundred missing persons reports a year in Copenhagen alone. Our budget is limited and gets more limited year by year. The special unit that you want to set up has been costed out as something over ten million kroner a year. The finance committee will not approve. It's just not cost-effective. Not just for a dozen girls a year ... forget it.'

Jens Jensen turned and headed for the door, saying over his shoulder, 'So I'll send Mr and Mrs Andersen to see the finance committee.' At the door he turned and looked at his boss. 'Perhaps they can explain to them about budgets ... and about "The Blue Ring".'

ONE

It was a hot late September evening on the small Mediterranean island of Gozo when Father Manuel Zerafa drove his old battered Ford to the house on the ridge. It was a very old, converted farmhouse which commanded superb views over the island and across the sea to the tiny island of Comino and the big island of Malta. He was sweating slightly as he pulled the old metal bell-handle set into a vast stone wall. After a minute the door opened. A big man stood there. He had close-cropped grey hair above a well-travelled square face; a long scar down one cheek, another on the chin, another on the right side of his forehead. The man was dressed only in a swimsuit. His body was large and tight and deeply tanned. It also bore scars; one from the right knee almost to the groin, another from the right shoulder to the waist. Father Zerafa knew the man well; knew that on his back were other scars. The little finger of his left hand was missing. Father Zerafa knew how the man had come by some of those scars. Mentally, Father Zerafa crossed himself.

He said, 'Hello, Creasy. It's bloody hot and I need a cold beer.'

The man stood back and gestured a welcome.

They sat under a bamboo canopy covered by vines and mimosa, the swimming pool was in front of them, looking blue, cool and inviting. Beyond it was the panoramic view. Father Zerafa decided that if he sat there for a hundred years he would never tire of that view.

The big man brought two ice-cold beers and then looked a question at the priest. They were very old friends and, although the priest often dropped by for a cold beer on a hot day, the man knew that this visit was not just a courtesy call.

'It's about Michael,' the priest started.

'What about Michael?'

The priest took a sip of beer and said, 'It's Thursday and I know he's in Malta today with George Zammit. What time will he be back?'

Creasy looked at his watch. 'He should have caught the seven o'clock ferry, so he'll be back in half an hour. What is it?'

'It's about his mother.'

Creasy looked astonished. 'His mother!'

The priest sighed and then said firmly, 'Yes, his mother. She's in St Luke's hospital, dying of cancer. Apparently she only has a few days to live.'

'So what?'

In an even firmer voice the priest replied, 'So she wants to see Michael before she dies.'

'Why?'

The priest shrugged. 'I got a call from Father Galea who ministers to the sick and dying at St Luke's. She asked him about her son. She asked him if he was still in the orphanage. She told him she wanted to see his face before she died.'

Creasy's voice was as cold as a glacier. 'She hardly saw his face when he was born. She abandoned him ... You know how she did that. You told me.'

'Yes, I told you.'

'Tell me again.'

The priest sighed.

'Tell me again, Father!'

The priest looked at him and said, 'The doorbell rang at night at the orphanage of the Augustine sisters in Malta. One of the sisters opened it. There was a basket on the doorstep covered with a cloth. A car was pulling away. In the car the sister saw the face of a woman and the face of a man ... obviously the face of Michael's natural mother and the face of her pimp.'

There was a long silence while the two men gazed out over the view, then the priest said quietly, 'Understand, Creasy. I have to tell Michael that she wants to see him. That's my duty.'

Harshly, Creasy replied, 'Your duty is to Michael. You raised him in the orphanage until I adopted him. He never knew his mother but you and I both know that he hated the thought of her. His mother was a whore, more interested in making money than in her own flesh and blood. You also know that Michael has been through hell. Why make it worse?'

Another silence. The priest's glass was empty. He looked up at the man and said, 'Go and get me another cold beer. When you come back I'll tell you.'

He spoke in a tone of voice that few people would ever use, or dare to use, to Creasy. For a long time Creasy looked at him through narrowed, slate-grey eyes. Then he shrugged, stood up and went into the kitchen.

With a fresh beer in front of him the priest talked quietly. He reminded Creasy of the time two years before when they had sat together on the church steps and watched a game of football between the orphanage and the village of Sannat. Michael had been seventeen then and was the most talented and co-ordinated player on the field. Father Zerafa ran the orphanage and coached the football team. Creasy had watched the game intently and enquired about Michael. Enquired in detail. The priest had explained that Michael's mother had been a prostitute in the Maltese red-light district of Gzira. Michael had been fathered by one of her clients, almost certainly an Arab, which gave Michael his dark looks. She had abandoned the child at birth and he had been raised at the orphanage in Gozo. Two adoption attempts had failed, then Creasy had watched him play football. Father Zerafa had been astonished at the adoption, for Creasy's wife and four-year-old daughter had been killed only a few months previously, on the terrorist bombing of Pan Am 103 over Lockerbie.

Creasy was a retired, legendary mercenary. The priest knew that his adoption of Michael had been a cynical arrangement to bind a young man to him and train him in his own image. To do so he had to enter into a contract of marriage with a failed English actress, who had been subsequently killed by terrorists. He and Michael had gone on to exact their own personal vengeance and in doing so had forged a bond as close as two human beings could ever accomplish.

The priest reminded Creasy of all this and of his own complicity in arranging the adoption, knowing what was behind it. He had watched Michael as Creasy had turned him into a finely tuned killing machine; waited while they went to the Middle East and exacted their vengeance. He had seen them return to Gozo and noted the extraordinary bond between them.

'Michael is a man,' the priest said quietly. 'You made him so. He must make his own decision. I made decisions for him in his childhood and you made decisions for him in his youth. This decision he must make for himself.'

TWO

'I know you,' Michael said. 'You are the woman on the wall.'

She smiled. A smile on the face of a skull. He knew that she was only thirty-eight years old, but he was looking at an old woman. A woman with no hair after weeks of chemotherapy treatment. A woman whose yellow cheeks had vanished into a face of skin stretched over bones. But he could recognise the face that he had seen almost every week of his younger life. A then beautiful face, framed by long black lustrous hair. When he was very young it had been the face of a young woman, almost a girl. Over the years as he grew up the face had aged imperceptibly, but had always remained beautiful. Now it was the face of death.

'You sat on the wall,' he said, bemused. 'Every Sunday. When we went to church at eleven o'clock in the morning you were always sitting on the wall across the road from the orphanage; and when we came back from church an hour later you were still sitting there. We used to watch you from inside the orphanage, wondering who you were. You always left at exactly twelve-thirty and walked down the hill to the harbour.'

She smiled again.

'Yes, to catch the one o'clock ferry.'

'Why?'

'I came to watch my son . . . to watch him grow up.'

'Why didn't you talk to me?'

'I could not. I had given you to the priests. I could not take you back.'

'Why did you give me to the priests?'

'I had no choice. No choice at all.'

He pulled his chair closer to the dying woman. His voice became hard. 'Tell me why you had no choice!'

THREE

There were two prostitutes, the old, stooped priest and Michael by the side of the grave. The two grave-diggers wearing denim shorts and dirty white T-shirts lowered the coffin into the grave. The prostitutes crossed themselves, the priest intoned prayers and Michael threw a lump of earth onto the coffin. Then they went away; the prostitutes to Gzira, the priest to his church and Michael to Gozo.

'Count me out,' Creasy said.

They were sitting under the vines and mimosa, eating a hot lamb curry. Creasy had cooked it two days before and it had matured into a rich, tangy example of the quintessential Indian speciality. There was a wide variety of side dishes and, of course, *popadums*. Creasy prided himself on his curries. Michael was an enthusiastic consumer.

Michael crunched a *popadum* and then forked some banana into his mouth to take away the heat of the curry. He said, 'I thought we were a team.'

'Your natural mother was a whore,' Creasy said. 'Face up to it. She abandoned you the day after giving birth. Any woman who can do that is no human being in my eyes.'

'She had no choice.'

'That's what they all say.'

Michael took a sip of cold beer. He was not frightened of Creasy, nor was he in awe of him, even though Creasy was the hardest man he had ever known or would probably ever know.

'You taught me about vengeance,' he said. 'You taught me about justice.'

Creasy sighed.

'OK, so she told you she was forced into prostitution. Forced into

15

being a drug addict and forced to give you up. That was twenty years ago and even if it's true – and I doubt it – what can you do? By nature prostitutes are notorious liars.'

Michael was looking down at his plate. Quietly he asked, 'Is Blondie a notorious liar?'

Creasy sighed again and shook his head.

'No, Blondie always tells the truth. If you talk to Blondie she will tell you to forget the whole stupid idea.'

Michael finished the last of the curry and said off-handedly, 'By the way, my father was an Arab. He was the one who made my mother an addict and sold her off to prostitution.'

'She told you that?'

'Yes, and much more.' The young man looked up. His eyes were defiant. 'She came to see me every week ... every Sunday. She sat on the wall near the orphanage and watched me go to church and watched me coming back.' Emotion crept into his voice. 'It must have broken her heart not to be able to talk to me.'

'She was a whore.'

Emotion left Michael's voice and it took on the edge of a razor blade. 'Blondie was a whore and still owns a whorehouse; but Blondie is a great friend of yours and you admire her.'

'Blondie is different.'

Michael stood up and stretched his frame and then began stacking plates. 'Maybe so,' he said. 'But tomorrow I go to Brussels to talk to her. She's been around a long time, maybe she knows something. Maybe she can point me in the right direction.'

'Maybe she'll tell you not to be a stupid idiot. Maybe she'll tell you that there are whores and different whores ... and that a whore who discards her child the day after its birth deserves no thought or compassion from that child nineteen years later.'

Michael gave him a belligerent look. A look that made Creasy realise that he was not talking to a child; he was talking to a nineteen-year-old man, made wiser far beyond his years. Creasy also realised that he could not let Michael just blast off alone on some crazy path of vengeance. It also entered his head that he himself had used Michael, and in a sense created Michael as an instrument for his own vengeance. He took a decision.

'OK, Michael. You want to be an idiot and expurgate this so-called duty ... then I go with you and hold your hand.'

Michael reacted very quietly. 'I don't need you,' he said. 'You trained me well. I can do it myself.'

Creasy looked down at the rough wooden surface of the table. His face was sombre, and that mood was reflected in his voice. 'Michael – in a way I feel a great guilt. You had no childhood. I plucked you from an orphanage and made you a soldier. You were seventeen. You should have been able to live like any other teenager, but you never had the chance. Now you're nineteen years old and seem like you're forty ... So that's past ... Nothing to be done. But maybe you'd let me help on this stupid thing you're doing? Anyway it will be good to see Blondie again, and Maxie and Nicole ... and I guess I need to be a chaperone between you and Christine.'

Michael smiled at him with an edge of affection.

'Somehow I don't see you in the role of a chaperone. Yes, come with me ... but Creasy, understand that this is my show.'

Creasy sighed and nodded.

They landed at Brussels airport at eight p.m. They only had hand luggage and within fifteen minutes were striding out of customs. Michael looked infinitely older than his nineteen years: six feet tall, jet-black hair, cropped short; a long, lean face above a long, lean body. He wore black jeans, a cream open-necked shirt and a black leather bomber jacket. Beside him Creasy moved along with his curious walk; the outsides of his feet coming into contact with the ground first. A bear of a man with his cropped, grey hair and scarred face the colour of pale mahogany. He wore dark blue slacks, a light oxford cotton shirt, a black cashmere sweater and a tweed jacket. An observer looking only at his clothes would have deduced that he was an English or Scottish country gentleman; but one look at the face would have dispelled such thoughts. This was a hard man in a bad mood.

As they came out towards the line of taxis Creasy suddenly stopped with a sharp grunt. Michael turned to look at him and saw the pain on his face. It was not the first time. Over the past months that short, sharp pain had recurred several times. Each time Creasy had brushed it aside, muttering something about indigestion.

'Are you all right?' Michael asked.

'Sure, let's go.'

They climbed into a taxi and Michael told the driver, 'The Pappagal, Rue d'Argens.'

The driver twisted his head in surprise. 'You know what that place is?'

'Yes, a high-class brothel.'

The driver engaged first gear and pulled away, saying over his shoulder, 'You don't waste much time.'

Michael grinned at Creasy, then turned to look out the window, taking in the scenery, remembering the last time he had been in Brussels, almost two years ago, sitting in a taxi on the same route. At that time he had been with Creasy and Leonie. The memory of Leonie brought a sick jolt to the pit of his stomach. He had loved her as a mother. He remembered the tears he had shed when she had been killed. He remembered Creasy tossing him a handkerchief in the room at Guido's *pensione* in Naples and telling him in that flat voice, 'Dry your tears. You're a man now. It's time for vengeance.'

Half an hour later Michael pressed the doorbell of a discreet building in a discreet side-street only a few blocks from the EC headquarters. They heard the click of the tiny shutter set into the door and knew they were being examined from the inside. A few seconds later the door opened. It was Raoul; tall, skeletal and with a face dark enough to frighten strong men. He moved past them and looked carefully down both sides of the street, then nodded. They strode into the plush, carpeted hallway, dropped their bags and shook the tall man's hand.

'How long will you stay?' Raoul asked.

'A couple of days,' Michael answered.

Raoul picked up their bags. 'Blondie's in the bar. I'll take your things upstairs.'

They walked down the corridor, opened a door and went through. It was an opulent room: deep-pile maroon carpet, crystal chandeliers, velvet walls, a small mahogany bar, deep leather settees and armchairs. There were four very beautiful and elegantly dressed young women sitting in the armchairs. Sitting at the bar was something entirely different. An old woman in an ankle-length gold brocade gown. She had ebony black hair, a face thick with pancake make-up and a red slash for a mouth. She had blue-white diamonds at her ears, around her neck and around both wrists and on every one of her fingers. Her age was indeterminate, but Michael and Creasy knew that she was in her mid-seventies.

The red of her mouth widened as she saw them. She slid off the bar-stool as though she were an eighteen-year-old coquette; her arms opened. First embracing Creasy and then Michael, who could feel the stiffness of her corset. She held Michael at arm's length, looking up at his face, and brushed a hand down his cheek, saying in her heavily

Italian-accented English, 'You have become beautiful ... Before you were ... just handsome.'

Creasy chuckled. Michael smiled and felt slightly embarrassed under the interested gaze of the four beautiful young women.

'Business seems slack,' Creasy commented.

Blondie's smile waned.

'It's not great,' she answered. 'But the night is young. What will you have to drink?'

As they eased themselves onto the bar-stools Creasy again gasped and his left hand moved to the centre of his chest. Blondie and Michael glanced at each other.

'What is it?' the old woman asked sharply.

Creasy was shaking his head dismissively. She looked at Michael who shrugged and said, 'He's been getting those pains over the last few weeks ... Says it's nothing, but they're getting more frequent.'

The atmosphere changed immediately. Blondie's face had turned very serious. She spoke to Creasy rapidly in French. He nodded reluctantly. Michael could not understand the language but he saw the genuine anger and concern on her face. Abruptly she turned to Michael and spoke to him in English.

'It has happened before with this fool who would be your father. He has so much metal in him it could be recycled into enough tin cans to supply a baked bean factory. Sometimes that metal moves.'

Suddenly she became a mother, mistress, manager and cyclone all in one. She snapped her fingers and Raoul passed her the phone. She dialled a number and spoke rapidly into it. Creasy tried to remonstrate but she cut him short with a look that would have withered an oak tree. Michael looked on in amazement. Blondie hung up the phone, turned to Michael and gave him his instructions.

'An ambulance will be here within a few minutes. You are to make sure that Creasy gets into it together with pyjamas and whatever else he may need in hospital. A top surgeon is waiting for him in a private hospital ... It is comfortable with pretty nurses. That surgeon will take out the piece of shrapnel that is working its way to that idiot's heart.' She gave Creasy another laser-sharp look. 'I can never understand how a man of your intelligence and knowledge of wounds can be so stupid when it comes to your own body.'

Creasy coughed irritably and said, 'You know I hate hospitals.'

Blondie smiled. 'I told you ... this one is exclusive, and the nurses are cute.' She turned back to Michael and her voice was tight with authority. 'So you get him there, Michael. And instruct that surgeon to X-ray Creasy from his toenails to the top of his head. If he finds any metal in there which needs to be taken out, he should do it now.'

Creasy coughed again, looked at Blondie and said, 'You're sure this guy knows what he's doing?'

She smiled at him sweetly. 'They say he's one of the best in Europe.'

'Must cost a bomb,' Creasy muttered.

She smiled and shook her head. 'His wife died five years ago. He compensates his grief by hard work. He does not contemplate replacing his wife, but he is a virile man. He comes here usually once a week. All my girls love him.' She gave a very Italian shrug. 'And in his way he loves them too ... His name is Bernard.'

Bernard Roche was a good surgeon. He had been ten years in the French army and had done his apprenticeship in Algeria during the war of independence. He recognised Creasy.

He looked at his face, straightened in his chair and said, 'First REP ... I set a broken arm for you about two weeks before you guys blew up your barracks and marched out of Zeralda, singing Edith Piaf's *Je ne regrette rien*.'

Creasy looked at him with suspicion and said, 'You must have been in nappies.'

The surgeon smiled. 'Just out of them. I was twenty-three years old. You were a legend. When I put that plaster on you my hands were shaking. You had a friend then ... an Italian called Guido something ... He told me if I didn't put you back into perfect condition he'd bury me neck deep in the desert and train a camel to piss on my face every day for the next thousand years.'

Creasy smiled at him. 'The arm turned out fine. I'm getting pain from an old wound.'

The surgeon stood up. He said to Michael, 'Go away and have a drink and come back in an hour.'

Michael drank half a bottle of red wine in a small bistro across the road from the hospital that looked no more than a large private house. On his return, the surgeon's face was sombre.

'It was close,' he said. 'The legend could have died within the next week or so. Why is it that such hard men are so frightened of hospitals and doctors?'

Michael shrugged. 'Have you operated?'

Bernard shook his head. 'No, in about two hours. Come and have a look.'

They walked over to a wall which held a series of back-lit X-rays. Bernard pointed to the first one. Pointed to a small, dark shadow. 'A grenade fragment,' he said, 'collected at Dien Bien Phu in Vietnam in the early fifties. It spent three decades working its way through muscle to the heart. We've caught it just in time.' He pointed at the next X-ray and another dark shadow. 'The fragment of a bullet... Apparently received in the Congo ... very close to the spleen ... I'll take that out as well.' He pointed at the next X-ray. Another dark shadow. 'That's a steel pin which some Italian doctor used to connect a small bone in his shoulder to his collar bone ... That was in Laos. That pin should have been taken out about six months later but somehow it got forgotten ... I may as well do it now ... I may have to replace the pin, but I won't know until I see how the two bones have fused.'

Michael had been listening carefully. He asked, 'Maybe leave that one well alone?'

Bernard shook his head. 'It will give him terrible arthritis later in life. Better it comes out now.'

Michael smiled as though to himself and then said, 'I agree. Do it all at one time. How long will he have to stay in hospital?'

Bernard thought for a moment and then said, 'At least ten days.'

Michael nodded in satisfaction. 'That's perfect.'

'Do nothing until I'm out of here.' Creasy's voice was emphatic.

Michael shrugged. 'Well,' he said, 'I'll just make some enquiries and sort of mosey around. I mean, you're going to be out of it for at least ten days and there's no point in my sitting on my ass doing nothing.'

Creasy gave him a very narrow look. He said, 'Put the mother situation on hold for a while ... at least until I get out of this place. But try to find out what's bothering Blondie.'

'Blondie?' Michael asked curiously.

Creasy nodded.

'Yes. Something's worrying her. I've known her many years and I can tell. I don't think she'll talk to me about it. She likes to be independent ... But something's wrong. Hang your ears out and try to get some kind of message.'

Blondie smiled at Michael across the kitchen table and said, 'So Creasy is locked up in hospital for a few days ... It's about time.' She leaned forward and said in a conspiratorial whisper, 'So tell me. Why are you here?'

He took a sip of his wine and answered, 'I came to ask for your advice and perhaps your help.'

'Tell me.'

So he told her. She knew the bare bones of the story and had been part of it, but he fleshed it out and went all the way back to the beginning: his adoption by Creasy and the dead English actress, Leonie, whom she had met and liked. Their revenge against the terrorists who had planted the bomb on Pan Am 103; his in-built hatred of the unknown natural mother who had abandoned him only one day after his birth. He explained about Father Manuel Zerafa telling him about that natural mother who was dying of cancer and wanted to see his face. He told her of his decision to see her. Told her of the woman with the ravaged bald-headed face lying on the hospital bed. Told her of the woman who had sat on the wall every Sunday during his childhood. Finally he told her of the reason why the woman on the wall had no choice but to abandon him the day after he was born. Then he told her what he planned to do, and again asked her advice and possibly her help.

She lowered her head in thought for a long time, then looked up at him and quietly said, 'Those people that you seek. Those people who forced your mother to abandon you. Those people who are the dregs of the earth. They have been around a long time. Many decades. They are very powerful and well-connected, both politically and financially, in several countries.'

'You know these people, Blondie?'

'I know of them. They have tried to do business with me in the past, but I don't deal with that filth. I don't need to. My girls work for me because they want to. I look after them. I take care of their money and when the time comes I make sure they leave the business in a better condition than when they joined it.'

He smiled and asked, 'Like Nicole?'

She nodded solemnly. 'Exactly like Nicole. You will see her, of course ... and Maxie.' She smiled. 'And that young sister of hers.'

Michael smiled in return.

'Of course. I'll go there for dinner tomorrow night. Why not come with me?'

Sadly she shook her head.

'It's not a good time for me to be away from the Pappagal.'

'You have problems?'

'Only small ones, but I have to be here.'

'Anything I can do?'

She shook her head, reached out and touched his cheek. 'You have problems of your own. These people you seek are dangerous. They kill without thought and they protect their interests with cunning and ferocity.'

'Who are they, Blondie?'

'They come and go. Different faces but from the same area. They work in southern Europe, the Middle East and northern Africa. I've heard a name, but I'm not sure whether it means anything.'

'What name?'

'I have heard that they are called "The Blue Ring".'

'Are they Mafia?'

She shook her head. 'They are worse than Mafia.'

Michael swirled the wine in his glass. 'Where would I start to look?'

She considered the question for a long time, then stood up and said, 'Wait.'

She came back five minutes later, holding a white business card. She put it on the table between them, saying, 'About six months ago a man came here and hired one of my girls. It turned out that he did not want to make love. He wanted to talk. Such things happen, even at three hundred dollars a session. Some want to talk about their fantasies without doing anything, some want to talk about themselves.' She tapped the card. 'This man did not want to talk about any of those things. He wanted to ask questions. He was curious about the modern white slave trade. My girl thought he was a nice man and sympathetic. He told her he was a writer researching a book. At the end of his hour she suggested he talk to me. We talked in the bar for a couple of hours and we became friendly. During the conversation he mentioned "The Blue Ring". At the end he admitted he was not a writer.' She tapped the card again. 'Perhaps you and Creasy should start by talking to this man.'

Michael picked up the card and read, 'Jens Jensen, CID (Missing Persons Bureau) Copenhagen, Denmark.'

FOUR

Michael was woken just after midnight by a gentle tap on the door. He pulled himself out of bed, padded across, unlocked the door and opened it. Raoul stood there with a silver tray in his hand. On it was a bottle of Hennessy Extra brandy and two glasses.

He said, 'I thought we might have a drink. I hope I didn't wake you.'

Michael yawned, smiled and said, 'You did, but let's have a drink anyway.'

He was puzzled because Raoul was a taciturn man, not given to conversation, conviviality or socialising. They sat at the small table and Raoul poured two large measures. Michael studied him. He was a man in his mid-forties, blessed with a face to frighten small children, old ladies and clients who got out of line. He had worked for Blondie for over ten years and was a combination of bartender, bouncer, handyman and silent companion. Blondie was the only person in his life that meant anything to him. He opened the conversation. 'How is Creasy?'

'Creasy's just fine,' Michael answered. 'That surgeon really is good. He mined a great deal of metal from Creasy's body.' Michael smiled at the recollection. 'He also filled him full of morphine ... It's one very happy Creasy lying in bed there, and he probably weighs half a kilo less.'

'How long will he have to stay there?' Raoul asked.

Michael shrugged. 'The doctor says ten days ... but knowing Creasy he'll discharge himself the minute he can walk ... I'd guess four to six days.'

Raoul nodded solemnly and said. 'Then I guess it has to wait a couple of weeks or more until he's fully recovered.'

'What has to wait?'

'You don't know?'

'Know what?'

Raoul was looking puzzled. He asked, 'You are here because Blondie called you?'

Michael shook his head.

'She never called us . . . What's happening?'

Raoul was confused. He rubbed the palms of his hands down his face, sighed and said, 'Blondie has problems. I thought she might have written to Creasy. In fact I suggested it, but obviously she didn't.'

'Not that I know of. Tell me about her problems.'

Raoul thought for a moment and then said, 'We don't have the Mafia here in Belgium, but we do have something similar. We call them *Les hommes de la nuit*. There are several gangs, but one has recently become predominant. It takes its name from their leader, Lamonte. They deal in drugs, prostitution, illegal gambling, protection rackets and coercion. Blondie has no affiliation with any criminal group or with any pimps. You know she treats her girls well.'

Michael's voice indicated his interest. 'So tell me.'

Raoul's face went gloomy. 'Recently, Lamonte's gang has been targeting up-market brothels for protection money. There are many such brothels in Brussels. They cater to the huge amount of civil servants who work for the EC and also for the businessmen who need those civil servants, and often invite them to places like Pappagal. Most of the brothel owners have buckled under and now pay protection money. But not Blondie. She refuses.'

'So what have they done?'

Raoul shrugged. 'They are very clever. They don't plant bombs or start fires or anything so obvious. But every night Lamonte has his men waiting on the street outside. They threaten our customers with blackmail and violence and, like common touts, they give them the cards of other brothels over which they have control.'

'And the results?'

Raoul spread his hands. 'Business is down by more than half. Blondie cannot even cover her costs. She is paying the girls minimum wages from her own pocket.'

For more than a minute there was a silence while Michael thought. Then he said, 'She should have told Creasy. She should have followed your advice.'

Raoul nodded. 'But she will not. She has her pride.' His dark face turned apologetic and his voice took on a different tone. 'You have to understand, Michael, I want to do something. Blondie is like a mother to me. But I am not like you or Creasy. Sure I look tough, and I can frighten people just by a look.' He tapped his suit under the armpit. 'And, yes, I carry a gun, but it has no bullets. It's an understanding we have with the police. It's just to frighten unruly clients.' He shrugged again. 'I am no match for Lamonte or his "soldiers". So we must wait for Creasy to come out of hospital ... I hope it will be in time.'

Michael shook his head.

'We will wait for nothing. I will have a gentle word with Lamonte myself.'

Raoul looked slightly startled and murmured, 'Maybe you should wait for Creasy.'

Again, Michael shook his head.

'I will do it myself ... Don't worry, Raoul. I am capable.'

Raoul looked into the young man's face and into his stone-cold eyes. 'If you want, I will watch your back ... I will get bullets for my gun and fuck the police.'

Michael smiled and shook his head.

'I would be honoured for you to watch my back, but your place is here, watching over Blondie. And, yes, do get bullets for your gun and fuck the police.'

'So who will watch your back?'

Michael's smile widened. 'Maxie MacDonald will watch my back. I'm having dinner at his bistro tomorrow night. He knows the city and will know all about Lamonte.'

Raoul grinned back. 'Yes,' he said, 'Maxie will enjoy the action. He's been out to pasture for too long ... And Blondie will know nothing?'

'Blondie will know nothing. But later, when business returns to normal, she may guess.'

Raoul smiled again. 'Let her guess.'

FIVE

Michael ate *moules marinières* followed by *coq au vin*, and drank half a bottle of the house wine. While he ate, Maxie made several phone calls. After most of the other guests had left, Maxie brought over an old unmarked bottle of Cognac and two glasses. The square ex-mercenary explained that Jacques Lamonte was in his mid-forties. He had muscled his way up to the top of the pile in the Belgian crime hierarchy. He was daring and ruthless. He was also gay, and owned several nightclubs which purveyed to the gay community in Brussels. He lived in a grand house in a prime suburb on the outskirts of the city. His home was extremely well-guarded and he never moved anywhere without very hard bodyguards, all well-armed. Diffidently Maxie suggested that Michael should wait until Creasy was out of hospital and fully fit.

Michael shook his head and explained. 'Maxie, you know how close Creasy is to Blondie. I have a feeling he will get so mad that someone like that pimp is threatening her that he'll kill him. That could be complicated. So I'll just give the guy a hell of a fright and Creasy needn't know anything about it.'

Maxie looked into the young man's eyes and said, 'My sister-in-law loves you, but sometimes, Michael, you can be a prick. You want to do this for Blondie while Creasy is indisposed. You're being a macho young guy.'

Michael started out on a retort, but Maxie held up a hand, smiled and said, 'That's OK. It's no problem. I understand. You need to make your own moves and come out from under Creasy's shadow. I'm sure you can take care of it.'

'I will take care of it. Where does Lamonte go at night?'

'He is almost always in one of his clubs, usually The Black Cat. It's on Rue Lafitte. He goes there to pick up young men.'

Lucette came and sat with them. She smiled at Michael and asked, 'Are you going to take me out tonight?'

'Yes, with your sister's permission. I want to enjoy tonight, because tomorrow I'm going to become gay.'

There were a few customers that always lingered late. At eleven o'clock Nicole saw the impatience in her sister's eyes and said, 'Go on, then. Don't wake us up when you come home.'

Lucette smiled and said demurely, 'I will not wake you up when I come home.'

First they went to a small bar around the corner. They sat in a dimly-lit banquette. Michael ordered champagne and they drank it, holding hands.

'Do you want to go to a disco?' he asked.

She squeezed his hand and shook her head. 'No.'

'Do you want to go home?'

'No.'

'Where do you want to go?'

'I want to go to a big warm bed. I want to stay in that bed the whole night and I want to watch your eyes open in the morning. I want to see the pleasure in them because the moment they open I will be doing something very beautiful to you.'

The big bed was in a small luxury hotel just around another corner. A hotel that catered for such assignations. They had only made love once before, about a year earlier, but he remembered how physically sensitive she was.

Very slowly he undressed her as she stood by the bed. First the pale green mohair sweater then the white cotton blouse. She wore no bra. Her breasts were small and high and made a triangle with the soft point of her chin. He loosened the belt of her black woollen skirt and it dropped to the carpet. She was left wearing only very brief white panties. He lifted her up and laid her on the bed.

She smiled up at him and asked quietly, 'Do you remember?'

He nodded as he took off his clothes. He did remember. He remembered virtually every word she had spoken to him the first night he had made love to her.

In the beginning it had been a disaster. Like many young men he had assumed a woman took pleasure from the pure physical act of sex, and that the harder he went and the longer he went, so much the better. She had stopped him after five minutes, pulled herself away from him, and then whispered in his ear in a humorous voice, 'Perhaps I'm not like your other girlfriends. Have you ever had a Belgian girlfriend?'

'No.'

'Then maybe we are different. Maybe we are the aristocracy of girlfriends. We are nervous like race horses. However, there are ways to handle us.' She had gone on to tell him in great detail how to handle her.

So he remembered. He made love to her very slowly, very carefully and very tenderly. At the end she lay with her head in the crook of his arm, her hand across his chest. In a voice as low as the purr of a cat she said, 'I love you because of your memory. I love you because you think you are so tough and so mean and so hard ... But you are just a little boy.'

He stared up at the canopy of the four-poster bed and then asked, 'Do you really see me as a boy?'

She moved up until her head rested against his shoulder and her lips were near to his ear. 'Oh, yes. You think that your youth has passed you by. Everybody thinks that. My mother and Maxie say that you have the mind of a forty-year-old ... It is not true.'

'No?'

'No. You are nineteen years old, but for me you are even younger. I don't talk of your mind or your body. I only feel the essence of you in my arms ... I feel a young boy.' Both her arms had now circled him and pulled him close. She waited for an answer, but he was silent. She lifted her head and in the dim light looked at his face and into his eyes. They were infinitely sad.

He murmured, 'You must be the only one to see me as a boy. Sometimes I feel a thousand years old.' His smile was half bitter and half humorous. He kissed her and said, 'But you are so wise. I am a boy, but I badly need to become a man. I need to stand alone.'

He saw the concern in her eyes. She said, 'That's why you go after Lamonte on your own?'

Slowly he nodded. 'And more. I told you about "The Blue Ring" ... I will go after them myself while Creasy recovers. At least, I will start the journey and plot my course.'

She wanted to tell him to be careful and to be cautious and to be patient, but she had the wisdom to kiss him and keep silent. She ran a hand down his body and felt the scar which she had not seen before.

'What happened?' she asked.

'Someone shot me.'

'Did you kill him?'

'I don't remember.'

She smiled and said, 'That's what Maxie always says about his past.' She moved and kissed the scar and then his lips. 'Are you really going to go gay tomorrow?' she asked.

'Yes, but only temporarily.'

She looked down at him, her blonde hair falling across his face. 'Afterwards,' she murmured, 'come back to me. I will straighten out your genes.'

SIX

The Black Cat was dark and dangerous, a mixture of discreet spotlights, chrome and black leather. The two bouncers at the door were gay and mean. Michael paid his fifty francs entrance fee and walked into the bar. He was wearing frayed denim jeans with a metal-studded belt, an olive green silk shirt and a gold earring in his left ear.

He ordered a *crème de menthe frappé* and studied the room. About sixty men, ranging in age from fifty to seventeen. Not a woman in sight. The bartender had a purple hair-do down to his shoulders.

Lamonte was sitting at a corner table with two men. Michael recognised him from Maxie's description. He was in his mid-forties, a tanned, handsome man wearing a sober business suit. Michael gazed into his eyes and then turned away and talked to the bartender about the weather. When he ordered his third *crème de menthe frappé* and tried to pay for it the bartender gave him the drink and waved away his money. With a wink he said, 'It's on the boss,' and gestured at Lamonte's table.

Five minutes later Lamonte eased himself onto the stool next to Michael, smiled disarmingly and said, 'I haven't seen you in here before.'

Michael answered, 'It must be Christmas.'

They left an hour later. Lamonte had a Mercedes 600 complete with mini-bar, telephone and miniature TV. He and Michael sat in the back. One of the bodyguards drove, the other sat silently next to him. Lamonte opened the tiny fridge in the mini-bar, took out a bottle of Veuve Cliquot, popped the cork and poured two glasses. They toasted each other. With his free hand Lamonte felt for Michael's penis.

'It takes time,' Michael said with a smile. 'But when it stands up,

31

it stays up.'

Lamonte grinned, leaned across and kissed him on the mouth, his tongue probing. Michael played his part.

There were two other bodyguards waiting at the house. One at the main gate and one inside the front door, who let them in. They proceeded straight up the stairs to the bedroom, both carrying their glasses of champagne, and Lamonte carrying the half-empty bottle.

In the opulent bedroom with its huge bed and silk canopy, Michael's first words were, 'First the money.'

Lamonte took out his wallet and counted out five hundred francs. Michael pushed the money into the back pocket of his jeans. With that action Lamonte took off his clothes and moved in, needing to use what he had purchased. He reached out his hand to move Michael's face closer. Michael kissed him, and then the stiffened fingers of his right hand moved in a blur to a precise spot just below Lamonte's rib cage. As Lamonte went down to the deep-pile carpet Michael's right knee smashed into his face, breaking his nose and dislodging four front teeth.

Lamonte woke up five minutes later. He was lying on the vast bed, naked and in excruciating pain. His thumbs were tied together. He looked up into Michael's eyes. Black eyes, and very cold. In a strange way the eyes were disinterested, as though looking at a boring object. The voice when it came was conversational, perhaps that of a young man talking to an uncle. It was a voice without menace and, under the circumstances, terrifying.

'Do you have a religion?'

Lamonte could not find his voice. His face was a pool of agony, his body chilled by fear.

'If you do,' the voice went on, 'now is the time to pray to your God. Now is the time to repent. Now is the time to consider your life.'

Lamonte took a deep breath to scream for help. The sound never came. Michael's right hand smashed into his mouth again, dislodging three more teeth. When he came out of the waves of nauseous pain he was looking again into the cold, black eyes and hearing that conversational voice.

'Lamonte, don't think of your bodyguards. You would be dead before they got through that door. You think you're a tough, hard man, but you know nothing of that kind of world. I got you here as easy as picking a baby from a pram. I'm going to let you live but with one name in your memory. The name of a woman called Blondie.

You threatened her. For sure I frighten you, but also be sure that you are lucky. There is another friend of Blondie's who would send you to hell in a basket of ice that would never melt. I will be a little generous. When you come out of hospital you'll go to the Rue d'Argens and apologise to Blondie. Otherwise I will come again and I will not be generous.' He reached forward and put his left hand over the Belgian's mouth. The side of his right hand smashed down on Lamonte's left forearm, cracking the bone.

SEVEN

The soft chimes of the doorbell at the Pappagal rang ten days later. Raoul came out of the bar, moved down the corridor, opened the peephole and peered through. He recognised the man standing outside. He noted the jacket hung over the shoulders, saw the white plaster on the man's right arm. Raoul opened the door.

The man said in a quiet strangled voice, 'I wish to speak to Madame Blondie.'

'Wait here.'

It was drizzling slightly. The man stood there, getting slowly wet.

Raoul went back to the bar and said to Blondie, 'Lamonte is outside. He wants to talk to you.'

Her face hardened in anger. 'I have nothing to say to him. Not now. Not ever!'

Raoul smiled and said, 'You don't have to say a word to him. I think he wants to say something to you.'

EIGHT

Jens Jensen was a good policeman. He had all the right instincts. He had a nose that smelled out everything. He knew when he was being followed. He could feel it at the nape of his wide neck, a tingling of the flesh. He carried his lunch bag across the park to a bench and sat in the sunshine. As he took the first bite of his salami sandwich a young, dark-skinned, dark-haired man sat down next to him.

'What do you want?' Jens asked.

'I want to talk to you about "The Blue Ring".'

NINE

Jens Jensen was apologetic as he ushered Michael through the door of his apartment in the Vesterbro district of Copenhagen.

'It's a bit small,' he said. 'We're not exactly overpaid in the Danish Police.'

It was small, and very warm and cosy. Very much a home. Michael shook hands with Jens' wife Birgitte, a slender, attractive woman in her late twenties. Then he solemnly shook hands with Lisa, their six-year-old daughter.

If the apartment was small, the dinner was huge. They started with smoked salmon on toast. On top of the salmon was baked egg, asparagus and cress. Then they went on to the main course, which was glazed ham with vegetables and oven-baked potatoes. For dessert Birgitte had made a delicious sherry mousse with hazelnuts and chocolate. Michael had hardly eaten since leaving Brussels, and he literally devoured the food, mostly in silence, while listening to a typical family conversation: Jens complaining about his boss; Birgitte, who was a school teacher, complaining about her students; and Lisa complaining about her teachers. But it was a conversation of good humour and Michael decided they were a comfortable and happy family.

After the meal Lisa went to bed and Birgitte cleared the table and went into the kitchen. Michael and Jens talked again about 'The Blue Ring'. Jens was quite sure that they worked out of three main centres: Marseille, Milan and Naples. He had heard that there was a strong Arab influence within the Ring and therefore thought that perhaps Marseille might be the main centre.

'That's where I'll start, then,' Michael said. 'I'll leave tomorrow. Do you have any contacts there?'

Jens nodded. 'Yes, a good one. He's my counterpart there, a man called Serge Corelli ... He's part Arabic.'

Michael smiled slightly. 'So am I,' he said.

Jens raised an enquiring eyebrow and on impulse Michael told him about his background, explaining in detail about being in the orphanage from his birth. By this time Birgitte had come back from the kitchen and sat down. Both she and Jens listened in fascination as Michael recounted his life. He felt strangely relaxed with these two people. He told them how Creasy had adopted him and very briefly about what he and Creasy had done in vengeance. He finally told them about listening to the story of his natural mother just before she died.

There was a long silence when he had finished, then Birgitte reached across the table and put her hand over his and said softly, 'I understand how you feel.'

Jens nodded. 'And why you are looking for them. But it's been a long time and maybe they won't be the same people.'

'It doesn't matter,' Michael said coldly. 'They come from the same pit. They practise the same filth.'

Birgitte went to the kitchen to make coffee and, very gently, Jens said to Michael, 'These are hard and dangerous people, Michael, and totally ruthless.' He gestured as if in apology and went on, 'You are a young man, with limited experience. This man Creasy you talked about. Will he not help you?'

'Of course. But right now Creasy is in hospital, all stitched up in three places and he'll need at least a week. Meanwhile I'll get in position and he can follow later.'

'I hope so,' Jens said. 'After all, you are a young man and against a mob like that the odds are not very good.'

Michael went very quiet. He was sitting across the table from Jens, his eyes still cold. 'Did you have training in the police – small-arms, unarmed combat and so on?'

'Of course, and I was damn good at it, and still am.' He touched his slight paunch and smiled. 'Even though I'm not quite as fit as I should be.'

Birgitte was just coming out of the kitchen carrying a tray when she heard Michael's words. She stopped abruptly, almost spilling the coffee, as Michael said, 'Jens. You worry about my ability. If I wanted to I could kill you within three seconds. If there were three of you sitting around this table, all well-trained, I could kill you all within ten seconds.'

37

Very quietly Jens asked, 'You are carrying a gun?'

'No.'

'A knife?'

'No.'

'No weapon at all?'

Without speaking Michael held up his two hands.

There was a silence and then Jens asked, 'Have you killed before?'

'I can't remember,' Michael said, and then smiled and the tension left the room.

Birgitte moved forward and put the tray on the table. She poured the coffee and then carried her cup back to the kitchen, saying over her shoulder, 'I'll leave you to it. I have to correct some test papers.' She closed the door behind her.

'I wish I could come with you,' Jens said. 'I'm fed up with sitting in an office reading reports and not being able to do anything about them. I look at an endless number of photographs ... sometimes the faces come to me in the night. All too often I have to talk to the parents of missing girls – that's the worst part of the job. They ask me what they can do, and I have no real answer. It's even worse than telling them their daughter is dead. At least then they know something and can come to terms with it. I wish to hell I was going with you.'

'Why don't you?' Michael asked.

Jens' smile carried no humour. 'What a joke,' he said. 'But not a funny one. Our budget is ridiculously small. There's just no money.'

'I have plenty of money,' Michael stated. 'Would they give you leave of absence for a month or two?'

Jens sat back, his face showing first surprise and then thoughtfulness. After a while he said, 'They might. It's a long shot ... but they just might.'

'It won't hurt to ask,' Michael said, and then gestured towards the kitchen. 'But what about Birgitte?'

Jens smiled and shook his head. 'That's no problem. She feels the same way I do. She has to put up with my frustrations. Besides –' he gestured towards one of the bedrooms – 'in ten or eleven years' our daughter will be wanting to go off to the Mediterranean on holidays. We both have nightmares about someone from my department knocking on the door and telling us that she's gone missing. That could still happen, but I would sleep better knowing that I'd tried to do something about it.'

Michael took a sip of his coffee and said thoughtfully, 'You'd be very useful with your contacts and knowledge.' He smiled. 'And I would try to keep you out of danger.'

Jens laughed. 'I'm twice your age and still rate myself a young man and you're going to keep me out of danger? If I get leave of absence the first decision I have to make is whether to take along a gun or a bag full of nappies.'

Michael also laughed. Then he said flatly, 'Jens, I'm serious. You have a wife and child. Your role would be to make the introductions and give me the benefit of your experience. When the time comes for the dirty work, Creasy and I will do that.'

'Well we'll see,' Jens answered. 'Anyway it's hypothetical. I'll see my boss first thing in the morning and he'll probably kick me out of his office.'

'You'd let him do that? I thought you were a hell of a tough guy.'

Jens smiled again. 'I am. But the bastard signs my salary cheques.'

TEN

Blondie bustled around the comfortable room, twitching curtains into place, straightening a Manet reproduction on the wall, rearranging the roses she had bought for the third time and generally behaving like a broody hen. Creasy surveyed her with fond amusement.

'So tell me what Michael is up to?' he asked.

She suddenly became serious, gave the question some thought and then answered, 'Michael told me not to tell you what he was up to. Michael wants to go off and do his thing without having his papa hovering over him.'

Creasy grunted in irritation. 'Tell me what he's doing.'

Blondie sat down at the foot of the bed, squeezed his left ankle and said, 'Michael will be angry with me, but I'm going to tell you.'

First she told him about Lamonte and his apology.

Creasy nodded thoughtfully. 'Maybe it was for the better,' he said. 'I would probably have killed the bastard. I seem to have less patience as the years go by. What has Michael been up to since then?'

'That's what worries me,' Blondie answered. 'You see, the ease of his success with Lamonte may have gone to his head. It's so easy to forget that he's only nineteen years old. His childhood and his experiences with you make him seem so much older. He has become over-confident. He wants to prove himself to you.'

'Where is he?'

'He left yesterday,' she answered. 'He didn't say where he was going. He said he'd phone in a couple of days to let you know how he was progressing.'

Creasy sighed. 'Yes, of course. He thinks I'm stuck here for a week or ten days.' He pointed at a steel cupboard in a corner. 'My clothes and shoes are in there. Get them for me.'

Blondie started to argue but then looked into his eyes and stopped. Creasy smiled at her and said, 'They only want to keep me in so that they can take out the stitches in a few days. Your surgeon Bernard did a good job, but I can take out the stitches myself. Where do you think Michael's gone?'

'Copenhagen,' she said over her shoulder as she went to get his clothes.

ELEVEN

Lars Pedersen was, within his limits, a good policeman. But one of his limits was a lack of imagination. He always went by the book. He was known in the force as being competent, knowledgeable and hard-working, but only really happy when he could act with all the facts in front of him.

He studied the man sitting on the other side of the desk. A big man with close-cropped grey hair, heavy-lidded eyes, a deeply tanned face with a scar down one cheek, another on the forehead, a third on his chin.

Slowly Pedersen shook his head. 'I'm very sorry, Mr Creasy. I'm not authorised to give you any information regarding my officers. I'd have to receive an official request through Interpol and I doubt that you could obtain that.'

His visitor's voice carried a slight American accent. 'I've reason to believe that my son is with your officer. Surely that's reason enough?'

Again Pedersen shook his head. 'I gave Jens Jensen two months' leave of absence as from yesterday. To be frank, I don't know where he is. To be even franker, I only gave him leave because he's been under quite a lot of mental strain lately. It was not easy. I had to clear it with the Commissioner. But Jensen is one of my best men and he needed the break.'

'Is he married?'

'Yes.'

'Can you give me his home address and phone number?'

Again Pedersen shook his head. 'I'm sorry, but that's against regulations.'

A small smile flickered across the American's lips and he said, 'If your Commissioner instructs you to co-operate fully with me, I assume you would do so?'

42

'Naturally,' the Dane answered coldly. 'But I think that's highly unlikely.'

The American stood up, glanced at his watch and said, 'I'll be back in half an hour.'

In Washington Senator James S. Grainger woke to the ringing of his bedside phone. He looked at his watch, cursed under his breath, picked up the receiver and barked into it, 'Grainger.' A moment later he was sitting up in bed listening intently. The man talking to him from across the Atlantic Ocean wasted few words, and he wasted few in his reply. He simply jotted down the names and numbers on his bedside pad and said, 'OK, Creasy, no sweat. I'll get onto Bennett at the FBI right away. He'll call their guy over there and sort it out. Anything else you need? ... OK. Give Michael a hug for me, and let me know when it's over.'

Grainger cradled the phone, pulled himself higher in the bed and tucked a couple more pillows behind him. The phone call had warmed him; a contact with a distant friend, a man who had been a stranger and arrived into his life and given him the satisfaction of vengeance; a man whom he respected to his core. Of course the conversation had been so abrupt as to be monosyllabic, but the contact and the voice had blown away a loneliness. He recalled the days gone by with Creasy. The man he had found drinking at the bar in his lounge late one night, the man who told him that together they would take vengeance on those people who had killed their loved ones. The man who had done what he had said he would do. Grainger knew all about Michael and what he also had done on that trail of vengeance. He decided to go right down the line on what Creasy had asked for. He picked up the phone, flicked through his personal directory and dialled the number of the director of the FBI.

When Creasy was shown back into Lars Pedersen's office he was greeted with deference and even given a cup of coffee. Forty minutes later he was drinking another cup of coffee and talking to Birgitte Jensen in her apartment.

'Marseille,' she told him. 'They left yesterday morning by air via Paris.'

'Do you know where they're staying?'

She shook her head, looking worried. 'No. Jens told me he would phone me in four or five days. He expected to be away about a month.' She paused and said tentatively, 'Michael told us something

43

about you, Mr Creasy, and I know why they've gone down there. Is there a great danger?'

He shrugged and said non-committally, 'I don't think so, but I'd like to be there. Do you know if your husband has any contacts in Marseille?'

'Yes. He will certainly have a contact in their Missing Persons Bureau.'

'Do you know his name?'

'No, but it will be on file at police headquarters here.'

'Would you mind getting Lars Pedersen on the phone for me?'

She smiled at the thought of phoning her husband's boss. A minute later Creasy was talking to Lars Pedersen and two minutes later he had the information he wanted. He turned to Birgitte and said, 'Your husband's contact is an Inspector Serge Corelli.'

'Will you phone him?' she asked.

Creasy shook his head.

'No. It's better that I wait until I get there. I'll be in Marseille by tomorrow morning. As soon as I arrive I'll call you and give you the name and number of my hotel. When Jens rings tell him to have Michael contact me there immediately and to do nothing until I talk to him. If Jens phones tonight, get a contact address and phone number.'

He moved to the door and as he opened it she said, 'I'm glad you're going down there. I feel better about it.'

He turned and for the first time smiled. 'Don't worry. Your husband will be just fine.'

He closed the door behind him and stood on the small landing. He moved towards the lift but suddenly stopped and leant against the wall. Pain went through him. It had only been three days since his operations. They had taken out the metal, but the pain was still there. He dragged in air and created a mind over matter situation. His body would do what his mind instructed. It had always been that way. Even when the blood flowed. He thought again about the woman he had just left. The last words he had spoken were for her comfort, but inside he had a suspicion that her husband might not be fine. Creasy knew Marseille well. He had joined the French Foreign Legion there many years before, and the one thing in his favour now was that he had good contacts in the city. As he pressed the button to call the lift, a thought struck him: Michael would need weapons. They had gone to Marseille via Paris, and Michael knew where to get weapons in Paris.

He turned back and knocked on the apartment door again. When Birgitte opened it he said, 'Sorry to bother you, but can I make a quick call to Paris?'

She nodded. 'Certainly.'

She understood French very well, but the side of the conversation she heard was puzzling. On getting through Creasy simply said, 'Do you recognise my voice? ... Good. Have you seen my son recently? Did you give or sell him something?'

If Birgitte could have heard the other side of the conversation she would have heard a male voice saying, 'Yes, two small silent ones. Did I do wrong?'

'No. Did my son leave a forwarding address?'

'No. He had phoned earlier. I met him at the airport with another guy. I guess they caught an onward flight.'

'Thanks. How's your father?'

'Getting old and bad-tempered.'

Creasy smiled and said, 'Give him my respects.' He hung up and turned to Birgitte. 'As soon as I contact your husband, I'll tell him to call you. Don't be worried.'

TWELVE

It had only taken six days for Hanne Andersen to become a complete heroin addict. She had not seen Philippe again. After that first time a different man brought the tray with her friend on it. He was tall, fair-haired, in his mid-forties and very handsome. During those six days he also appeared to be charming, talking to her gently and reassuringly. He told her that his name was Carlo. On the first occasion he had freed her from her ropes and she was able to move around the windowless room. He had also brought her a new red tracksuit and some cloth slippers and three pairs of white panties. He spoke English with an Italian accent. The only other person she saw was the old woman who brought her food and took her to the bathroom down the corridor. She was only allowed to go to the bathroom shortly after she had been injected so that she was completely placid.

After the sixth day the injections stopped. They had allowed her to keep her watch. It was a silver Georg Jensen, an eighteenth birthday present from her parents, and her most valued possession. By the sixth day she knew that Carlo would bring her the heroin every six hours, just at the time when she was beginning to feel the pangs for it. At first the pangs were minimal, but as the days went by they grew sharper.

On the sixth day she kept glancing anxiously at her watch. The six hours stretched out. After nine hours she was lying on the bed, shivering. She leapt up when the key of the door turned. It was the old woman with the tray. On it was a bowl of soup and a bowl of *spaghetti*.

'Where is Carlo?' Hanne asked in a tremulous voice.

The old woman silently walked across the room, placed the tray on the bedside table and turned back to the door.

'Where is Carlo?' Hanne asked again, and then repeated the question in French more loudly.

Without a word the old woman went through the metal doorway and the door clanged shut behind her. Hanne heard the key scrape in the lock and the bolt slide home. She sat up beside the bed and reached for the spoon. Her hand was shaking, and she could hardly get the soup to her mouth without spilling it. It tasted of nothing, and she dropped the spoon back into the bowl. For several minutes she sat shivering on the bed, staring at the wall, and then she rolled onto her back and pulled the blanket over her and suffered through the night.

He came at seven o'clock on the morning of the seventh day. He was holding the small metal tray with the syringe. She was sitting in the corner of the room, her knees pulled up against her chest, her arms wrapped around her knees, her eyes only half open. He smiled at her.

She pushed herself to her feet, asking querulously, 'Where have you been?' Her eyes were not on him. They were focused on the tray in his hands. He smiled and held out the tray as though it were a present to a small child.

'Here is your friend,' he said.

She moved across the room, pulling up the sleeve of her tracksuit. He put the tray on the bedside table. She moved towards it eagerly, but he held up his hand.

'Wait. First I want you to do something.'

'What?'

He smiled disarmingly. 'I want you to kiss me.'

At first her face was puzzled. 'What?'

He smiled again and spread his hands. 'To kiss me, is that so difficult? Am I so ugly?'

She took a step backwards, her face now showing alarm. She shook her head as though clearing it from a blow. 'No,' she mumbled. 'No.'

He shrugged, picked up the tray and walked towards the door.

'No,' she called loudly. 'Don't go! Please give it to me.'

He turned with his hand on the doorhandle and said, 'I will give it to you if you give me a kiss.'

Again she shook her head as though in bewilderment, then said, 'No ... But I need it ... I need it badly ... I'm feeling very ill.'

Abruptly he turned the handle of the door and went out, saying over his shoulder, 'I'll be back in an hour. Think about it.'

An hour later she kissed him. He held her close with his hands behind her head, his tongue probed into her mouth. She felt nothing. Her mind was concentrated on the tray on the bedside table. The tray with the syringe.

Afterwards she lay down on the bed while he let himself out. She felt the warmth spreading over her, felt the knots in her belly unravelling, felt the tension in her arms and legs ease away. He came back eight hours later, carrying the tray. For the past two hours she had been looking at her silver watch every two or three minutes. Those two hours had seemed like two years of her young life. This time to get the injection she had to kiss him and let him caress her breasts and bottom over the tracksuit. The third time she had to let him caress her whole body under the tracksuit. The fourth time he came clad only in a dressing-gown and told her that to get the injection she would have to let him make love to her. She refused and he went away with the tray, leaving her pounding on the metal door and screaming abuse at him in her native Danish. He came back two hours later and she let him make love to her. Lying naked on her back she felt nothing. Her eyes never left the tray a metre away from her head.

And so it went on. Within a week she was performing acts of degradation that she had never known existed. A few days later he was accompanied by another man, a tall, thin, dark-skinned man with a black moustache. They used her body separately and together. Sometimes it was painful. After two hours the dark-skinned man got dressed and left. Carlo gave her the injection and then lay naked on the bed, smoking a cigarette, watching her as the pain and humiliation ebbed away with the effects of the drug.

Conversationally he said, 'Tomorrow you are moving to a different city.'

'Where?' she asked dully.

'It doesn't matter,' he answered. 'It's a different country.' He smiled at her. 'A nice country.'

She took this into her drugged mind and then asked anxiously, 'Will you be coming with me?'

He shook his head. 'No, my job is done now.'

Anxiety registered in her mind. She pointed at the syringe. 'What about that?'

He smiled again. 'Don't worry about that. Someone will be there to give it to you.'

She tried to think through the haze of her brain. 'Will I have to do those things before they give it to me?'

'Yes,' he said nonchalantly. 'But as time passes you won't mind so much.'

She turned away, knowing that she was now a slave.

THIRTEEN

The sun was setting over the fishing harbour. Jens Jensen sat on the small balcony of the apartment and took pleasure in watching the coming and going of the boats. He loved the sea and its traffic, and his ambition was to own a house or apartment in one of the small towns north or south of Copenhagen, which fronted onto a harbour.

He reflected on the last forty-eight hours since Michael had come into his life and marvelled at the composure and confidence of the young man. Jens had been a policeman throughout his working life and had seen and done a great deal. He had worked in the CID, the Vice department and the Drugs department. He was twice Michael's age and yet, since the moment they had got on the plane at Copenhagen's Kastrup airport, he had deferred to Michael as the leader of this particular operation. His first surprise had been at Charles-de-Gaulle airport in Paris, where they had a two hour wait for the connection to Marseille. Michael told him that they would not stay in the transit lounge but check through Immigration. They had gone to the coffee shop, sat in a corner and both ordered cappuccinos.

After five minutes a thin, dark-haired man in his late forties had slid onto a chair beside Michael. No greetings had been exchanged. The man passed Michael a very small briefcase and asked, 'How's your father?'

'He's well,' Michael had replied, 'And yours?'

'Getting old and bad-tempered.'

Michael smiled and said, 'Give him my respects.'

The man nodded, and said quietly, 'Nine zero nine,' and then went away.

'Who was that?' Jens had asked.

'He's called Corkscrew Two,' Michael replied, straight-faced, then smiled at Jens' puzzled look. 'His father was called Corkscrew. He took over the family business when his father retired a few years ago.'

'What business?'

Michael thought for a minute and then replied in a low voice. 'He's based in Brussels, which used to be the centre for recruiting mercenaries and similar types. His father has known my father for years. Corkscrew got his nickname because he could get into anywhere in the world and then get himself out. He could obtain almost anything from weapons to information. He passed on his knowledge and skills to his son, who naturally became Corkscrew Two. It was Corkscrew Two who set up the safe houses and equipment that we needed on that operation in Syria a couple of years ago.'

Jens had been intrigued. He had tapped the briefcase on the table. 'What's in it?'

'The keys to an apartment in the old fishing harbour in Marseille,' Michael had replied. 'Plus a detailed street-map of the city.'

'That's all?'

Michael had shaken his head. 'No, there'll be a pistol for shooting very effective tranquilliser darts, two flick-knives and two pistols with silencers and plenty of ammunition in spare magazines.'

Jens' gaze had been on the small black briefcase, but at that moment it had risen sharply to look at the young man. 'Are you crazy?' he had hissed. 'You're going to carry that through the security checks? Don't you know they check everything?'

Michael nodded, then tapped the bag on the other side of his chair. 'The briefcase will go in my bag which I will check through. The bag will be X-rayed as usual. The X-ray will show the outline of the briefcase and the outline of its contents. That outline will not resemble anything that I have told you about. The flick-knives will look like two marker pens, which is what they would look like even if you held them in your hand. The guns and ammunition will look like video cassettes, which is what they are in – very special lead-lined cassettes. Superimposed above the lead-lining is the embossed outline of a real cassette. Even if the bag and briefcases are searched it would take an extremely clever inspector to find its real contents. It's an acceptable risk. There will also be various innocuous business files in the briefcase.'

Jens had been impressed but still felt nervous. 'You set all this up on open line from your hotel room in Copenhagen?'

Michael had nodded. 'Certainly. I rang an old friend without mentioning names. We had a brief conversation which contained several code words. I don't know what make the pistols will be, but they'll be the best: nine millimetre and untraceable. You'll have noticed that Corkscrew Two was wearing gloves – no fingerprints on the briefcase or on its contents.'

His total confidence had reassured the Dane, as had events when they arrived at Marseille's Marignane airport. They collected their bags and walked through customs and had another coffee at the airport. Michael took the briefcase out of his bag, set the combination lock at nine zero nine and opened it. Jens had leaned forward. The contents were exactly as Michael had described: three video cassettes, two fat 'Bon' marker pens, a fat street-map of Marseille and two keys on a key-ring, plus half a dozen files.

Michael had taken out the street-map and opened it. He had pointed to an inked circle near the old fishing harbour. 'That's our base. Let's go.'

They had taken a taxi to the modern city centre, then walked for half a mile with their bags, then taken another taxi to within half a mile of the apartment. They walked the rest of the way, stopping several times to look at shop windows like a couple of tourists.

Again, as an experienced policeman, Jens had been impressed with the technique, especially when they actually reached the apartment. It was on the top floor of a three-storey building, old but in good repair. At the door Michael had taken two pairs of dark blue thin cotton gloves from a side pocket of his bag and handed one pair to Jens, saying, 'While we're inside we wear these at all times.'

The apartment itself had two bedrooms, a bathroom, a small kitchen and a combined lounge and dining room. It was sparsely but adequately furnished. Jens had opened the curtains and seen the balcony and fishing harbour below and strangely felt immediately at home. It was the sort of place that hopefully, in a few years, he would be looking for in Denmark. Michael had gone straight to the telephone, unscrewed the base and peered into its insides. Satisfied, he reattached the base and went prowling around the apartment, checking light sockets and plugs.

'You're very cautious,' Jens had remarked.

'It's been drummed into me over many months,' Michael had answered. 'I don't expect to find anything, but you can't be too sure. What do you like for breakfast?'

'Breakfast?'

'Yes. There's a small supermarket around the corner; I'm going to stock up for a few days, while you rest those old bones.'

Jens grinned and tapped his slight paunch. 'I'm coming with you and getting all the fattening things that Birgitte won't let me eat at home.'

Michael had gestured to the phone. 'OK, but first call your contact and set up a meeting for early tomorrow morning. Do you think he'll let us look at his files?'

'Yes, I think so. I've met him a couple of times at seminars and we get on well.'

'How much are you going to divulge?'

'Nothing,' Jens had answered. 'He'll understand that. I'll explain that I'm on a private case, earning a bit of money on leave of absence, financed by a missing person's family. I'll tell him I'll brief him later on, by which time we'll be long gone.'

Michael had nodded approvingly.

For breakfast Jens ate smoked salmon, toast, half a Camembert, smoked ham, salami and a large tin of fruit salad. Michael had a cup of tea and a piece of toast.

At nine o'clock they were in Inspector Corelli's office. He was a tall, grey-haired, hook-nosed man, wearing an elegant grey suit, a pale blue shirt and a maroon tie. He was also very friendly. Jens introduced Michael as his new assistant and explained briefly that to satisfy a wealthy family they were going through the motions of an on-sight investigation. Corelli had nodded understandingly; it was not an unusual occurrence. He found them an empty office, called in an assistant and told him to supply them with whatever files they wanted plus coffee when they asked for it.

Jens had brought along his newest toy, a small Sanyo lap-top computer. During the next four hours they went through a stack of files together and Jens transcribed all the relevant material onto the computer. They thanked Corelli for his help, and Jens promised to call him in a few days to invite him out for lunch or dinner. On good expenses, Jens explained with a smile. Then they found a good restaurant a couple of blocks away which had tables wide enough apart to allow private conversation. Michael had wanted to order *bouillabaisse* but Jens, who had been in the city once before, a long time ago, told him to save that famous dish for an equally famous restaurant on the outskirts of Marseille. Instead they both had steaks and discussed what they had learned that morning.

During this discussion Jens learned something else about the young man. Not only was he intelligent and highly competent, both in fieldcraft and tactics, but he was totally ruthless. His plan was simple. They knew from Corelli's files that the top criminal in Marseille dealing with vice and drugs was a certain Yves Boutin. He operated out of the red-light district between the Opéra and the Vieux Port. He had connections with the Italian Mafia, the Spanish underground and, reportedly, criminal elements in North Africa. He had been arrested several times but never convicted. His political connections in the city, the police department and in Paris were known to be very strong.

The bars and brothels that Boutin was thought to own or control were listed on Jens' computer, as was the address of his villa on the coast and his luxury apartment in the city itself. He was married with two children: a fourteen-year-old boy and an eleven-year-old girl. He had two younger brothers, both in the business. Georges, the elder, ran the drugs side, and Claude, the prostitution side. Yves himself was the nominal head of a seemingly legitimate construction company which somehow got a lot of municipal contracts. Jens explained that Marseille was one of the most corrupt cities in France, if not the whole of Europe. At police headquarters they had studied many photographs of Boutin, both official police mug-shots and others taken unawares. He was a squat man in his late fifties, completely bald, but with a dark-brown moustache. They had also studied similar photographs of his brothers, his lieutenants and a score of lesser gang members. There was one item of particular interest on the files. He was particularly devoted to his young mistress, a striking blonde called Denise Defors. For five years he had kept her in a city apartment and spent most nights with her during the week. She worked as nominal manageress in his flagship nightclub, The Pink Panther, which had about forty top-class hostesses and strippers and a plush brothel upstairs.

Jens and Michael discussed the cast of characters during their lunch and then, while Jens was tucking into a huge portion of pavlova, he discovered just how ruthless Michael could be.

'I will take one of the children or the mistress.'

Jens looked up from his pavlova and through a mouthful mumbled, 'What?'

'It's obvious,' Michael answered. 'We need to have a serious discussion with Monsieur Boutin. There's been a lot of inter-gang killings in the past months and years, and for sure Boutin will be heavily guarded. I'm not just going to be able to walk up to him and ask to have a chat about his business. But if I'm holding someone dear to him then for sure he'll talk. The question is, a child or the mistress?'

'You mean, kidnap them?'

'Of course.'

'But that's a crime!'

Michael smiled. 'You're kidding! I never realised that.'

Jens put down his spoon, looked at the young man and said, 'Listen, Michael, I'm a policeman, for Christ's sake. I can't go around kidnapping people, even if they are the children or the mistress of a gangster.'

'You're not going to,' Michael answered. 'You're going to stay in the apartment, sitting on the balcony, drinking good wine and watching the view.'

A long silence. The conversation had definitely unsettled the Dane. He even pushed away the small unfinished portion of his pavlova.

'Do you have a better idea?' Michael asked.

'No. But I thought we'd sort of scout around and get familiar with this operation.'

Michael nodded. 'We will, of course. In fact, we'll start tonight. We'll check out The Pink Panther first. Meanwhile, it would help if we had details of where Boutin's children go to school and anything else we can find out. Maybe your friend Corelli would know. Also tonight we'll find out what time the mistress leaves the club and how she gets home. Jens, it has to be done that way. If I take one of his brothers or a top lieutenant it may not be so effective. Boutin is nothing if not ruthless.'

'He's not the only one,' Jens murmured.

The words washed over Michael unheard. His mind was back in Brussels in that small hospital. His mind was confused. He felt like a fledgling bird who had tumbled out of the nest and was flapping its wings but still descending rapidly. Sure he was tough. Hard as a nail. Trained to perfection. He looked at the Dane, who looked back at him with an expression of respect. Tomorrow, Michael thought, tomorrow I phone Blondie and pass on all the information so she will tell Creasy. When he gets out of hospital he will come down here and let me do what I have to do, but be there in the shadows, just in case … tomorrow.

Inspector Corelli took the call just after three o'clock. He listened to Jens and said, 'Wait just a minute.' He tapped the keys on his PC, looked at the screen and said, 'They both go to a private school, called École St Jean. It's a boarding school in Switzerland just outside Geneva. Naturally very exclusive and expensive. Anything else you need?'

Jens said, 'No, thanks very much. I'll call you in a few days.' He put down the phone and turned to Michael. They were back in the apartment. 'The kids are both in an exclusive boarding school in Switzerland. They probably come home for weekends. I can check that out if necessary.'

Michael shook his head.

'No, it's only Tuesday now. We can't wait that long. It has to be the mistress. We'll check her out tonight ... or maybe it's better if I go alone?'

'No,' Jens said emphatically. 'I've been thinking about it. I'll go with you. Nothing's going to happen tonight.' He gestured at the dining-table. 'Do we take the guns?' They were lying side by side. Two black nine millimetre Berretas.

'No,' Michael answered. 'The club will have bouncers and doormen and with that kind of club they often frisk the customers.'

'They don't in Copenhagen.'

Michael smiled. 'This is not Copenhagen.'

In his office Inspector Corelli had also hung up. For several minutes he sat looking thoughtfully at the phone. Then he picked it up, punched the number and held a three minute conversation, at the end of which he gave a detailed, policeman-like description of Jens and Michael.

FOURTEEN

The suite of offices was typical of a small, individual, highly successful business. A severely attractive, middle-aged secretary sat in the outer office, working at a computer console. Opposite her were a coffee-table and three comfortable leather chairs. There were original oil paintings on the walls depicting seascapes. It had been six years since Creasy had been in that office in Marseille. As he walked in through the door the secretary glanced up and then back at her console. She then did a complete double take, jerking upright in her seat, a look of astonishment on her face.

'I thought you were dead,' she stammered.

'Yes. I sort of came back to life.' He gestured at the door to the inner office. 'Is he in?'

She had recovered her composure. 'Yes. But he has someone with him.' She reached for the phone. 'I'll tell him you're here.'

He shook his head. 'No, I'll wait. Any chance of a coffee?'

She stood up and bustled over to a percolator in the corner. When he tasted the coffee he looked up and said approvingly, 'What a memory you have. It's been about six years since I was in this office and you remembered that I don't take milk or sugar.'

She smiled at the compliment, at the same time thinking that this was a man nobody would forget. She wondered what her boss' reaction would be when he set eyes on him.

It happened about two minutes later. A very dark negro wearing a well-cut suit came through followed by Leclerc, who was saying, 'You'll have my fax on Thursday but, believe me, the prices will be final and the letter of credit is essential.'

At that moment Leclerc's eyes found Creasy. He paused briefly in his stride but his face showed nothing. Leclerc had always been a good poker player.

The negro was ushered out and Creasy stood up. Leclerc turned and the two men studied each other in silence. Leclerc was about Creasy's age, tall, florid, running slightly to fat. Dressed in a dark blue suit with a faint pinstripe, he looked like a banker. In fact he was an ex-mercenary who one day had discovered it was more profitable selling weapons than using them himself. And much safer. He had become one of the most succesful arms dealers in Europe. Six years earlier, when Creasy was about to take on a whole Mafia family in Italy, he had turned to Leclerc for his weapons. They were not friends; they never would be, but they respected each other.

Leclerc gestured at the open door to his office and Creasy went through, carrying his cup of coffee. The office was luxurious, but these walls were adorned with large photographs of weapons ranging from tanks and armoured personnel carriers to submachine-guns. Leclerc sat down behind the wide mahogany desk and Creasy sat in front of it.

'I had heard rumours,' the Frenchman said. 'Rumours that you were alive, that you had not died in that Naples hospital. Rumours that it had been fixed. I did not believe the rumours, but then I heard more rumours a couple of years ago. They were rumours that you had been seen in America and the Middle East. There was another rumour that Maxie MacDonald and Frank Miller did a job for you.' He smiled slightly. 'Old friends of yours. I began to believe the rumours.'

'Yeah, I did fake that death. It seemed like a good idea at the time. Half the damned Mafia in Italy was looking for me.'

Leclerc's smile grew wider. 'Hardly surprising. You wiped out their top family. That arsenal I supplied you with was apparently effective.'

'It was,' Creasy conceded. 'And I remain grateful.'

Leclerc inclined his head in acknowledgement and asked, 'What can I do for you now?'

Creasy gestured at the window. 'You know this city better than anyone. I need a briefing on certain underworld elements. Depending on that briefing, I might need some light weapons. The problem is that if I need them, I need them today.'

'If you need them you'll get them today. What information do you want?'

'I know the crime situation here is pretty well compartmentalised. The man or men I'm looking for will be paramount in the vice and drugs sector. If there's any white slavery going on in the city they'd be involved or know all about it. I need to know his or their location and what forces they have available.'

Leclerc's answer was immediate. 'Your man is Yves Boutin. He more or less controls prostitution in the city and much of the Riviera. He's one of several gang leaders in the drug business, but when it comes to vice he's the king-pin.' He went on to describe Boutin, his family, his brothers, his mistress, his chief lieutenants, his homes and his clubs. Finally he said, 'He's very well-connected politically and with the police.'

At this Creasy leaned forward and asked intently, 'How good are your connections and knowledge concerning the police?'

Leclerc smiled and spread his hand in an eloquent gesture. 'In my line of business they have to be perfect. The police force in this city is massively corrupt. It always has been and always will be.'

Creasy leaned further forward. 'Do you know an Inspector Serge Corelli?'

'Yes. Very well.'

'Is he corrupt?'

Leclerc burst out laughing and then said, 'That's an under-statement! He's the leader of the pack. A very very rich man, and getting richer by the day. Thanks in part to large contributions from Yves Boutin ... They're practically partners.' He noted the sombre expression on Creasy's face and asked, 'What's it all about?'

Creasy was deep in thought and when he spoke it was not to answer the question. 'If I or anyone else had gone to see Serge Corelli and asked detailed questions about Boutin, would Corelli inform Boutin?'

Leclerc smiled and said, 'Immediately!'

'Even if the person asking the questions was a police officer from another European force?'

Leclerc smiled again. 'In that case, he'd inform Boutin even more immediately.'

Another silence and then Creasy said, 'I'm going to need those weapons.'

'What do you want?'

Suddenly Creasy's voice became brisk and businesslike. 'Do you have a Colt 1911?'

Leclerc nodded. 'Always.'

'I need three extra mags.'

Leclerc nodded.

'I also need an SMG, small and easily concealed. Like an Ingram 10 with a folding butt.'

'I've got them,' Leclerc said, 'but I also have something better. Very new. Perhaps you haven't seen it.' He stood up and moved to one wall of the office. It was panelled in oak. He pressed a hand against a panel and slid it to the right. A huge wall-safe was revealed. He worked the combination lock, pulled open the heavy door and took out several metal boxes. Creasy also stood and watched as Leclerc opened them. One box contained a Colt 1911. Creasy picked it up and felt the familiar grip and then replaced it. He then looked into the other box and asked, 'What the hell is that?'

With satisfaction Leclerc replied, 'That's brand new. It's a miniature SMG made by Fabrique Nationale, it's called FN P90. It's very different. The body and magazine are made of plastic and detachable from the other metal components.' Quickly he disassembled the weapon. It took only seconds. Then he reassembled it and handed it to Creasy, saying, 'It's only as long as your forearm, but it will pierce body armour at one hundred and fifty metres. It's superior to any NATO rifle or compact SMG.'

Creasy was impressed. The weapon was very easy to conceal, using a shoulder-strap under a jacket or coat.

It was as if Leclerc was reading his mind. 'I can get you a shoulder-strap and a suppressor, which is a little bulky but fits under the other arm, also on a strap.'

Creasy nodded. 'I also need a silencer for the Colt.'

'No problem. What else do you need?'

'Four frag. grenades, and four phosphorescents and the webbing to sling them. Also a pair of goggles against the phosphorescents, and, yes, three pairs of handcuffs.'

'No problem,' Leclerc said, making a note on his pad. 'I can also arrange a practice session with the SMG down at my warehouse. Being light it's got quite a kick.'

Creasy shook his head. 'I don't have time. This afternoon I have to do a recce, then I have to make my move tonight. There is one other thing which you may or may not have. Do you remember, last time you supplied me with the components to make a very small, but very powerful bomb using plastic explosive with a tiny detonator and small remote control? Good for up to a couple of hundred metres?'

'I remember,' Leclerc answered. 'And I remember reading in the newspaper what you used it for in Italy. Not a nice way to send a man to hell.'

Creasy shrugged. 'He was not a nice man. Can you get it for me?'

Leclerc picked up one of the three phones on his desk, punched a number, listened for a moment and then spoke rapidly in French, listened again, then asked Creasy, 'Do you want it assembled or in components?'

'In components,' Creasy answered. 'I'll assemble it myself.'

Leclerc spoke again into the phone, rapidly and persuasively. Then he hung up and said. 'The components will be delivered here at six p.m. together with the other stuff. What else do you need?'

Creasy pondered for a moment. 'I need a safe hole and a good fast car, which is clean and has a green card and all other documentation for crossing borders within Europe. It should be fully fuelled with a few hundred extra litres in cans in the trunk. The car may not be returned, so cost it in. Both the hole and the car should be stocked with easy rations for three people, for three days. You know the drill.'

Leclerc made notes on his pad and said, 'No problem. Your safe hole will be an apartment in the same block where I have my penthouse. I own the whole block, but no one knows that. The local BMW dealer's a friend of mine. I'll get a good second-hand car from him and make sure it's serviced this afternoon.'

He sat back and looked at Creasy steadily, and then said quietly, 'I'm going to repeat what I said when you were last here. We've never been friends. Apart from Guido in Naples I doubt that you've ever had a really close friend. You're not that kind of man. But like I said then, I owe you. You saved my life in Katanga. That alone would be enough, but I also owe you for Rhodesia. You helped me land a very profitable order.' He spread his arms and said, 'Now you're in my city and apparently going up against Boutin, who has a lot of "soldiers". Do you need any back-up? I know some good people that can be trusted.'

'I appreciate it. But no thanks ... you know me.'

Leclerc nodded slowly. They both stood up and the Frenchman said, 'Everything will be here at six o'clock, including the info on Corelli. Then we can check out your hole and the car. If you need anything else at all just call me. You have my home number.'

'Thanks, I will. Now, what do I owe you for the stuff?'

Leclerc's face looked pained. 'Please, Creasy ... Don't insult me.'

They shook hands and Creasy left. Leclerc moved to the window and stood looking down at the street four floors below. He saw the American come out from the front door, cross the road and walk briskly away. There were plenty of taxis around but Creasy was not the sort of man who would come out of such a meeting and jump into a taxi at the front door. First he would make sure he had no tail.

Leclerc turned and went to the door of his office and opened it. He asked his secretary, 'How many shares do I have in Boutin's construction company?'

She fingered the keys of her console, looked at the screen and answered, 'Seventeen thousand. They went up four points last week and look good. They're sure to get that new bridge and flyover contract next month. It's a huge project.'

Tersely he said, 'Sell those shares before close of business today.'

FIFTEEN

She stood leaning back against the desk, gazing through the long one-way mirror. She had the sort of beauty that would stop traffic in any of the world's capitals: long-limbed with high breasts and a tiny waist flared into a high bottom and long flanks. Her ash-blonde hair fell to her shoulders, a contrast with the full-length, midnight blue satin dress.

She was looking through the one-way mirror which ran the length of the bar, and from her position she could survey the entire basement club. There was a small stage to her right and next to it, raised a little higher, was a dais with a four-piece band. There were intimate, velvet-covered banquettes around the walls, surrounding a polished wooden dance-floor. Customers were mostly middle-aged businessmen. The girls were almost uniformly beautiful and were also dressed in long gowns. The waitresses on the other hand wore cream silk blouses, slashed to the waist, and very short black, lycra mini-skirts above dark, fishnet stockings and black patent leather knee-high boots.

She turned her head to see the two men being ushered through the door. One was blond and fair-skinned and slightly plump. She guessed his age at approaching forty. The other was much younger, with jet-black hair and dark skin. He had sharp features and she decided he was very handsome. They sat at the bar almost in front of her and for a moment her view was obscured as the barmaid took their orders. She reached behind her and flicked one of a row of switches. Immediately she heard their voices. They spoke in English. The blond one ordered a whisky soda, and specified Chivas Regal. The young one ordered a Campari and fresh orange juice. As she mixed the drinks the barmaid chatted to them as she had been trained, first asking where they were from. The blond said he was from Stockholm and the handsome one said he was from Cyprus. The barmaid told them that the floor-show would start at midnight and to let her know if they wanted a table. The young man answered that they would stay at the bar.

The barmaid then moved away to serve another customer, and the beauty behind the mirror studied them again before reaching for the telephone. She dialled a number which was answered immediately.

She said, 'Yves, they are here ... Yes, they fit the description exactly.' She listened for a moment and glanced at her watch and said, 'OK, about halfway into the floor-show.' She hung up, pushed herself away from the desk and moved towards the door.

Michael and Jens' heads moved in unison to the left as she appeared from the recessed door. She came towards them smiling, knowing the effect she had on them, the effect she had on all men who were not senile or gay.

She held out her hand to the blond, saying, 'Welcome to The Pink Panther. I'm Denise, the manageress.' She squeezed his hand and he squeezed hers in return, looking slightly flustered. She withdrew her hand, reached across him and shook the young man's hand and also squeezed it. He did not squeeze hers and he did not look flustered, nor did he look at her high breasts. He just gazed at her face. Not disinterested but not overwhelmed. He was, she decided, extremely handsome. She chatted with them for several minutes, asking the usual questions and then explaining that if they wanted company it was readily available, and intimating that such company could become very intimate indeed in other, more private parts of the club upstairs.

'We have a very good floor-show here at midnight,' she said. 'But at one o'clock we have a more ... how shall I say it? A more erotic show. In fact, a very erotic show upstairs. Usually that's reserved for only those customers who have hired a hostess, but since this is your first visit you'll be my personal guests.'

Jens started to say something, but Michael cut in. 'That's very kind of you. We'd be honoured.'

She smiled and gave him a look that sent him a definite promise. She said, 'I'll come to collect you just before one o'clock.'

She turned and walked back to the recessed door. Both men watched her swaying bottom and then Jens murmured, 'Do you want to see a sex show? I did three years in the Vice Squad in Copenhagen and I can tell you they're not very erotic.'

Equally quietly, Michael replied, 'It's necessary. I need to see as much of this building as possible, so I can draw up a plan for the "snatch".'

The Dane nodded, and then said, 'I'm not surprised you want to take her rather than one of the kids.'

SIXTEEN

In some respects Serge Corelli did not have the same natural instincts as Jens Jensen. He did not realise he was being followed. He left the office late, just after seven o'clock, driving out of the basement garage in his red Renault 19. He never brought his Mercedes 600 to the office.

He did not notice the rented Citroën across the road which moved out into the traffic behind him. He drove to the O'Berry Bar on Rue de l'Eveche and parked outside a No Parking zone. He did not bother locking it; every petty thief in Marseille knew whose it was. A minute later he was drinking the first of his regular vodka tonics and chatting to the heavy-breasted barmaid with whom he'd had a brief fling some years before. He drank until nine o'clock, then belatedly rang his wife and told her he had to stay out to dinner on business. He drove four blocks to the Rue de Lorette and parked in the alley beside the Chez Etienne restaurant, again leaving the car unlocked. He ate a leisurely dinner of vegetable soup, fillet steak with truffles and *pomme soufflé*, followed by *crêpes suzettes flambées*, all washed down with a bottle of Chateau Margaux. He then had coffee and a vintage Cognac. It was an expensive restaurant but when he rose from the table just before midnight he received no bill. The owner merely shook him deferentially by the hand.

It was dark in the alley and, even though he could hold his liquor well, Inspector Serge Corelli was a little unsteady. He opened the door to the Renault and slumped into his seat. He pulled the door shut and reached for the ignition key. Then he felt something cold on the back of his neck and heard a quiet voice speaking in fluent, accentless French.

'This is a Colt 1911 with a soft-nosed forty-five shell. You do exactly what you're told or that shell goes through your brain.'

Corelli stiffened, feeling the adrenaline surging through his blood, trying not to panic. 'Who are you?' he blurted out. 'Do you know who I am, you fool?'

From behind him the cold voice said, 'You're Inspector Serge Corelli and you'll keep silent or you'll lose most of your head. Now start the car and drive towards the old fish market district. Drive carefully at a normal speed. I seriously don't care if you live or die, so if you try and pull a stunt, it'll be the last thing you ever try to do.'

Corelli drove carefully, his mind racing, trying to think who the man behind him could be. He had a pistol in the glove compartment but that was locked and the key was on the same ring as the ignition key. His only chance would be when they arrived at the destination. When he turned off the ignition to pull out the key the man would have to get out of the car, and he might get a second or two to open the glove compartment.

They approached the old fish market area, and the man gave brief directions. Finally they arrived in a dimly-lit street behind a row of garment factories. It was lined with dilapidated garages, some of which had For Rent signs on them. It was about half past midnight and the street was deserted. The voice told him to pull over and stop. Then it told him to put the car into neutral and apply the handbrake. As the handbrake ratcheted tight he felt the pressure on the nape of his neck withdraw. He tensed himself to make his move, but a split second later his brain flashed white and then black, as the butt of the pistol smashed into it.

The policeman came around, lying in a heap in the corner, his arms pulled behind him, his hands locked into handcuffs. Painfully, he pushed himself into a sitting position against the wall and focused his eyes. The garage was lit by a single, shadeless lightbulb hanging from the ceiling. He saw an old wooden table with a chair on each side and a big man dressed in black looking at him. The man reached forward and picked up the heavy black pistol. It was fitted with a silencer. Without seeming to aim, the man pulled the trigger. The bullet entered the wall six inches above Corelli's head, showering him with plaster. With a moan he scrambled away on his knees. Another bullet smashed into the wall just in front of him. Corelli froze in terror. The man's voice was quiet. He pointed to a chair.

'Stand up, and sit there.'

Corelli did not move for several seconds. He crouched, looking at the oil-stained, concrete floor.

'Do it now and do not ask questions. Do not open your mouth until I tell you.'

Corelli pushed himself to his feet. The pain in his head was intense. Carefully he moved across the room and sat on the edge of the chair. His eyes focused again on the man across the table. He noticed the cropped grey hair and the scars on the face and the cold, slate-grey eyes. He looked down at the table. There were several objects on it which he did not recognise: two round, recessed metal discs with bevelled edges, a lump of what looked like Plasticine, a small metal tube with two wires attached, and a small metal box with two buttons on it.

'Do you know what those are?' the man asked.

'No,' Corelli murmured.

'They're the components for a small, but very powerful bomb.' The man leaned forward and pointed at the larger metal disc. It had a diameter of about six inches. 'That's the back casing.' The man pointed to a smaller disc, which had a diameter of about four inches. 'That's the front casing.' He pointed to the small grey lump. 'That's plastic explosive.' The finger moved again to the small black metal box. 'That's the remote control.' The voice took on a conversational tone. 'Now that bomb is not big enough to blow up a house, but when it's assembled and strapped at the base of your spine, and when it explodes, it will definitely blow you in half.'

Corelli's eyes were fixed on the objects, mesmerised.

The man went on, 'You and I are going to spend some hours together. You are going to answer some questions and, based on your answers, we'll be making a little trip. You'll have the bomb at the base of your spine. I will have the detonator in my pocket and a finger on the button. Just pray that I don't bump into something, or that something or someone doesn't bump into me.'

The Frenchman lifted his head and looked again into the man's cold eyes. His question came out as a croak: 'Who are you?'

'For you I'm life or death. It will be your choice.'

'What do you want?'

The man leaned forward and started to assemble the bomb. The policeman watched in dreadful fascination and heard the words: 'You had a visit from a Danish policeman called Jens Jensen, probably this morning. He would have asked you questions about certain criminals in the city and maybe asked to see your files.'

He looked up from his work and again Corelli asked, 'Who are you?'

The man put the components on the table, stood up, walked around, grabbed the Frenchman by the hair, pulled him upright and in a blur of speed hit him three times to the body with a stiff-fingered hand, each blow to a different nerve, each nerve sending an agonised signal to Corelli's already agonised brain. He was dumped back in the chair and Creasy moved back around the table, sat down and continued working on the bomb.

He said quietly, 'If you don't answer my questions, I'm going to do that again ... and again ... and again. Only harder. If you don't answer then I'll shoot your fingers off one by one. Then your toes.'

Corelli was slumped over the table, his whole body wracked with pain. Slowly he lifted his head and looked into the man's eyes and knew for certain that he meant it. In an almost inaudible voice he said, 'Yes, this morning with another man ... a young man. He said he was his assistant but I didn't believe it. Too young and he wasn't Danish.'

Creasy had finished packing the plastic explosive into the recess of the larger disc. He unscrewed the small metal tube and checked the cadmium cell battery, then connected the two wires and carefully pushed the detonator into the plastic explosive.

'Did you show them any files?' he asked without looking up.

'Yes.'

'What files in particular?'

'Vice and drugs.'

'What gang in particular?'

Corelli was feeling waves of nausea sweeping over him. He swallowed deeply several times and then shook his head. 'I don't know, I wasn't there. I don't know. I gave them an office.'

Creasy was screwing the front casing onto the bomb. He looked up and said, 'Who is the leading gangster in vice and drugs?'

There was a silence and then Corelli answered, 'A half-Arab called Jahmed ... Raoul Jahmed.'

Carefully Creasy put the bomb on the table, stood up and walked around, grabbed the Frenchman by the hair again and hammered blows into his body. Two minutes passed before Corelli could sit upright again. His face was a picture of pain and he began to beg. 'Why? ... Why did you hit me? ... I'm answering your questions.'

'You lied,' Creasy answered curtly. 'You're trying to protect your friend Yves Boutin. He's the biggest in the city by far. He pays you big money. If you lie again you'll regret it. Keep it in your head that I know most of the answers to the questions, and I know when you lie. When was the last time you spoke to Yves Boutin?'

Corelli was looking down at the table again, not knowing who his tormentor was or how much he knew. But he did know the pain and that he had reached his limit.

'This afternoon,' he said, 'about three o'clock, on the telephone.'

'What did you tell him?'

Another silence and then Corelli raised his head and said, 'I told him that a Danish policeman from the Missing Persons Bureau was asking questions about him. Asking where his children went to school.'

'Where do they go to school?'

'Privately. In a Swiss boarding school.'

'Are they there now?'

'Yes.'

'Is Boutin close to his wife?'

Corelli began to offer information. 'No, he's closer to his mistress. Denise Defors. He keeps her in an apartment in the city. She fronts up his top club, The Pink Panther.'

Silence while Creasy thought. While he put himself into Michael's mind. It was not difficult. He had partly created that mind. Michael's strategy would have been to 'snatch' someone close to Boutin. If the children were away in boarding school then the obvious person would be his mistress. Michael would have gone to the club on a recce. He glanced at his watch. It was just after one a.m. He asked, 'Presumably you gave Boutin a description of Jensen and the young man?'

'Yes, a detailed one.'

Again Creasy was silent while he thought. Then he pointed and said, 'Kneel down there.'

The fear showed vividly in Corelli's face. 'Why?'

Creasy stood up, leaned across the table and said, 'Do it now or I'll hit you again.'

Slowly Corelli got up, moved to the spot in the centre of the garage and went down on his knees. Creasy picked up the bomb and the roll of masking tape. He straddled the Frenchman from behind, pulled up the back of his jacket and with his elbow forced the Frenchman's head forward until it almost touched the floor. He tore off a four-foot strip of masking tape and laid it, sticky side up, beside the Frenchman. Then he placed the saucer-shaped bomb into the centre of the masking tape, the front casing facing up. Very carefully he positioned the bomb at the base of Corelli's spine and then reached round with the masking tape to secure it. Corelli was moaning deep in his throat. Creasy ignored it. He picked up the roll of masking tape and wound it round the policeman's body many times, securing the bomb tightly. Then he grabbed Corelli by the back of his collar, pulled him upright and adjusted his jacket. He walked around the Frenchman and said, 'No one would notice you're a walking bomb. Sit down again very carefully on the edge of the chair.'

Corelli did as he was told, moving as though he was walking on thin ice and sitting down very, very slowly. Creasy walked to a leather bag in the corner, unzipped it and pulled out a mobile telephone. He placed it on the table in front of Corelli, then he carried the other chair around next to Corelli. He sat down, reached across the table and pulled the detonator across in front of him. He put his index finger very close to the red button and said, 'That's what I push if I decide that you're showing the slightest lack of co-operation.'

Corelli's eyes flickered to the button with the finger hovering over it. He noticed the burn marks on the back of the thick hand and guessed how they had been caused. At one time his tormentor had been the tortured himself.

'I'll co-operate,' he said harshly. 'Just be fucking careful with that thing.'

He looked up into Creasy's face and heard the words: 'I only get careless with these things when I get angry. I'm quite safe sitting here. It's not a fragmentation bomb. If I press that button the outer casing will hit the back wall.' He pointed at the wall in front of Corelli. 'And the inner casing will hit that wall, together with your blood and guts. It will probably take you quite a few very painful minutes to die.' He picked up the phone and said, 'Now you're going to call your good friend, Yves Boutin, and ask him what happened to Jens Jensen and his friend. If he's holding them you want to know where, because you want to question them yourself before he disposes of them. I'll be listening to the conversation and if I think you're not being sincere or convincing enough, I hit the button.'

The mobile phone was a handless, speaker-phone type. Creasy positioned it between them and asked, 'What's the number?'

'6854321 ... That's his personal mobile, which he carries with him ... Even to bed.'

Creasy pressed in the numbers and pushed the 'send' button. Then he sat hunched over, one finger poised over the 'end' button and one finger of the other hand over the red button on the detonator. Corelli drew a deep breath.

A few seconds later Boutin's cold, harsh voice came out of the speaker. 'Boutin.'

Corelli's eyes flickered to the speaker. 'Serge,' he said in a voice which didn't betray his tension. 'Did those two show up?'

A laugh came out of the speaker. 'Sure, they're in The Pink Panther right now. They've seen the cold show and Denise has persuaded them to go upstairs to see the hot one. We'll take them out in a few minutes.'

'To where?' Corelli asked sharply.

'The usual place.'

'Don't do anything until I get there,' Corelli said. 'I want to question them myself first.'

Boutin's voice showed a trace of surprise. 'Are you sure? Even if they're blindfolded they may recognise your voice.'

'It won't matter,' Corelli replied. 'When it's over they can go to the fish.'

Immediately after the word 'fish', Creasy's finger hit the 'end' button on the phone. 'What's the "usual place"?' he asked.

'It's a big old house, about five kilometres outside the city on the coast. It has its own small harbour and Boutin keeps a couple of fast motorboats there.'

'Tell me more.'

'It stands in its own grounds, surrounded by a high stone wall.'

'Guards?'

'Always.'

'How many?'

'Never less than four, sometimes more.'

'Armed?'

'Yes ... with hand-guns.'

'What goes on in that house?'

The policeman sighed and tried to look mournful. 'He keeps drugs there and processes them.'

'What else?'

Another sigh and the policeman answered, 'Sometimes girls.'

'What kind of girls?'

The policeman was silent, looking down at the table, but when Creasy started to move, his head jerked up and he said hurriedly, 'Lost girls.'

'Explain.'

The policeman explained. He explained how the girls, mainly from northern Europe, were abducted and then forcibly made heroin addicts and sold into prostitution in other parts of the Mediterranean, in the Middle East and North Africa.

Creasy's voice was very low, but it drove straight into the policeman's brain. 'You mean he "processes" them like he "processes" the drugs?'

A pause, then Corelli nodded, his eyes again looking down at the table.

'You're a wonderful human being,' Creasy said. 'Head of the Missing Persons Bureau and duty-sworn to protect such innocents. You are conspiring to do exactly the opposite. I don't know if there is a heaven or hell, but I'm damn sure there's a place for people like you.'

SEVENTEEN

Jens was wrong. It was erotic. Denise led them into an expensively furnished room at the end of a long corridor. In the middle was a white-carpeted, round dais with two steps leading up to it. On the dais was a solitary white cane chair. On it was a pair of black high-heeled shoes. Draped over the back of the chair was a flame-red silk gown and on top of that a pair of sheer black stockings, suspender belt and ivory-coloured silk French knickers. Beside the chair was a small white cane table. On that lay an open white leather box and next to it was a plate-sized mirror on a stand.

Circling the dais were a dozen embossed black leather settees of the type normally found in exclusive gentlemen's clubs in London. Half of them were occupied by middle-aged business types. Michael noted that two of them were Arabs; the others were Europeans and one oriental, probably Japanese. They all had hostesses beside them. In front of each settee was a low table with an ice bucket containing vintage champagne. One of the Arabs was already fondling the breasts of his companion under her gown, while she licked his ear.

Denise guided them to a settee and whispered with a smile, 'This has the most strategic view.'

Jens was surprised at the choice of music floating out from the quadraphonic speakers. It was Vivaldi's 'Four Seasons', one of his favourites. With a twitch of guilt he realised that he often played it while making love to Birgitte. Especially the 'Summer' movement.

Denise sat between them. They could both feel the warmth of her thighs and inhale the musk of her perfume. As she leaned forward and poured three glasses of champagne, a door opened to her left and a woman emerged.

She was tall, almost six feet, and in her early thirties. A dark brunette with slightly curly hair falling outwards and down over her shoulders. She was slender, almost thin. Her face had no make-up. Her legs and her neck were so long as to be almost out of proportion but not quite. In spite of her height she walked to the dais like a ballerina. She was totally naked.

There had been a murmur of conversation around the room, but it stilled completely as she walked up to and on to the dais. She did a slow pirouette, her green eyes lingering on each man in turn. Each man was convinced that they lingered on him the longest. The Arab had stopped stroking his companion's breasts. In a matter of fact, contralto voice she spoke a single sentence: 'I prepare myself for a man.'

She turned, stepped up to the small table and looked into the white leather box. The only sound in the room was Vivaldi, entering the 'Summer' movement. Jens squirmed with some embarrassment against Denise's thigh. His erection was building. He glanced across to Michael whose eyes were transfixed on the naked woman. He noted that Denise's right hand was resting on Michael's left thigh. His eyes were drawn back to the dais. The naked woman had taken several items out of the leather box. They were cosmetics. For the next fifteen minutes she applied light make-up to her face, leaning low to study herself in the mirror. Her legs were straddled.

Jens and Michael did have the most strategic view. Jens had been faithful to Birgitte since their marriage, but still had to admit that ten feet away was the most perfect bottom he had ever seen. Finally, satisfied with her make-up, she turned to the chair, picked up the suspender belt and fastened it around her slim waist. She sat down and slowly rolled the sheer black stockings, first one, then the other, up to her thighs and hooked them to the suspender belt. She did it naturally and without any overt eroticism. Then she rose, picked up the French knickers, stepped into them and pulled them up to her waist. She stepped into the shoes and then picked up the wispy gown, pulling it up to and just over her small breasts. It shimmered from the alabaster white of her shoulders to the jet black of her shoes.

For the first time she lifted her head again, surveyed the men, and said in a quiet, sad voice, 'I have wasted my time.' She made a small smile and lifted her hands in front of her face and said, 'No, I have not wasted my time ... I have made myself beautiful for myself.' Her shy smile broadened. 'If I don't have a man to take me, I will take myself.' Slowly she pirouetted again, looking at each man and saying, 'Have you ever seen a woman take herself? We all do it differently. I do it with my thumbs.'

74

Slowly she reached down and pulled up the front of her dress exposing her French knickers and then sank to her knees on the shag carpet and rolled forward onto her stomach. The audience watched in total silence as she pulled her arms underneath herself and slid her hands between her thighs. Only her elbows were visible and they were trembling. The dais very slowly started to rotate. Her bottom began to rotate at about the same speed. Her chin was flat on the carpet, her neck and back arched as each man in the audience came into her view. She looked them straight in the eye. She had a gentle smile on her lips. Every man was imagining her long, slender, red-tipped thumbs sliding against her clitoris. At this point all their companions had been forgotten and they were leaning forward, watching avidly.

The woman spoke again. Her soothing contralto voice had grown husky. 'It's good ... so very good ... but never as good as a man inside me.' Then she spoke very slowly and even huskier, during the course of one rotation of the dais. 'Is there no man who can take me?' She kept repeating the phrase, emphasising the word 'take' as she looked directly into the eyes of each of the men. Her bottom began to rotate even faster and it was obvious that what she was feeling was genuine. Abruptly the Arab who had been fondling his hostess' breasts rose to his feet, unzipping his trousers. He jumped onto the dais, pulled out his engorged penis, pulled up the back of her skirt, knelt between her legs, pushing them further apart, pulled aside the French knickers and with a grunt plunged into her. She did not remove her hands but continued rubbing herself, but she turned her head and said, 'That's perfect now.'

Denise leant forward between Jens and Michael, who were watching the tableau intently. Occasionally she moistened her lips with her tongue. Her right hand had moved to Michael's crotch, kneading the hard lump. With her left hand she made a gesture towards the abandoned hostess, who immediately rose to her feet and stepped up onto the dais in front of the woman. This hostess was seductive like a fox was crafty. Her movements were graceful, as natural to her as the raw sex she enjoyed. Kneeling down, she raised her skirt, showing her slender thighs which were encased in sheer white stockings. She wore nothing else. With her right hand she masturbated inches away from the brunette's glazed eyes. At that moment Denise took her hand away from Michael's crotch, put her hand behind both men's heads, pulled them towards her and said huskily, 'This is a little tame.

75

Something more interesting is about to start in a room above. Follow me.'

They followed her like lambs. As they left the room they could hear the brunette moaning into her orgasm.

Denise opened another padded door halfway down the corridor above and ushered them through. The room was dimly lit, but they could see the three men standing in a line in front of them, each holding a silenced pistol. They heard the door close behind them and the suddenly hard voice of Denise.

'We are going to have a different show ... and you are going to be the stars.'

EIGHTEEN

'I'll make a deal,' Corelli said flatly.

Creasy looked up from the canvas bag in the corner of the garage. Corelli was still sitting in front of the table, leaning forward intently, his hands still cuffed behind him.

'I'll make a deal,' Corelli repeated.

Creasy picked up the canvas bag, carried it to the table and unzipped it. 'What deal?' he asked.

'I'll guarantee your friends are released unharmed. My personal guarantee.'

Creasy was taking several items out of the bag and laying them on the table. Casually he said, 'Your personal guarantee isn't worth a dog's turd.'

The Frenchman's voice took on an insistent tone. 'I have the power. If I tell Boutin to let them go, he'll do it ... he needs me.'

Creasy's laugh was short and mirthless. 'He needs you like a second left foot. From what I hear he's paying off half the Marseille police force. If you call him up and tell him to let them go, they'll vanish forever and he'll deny any knowledge of ever having heard of them. And I guess within a matter of days you'll be dead meat as well. You're just a crooked cop, Corelli. Boutin is way above your league. You're his puppy and nothing else.'

Creasy had been preparing while he had been talking. He had taken off his black jacket and slipped into the black webbing and the two sling shoulder-holsters. Corelli watched in mute fascination as the eight grenades were clipped onto the webbing. Then Creasy stripped down the submachine-gun, reassembled it, inserted a magazine and clipped it onto the holster under his left shoulder. It fitted snugly under his arm. Three times in quick succession he practised releasing it and aiming. It was a blur of motion. Then he clipped the Colt under

77

his right arm and again practised the release. Satisfied, he slid the spare magazines and the SMG into the pockets of the webbing, near the waist. He stepped back and the policeman watched in awe as Creasy released the SMG, changed the magazine and reclipped the weapon in about three seconds.

Like all modern forces, the Marseille police force had its own regional special assignment group, trained to react to hijackings or any other criminal or terrorist activity. Corelli had watched them train. They were good. But he realised that none of them could compare to the man in front of him.

Finally Creasy took out a black three-quarter-length denim coat and slipped it on. It was loose and came down to his thighs; even unbuttoned it concealed the weaponry. He reached forward and picked up the small black remote control. Corelli stiffened in his chair. Creasy slipped it into his right-hand pocket and said tersely, 'Stand up.'

Nervously the Frenchman stood. Creasy moved around behind him, unlocked the cuffs and slipped them into the left-hand pocket of his coat. The other two pairs were already in the same pocket.

'Let's go,' he said. 'Let's go and meet this sweet partner of yours.'

NINETEEN

In his life Jens Jensen had never received a severe beating. It terrified him both mentally and physically. The worst part was the mindlessness and casualness of it all. He lay on the floor, curled up while the two men kicked him. It went on for several minutes. They were not in a frenzy, but taking turns, just placing their kicks where they wanted. On the other side of the room he could hear Michael grunting as he got the same treatment from two other men.

They had arrived in the back of a van, with guns at their heads, and had been taken through the back door of a large house, through the kitchen and down the steps to the basement. They had been ordered to lie on the floor with their arms in front of them and not to look up. A few minutes later they had heard echoing footsteps. From a prone position Jens had seen two pairs of shoes approach and come to a stop. One pair was brown, highly polished alligator leather; the other was high-heeled and black: the shoes of Denise Defors. Jens assumed that the man was Yves Boutin. The man spoke to them in English with a heavy French accent.

'In exactly ten minutes, I'm going to ask you some questions. Between now and then my men will give you a very slight example of what will happen to you if you don't answer them, and answer them truthfully.'

Boutin and the woman had walked away and other shoes started pounding into his body. He had heard Michael shout, 'Curl up! Don't resist.'

Irrationally, through the agony, something came into Jens' mind. He remembered, all those years ago at school, the physics master trying to explain Einstein's Theory of Relativity: 'If you sit on a scalding hot oven for two seconds, it feels like two minutes, but if you kiss a beautiful girl for two minutes, it feels like two seconds.'

The ten minutes of the beating felt like ten hours. Then it stopped, and he lay there, still curled up, moaning with the pain. The two men above were discussing whether Marseille would beat Monaco at football the next afternoon. Then one of them said, 'Straighten yourself out. Lie on your stomach with your hands outstretched. Both of you.'

Slowly Jens began to uncurl, every limb in agony. He was too slow. The man stepped forward and drove a foot into his kidneys. Jens yelled in pain and rolled over onto his stomach. The alligator shoes returned to within inches of his outstretched hands. Beyond them he could see the woman from the waist down, standing a few feet away.

'What is your name?' the voice asked.

In an instant terror changed to anger. 'I'm a fucking policeman,' Jens snarled. 'And you'll pay for this.'

One of the alligator shoes moved out of sight and then slammed down on Jens' right hand. The Dane screamed again and then heard Michael shouting, 'Answer his questions! All of them! Truthfully!'

Jens then heard a dull thud and a grunt from Michael, as a foot slammed into him. The voice said to Michael, 'If you open your mouth again without being told, you'll get a bullet in the leg.'

A silence, then the voice asked Jens again, 'What's your name?'

Jens answered through waves of pain. 'My name is Jens Jensen.'

'What are you doing here?'

'I was forced here at gunpoint.'

The voice said, 'If you get clever you'll suffer. What are you doing in Marseille?'

'I came to confer with a colleague here.'

'About what?'

'Missing persons.'

He heard the woman laugh. Boutin said harshly to her, 'Shut up!' To Jens he said, 'So why were you asking questions about me? And why did you come to my club?'

'Because you're known to deal in both drugs and women. The two go hand in hand.'

At that moment, Creasy was looking at the house from a rise in the road three hundred metres away. He was sitting in the passenger seat of Corelli's Renault. Corelli sat behind the wheel, speaking.

'There will be one or two guards at the main gate and a third somewhere in the grounds. The guards at the main gate will let us through. I'm expected.'

'But I'm not,' Creasy stated.

'I'll introduce you as a colleague,' the Frenchman answered. 'There will be no problem at the gate. I have brought colleagues here sometimes in the past.'

'For what?'

A long pause, then Corelli said quietly, 'For pleasure.'

Beside him Creasy grunted. 'What a pigsty you all live in! What happens when we go into the house?'

'There will be one or two guards inside the front door. They will definitely search you for weapons.'

Grimly Creasy said, 'They're going to find them ... in the very nicest way. Will they have guns in their hands, or under their jackets?'

'Under their jackets.'

'Let's go.'

It went as the policeman had predicted. The massive gates were opened and a man stepped out and shone a torch into the car, first onto Corelli's face and then on Creasy's.

'He's a colleague,' Corelli explained.

The guard nodded and waved them on. They drove up a gravel driveway and parked next to a red Mercedes sports car.

'Is that Boutin's?'

'No, his mistress'.'

They climbed out of the car, walked up the steps and Corelli pressed a button. They heard the chimes inside and a few seconds later the door opened and they went through.

There were two of them, both hard-faced; one tall and so thin as to be almost skeletal; the other was short and stocky. Both wore loose-fitting suits. They nodded respectfully to Corelli but gave Creasy a suspicious look.

'A colleague,' Corelli explained. 'Your boss is expecting me.'

'He's in the basement,' the short one said, and then gestured at Creasy. 'Are you taking him with you?'

'Yes.'

'Then I'll have to check him.'

'Go ahead,' Creasy said affably and unbuttoned his coat.

The guard moved forward, raising his hands to pat him down. He was about six inches shorter than Creasy. Neither the guard nor Corelli saw the uppercut coming. It was just a blur; a sharp crack as the guard's jaw snapped shut, and the man was lifted off his feet by the force of the blow. The tall guard was fast but not fast enough. His right hand had vanished under his jacket before the unconscious

81

guard had hit the floor. But as his pistol came out, he knew he was too late. He saw the levelled Colt with its fat silencer. A split second later he felt the impact of the first bullet into his heart. He was punched back onto the wall. The second bullet went through his forehead an inch above his nose and splattered his brains against the wall. Unfortunately, he had time to flick off the safety of his pistol. It hit the flagstoned floor and fired a bullet which narrowly missed Corelli's feet. The pistol had no silencer and the shot echoed around the room.

Instantly Creasy turned and fired two shots into the heart of the unconscious guard and a third into his brain. Then, within seconds, he had unscrewed the silencer and changed the magazine. Corelli stood frozen as Creasy reholstered the pistol and unclipped the SMG.

'Move!' the American said. 'I follow you to the basement and no tricks. I've got my thumb on the button.'

In the basement they heard the single shot. Boutin's head jerked up in surprise and he turned to the open door and the long flight of stone steps leading up to the kitchen.

'Get up there,' he snapped at one of the guards, and to another he ordered, 'Cover the steps.'

The first guard ran up the steps three at a time, his pistol out-stretched. The second guard took up position at the open door, gun raised.

Michael lifted his chin and looked up and around the room. Boutin had grabbed Denise's arm and had pulled her away from the line of fire into a corner. He was holding a pistol. She looked frightened. A guard was standing over Jens with his pistol pointed at his head. Michael assumed that the remaining guard was doing the same behind him; he decided to wait before making any move. From above he heard a two-second burst from an SMG and a scream, and knew that Creasy was in the building. Michael's brain shifted into high gear. If it was Creasy and he had an SMG he would have other weapons. He definitely would not come down those stairs unpro-tected, and he wouldn't come down firing, in case Michael or Jens were hit by a stray bullet. No, he would neutralise everybody in the room first. Michael tensed.

Upstairs in the kitchen, Creasy stepped over the body of the guard he had just shot. Corelli was immobilised, handcuffed by one hand to a steel pipe by the big oven. He stood and watched, his face ashen.

Creasy moved up to the top of the steps, pulling out the dark goggles and adjusting them over his eyes. He reclipped the SMG and unclipped a phosphorescent grenade. He edged to the open door and, in a fraction of a second, took a glance down the stairs, then took the pin out of the grenade, set the lever free, counted in his head and with great force hurled it down the steps. It hit the floor between Jens and Michael, ricocheted off the back wall and then exploded in a blinding white light. Everyone in the room instinctively covered their eyes.

Michael shouted, 'Jens, don't move!' Then he shouted again, this time up the stairs: 'Three of them armed! One unarmed.'

Boutin was shouting something which Michael could not understand. Then Michael heard a thud and two short bursts from an SMG. Then a single shot. The woman was screaming in terror. Michael knew that the thud would have been Creasy, rolling into the room. Two short bursts would have taken out the two guards. Then Creasy would have changed the SMG to single shot and disabled Boutin.

Slowly the glare on the other side of Michael's eyelids diminished and Michael opened them. The scenario was exact. Creasy was crouched just inside the door. Michael noted the webbing under the open coat, holding the grenades and spare mags. He saw the blur of Creasy's right hand as he changed the mag of the SMG. The guard by the door was lying face down. Michael turned his head. The guard who had been standing over him was lying crumpled in the corner. Boutin was on his knees, one arm across his eyes, the other clutching his shoulder. His gun lay on the floor a few feet away from him. The woman was slumped against the wall, both hands across her eyes.

Creasy's voice snapped out. 'Jensen! Stay still! Michael, move! Get Boutin's gun.'

Michael scrambled to his feet, ran over and picked up Boutin's gun. By now the light in the room was returning to normal. Creasy rose, pulled off the goggles and dropped them into his pocket.

He said, 'Michael, the guards are kaput.' He gestured at Boutin and his mistress. 'Cover those two from the other side of the door. There are other guards in the grounds. They'll be on their way.' He disappeared up the steps.

Boutin's eyes were open now. He looked up at Michael and then at his two dead bodyguards. His mistress had sunk to her haunches, trembling in shock. Boutin took his hand from his shoulder and looked at the blood on his palm. He started to say something, but Michael's voice cut him off.

'Shut your mouth or I'll put a bullet through it.'

From upstairs they heard two more bursts from the SMG, and then nothing.

From the floor, Jens asked in a dazed voice, 'Who the hell was that?'

Michael grinned down at him.

'That was my old man.'

'Jesus Christ,' the Dane muttered. 'Can I get up now?'

'No. He said to lie still. It won't take long.'

It took a minute, then Creasy's voice called down the stairs. 'Michael?'

'Yes. Everything OK here.'

'Good. Does Jensen know how to use a gun?'

Jens provided the answer himself in a pained voice. 'Yes! Jensen does know how to use a gun and he's fed up lying here doing nothing.'

Jensen heard a short laugh and then Creasy shouted, 'Get one of the guard's guns and come up here.'

The Dane scrambled to his feet, moved to the guard near the door and rolled him over onto his back with his foot. The pistol was lying under him, its barrel covered in blood. Quickly Jens picked it up by the barrel, wiped it against the guard's jacket, checked the safety was off and that the magazine was full, and then ran up the stairs.

He found Creasy in the kitchen with Serge Corelli.

'What the hell?' Jens asked, astonished.

'Later!' Creasy snapped. 'We don't have much time. The outside guards are dead and I doubt there are any more upstairs. They'd be here by now, or they might be hiding. Let's check it out. I'll go first. You watch my back, from about five metres.'

There were no guards upstairs, only an old woman, cowering at the end of the corridor. There were also two drugged girls in separate cell-like rooms. Jens recognised the first one immediately.

'Hanne Andersen,' he said. 'I was studying her file only a few days ago.'

She sat on the bed, looking back at him with glazed eyes. He spoke a few words in Danish to her, mentioning her name, and her eyes cleared for a moment and she nodded.

'Later,' Creasy said. 'Let's check the other rooms.'

They found the other girl in the next one. She was sitting in a corner with her arms around her drawn-up knees. There were bruises on her arms and face. She was very young, dark and beautiful, and very frightened. She cringed further back into the corner, mumbling in English, 'No ... No ... Please ... No more.'

Jens moved forward, speaking to her softly, but she only cowered lower, her eyes reflecting fear and despair.

Creasy said, 'Let's get the hell out of here. First we'll get them to the car and you stay with them while I collect Michael. I'll take care of the old woman.'

Startled, Jens asked, 'Are you going to kill her?'

Creasy shook his head.

'No, but she deserves it, being part of this slime.'

He walked quickly down the corridor to the woman, who watched his approach and started speaking rapidly in French. He did not answer, he just grabbed her by the hair and slammed his fist into her jaw. She crumpled to his feet. He turned away.

In the basement, Denise Defors had recovered some of her composure. She tried pleading with Michael, telling him that the business had nothing to do with her. He told her to shut up. Then, with the instinct of any cornered animal, she tried to escape. Her life had been such that anything she had ever wanted from any man she had always received. She could not conceive that any man would willingly shoot her. She pushed herself away from the wall and ran for the door.

Michael shot her in the back. As she slumped against the doorpost, he shot her again in the back of her head, then immediately levelled the pistol back at Boutin, who put up his good hand as if to ward off a blow.

'No ... Please, no,' he stammered. His face was dripping with sweat.

'Just shut up,' Michael said harshly. 'There's a small chance you might live.'

A minute later, Creasy came down the steps, glanced at the dead woman and then at Michael.

Michael said, 'She made a run for it.'

Creasy nodded, took out a piece of paper from his pocket, gave it to Michael and said, 'Jens is in the Renault outside –' he gestured at Boutin – 'together with two of this bastard's victims. Take the Renault and wait for me outside the main gates. The kitchen window faces the road there. If you hear any police sirens, fire a bullet through it. Do the same if any car goes through those gates – there's a mobile phone on the driver's seat – then drive away and phone the number on that bit of paper. The man at the other end will give you directions to a hole. Wait for me there. Otherwise I'll be finished here in five minutes. I'll meet you at the car.'

Michael simply nodded and headed out through the door. Creasy looked at Boutin expressionlessly and said, 'We're going up to the kitchen to have a brief but informative conversation.' He gestured with his gun. 'Move.'

With a grunt of pain, the Frenchman moved.

Outside, Michael found Jens in the back seat of the Renault with the two girls. One of them was slumped against the window, seemingly unconscious. The other was holding Jens' hand, while he was talking to her quietly in what Michael guessed was Danish. Michael got into the driver's seat without a word, turned the ignition and drove the car down the driveway to the open gates. He turned right and parked the car fifty metres down the road, took out the pistol and watched the window of the kitchen about one hundred and fifty metres away.

'What now?' Jens asked.

'We wait,' Michael said, and explained Creasy's instructions. 'What shape are those girls in?' he asked.

'Very bad shape,' the Dane answered bitterly. 'They were damn lucky – one of them was due to be shipped out tonight. The other wasn't quite ready yet. Bastards!'

'We were lucky too,' Michael said quietly. 'First, very stupid, then very lucky.'

'I wonder what Corelli was doing there? Handcuffed . . .?'

'We'll find out soon enough,' Michael answered.

Six minutes later, Creasy slipped into the front passenger seat.

'No movement,' Michael said. 'Did you let them live?'

Creasy answered, 'I handcuffed Boutin to Corelli, back to back. Someone will find them.'

From the back seat, Jensen said with bitterness, 'I'm a cop. But men like that don't deserve to live. The way things are here they'll probably get away with it.'

Creasy turned to look at him and then showed him the small black box in his hand, and very quietly said, 'Not this time.'

The Dane watched Creasy's thumb depress the button and heard the dull explosion from the house.

Creasy said, 'Well, they'll only find bits of them. They've just gone to that special hell reserved for such people.'

TWENTY

It was a comfortably furnished, three bedroom apartment. Jens and Michael sat at the dining-room table, drinking coffee. Creasy came out of one of the bedrooms and gently closed the door. His face showed little emotion, but the two younger men could feel rage and disgust emanating from his whole body.

He looked at them for a moment and then said quietly, 'I've killed many people in my life and sometimes regretted it. But I have no regrets about those bastards we left back there. Only human beings do that to their own kind. The lowest form of animal life would never understand it.'

They said nothing. Just watched him. He moved to the phone on the sideboard, picked it up and punched a number. Although it was five in the morning, he received an immediate answer. He talked into the phone in rapid French. Michael did not understand, but Jens caught the drift. Creasy indicated that everything had gone well. He then ordered what were obviously medical drugs. Jens recognised only one: methadone.

Then Creasy said, 'My friend, I'm going to need one of your men for maybe up to a week. He should be compassionate as well as tough ... Yes, I said compassionate. I'll call later in the morning. Try to have the drugs here as early as possible with your man. Tell him to use the code words "Red Three". The answer will be "Green Four" ... Thanks again.' He cradled the phone and came over to the table. Michael poured him black coffee.

'That was Leclerc,' Creasy said to him. 'Remember me telling you about him?'

Michael nodded. 'Yes, the arms dealer. I guess you got your arsenal from him.'

Jens interjected, 'We have to get those girls into a clinic as soon as possible.'

Creasy shook his head. 'Mr Jensen –'

Jens interjected again 'After what has happened tonight, maybe you can call me Jens?'

Creasy nodded solemnly and continued, 'Jens, you're a policeman, and obviously you have to think and, as much as possible, act like one. But this situation is different. Normally you'd pick up the phone and call the Marseille police headquarters or even police headquarters in Paris. But what would you tell them? That you've just been in a full-scale battle, involving pistols, grenades, SMGs and a bomb that killed the number one criminal in the region, together with the corrupt head of the Missing Persons Bureau in Marseille. How would you explain that? How would you explain myself and Michael? Bear in mind that I just killed seven men and Michael killed one woman. We'd all be stuck in this city for months. Including you. Michael and I would be arrested and held in a jail which no doubt is run by other corrupt officials. That's definitely not on my agenda.'

Jens thought about that and said, 'I could call my top boss in Copenhagen and he would call the top man in Paris.'

Michael said, 'They would still want answers, and we still could not provide them.'

Jens thought again and slowly nodded. 'So what do we do? What about those two girls? They need treatment, and soon.'

'They'll get it,' Creasy answered. 'I've had experience in such cases. First, let's examine their situation. I was able to talk to them both. They speak good English. Hanne's situation is infinitely better than the other girl's ... Her name is Juliet. She wouldn't tell me her second name. Hanne has a Danish policeman sitting right outside her bedroom door. She was reassured as soon as you showed her your ID. She comes from a wealthy and loving family. We have to get her back to Copenhagen.' Creasy looked at Jens. 'You can't just take her on a plane, not in her condition. I assume that her passport and clothing are being held by the Marseille police?'

Jens nodded.

'In that case,' Creasy went on, 'we'll have to get her a false passport.'

'How do I do that?'

'You don't. I do.'

'And how do I get her back to Copenhagen?'

'You drive her back,' Creasy answered. 'Together with another

88

man. The car's in the basement garage, fully fuelled with spare jerrycans of petrol in the trunk. You make it in one go. Her passport will give her the identity of your sister: she ran off with a low-life character while on holiday. He mistreated her and you came down to bring her home. It's a common enough story. We'll go into details later.'

Michael leaned forward and asked, 'What about the other one ... Juliet?'

Creasy shook his head. In a flint-hard voice he said, 'Her situation is very, very different. She's American. Her father was a GI with an American unit at Wiesbaden Airbase in Germany. He was killed during exercises three years ago, when Juliet was ten years old. Her mother had a secretarial job at the airbase and stayed on there. About a year ago she remarried. It seems that Juliet's stepfather's a total bastard. Within weeks he was abusing her mentally and physically. Her mother did little or nothing to stop it.' He sighed and then went on, 'About a month ago she stole some money from the house and ran away. She had some romantic notion about Paris and managed to get there, where she was quickly spotted by one of Boutin's scouts, who no doubt showed her great sympathy. Well, she ended up in that villa, up to her eyeballs in heroin ... I'd guess she was destined for the Middle East within a few days.'

Michael muttered, 'Animals ... fucking animals!'

Jens was shaking his head. 'No ... like Creasy said, animals don't do that to their own.' He glanced at Creasy. 'So what do we do with her?'

As though talking to himself, Creasy said, 'There's no way we can send her home. There's no way we can hand her over to the authorities here, or anywhere else for that matter. They would put her in a detox-centre and then either into a social centre or maybe send her back to her mother. Either option would be a disaster.'

'So what do we do with her?' Jens persisted.

Creasy was looking at Michael, who was staring at the top of the table and his empty coffee cup. Slowly he stood up, walked to the kitchen counter, refilled his cup from the percolator and, over his shoulder, said, 'We have no choice.'

'I agree,' Creasy answered.

The puzzled Dane looked first at Michael and then at Creasy. 'You agree what?' he asked.

Michael came back to the table and sat down and provided the answer. 'We keep her,' he said.

'Keep her?' Jens asked.

'Yes, keep her,' Creasy said. 'We take her back to Gozo. She'll have to go cold turkey to get off the heroin, then she'll need a hell of a lot of counselling to get her mind together. Gozo is the best place for that.'

Jens' face showed his incredulity. He stated flatly, 'You're both crazy! You're talking like she's a stray puppy or kitten that you picked up off the street.'

Creasy nodded. 'That's more or less it. But instead of fleas, she's got a dope addiction. Instead of a flea bath she goes cold turkey.'

The Dane shook his head in exasperation then also stood up, carried his cup to the kitchen counter, poured coffee into it, came back, sat down and started talking in a firm policeman's voice. He explained in emphatic terms that basically they were abducting the thirteen-year-old all over again. He pointed out that they had no right to do such a thing. He told them that there were strict procedures in every civilised country for handling such a situation. His voice grew louder, and his right hand thumped gently on the table-top as he emphasised his points. Nobody had the right to decide the future of any other human being. In every civilised country there were laws and social structures to deal with such cases. The girl was in no condition to make a judgement for herself. She should be taken immediately into care and given professional counselling. He emphasised the word 'professional' with a particularly hard thump on the table. Then he gave them both a very stern look.

Creasy was looking at his empty coffee cup. He said, 'Well, I'm sitting here with two very uncivilised, very bad-mannered people.'

'What do you mean?' Jens asked.

Creasy gestured at his coffee cup. 'In the last five minutes you've both gone and helped yourself to more coffee and no one offered me a cup.'

Michael smiled slightly, pushed himself to his feet, picked up Creasy's cup and went to the counter.

Creasy looked at the Dane. 'You talk to me about civilisation. Yes, the French pride themselves on their civilisation.' He gestured at the closed bedroom door. 'You call that civilisation? You call that a social structure? I've seen more civilisation and social structure in a mud hut village in the middle of Africa. I've seen more civilisation and social structure in the slums of Rio de Janeiro or Calcutta.' He leaned forward, his voice growing more intense. 'What you're saying is that we take that stray kitten to a vet. You know what vets do with stray kittens? They usually make a half-assed attempt to find it a home ... enter your professional social workers. If that doesn't work they put it to sleep.' He gestured again at the bedroom door, a gesture of anger this time. 'Michael and I killed to pick up that stray. You also risked your life.' He leaned even further forward towards the policeman. 'There's no way that stray is going to the vet.'

Jens looked into the slate-grey eyes, shrugged and said, 'You're taking on a big commitment.'

Michael returned to the table, put the coffee in front of Creasy and sat down. As far as he was concerned, that angle of the discussion was over. 'What's our next move?' he asked Creasy.

Creasy was still looking at the Dane. Jens saw the question in his eyes. He sighed, tapped the table once more and made up his mind. 'OK,' he said reluctantly. 'What is the next move?'

Creasy took a gulp of coffee and again gestured at the bedroom doors. 'Jens, go and sit with the Danish girl for a while. I have to talk to Michael, and afterwards he will go and sit with Juliet. Both of you try to reassure them. By now they'll be getting the craving.' He looked at his watch. 'The methadone will be here in a couple of hours.'

'Your friend will need a prescription for that,' Jens said.

Creasy nodded. 'My friend will get what he needs in this civilised country.'

The Dane thought about that for a moment, nodded, stood up and quietly went into one of the bedrooms, closing the door behind him.

Creasy looked quizzically at his son.

'So, tell me, Michael. How did you come to be lying on the floor in that basement, getting your ribs kicked in?'

Michael stood up and paced up and down across the room. Creasy held his tongue, realising that something was building up in Michael's mind and that it would soon come out. It came out sheepishly but with an underlying defiance.

'So I was stupid,' Michael said. 'I don't have your experience. You had to get me out with Jens.' He stopped pacing and turned and looked at Creasy. 'One day I'll get you out, just like that. Same scene, same situation!'

Creasy felt a warmth but had no way to show it. He simply shrugged and said, 'Tell me exactly what happened.'

Michael outlined his plans to snatch Boutin's mistress and get information. He told Creasy how they had gone to the nightclub on a recce and been led into the trap.

When he finished he looked up and said, 'OK. First, I should have realised that Corelli might have been corrupt. Second, I should have done the recce alone.'

Creasy nodded and asked, 'What did you hope to find out?'

Michael shrugged and said, 'I believe that "The Blue Ring" does exist ... Jens does too, and so does Blondie. My guess is that Boutin's relatively low-level. I wanted to find out the structure of the "Ring" and who was the next rung on the ladder ... and I made a couple of mistakes.'

Creasy said thoughtfully, 'Your strategy was good, but too hasty. You should not have gone with Jens to police headquarters and he should not have gone with you to the club. That way you could have checked things out without arousing suspicion. Then you should have taken one of the hostesses to bed, made love to her and out of totally natural curiosity, asked her about the manageress. Such women always like to gossip. Then you should have planned the "snatch".' Another brief smile flickered across his face. 'So you learned two lessons: never trust a policeman and never be led by your prick.'

'Weren't you ever?'

'Only once. I was younger than you. I lost my wallet and a little pride. You were about half an hour from taking a very deep dip in the sea and staying down there.'

Michael let that sink in and then asked, 'How did you find us?'

Creasy explained how he tracked them down, first through Blondie, then through Birgitte, then how he had learned about Corelli from Leclerc. After that it was straightforward.

'I'm sorry,' Michael said quietly.

Creasy took another sip of coffee. When he spoke his voice took on a different tone. 'No. Don't blame yourself. Lay it on my head. I have to realise that you are a man, and that years mean nothing. I should have supported you in this matter; been alongside you, not behind you. Be sure I'm with you now.'

Michael grinned.

'You were in hospital, for God's sake! What else could you do?'

Creasy shrugged.

'I could have supported you from the very beginning, so you would not have gone off trying to prove yourself ... Don't let me do that again.' He stood up, walked to the window and stood looking down at the street five floors below. A light rain was falling. The lights of an occasional car passed by. He turned and looked at Michael and then surprised the young man again. He spoke of his emotions. An event as rare as snow falling in the desert. He gestured at the bedroom door. 'Michael, something happened to me in there. I killed those people back at the house to get you out. But after I saw those girls and talked to them, especially the child, I felt the urge to go back and make sure there wasn't a flicker of life left in them. I also had the urge to kill the old woman. I don't often have the urge to kill. It was never like that with me. I worked as a mercenary because it was all I knew, but I never worked for people I didn't believe in. I never killed without having to.' He turned and looked down at the road again. A police car sped past, lights flashing and sirens wailing. Over his shoulder he said bitterly, 'I looked at those girls, especially Juliet. I saw the fear in her eyes and something worse. I saw desperation.' He turned again and said, 'Tell me exactly what your mother told you that day at the hospital.'

Michael also stood up and moved to the window, and they both stood looking down at the wet street.

Michael said, 'Like me, she was an orphan. She ran away from the orphanage when she was sixteen. It was not like the orphanage in Gozo; she was often beaten. She met up with a young Arab. He was wealthy and gave her a good time and hid her from the police. He introduced her to drugs and she became an addict. Then he started selling her to other men. When she refused, he took away the drugs. She thought he loved her, and she decided that if she got pregnant, he would not sell her body to other men. She kept it a secret until very late. When he found out, he beat her and took her to an abortionist. But the abortionist told her it was too late. When she had me, he forced her to give me to the orphanage the next day.'

'How did he force her?' Creasy asked.

'In a very simple way.' Michael gestured, his voice deep with emotion. 'He told her that unless she gave me to an orphanage, he would strangle me. I was born without a doctor, just another prostitute to help my mother. Nobody knew I was alive. She had no choice. She left me on the doorstep of the Augustine convent.'

'You should have told me that in Gozo,' Creasy said.

Michael smiled briefly and answered, 'At the time you didn't seem very receptive.'

'That's true,' Creasy murmured. 'Now I want to know all about it. I want to be part of it, just like you were part of the Lockerbie thing.'

Michael turned and smiled. 'So we do it together?'

Creasy nodded gravely. 'Yes, we do it together.'

'What kind of men are we dealing with?' Michael asked. 'Apart from the fact that they're evil.'

93

Creasy thought about that for almost a minute, slowly sipping his coffee, and then he started talking, as though he were thinking out loud. 'I have no religion. Neither do you. Most religions have a clear-cut distinction between good and evil. But in my experience there are many different ways to be evil. Perhaps the worst is the evil of sadism. Most human beings have it in them, to some extent or another, just as most human beings have a measure of masochism. It's not easy to understand sadism but I've seen a lot of it at first hand and one thing is for sure: the breeding ground for sadism is power. The more power a sadist has, the more evil he becomes. In fact, sadism is synonymous with power. It's a disease without a cure, a disease of the brain. There is no antidote. It's the reason why sadists are drawn to powerful people and dictatorial situations.' He put down his empty cup, glanced at Michael and continued. 'Sadists were drawn to the SS in the last war, just as they were drawn to Genghis Khan centuries ago. In any army at war the sadists soon show themselves, whether it's a mercenary in Africa, a drug baron's bodyguard in South America, or an American soldier in Vietnam. Sadism cuts across race, culture, creed or sex. It reaches its nadir when the sadist has a willing maso-chistic subject. Juliet's mother for example, did nothing while the stepfather beat her daughter up. You can imagine the mental impression that must have made on the child.'

Michael asked, 'What about Boutin?'

Creasy nodded grimly.

'Yes. Sadism was at the core of Boutin's character. He talked before he died. He talked and begged for his life. When a man begs for his life he tells the truth. He told me that he processed between six and eight girls a month during the summer and sold them on to "The Blue Ring" for one hundred thousand francs each. That's about eighteen thousand dollars. It sounds like a lot, but in reality it's nothing, compared to what Boutin made in his other businesses. For him it was a sideline to satisfy his sadism ... a little fun on the side, you might say. A chance to exercise total power over an innocent. As we get in among "The Blue Ring" we're going to find many more like him, perhaps worse.' He glanced at his watch. 'Go in to the child now, Michael. I have to phone Leclerc to arrange papers for the girl and the child. And I have to phone Gozo and get hold of Joe Tal Bahar.'

Michael looked up in surprise. 'Joe?'

'Yes. He's just bought that new fifty-foot Sunseeker. It cruises at thirty knots, and he can be here in a couple of days. He'll smuggle you and the child into Gozo, probably using a fishing boat for the last leg at night. You'll have to put the child in the wine cave behind the house and lock her in there until she's got the drug out of her. It will take about ten days and she'll go through hell ... so will you. Worse, if that's possible. You will have no help. Nobody must even know she's in the house. Clear everything out of the cellar. Just put in a mattress and run a hosepipe in there, and put one of those big, round barrels we use for winemaking in there too. Fill it with water. And put in a pile of blankets, a dozen or more. When you've done that, give her a last shot of methadone. The hell will start about twelve hours after that. I'll take you through the sequence of what will happen to her later. After the last shot of methadone, go down to the village and tell Theresa that you won't need her until further notice ... tell her you'll clean the house yourself. Also stock up on enough food for two weeks.'

'What if she gets really sick?' Michael asked. 'Do I call a doctor?'

Creasy shook his head.

'What if she dies?'

Creasy looked at his son and said, 'You bury her at the bottom of the garden between the pomegranate trees. You bury her deep. At least eight feet. Meanwhile, put a notice on the garden door that you're not to be disturbed until further notice.' He thought for a moment and then said, 'Run an extension from the phone into the cave, but when you're not in the cave take it out with you ... and make sure that cave door is always locked.' He pointed with his chin at the bedroom door. 'Go to the child now. Tell her the medicine's on the way.'

As the door closed behind Michael, Creasy reached for the phone.

TWENTY-ONE

The outside door intercom buzzed at ten minutes after six a.m.
Creasy had been dozing in his chair. His head jerked up and he
glanced at his watch, and quickly moved over and pressed the button.
He asked, 'Yes?'

A voice answered in French, 'Red Three.'

'Green Four,' Creasy replied and pressed the button to open the
downstairs door. He went to the table, picked up the silenced Colt
1911, checked the magazine, moved to the door of the apartment
and waited.

The soft tap on the door came two minutes later. He pulled it open,
moving back behind it, the gun levelled at waist height, and called,
'Come in.'

A man came in carrying a black briefcase and a leather flight bag.
He put them both on the floor, studied Creasy for a moment then
nodded, held out his hand and said, 'My name is Marc.'

Creasy transferred the Colt to his left hand, pointing it downwards.
They shook hands, and then Creasy gestured towards the table and
asked, 'Coffee?'

The Frenchman nodded. He was short, plump, and wearing thick,
rimless spectacles. He looked like a school teacher or a bank-teller.
He was dressed in a sober grey suit with a blue tie. He noted Creasy's
appraisal and smiled slightly.

'I know,' he said, 'I don't look tough, but that's been my biggest
advantage in this life. Nobody takes me seriously ... so I always get
first strike.'

Creasy returned the smile and went to the kitchen counter to pour
some coffee. The Frenchman put his briefcase on the table and opened
it. With the two mugs of coffee, Creasy sat down next to him. 'Are
you carrying?' he asked.

The Frenchman nodded and patted his left armpit.

'You have to leave it here,' Creasy said. 'And the holster.'

For a few seconds the Frenchman looked him in the eyes then stood up and took off his jacket. The pistol was a Beretta 9mm, nestling into a Henny, snap-release shoulder-holster. The Frenchman wriggled out of it and laid it on the table. Creasy pulled out the Beretta. He checked the breech and the safety, then took out the magazine and slipped it into his pocket. The Frenchman watched in silence and then spoke.

'I've worked for René Leclerc for fifteen years. He trusts me with his life. I know all about the man called Creasy. When Leclerc sent me he gave me one instruction: to treat you as I treat him.'

Creasy studied his face for a moment, then picked up the Beretta, pulled the magazine out of his pocket, rammed it into the butt of the pistol and put the pistol in front of the Frenchman.

He said, 'OK, Marc. Keep it while you're here. But leave it here when you go with my friend.'

'What's the job?' the Frenchman asked.

'Nothing onerous. I want you to accompany my Danish friend to Copenhagen with a girl. It will be about a forty-eight hour drive. You'll take turns at the wheel. The girl is a heroin addict and will have to be sedated all the way. My friend is a Danish policeman.'

The Frenchman's eyes widened, and Creasy said, 'Don't worry. He's a good one. After you leave them in Copenhagen you bring the car back here. You will be well paid.'

The Frenchman shook his head. 'You will pay me nothing. I work for Leclerc. He pays me.'

Creasy nodded in assent, stood up and peered into the open brief-case. He reached out and shuffled around the medicines inside. He found the disposable syringes of methadone. He put two on the table, and asked, 'You know how to administer this?'

Marc nodded, and then said, 'Can I ask you a question?'

'Go ahead.'

'On the car radio on the way over I heard a news report of a gang battle out in Boutin's villa on the coast ... a lot of dead. You have anything to do with that?'

Creasy merely shrugged but it conveyed the message.

'Is Boutin dead?' the Frenchman asked.

Almost imperceptibly, Creasy nodded. The Frenchman stood up and held out his hand. Creasy shook it.

The Frenchman asked, 'Did the girl come from that villa?'

'Yes. And one other in the other bedroom. A child of thirteen.'

Creasy saw the anger and hatred in the Frenchman's eyes.

'Are you sure Boutin is dead?'

Again Creasy nodded slightly, and said, 'Boutin is in very small pieces.'

The Frenchman said simply, 'Now we are friends.'

Creasy wrapped the two syringes in a white napkin, together with some cotton wool and a small bottle of surgical spirit. They went to the first bedroom. Creasy tapped on the door. When Jens opened it, Creasy introduced him to Marc. Hanne was sitting up in bed. She was shaking slightly, and her face was so pale as to be almost white. Jens spoke to her quietly in Danish, gesturing at Marc. The Frenchman smiled at her. It transformed his face. He looked like everybody's favourite uncle.

'Do you speak French?' he asked her.

She looked at him, and then said in a quivering voice, 'Just a little.'

'English?' he asked.

'Yes, I speak it well.'

'Good. Then we shall talk in English. Mine is not so good but over the next two or three days you will help me to improve it. We will be friends.' He smiled again and she replied with a very tentative smile.

On impulse, Creasy handed the Frenchman the white napkin and said, 'You do it. And again every eight hours until she is safe in Copenhagen.' He gestured at Jens and they left the room and closed the door.

'Who is he?' Jens asked.

'A friend of a very close contact. He doesn't look tough but I'm very sure that he is, and that you can trust him totally. He will drive with you to Copenhagen. Her papers will be ready tonight and you leave as soon as they are here.' He gestured at the telephone. 'You had better phone Birgitte now, before she goes to school. Keep it very brief. Just tell her you are fine and that you'll be home within seventy-two hours. Instruct her to tell nobody else. Do not make any other phone calls until you've crossed the Danish border. Then call your boss. Make arrangements to drive her straight to the clinic. Only then do I suggest you call her parents.'

Jens nodded thoughtfully and asked, 'What about you, Michael and the child?'

Creasy glanced at his watch. He said, 'In an hour I call Gozo. Within a couple of days a friend will come in a fast boat, pick up Michael and the child and take them home.'

'Home?'

'Yes. Home to Gozo.'

'And you?'

Creasy shrugged.

'I go to Milan to have a conversation with a man who buys girls.' He gestured at the phone again. Jens moved to it and dialled the number. After a moment he spoke a few brief words in Danish and hung up. Creasy noted with satisfaction that he did not identify himself or mention her name.

'No questions?' he asked.

Jens shook his head and smiled. 'She's a policeman's wife.'

Marc came out of Hanne's bedroom, closed the door quietly and said, 'She is calm. She will sleep within a few minutes.' To Jens he said, 'I suggest you stay with her until then ... she trusts you.' He gave a wry smile. 'Although I can't think why anyone would ever trust a policeman.'

Jens grunted something about not being French, and moved past him to the bedroom. Marc was still carrying the white napkin. Creasy tapped on the other bedroom door and Michael opened it. Creasy made the introductions and they all looked at the child lying on the bed. It seemed as though her dark eyes dominated her face; eyes filled with desperation. The Frenchman looked at her and the other two men heard the almost inaudible curses coming from his lips.

Quietly, Creasy said, 'Michael, introduce her to Marc. He will show you how and where to inject the methadone.'

Half an hour later the four men were sitting around the kitchen table. It was now seven-thirty a.m. A curious bond had grown between them. It was as though they were a sports team, about to go into action. Marc had brought with him detailed road-maps covering the area between Marseille and Copenhagen. Together with Jens, he traced their route and calculated that, without stopping, and depending on traffic, they could reach Copenhagen in under forty hours. Creasy made his phone call to Gozo. Again it was very brief. Joe Tal Bahar had left Gozo at the age of eighteen to seek his fortune in New York. He had returned ten years later with a fortune beyond his dreams. Having spent a fraction of his fortune on every conceivable toy a man could want, he was now bored. The little jaunt that Creasy outlined in euphemistic terms quickly sparked his imagination. Yes, he could be up the coast from Marseille with his Sunseeker within a couple of days and yes, his 'guests' would arrive in Gozo very discreetly. Creasy arranged to phone him back with a landing site. Marc made a couple of quick phone calls and then from his briefcase took a Polaroid camera.

'I need photos of the girls for their papers,' he said.

Jens and Michael started to stand up, but the Frenchman held up a hand.

'Stay here. They are tranquil.'

He went into the first bedroom, leaving the door open. They heard his gentle voice and Juliet's calm answer.

Jens turned to Creasy and asked, 'Who is the man in Milan with whom you want to have a conversation?'

'I only have a name,' Creasy answered. The name was given to me by Boutin as he begged for his life. It was only a surname ... an Italian surname ... Donati.'

'That's all you have?' Michael asked. 'Just one name?'

'There was another,' Creasy answered. 'But not very clear. You have to understand that Boutin was in trauma. He was talking, even babbling, but knowing he was about to die. Apparently, this man Donati had an emissary. In a sense he was a cut-out between Boutin and Donati. Boutin thought that he was half-French, half-Italian because he spoke both languages fluently. This cut-out had no name, but referred to himself only as The Link.'

'You have a description?' Michael asked.

'Yes, but only one thing of note. He was totally bald, about forty years old, very fit and a man of few words. However, Boutin indicated that whenever he came to Marseille he enjoyed using the girls. He had one other habit. He only drank Campari on the rocks, and in copious quantities.'

'Not much to go on,' Michael commented. 'I guess we have to concentrate on Donati. At least it's a name. Is he Mafia?'

'No,' Creasy answered quietly. 'According to Boutin he is "Blue Ring". He's the only contact that Boutin had with the organisation. Whenever he had a girl ready he would phone a number and be told where to send her and how.'

Thoughtfully Jens said, 'My department has contacts with the Italian police and the *carabinieri*. Maybe I can get a lead on him.'

Total silence. Then Michael said, 'A lead like Corelli?'

Jens took the rebuff well, but when he spoke his voice was defensive. 'Well, I can check our own files in Copenhagen.' A thought struck him. 'By the time I get back there, I'm still going to have seven weeks' leave of absence. What am I supposed to do – twiddle my thumbs?' He gave them both a belligerent look. Creasy smiled but then his eyes turned thoughtful.

'Maybe you can help,' he said. 'Maybe I can use you as a point man.'

'What the hell is that?' the Dane asked.

Creasy glanced at Michael and explained. 'A point man goes out in front at an angle and diverts the opposition. In this case it will not be dangerous. You would be blundering around in an official capacity, not posing any real threat to them. They would see you as a bumbling policeman and not get nervous.'

Michael laughed and the Dane got angry.

'What does "bumbling" mean?' he asked.

Creasy smiled to take away any hint of offence. 'A sort of Inspector Clouseau,' he explained. 'While they're laughing at you, I'll be sneaking in the back door.'

Jens digested that, and then said, 'I've never "bumbled" in my life! But if it helps I'll learn.' He said the last words seriously. He was obviously keen to stay in the team.

Creasy said, 'We may well need you, Jens. I'll know within a week. Hopefully Michael will be free to travel again in about three weeks. This will not be a quick operation. I have to activate past contacts in Italy.'

'Like who?' Michael asked.

'First of all your nominal Uncle Guido in Naples. He's passive but still has incredible contacts, and always gives good advice.'

Jens' face mirrored his curiosity. Creasy explained that Guido Arellio was his best friend. They had served in the Legion together and for many years afterwards as mercenaries in all corners of the world. The partnership had ended when they found themselves in Malta many years before, and Guido had fallen in love with Laura Schembri's eldest daughter Julia. They had married and gone to live in Naples, where they ran a small *pensione*. A few years afterwards, Julia had been killed in a car crash. Subsequently, Creasy had married her sister, Nadia, who in turn had died with their daughter over Lockerbie on Pan Am 103.

'I will also contact a Colonel Mario Satta,' he said.

Now even Michael's face showed curiosity. Creasy explained.

'He's another old friend. An unusual one. For many years he was head of *carabinieri* Intelligence against the Italian Mafia. Some years ago, I had a war with a family of the Mafia which stretched from

Milan to Sicily. I did not know Satta then. But he knew about me and what I was doing. He gave me a clear field, even though I was assassinating Italians right down the country. Sure, they were *mafiosi*, but by law he should have tried to arrest me. Instead he pulled off all his men until the last battle in Palermo when I killed the head *don* and most of his lieutenants. I was badly shot up myself and damn near died. Satta's elder brother, the senior surgeon at Cardarelli hospital in Naples, pulled me through. He also signed my death certificate, so that the remains of that Mafia family did not waste time trying to find me.' He smiled briefly at the memory. 'I'm told it was a lovely funeral.'

'So that's how you got your Gozo nickname,' Michael said. He turned to Jens and remarked, 'Everyone in Gozo has a nickname.'

'What is it?' Jens asked.

'*Il Mejjet*,' Michael answered. 'It means "the dead one". They also call him *Uomo*, which is Italian for "man".'

Jens was intrigued. 'What's your nickname?' he asked Michael.

Michael looked uncomfortable.

Creasy laughed and supplied the answer. 'They call him *Spicca*. It means "Finished". He got that nickname after they brought him home after his first time at a disco. The name's stuck.' He turned to Jens and said seriously, 'We have to give you a nickname now. It will also serve as a code word. If anyone calls you by that name you will know they come from me or Michael.' He looked at Michael and said, 'What shall we call him?'

Michael thought for a moment and then grinned. 'We'll call him "Pavlova". Jens is very partial to exotic desserts,' Michael explained, 'as you can see from his waistline.'

'Perfect.' Creasy nodded. 'From now on you're "Pavlova".'

Marc came out of the second bedroom, carrying the camera and several prints. He laid them on the table and pointed to one of them. It was Juliet. He said, 'That girl is quite a character. She insisted on borrowing my comb before she would let me take her photo.'

He scooped them up and dropped them into his briefcase, together with the camera. Then he slipped into the harness of his shoulder-holster and clicked the Beretta into it. He picked up the briefcase, saying, 'I'll be back in a couple of hours with all the papers.'

He turned to go, but Jens' voice stopped him. 'Wait, Marc. Do you have a nickname?'

The Frenchman muttered, 'Not really.'

'What is it?' Creasy asked sharply in French.

There was a pause and then the Frenchman tapped his thick round glasses and said, 'If you must know, they call me "The Owl".'

The other three men smiled and Creasy said, 'That is your password. If we ever get a phone call from The Owl we know who it is. Never use your real name.'

The Frenchman grimaced and went out, muttering something under his breath which included the word 'crazy'.

TWENTY-TWO

Grete and Flemming Andersen lived in the wealthy part of the Hellerup suburb of Copenhagen, in a large old house with a sprawling, tree-enclosed garden. The house was too big for a couple with only one child, but when they bought it they had hoped for several children. They were in bed when the phone rang at ten minutes to midnight. Sleepily Flemming reached for the bedside extension. He listened for half a minute and then abruptly sat upright.

'What is it?' his wife asked anxiously.

He held up a hand for silence and then said, 'Yes ... yes, of course.' He looked at the bedside clock. 'We'll be there in half an hour.' He put the phone down and scrambled out of bed saying, 'Come, Grete! Quickly. It's Hanne ... They've found her!'

Jens waited at the entrance to the clinic. He had arrived two hours earlier. The Owl was waiting for him in the BMW. The journey had been swift and uneventful. He saw the lights of the silver Mercedes sweep into the car park and in his mind went over again how he would explain to the Andersens. From his files and from the meeting he had had with them in his office several weeks earlier, he guessed that they were strong people. Flemming Andersen had made his fortune in heavy construction, much of it in the inhospitable terrain of Greenland. He was a self-made man and used to adversity. His wife, Grete, had been his childhood sweetheart and had supported him through the early, difficult years. Although she had been distraught and had wept in his office, Jens believed she was strong enough to face up to the truth now.

They hurried up the steps to the entrance, their eyes anxious but at the same time hopeful. He opened the door for them and ushered them through and then into a small waiting room. As they sat down,

Grete began asking questions. One of them was, 'Why is she in this particular clinic?' Her husband put a hand on her arm and said, 'Wait, darling. Mr Jensen will explain.'

Jens did explain. He explained in detail. He kept his voice sympathetic but firm. He told them of the ordeal their daughter had gone through. He told them of the difficulties facing them in the weeks and maybe months ahead. He finished by saying that she was in very good hands in the clinic, and he was sure she would be in good hands when she was allowed home. He stressed that she had been a totally unwilling victim and no blame could be laid on her.

At this point the father had lifted his gaze from the carpet and said quietly, 'The only blame is for the men that abused her. Have they been arrested?'

Jens shook his head.

'They have not ... and they never will be. It may not be much satisfaction, but I can tell you that they died a violent death, and they died knowing why. Your daughter is not the only one. She is very lucky – first to be alive and second to have such parents.'

Grete had been crying. Now she lifted her face and wiped away her tears. 'Did you kill them?' she asked.

Again, Jens shook his head.

'No. But I was there. I cannot tell you the story, because it would endanger the men who rescued your daughter and who sent her home. There will be no publicity about this. Nothing in the newspapers.'

The Andersens were silent and then Flemming asked, 'The men who rescued her and killed those animals ... Can I reward them? As you know, I'm not a poor man.'

Jens looked at him and nodded solemnly.

'Yes, you can certainly reward them. When she's well again ... when she is smiling, take some photographs of her. Send them to my office. I will pass them on. That is the reward they would want.'

He stood up, went to the door, opened it and beckoned. A middle-aged man dressed in casual jacket and trousers came in. Jens introduced him as Doctor Lars Berg, the head of the clinic and Denmark's foremost drug rehabilitation expert. He said, 'Doctor Berg will brief you and explain the procedures. I will keep in touch with the clinic.'

He turned to go, but at the door the mother's voice stopped him. She moved to him and put her arms around him. She was crying and trying to thank him at the same time. He kissed her wet cheek, hugged her back and eased himself away. One of the rare occasions when he felt total job satisfaction.

The Owl slept on the settee. Jens slept on the double bed in the bedroom. Birgitte lay wide awake next to him. She ran her hand over his naked body. Over the black and blue bruises. She had opened the door to them ten minutes earlier. They had not wanted food or drink. Just sleep. There were things she did not understand. When the other man was lying on the settee and Jens had gone into the bedroom, he had called out, 'Goodnight, Owl.'

The man had raised an eyelid and said, 'Goodnight, Pavlova.'

She sighed and kissed a purple bruise on his left buttock. No doubt she would find out all about it in the morning.

TWENTY-THREE

There was no moon. The sea was black. But Joe Tal Bahar kept the Sunseeker at a steady twenty-eight knots across the low swell. He sat next to Michael on the flying bridge and pointed at the radar screen.

'We are thirty miles south of the western coast of Sicily, and we're just entering one of the busiest shipping lanes in the world. Cargo vessels and tankers heading for eastern Italy, Greece and the Middle East and Far East via the Suez Canal.'

Michael leaned forward and looked at the screen. There were dozens of blips. 'How the hell will you pick up Frenchu's fishing boat?' he asked.

Joe laughed. He was enjoying himself. He looked at his watch and said, 'In about fifteen minutes, Frenchu will raise a special transponder up his mast. This radar has been adapted to recognise it.'

Michael glanced at him. 'I guess it's not the first time the two of you have done this kind of thing.'

Joe grunted in agreement. 'True. But it's the first time we've handled people not merchandise. What's the story, anyway?'

Without hesitation, Michael said, 'Joe, you'll have to ask Creasy when you next see him ... You know how it is.'

'Sure,' Joe answered cheerfully. 'It's just that she seems like a nice kid, and from the brief look I had of her she's been badly abused.'

They cruised on in silence. Away to port, Michael could see the lights of the accommodation structure of a supertanker sitting up in the water like a small city. He looked to his right and saw several lights. Joe was watching him.

'That's a fishing fleet,' he said, 'out of Porto Palo on the south-east coast of Sicily. They're trawling for king prawns. Usually I stop and trade a bottle of Black Label Scotch for a box of them ... but not tonight ... Listen Michael, if you need any help with that child, let me know. I don't know what's behind it, but I guess she's on drugs. I had experience with that kind of thing in New York. It's bloody hell getting them off it.'

'I'll let you know,' Michael said. 'As far as possible, Creasy wants me to handle it myself. The main thing is that nobody finds out she's on Gozo. At least until Creasy gets back with some decent papers.'

'It's no problem,' Joe answered. He gestured at the deck below him. 'Wenzu knows how to keep his mouth shut, and so do Frenchu and his sons.'

They sped across the sea in silence for another ten minutes. Joe was not looking ahead, nor left nor right, just at the screen set into the dashboard panel. Abruptly he grunted, leaned forward and pointed. Among the dozens of blips another one had appeared, brighter than the others. Joe laughed softly.

'That's Frenchu. From that blip you'd think he was a supertanker instead of a sixty-foot fishing boat.' He watched the moving blip for a couple of minutes and nodded. 'That's him all right. He's moving sou' sou' west at about ten knots.' He punched some buttons on the computer next to the radar, checked the screen and said, 'We'll rendezvous in sixteen minutes.'

Michael looked at his watch and asked, 'Can you calculate what time Frenchu's boat will get back to Gozo?'

Joe punched some more buttons and said, 'Assuming he cruises at twelve knots, which he will, you'll be there at about five a.m. An hour before dawn.'

'I'll go below, then,' Michael said, 'and check the girl out.'

He found Wenzu sitting outside the door of the aft cabin. Michael nodded, opened the door and went in. She was sitting half-propped up on the large double bed. She was wearing jeans and a black long-sleeved T-shirt. She looked at him with anxious eyes.

'Are you all right?' he asked.

She shook her head. 'I feel lousy. I need some of that stuff again.'

'It's a bit early,' he said, 'but better now than on the other boat.' He unlocked a drawer and took out a small box as she rolled up the right-hand sleeve of her T-shirt.

TWENTY-FOUR

It was a Friday night. Colonel Mario Satta always dined alone on a Friday night. He sat at his favourite alcove table in his favourite restaurant in Milan; he was a man of few habits but this was one. During the meal he would think over the events of the preceding week, and map out plans for the coming one. He did not look like a colonel in the *carabinieri*. He looked like a successful grand prix driver or an avant garde playwright or the owner of a television company. His clothes were a master tailor's dream. The dark grey double-breasted suit had the faintest black pinstripe; it had been tailored by Huntsman's of Savile Row. His cream silk shirt had come, like all his others, from a small shirtmaker in Como. His maroon silk tie was by Armani. His kid leather shoes were made from his personal 'last' at his cobbler's in Rome. His face caught attention, especially from women. It was not conventionally handsome, but his deep-set dark eyes and slightly aquiline nose gave him an air of both authority and mystery. He came from a wealthy and somewhat aristocratic family, which his mother dominated. She could never understand why, with her wealth and connections, her younger son had chosen to become what, in her eyes, was a mere policeman, even though he constantly pointed out that he was in the *carabinieri* and the youngest colonel in that corps. She would simply sniff and remark that, no matter how beautiful his uniform, he was still a policeman. Her elder son had studied medicine and gone on to become one of Italy's most eminent surgeons. Even that did not satisfy his mother. She referred to him as an over-educated butcher. She would have preferred her sons to go into commerce, industry or politics. She would also have preferred them to be married to prominent, acceptable socialites from the right sort of family. Instead, her elder son had married a nurse from Bologna, no less, and Mario seemed to have endless affairs with nubile young actresses. She despaired of her sons but she loved them both, and the love was returned.

Colonel Mario Satta had made his reputation by deep research into the workings of the Italian Mafia. Over a period of years and with the help of his dedicated assistant, Bellu, he had built up dossiers on every major family. It had been at first rewarding and then frustrating and then heartbreaking. His dossiers had been used by the senior prosecuting magistrates in Palermo and elsewhere. One by one he had seen those magistrates and their bodyguards shot or bombed as they closed in on the quarries that he had identified. They were brave and good men, and he had been unable to help beyond passing on his information. Politics and corruption and a combination of both had always protected the killers. Finally, in frustration, he had requested a transfer and a few months earlier had been assigned to the department which investigated political corruption in Italy's northern industrial heartland. He had taken Bellu with him and, although they had only been at work a few months, many politicians were already looking nervously over their shoulders.

Colonel Mario Satta's three main passions in life were good food, beautiful women, and backgammon. More or less in that order. For him, the perfect evening was a meal in a fine and intimate restaurant, or else at his apartment, prepared by himself, together with a beautiful woman and afterwards several games of backgammon – which of course he must win – followed by a satisfying session in bed. But on this night he dined alone with the added anticipation of a date with a beautiful woman on Sunday night. She was not an actress but a television presenter with titian hair.

He had ordered one of his favourite meals: a special *antipasto* followed by *cappon magro*. For the dessert he had spoiled himself and ordered his favourite *gelato di tutti frutti*. He was always conscious of his waistline but indulged himself on Friday nights. He had just finished the *cappon magro* together with the last of the Barolo, which was of course a little heavy, but a nice contrast to the dessert which was coming. He looked up as the restaurant door opened and slowly lowered his glass to the table. He saw the man's gaze sweep the restaurant and alight on him. The man wove his way through the tables towards him. He had a curious walk; light, but as if the outsides of his feet touched the ground first. Slowly, the Colonel rose to his feet and moved around the table. Some of the other diners stopped eating to watch. They saw the Colonel embrace the man warmly and kiss him on both cheeks. No one, not even the maître d' or the waiters had ever seen Colonel Mario Satta do that before. The men sat down and looked at each other across the table. The maître d' hovered a couple of metres behind the newcomer.

'Have you eaten?' Satta asked.

Creasy shook his head. 'I had a sandwich on the plane, a couple of hours ago.'

Satta nodded to the maître d', who moved forward. Without being asked, the Colonel ordered for Creasy: *spaghetti alle vongole*, to be followed by *osso buco*. He told the maître d' to hold his dessert and then bring a double portion when the *osso buco* was finished. He also ordered another bottle of Barolo.

Creasy smiled as the maître d' hurried away.

'You don't forget much, Mario.'

The Italian grinned. 'That was the last meal you ordered at the Cardarelli Hospital the night before your funeral.'

Creasy nodded at the memory, and asked, 'How is your brother?'

'He is well, but, as always, works too hard.'

'It's his vocation.'

'True,' Satta replied. 'I also have a vocation, but I don't work fourteen hours a day. What brings you to Milan? Apart, of course, from my fascinating company and the possibility of losing a large amount of money at backgammon.'

The wine waiter appeared with the Barolo, ritually uncorked it and poured a sample into Creasy's glass. Creasy tasted it and nodded his approval. As the waiter left Creasy said, 'I came to throw a name at you. All I have is a name and a possible connection to a white slave ring.'

'Throw away,' Satta said.

'Donati.'

'Christian name?'

'I don't have it.'

'He lives in Milan?'

'He's based in Milan.'

The waiter brought Creasy's *spaghetti*. He ate in silence, occasionally glancing up at the Colonel. He knew that Satta's memory was legendary. Right now he was picking through all the compartments of his mind.

Finally he said, 'I know of three Donatis living in Milan. One is a priest, one is a junior conductor at La Scala and the third bakes the best bread in the city. I doubt that any of them have connections with a white slave ring.' He shrugged and then smiled. 'But who knows?

Last month the priest bought a new car ... a BMW ... not a big one, you understand, but it was new.'

Creasy smiled through a mouthful of *spaghetti*, swallowed, and said, 'Have you ever heard of "The Blue Ring"?'

Again Satta's mind went through its computer exercise. Creasy had finished the *spaghetti* before he got an answer. He drank half a glass of wine and then heard Satta say, 'There is a faint little bell ringing in my head, but I can't place it right now. I take it that this Donati is connected with "The Blue Ring" which is involved in white slavery?'

'Yes. It's been established a very long time; probably operates in most southern Mediterranean countries and has tentacles into North Africa and the Middle East. I only have the name Donati, nothing else. Between Donati and the man who gave me the name there was a complete cut-out. Very professional. I suspect that Donati is just the next rung on the ladder, and that there will be very complete cut-outs between every rung all the way to the top of that ladder.'

'And what is your involvement?'

Creasy sighed and said, 'This will take some time to explain. I will have to go back to the last time I saw you ... about six years ago.'

It took over an hour. Creasy talked and Satta listened, occasionally interjecting to clarify a point. Creasy finished his story as they both finished the *gelato di tutti frutti*.

Satta wiped his mouth carefully with a napkin, drank the last of his wine, smiled and said, 'Is this the Creasy I used to know? I find you now with a fully-grown son and possibly a daughter ... By the way, I never wrote to you with my condolences about Nadia and Julia.'

'I got your message via Guido,' Creasy said quietly. There was a silence while he remembered that message. It simply said, 'The sun sets and in time it always rises again.' Creasy looked at his friend across the table and said, 'Good words from a good man.'

Satta shrugged and dismissed the subject. 'Anyway. I can tell you that this "Blue Ring" is not connected with the Mafia. If it was I would certainly know about it. Therefore it must be secretive in the extreme because, assuming that it's lucrative, the Mafia would want a part or all of it. It must also be very powerful and I assume ruthless. I have a colleague who deals with these matters. He is trustworthy. I will confer with him in the morning. How long will you stay in Milan ... and where?'

The waiter appeared to clear away the table. Satta ordered two espressos and two double Armagnacs.

Creasy said, 'I stay as long as it takes to get a lead on Donati. I checked into a small hotel near the station.' He smiled wryly. 'It's called The Excelsior and somewhat less comfortable than its namesake ... but it is discreet.'

'I would offer you my spare bedroom,' Satta said, 'but I know you. You prefer to come and go like a ghost.'

Over the coffee and Armagnac they talked about old times, and especially about Guido Arellio. Since those days, when Creasy was fighting the Mafia, Satta and Guido had become good friends. Satta often visited Guido's *pensione* in Naples, firstly for the company, secondly for the food, and thirdly in a vain attempt to recoup his losses from the many backgammon games he had lost to Guido over the years.

They were the last to leave the restaurant. On the street outside they embraced again briefly, and went their different ways.

TWENTY-FIVE

It was the second day. Michael was very frightened.

He had followed Creasy's instructions to the letter. They had come ashore at Mgarr I'Xinni an hour before dawn. Frenchu's Land-Rover had been waiting and one of his sons had driven Michael and the girl to the house on the hill. The girl had been sedated and asleep, and Michael wrapped her in a blanket, and carried her in his arms.

He had placed her on his own bed and then for the next two hours worked feverishly, clearing all the wine out of the cave and other odds and ends which had found their way in there. He stored everything in the spare bedroom, then fetched the mattress and a pile of blankets. He rolled an empty barrel into the cave, connected a hosepipe to a garden tap and filled it up. He had checked the single light set high above the door, then he had gone back to his bedroom. Juliet had been awake. He had sat next to her on the bed, taken her hand in his and talked to her quietly. During the preceding hour he had decided to tell her the truth.

She had listened without expression and then asked, 'Will you be with me?'

'Yes.'

'All the time?'

'Yes. Except for a few minutes once in a while, when I have to go into the house to get food.'

She had nodded and squeezed his hand. So he had injected her with the final dose of methadone and then taken her into the cave. She had been wearing just a pair of jeans and a T-shirt. No shoes or socks. She had looked around the cave with apprehension and he had explained that it had been used to make and store wine, and that it was better she stayed there, in case anyone passed by. She had lain down on the mattress and he told her he would be back in an hour.

In fact, it had only taken him half an hour to go down to the village. The sun had been up by then. Theresa had been surprised, but happy to see him. And then mystified when he told her that she was not to go near the house until further notice, and that she was not to mention that to anybody. He then went to the small grocery and loaded several boxes with provisions, mostly tinned food, fruit, pastas and soft drinks. He had decided not to drink any alcohol for the duration. Back at the house he had stored the provisions and rigged up an extension lead for the phone out to the cave. When he had opened the heavy door into the cave he found her asleep on the mattress. He had gone back out and fetched a folding canvas chair for himself.

The ordeal had begun about twelve hours later. He had recognised what was happening to her from Creasy's detailed description. A sense of uneasiness began to come over the girl. She sat cross-legged on the mattress, her back to the rock wall. She began to yawn frequently, and then to shiver. Her eyes moistened and then a watery discharge began to pour down from her eyes and nose. He had told her that he would be back in a moment, gone out and locked the door behind him. From the kitchen, he had fetched several boxes of tissues. Back inside the cave he had opened one and given it to her, but nothing could stop or stem the flow from her eyes and nose. Her T-shirt and jeans became wet with sweat. For several hours he sat with her on the mattress, holding her shivering hand. She began to moan in her throat. The moan of a small animal in pain. Then almost abruptly she had fallen into a deep sleep. He had known that this was what the addicts called the 'yen sleep'. It would last for several hours, after which she would sink deeper into hell. He had gone out and locked the door behind him, his mind numb.

It had become night again, and he had walked out past the swimming pool and looked out over the lights of the villages of Gozo and of Comino and in the distance, of Malta. His whole body was suffused with hatred for the men and women who had done this to Juliet. He had thought of Creasy, who by now would be in Milan, hunting them down. He offered up a kind of personal prayer that his father would find them. He had looked into the cave a couple of hours later. She had still been asleep, so he had gone back to the swimming pool, stripped off his clothes and swum fifty fast lengths.

Two hours later she had woken. It was about twenty-four hours after the last dose of methadone, and she had entered the depths of her personal hell. He had sat in his canvas chair and watched her torture. She began to yawn so violently that he worried she might dislocate her jaw. Watery mucus poured from her nose and floods of tears came from her eyes. Her pupils were widely dilated. The fine dark hairs of her skin stood up, the skin itself cold and covered with goose bumps. From Creasy's description, Michael knew that she was going through cold turkey.

Then the misery deepened. Her bowels began to act with shuddering violence. Her jeans stained, and the stench drifted across the cave. Feverishly, she pulled them off, and then her stained knickers and finally her sodden T-shirt, until she was naked. It was as though he was not in the cave, but then he saw her imploring eyes rest on him, and heard her strangled voice begging him to give her an injection. He stood up, went over to the barrel of water, picked up a wooden ladle and splashed the water over her. He repeated the process several times, but there was no way to keep her clean. She started vomiting; just lying there, vomit coming out of her mouth and excrement from her bowels. He had noticed that there was blood in the vomit and his anguish deepened almost to despair. He noticed too that her stomach was rippling, as though there was a tangle of snakes under the skin. He remembered Creasy's words, and knew that it was caused by extreme contractions of the intestines. Knowing what caused it gave Michael no relief. He knew that from this point on the child would know no rest nor sleep until she either pulled through her hell or died. Irrationally, he thought that the grave he would have to dig would not be very long or very wide.

Over the next hour he sluiced her down from the water barrel several more times. She was wet, the mattress was wet and the floor of the cave was wet. He looked around him, the ladle dangling from his hand. He had no sense of time, and if he had not been wearing a watch he could not have judged whether he had been in that cave for hours, days, or weeks. His whole body ached and his mind was numb with the shock and the pain of it all. He knew that she had been about thirty-six hours without the drug. He knew that it would take another four to five days before she passed through it or died.

Then she started talking to him in a hoarse, grating whisper. An imploring voice, begging him to give her the injection. He went to his canvas chair and sat down and tried to avoid her eyes. It was impossible. His eyes were constantly drawn to the small, white, shaking figure on the filthy mattress. She had offered him everything she had, which was only her naked body. She cupped her breasts and offered them to him. She opened her legs and stroked her crotch and tried to look coquettish. He tried to fix his eyes on the mark on the rock wall above her. Then she had begun to curse him and scream at him. Vile words from a child of thirteen. Finally her legs had begun to twitch and then kick out violently. It went on and on, as she thrashed about on the mattress. He began to wonder how any human being could produce such a sustained and violent action. He began to wonder how even a strong man could live through it, let alone a weak and ravaged child.

Michael was very frightened. And then the phone rang. She was oblivious to the noise and continued thrashing around, her legs kicking convulsively. Michael picked up the phone. He heard the click and a hum of an overseas call and then Creasy's voice.

'Is that you?'

'Yes.'

'What's our situation?'

Michael took a deep breath and answered as calmly as he could. 'I'm in the cave ... I think she's dying.'

'Describe it.'

Michael took another deep breath. 'She's convulsing. Kicking like hell. Begging for a shot.'

Creasy's voice was controlled. 'Has she been shitting and vomiting?'

'Yes.'

'Have you seen the snakes in her belly?'

'Yes.'

'Did she have a long sleep?'

'Yes, she woke up a few hours ago ... Creasy, she's only a child ... her body can't take much more.'

There was a brief silence, and then Creasy asked, 'When did you give her the last shot?'

Michael looked at his watch and answered, 'Thirty-eight and a half hours ago.'

Another silence. Creasy said, 'If she gets through the next twenty-four hours she might make it. Have you had any sleep?'

'No.'

'Then listen to me carefully. What she's going through now is what addicts call "kicking the habit". Michael, whatever happens ... no matter how bad you feel ... don't give her another shot. No matter what she does or says.' The voice turned hard. 'And Michael, no matter what she does or says, don't even think about calling a doctor or anybody else. A doctor would give her a shot and send her to a detox centre. With some addicts that might be the best thing to do, but with Juliet my gut feeling is that her only chance is over the next few days in that cave with you. Now I want you to lock her in and go and get at least four hours' sleep. Set your alarm. If you fall asleep in that cave anything could happen.'

Brusquely Michael said, 'I can't just leave her!'

'You have to! Get out of that place for four hours and take away anything she might damage herself with.'

Michael looked at the thrashing girl and then at the door. Exhaustion swept over him. His eyes felt as though they were filled with sand. His whole body ached. Juliet was pulling at the pile of blankets, shaking them loose and covering herself with them. Michael relayed this to Creasy.

'It's the next stage,' Creasy told him. 'She's being wracked by chills. It will go on for many hours. She will not sleep. Cramps in her stomach will keep her awake. They may kill her, but there is nothing you can do. If she lives she will need you later. Go and get that sleep!'

Michael made his decision. 'I will. What's your situation?'

'I've got a lead on the name I was given in Marseille. I'm tracking it down. I'll call you again in two or three days . . . Be strong, Michael.'

The phone went dead.

TWENTY-SIX

Creasy threw a double four. Satta rolled his eyes to the ceiling and muttered something about luck and the devil. Creasy took his last two counters off the board, glanced at the doubling dice, made a quick calculation and said, 'It adds up to four hundred and twenty thousand lire.'

Satta swore under his breath, stood up, stretched his limbs and walked over to the drinks cabinet.

They were in his elegant apartment. It was Saturday afternoon, and they were both dressed casually in slacks and open-necked shirts. For two hours they had been waiting for a phone call, and had passed the time playing backgammon. Creasy also walked to the cabinet, which was high enough to double as an elbows-on bar. He glanced at his watch.

Satta handed him a vodka soda in a tall, frosted glass and said, 'He'll phone soon. He's reliable, and if anyone can get a line on this man Donati, he can.'

Creasy smiled.

'I'm not impatient, Mario. On the contrary, I don't mind sitting here playing backgammon all day.'

The Italian grimaced and said, 'I don't know who is the most gloating winner, you or Guido ... By the way, who usually wins when you play each other?'

'It's about even,' Creasy answered, 'but we never play for money.'

'Why not?'

'We just play for practice, so we can fatten our wallets from overpaid *carabinieri* colonels.'

Satta was about to retort when the phone rang beside him. He listened for about two minutes, then he said, 'Thank you', hung up and turned to Creasy. 'Maybe ... it's just a maybe. There is in this city a man called Jean Lucca Donati. He is a respected businessman, age sixty-one. He is a native of Naples but has been living and working in Milan for the past thirty years. He has no criminal record. In fact he is well-respected in the business and banking community. Over the past fifteen years he has been quite successful. He owns a large trading company which deals in the Middle and Far East, both importing and exporting textiles and garments of a high quality. He travels extensively. He is a widower with three grown sons who are all in the business. He has a penthouse apartment here in Milan and also keeps a small villa on Lake Como.'

Creasy had been listening intently. Now he took a sip of his drink and asked, 'So?'

Satta shrugged. 'My colleague is suspicious of him.'

'Why?'

Satta gave a slight smile.

'He pays his taxes.'

'So that makes him a crook?'

'This is Italy,' Satta said seriously. 'Very often the only way we can get to a criminal is on a tax evasion charge. The Americans finally got Al Capone for that reason. The last few years I've been specialising in corruption between industry and our beloved politicians. In those years I have not come across a single businessman or industrialist who honestly pays his taxes. So why does Jean Lucca Donati make like an angel when it comes to paying taxes? There are so many ways to evade it. It throws up the possibility that he is keeping a clean image in a relatively small business to cover the profits of a much larger and perhaps illegal business.'

Creasy was not impressed. 'So all you have is suspicion.'

They had been talking in Italian. Creasy had learned the language during the years he had spent with Guido, both in the Legion and later as mercenaries. In turn, he had taught Guido English. The result was that Guido spoke English with a slight southern American accent and Creasy spoke Italian with a definite Neapolitan accent. He spoke it so well that an Italian would only guess he was not native-born because he did not use his hands to emphasise his words. By contrast, Satta was so eloquent with his hands that if they were tied behind his back he would be struck dumb.

'Call it more intuition than suspicion,' he said. 'Also bear in mind that we have not been able to locate any other Donati who could possibly be involved in the white slave trade ... not on the international scale you are suggesting.'

He picked up the phone and within a few seconds was talking to his assistant, Bellu. Creasy listened as he gave precise instructions, which included an in-depth check of Donati's finances, his recent movements and his business associates overseas.

He cradled the phone, turned to Creasy and said, 'If nothing turns up during the next forty-eight hours, I'll tap all his phones and put a twenty-four hour watch on him.'

'Why?'

'Why what?'

'Why are you doing this? You have a million other things to do. This is just a tangent. You're busy from dawn till dusk. Why?'

Satta had no immediate answer. He had to think, but then his thoughts crystallised into eloquence.

'Creasy. You are such a stupid asshole. Don't you know you have friends? Don't you understand that you don't live in isolation? Don't you know that Guido would die for you? That there are other people scattered around the world who would do the same? You have a brain that is stuck in mud. You look at everybody in the same light as you see yourself.' The Italian became agitated, even angry. He saw that the glasses were empty and poured more drinks. He was a man who rarely showed his emotions. On this night he let himself go.

'I have known you for six or seven years, and I know the loyalties that you create. But you do not understand them yourself. This "Blue Ring" you talk about – maybe it exists and maybe it doesn't. If it does you will destroy it. But as an old friend I have to tell you – that you are no longer in your youth. All your life you have acted independently and turned yourself into your own guts and needed no one. But now you need those that you have created ... Of course I am always in touch with Guido. I know him as a brother ... and my brother knows him as a brother. Occasionally, after a long night, good food and good wine, he talks about you. No secrets, just memories of the days in the Legion, the days in Africa, the days in the Far East and the days in Vietnam. You came into my life, intent on destroying the Mafia family who had abused a child that you loved. I should have arrested you but I let you go. You put those Mafia bastards back ten years. I do not know about this "Blue Ring" you talk about, but I will find out about it. You can call so many people to your cause. Do not go alone. Use your history. These people you look for are more dangerous than you understand. I think that, because of what you tell me, they have existed for very many years; and we know nothing about them, and so they must be organised and clever in the extreme.' His voice was now filled with emotion. He took another gulp of his drink, nodded firmly and said, 'It is as though we go back six years. I see you as a smoking bomb. I have no doubt that in the weeks ahead I will come under pressure to find you and arrest you. I will avoid that pressure.

'My life now is involved in catching corruption. What is the result? I catch them and they pull the strings of politics and get off with a slap on the wrist. Creasy, indulge me ... Lately, life has been boring. I think the Donati we have identified is your first major link ... OK ... intuition, but go for him. You know my assistant ... I have to correct myself, my associate ... Bellu ... you know him well. He has the kind of mind to help you. He needs a long holiday. I will suggest that he helps you. I will give you the umbrella of legal sanction. But I urge you to call on those people you know and trust to help you break these animals. There is no legally constituted body in this country – or in any country in Europe – that could attempt it.'

A long silence. Then Creasy half smiled.

'At the end of it, will the *carabinieri* give me a pension?'

Satta also smiled, a smile of emotion.

'I talk tonight in a way that you will never hear me talk again. The evil that you look for will never be tried in a court of law. The only retribution will be death. I will cover you for that ... In the meantime, Creasy, you must be careful when you're in this city or in any other city in Italy. Don't forget, your face is well-known and, for sure, any Mafia family would love to get their hands on you.'

Creasy shrugged. 'That is why I stay in a lousy little hotel and keep to myself.'

The Italian nodded thoughtfully, then pointed at the telephone. 'Make your dispositions.'

Creasy looked at him. 'Is this phone secure?'

'Believe it.'

Creasy dialled a number. It was Blondie in Brussels. He spoke in euphemisms but she understood every word.

'A base,' he said.

'You have it.'

He told her about the people with whom she could be frank and open. 'Michael, of course, and in time maybe a child called Juliet. A policeman in Copenhagen whom you once met. A Frenchman from Marseille who will identify himself only as The Owl. His boss is another Frenchman whom you knew in Algiers. He was a legionnaire. Now he lives in Marseille.'

He heard her rich chuckle and she said, 'Yes, I know him ... not entirely ugly.'

'Yes, of course,' he said. 'You knew every good-looking legionnaire in North Africa.'

She laughed again and then said, 'A good man, and he respects you. Who else?'

'Maxie, of course. Also contact the Australian and the Frenchman who helped me on the last job in the States and put them on standby ... The usual rates ... plus job satisfaction. I'll be with you in a couple of days.' He cradled the phone and looked at Satta, who was grinning from ear to ear.

'So the war starts,' Satta said with satisfaction.

'It starts as soon as you give me a definite lead,' Creasy answered, then picked up the phone and dialled another number. The phone rang and, on a sudden impulse, Creasy hung up.

Satta's face showed surprise.

'What is it?'

Thoughtfully Creasy said, 'Is there any chance that Guido's phone might be bugged?'

Satta smiled and shook his head. 'I stay at his *pensione* quite often, and I have his phone and the *pensione* swept regularly. His phone is not bugged.'

Creasy punched the number and in a few seconds was talking to Pietro, the semi-adopted son of Guido, who did most of the work at the *pensione*. He had been dispatched to Gozo during those traumatic weeks when Creasy had been destroying the Cantarella Mafia family all those years ago. The conversation was brief but affectionate.

'How are you, you miserable little prick?'

'I recognise your asshole voice. What do you need?'

'Is the man around?'

'No he's with his mother ... she has a headache.'

Creasy laughed softly and said, 'Listen carefully and pass it on. There may be calls from the following: myself, Michael, Satta, Bellu, Corkscrew Two, Blondie, a girl called Juliet, Pavlova, The Owl, Laura, Maxie, Nicole, Miller, Callard ... only those. Tell the man and, understand yourself, take messages. Listen to nobody else.'

There was a pause as Pietro took notes. Then he said, 'Will we see you?'

'In a few days.' Creasy put down the phone, looked at Satta and said, 'Two or three more phone calls and I'll be ready.'

Satta nodded and refilled the glasses. Creasy dialled Leclerc in

Marseille. They chatted about inconsequential things and people such as a cousin in Milan and an old aunt in Naples. Creasy dropped a few nicknames which would be incomprehensible to any covert listener. They were certainly incomprehensible to Satta, who was listening with interest. But he knew who Leclerc was, and he surmised that Creasy was ordering weapons to be delivered to both Milan and Naples.

Finally Creasy said into the phone, 'I hear that The Owl did a good job. Perhaps I could use him on this one too?' He listened for a moment, nodded in satisfaction, said, 'Good' and hung up the phone. He then phoned Michael in Gozo, heard the anguish in his voice and gave his advice. He put the phone down and Satta noted the pain on his face.

'What is it?' the Italian asked.

Creasy explained about Juliet. Satta was one of the very few men that understood Creasy, understood the thick shell that surrounded him, and the small centre that held emotion.

He put a hand on his friend's shoulder and said quietly, 'You tilt at windmills. You slay the dragon. If that evil exists, you will obliterate it ... and then where will you go ... back to your island?'

Creasy drained his glass, nodded and said, 'Back to my island ... and to my son ...' He paused and thought, and his voice became sombre. 'And in the next forty-eight hours it's possible that I will go back to a daughter.' He lifted his head, stretched his tired body and then said in a soft voice, 'Mario, can you imagine me of all people, after what has happened, with a son and a daughter? I had a wife and a child, and life ended, and now just maybe I have a son and a daughter.' Seconds ticked by within a silence, then Creasy added something else. Very softly he said, 'Mario ... I know you have religion. When you can find time tonight ... please find time to pray for my daughter.'

TWENTY-SEVEN

God created the world in six days. On the seventh day he rested. But a millennium later he took time off from his rest to bring through one of his creations.

In the early morning she started to have violent physical orgasms. She clutched at her crotch and her child's body arched from one spasm to another. Michael sat in his canvas chair and watched, but could not stay. He knew it was the last phase. He also knew that her young heart had been greatly weakened from the excesses the drug had imposed on it. He knew that this phase would last an hour or more, and that she might well attack him physically, either out of inflamed sexual desire, or inflamed hatred. He took his chair and the ladle and the telephone and left the cave, locking it behind him. He set his alarm and slept for an hour by the pool and then, with massive trepidation, went back into the cave. She would be dead or asleep.

At first he thought she was dead. She lay so still; her body was wet, on the wet mattress. He moved forward slowly. He had been taught how to check for a dead body. She was curled up in a foetal position. He touched her shoulder. It was cold. He pulled her head away from her chest and put the back of his hand under her chin against her artery. The rhythm was slow and so faint that he could hardly feel it ... but it was there. He stood up and looked down at her exhausted, soiled body. He was looking at the most beautiful thing he had ever seen or would ever see.

In vain, he called her name, knowing that she could not hear. He picked her up and carried her out of the cave. At the main door to the house he paused, then carried her to Creasy's bedroom, laid her on the vast bed and went into the bathroom. He ran luke-warm water into a high-sided pine tub in the Japanese style, then picked her up, carried her into the bathroom, laid her in the bath and carefully washed every part of her. Then he wrapped her in a big towel and laid her back on the bed. She had murmured occasionally, but had not moved. He went back to the bathroom and took a scalding hot shower, as though to wash away the memories of seven days of hell. In the bedroom he checked her breathing. It was shallow but regular.

He went to the kitchen and began to cook. First, he took the carcasses of two large chickens, cut them up, braised them briefly in the frying pan with a little olive oil and put the pieces in a large cooking pot and covered them with water. He then chopped up onions, carrots, tomatoes, broad beans, fennel, parsley and basil and dropped all of them into the pot. He turned the flame down low, covered the pot, and went back to the bedroom. He lay with her and held her through the night. Her body was still agitated and she twitched and turned, but always came back to his arms. Had she been conscious, she would have felt the wetness of his tears on her cheeks and shoulders. But she slept the sleep of an angel, and he slept the sleep of a martyr.

In the morning he stirred the broth, and brought it to her in a cup. He held her head and gently fed it into her mouth. She slept again, and after a few hours woke again and drank more broth. He noticed her looking at her naked body with slight embarrassment, and in a drawer he found one of the colourful sarongs that Creasy always wore in bed. He wrapped her in it and kissed her cheek and told her to sleep.

The papers came two days later. They came from Marseille, from the arms dealer Leclerc, in a large envelope, delivered by courier. He took it at the gate, signed for it, walked into the kitchen, made himself a strong black coffee and opened it. Inside, he found adoption papers for a thirteen-year-old girl called Juliet Creasy. She had been adopted two years earlier by one Marcus Creasy and his wife Leonie. The papers indicated that she was of Belgian nationality and an orphan. It named the orphanage in Bruges. They looked totally authentic, as did the Maltese passport and her photograph.

Michael smiled and took the papers into the bedroom. She was barely awake, but she smiled as she perused the papers and the passport. She reached up an arm around his neck, pulled him down and kissed him on the cheek.

'You have a sister,' she said.

'You have a brother,' he answered.

TWENTY-EIGHT

Massimo Bellu was the antithesis of his boss, Colonel Satta, in every way except two: the quality of his brain, and his dedicated application in using it. Otherwise, no two men could have been more different. Satta was handsome, elegant, sardonic, cynical and an aristocratic gourmet. Bellu, on the other hand, was short, plump, and balding. He dressed like the most junior clerk in a seedy trading company and his main culinary delights ranged from a hamburger with an extra layer of onions to *spaghetti carbonara*. He also hated to play backgammon and a couple of years earlier had finally put his foot down and refused to play against his disconcerted boss during the many nights they spent together, waiting for a phone call or something to happen.

He had worked for Satta for eight years. During the first year he had spent much of his time trying to think up a viable reason to apply for a transfer to another department. But after that year he had begun to appreciate and understand the subtlety of Satta's mind. At the same time, Bellu's younger sister, who was highly qualified, had applied to enter Catanzaro University to study medicine. There were very few places and it was very hard to get in without a connection. She had been turned down, but a week later had received a letter reversing the decision. Many weeks had passed before she had learned that a certain Professor Satta, senior surgeon in Naples' Cardarelli Hospital had intervened on her behalf.

Bellu had confronted Colonel Satta, who had simply shrugged, and said, 'You work with me. Of course I had to do something.'

All thoughts of a transfer had left Bellu's head. It was not what Satta had done but simply the words he had spoken: 'You work "with" me, not "for" me'. Over the years they had developed a very relaxed working arrangement, which had slowly turned into a partnership.

Now Bellu sat late in his office, in front of his pride and joy, a new Apple Mackintosh computer. He had an affinity with computers and their progeny; the department's computer expert could teach him nothing. Within weeks he had transferred a vast amount of information onto the Apple's hard disc. On this night he sat and watched the screen, looking for something that might give him a clue into the workings of Jean Lucca Donati's mind.

When it came he did not see it at first, but two minutes later something in his brain clicked. He tapped his keyboard and went back, studied the screen for several minutes and then pushed more keys and went into a different file, the file of a man called Anwar Hussein. This was an Arab. In fact a Nubian Arab with antecedents in Egypt. Also a trader, with excellent contacts in the Middle East. He, too, had an impeccable reputation, and had lived in a luxurious villa on the outskirts of Naples for the past twenty years. He also paid his taxes. The only possible blemish on his reputation had occurred some two years earlier, when Saudi Arabian customs had discovered a small quantity of child pornography and associated Satanism in a container of fashion garments shipped to Riyadh by one of Hussein's Italian companies. It had been traced to an underling whom Hussein had promptly fired.

The faint link between Jean Lucca Donati and Anwar Hussein was that they were both members of the cultural group, the Italian Arab Circle, and four years earlier had both served on the committee. The only reason that Bellu had a file on the Italian Arab Circle was because in the late sixties and early seventies it had been thought that it may have been a front for one or more Arab intelligence services; much as suspicion had been directed at the British Counsel, Alliance Française and the Goethe Institute. In the case of the Italian Arab Circle, these suspicions had proved groundless.

Bellu went back and forth through his files, and then discovered another common denominator. Jean Lucca Donati was an honorary consul for Egypt in Milan and Anwar Hussein held the same honorary position in Naples. It gave them both access to the diplomatic bag. He switched off the computer and looked at his watch. It was close to midnight but he phoned Satta anyway and briefed him on his discovery. Satta instructed him to put full surveillance on both men and their families. Then Satta phoned Creasy at his hotel. He caught him just as he was leaving to catch a night flight to Brussels. He passed on the information. Creasy remarked that it looked pretty flimsy. Satta laughed softly and commented, 'Two men who pay their considerable taxes and enjoy the confidence of the Egyptian government ... Not so flimsy, I think.'

TWENTY-NINE

Michael took Juliet to the Schembris' for Sunday lunch. It was a sort of ritual. When he and, or Creasy were in Gozo, they always went to the Schembris' on alternate Sundays. On the other weeks the Schembris would come to them for a barbecue.

Before leaving the house he took her into Creasy's bedroom and said, 'There is a safe in this room. It is well-concealed. Since you are now a member of the family you must know how to open it.'

He was carrying a folder containing her newly-arrived passport and papers. He went to the head of the wide double bed and pointed to the top right-hand corner of one of the huge slabs of limestone which made up the thick wall.

'You count up four slabs from the floor,' he said, 'and then press it firmly here.' He pushed the heel of his hand against the limestone and it silently swung open. Behind it was a metal door about one metre high and half a metre wide. Set into the metal was a handle and, alongside that, a dial for the combination lock. 'Do you have a good memory?' he asked. She nodded solemnly. He could see that she was impressed, as any child would be, with the confidence shown her. '83 ... 02 ... 91.'

She repeated the numbers twice and then nodded. He reached forward, dialled the numbers and pulled open the heavy door. Inside were several shelves. He pointed to the top shelf which contained bundles wrapped in chamois leather.

'Weapons,' he said. 'Hand-guns and two small submachine-guns plus suppressors and ammunition. Later on I'll teach you how to use them.' He pointed at the middle shelf which contained several thick files. 'There are various files on people, some are enemies and some are friends.' He pointed at the bottom tray. There were more files but they were thinner. 'These are personal papers.' He took one of the files out, opened it and dropped her passport and adoption papers into it. Beneath the bottom shelf was a thin drawer. He pulled it out and pointed. She leaned forward to look and saw the tightly wrapped bundles of paper currency.

'There are US dollars, Swiss francs, pounds sterling, deutschmarks and Saudi Arabian riyals.' He lifted out a small canvas bag and shook it. She heard the clink of the coins. 'Gold sovereigns and krugerrands. Very useful as currency in the Middle East.' He dropped the bag back into the drawer and slid it closed. Then as he closed the door of the safe and spun the dial he said, 'In total, there's more than the equivalent of five hundred thousand US dollars in that drawer. In a crisis, and if Creasy and I are not around, use what you need.' He gave her a mock stern look. 'But next week I don't want to see you driving around in a new Mercedes sports car.'

She smiled, and he decided that as she recovered and as she grew older she was going to turn into a very beautiful young woman. She had been made thin and gaunt by her ordeal. The bone structure of her face was clearly etched and her limbs were little more than sticks. He calculated that while going cold turkey she had lost at least up to twelve kilos, about a quarter of her body weight. But she had been eating well since then, and within a week or so her body and face would start to fill out. She had also begun to exercise, swimming several lengths of the pool in the mornings and evenings.

As they drove through Rabat and on to Nadur, he told her in detail about Paul and Laura Schembri and their son Joey and his wife of two years, Maria, who would also be at the lunch. He explained the long connection between the Schembri family and Creasy and himself, summing it up succinctly. 'We consider them our family, and they reciprocate.' He turned to glance at her and went on, 'So, in a way, now they become your family and you theirs. You can trust them all totally, and respond to any trust they give you.'

She was silent as they drove down the winding dirt road towards the farmhouse. She sat in the jeep, looking out over Comino to Malta, and then she said in a quiet voice, 'I hope they like me.'

He glanced at her again and saw that she was nervous. He took a hand off the wheel and squeezed her shoulder.

'Don't worry. Just be yourself. Offer to help Laura and Maria with the washing up. They won't let you ... but offer.'

They did like her. Michael had not told them who she was, but when he had rung up had simply said he was bringing along a friend. As the jeep pulled up in the courtyard they all came out to greet them. He introduced her simply as 'Juliet ... my new sister,' and then laughed at the expression on their faces. He gave Laura and Maria a hug and a kiss on both cheeks. 'I'll explain over lunch.'

As usual, the lunch was enormous. *Tortellini* to start, followed by a lamb casserole and a vast array of vegetables from their own fields. The others were all silent during the meal while Michael related Juliet's story.

At the end of it Laura spoke with an angry edge to her voice. 'You should have called us the moment you got back. We would have helped ... taken it in turns to be with her. You know we can be trusted, all of us.'

Before Michael could open his mouth in defence, Juliet leaned towards Laura and said very seriously, 'It was better that Michael did it alone. He knew what to expect and was prepared for it ... besides by the time it started I knew him, and I trusted him, and I felt no shame. You cannot imagine how much shame I would have felt if there had been any strangers there to see me at that time.' Her voice dropped and she looked down at her plate. 'I know that I almost died several times ... if anybody but Michael had been there I think I would have died.' She looked up straight into Laura's eyes. 'I know that for sure.'

Slowly, Laura nodded her head in understanding.

'Perhaps you are right. We cannot imagine what you went through, but if anything like that ever happens again and there is no Michael or Creasy, then you must come to us.'

Juliet smiled and nodded.

'I will.' She gestured at the steaming pot of lamb. 'Especially with such food.'

In answer, Laura ladled more from the pot onto the girl's plate, despite her protests.

'How will you explain her?' Paul asked Michael.

The young man shrugged. 'It will have to remain a mystery for most people. We have adoption papers dated two years ago from Belgium. We also have a Maltese passport.'

'Forgeries, I suppose,' Joey said.

Again, Michael shrugged. 'No one except an expert would know.'

Then Maria, who worked as a clerk in the Malta police force, said, 'It's taken a long time, but over the past few months all immigration records, passports, ID cards etc have been computerised. If she passes through immigration coming in or going out of the country her passport number will not show on the computer and questions will be asked.'

Michael smiled. 'I am sure that before Creasy left Marseille he would have sent a letter to George Zammit.'

Juliet was looking puzzled.

'George is my nephew,' Paul explained, 'and a very senior policeman, who also happens to have immigration within his departments. Creasy has done him some favours in the past.' He glanced at his daughter-in-law and asked, 'Do you have access to the immigration software?'

'Yes. First thing in the morning I'll check out if a certain Juliet Creasy holds a Maltese passport.'

Juliet still looked puzzled.

'How can you do all this? I mean, it sounds like something in the Mafia!'

They all laughed and Joey said, 'We don't have the Mafia here.'

'That's true,' Laura said seriously and Juliet saw the twinkle in her eye. 'In fact, they come down here occasionally ... but only to learn.'

When Maria started to clear away the plates from the table, Juliet immediately stood up to help.

Very sternly, Laura told her to sit down. 'Guests don't help here,' she said.

Juliet did not sit down. Equally sternly, she said, 'I'm not a guest ... I'm family.'

They liked her.

THIRTY

'You want to go, don't you?'

Nicole spoke with a wry smile. Maxie glanced at her and shrugged.

'It's only natural, Nicole. When you've got good friends, and when you've been doing that kind of work most of your life, it's only natural.' He punched her lightly on the shoulder. 'But don't worry, I made you that promise two years ago and I'm going to keep it. You know I'm happy. Sure, I get restless feet once in a while, but not enough to make me want to lose what I've got here with you.'

It was after midnight and they were standing behind the bar of the bistro. Maxie was polishing glasses. Nicole had her elbows on the bar. A glass of Armagnac was in front of her. She picked it up and took a reflective sip, looking again at the last three customers. They were sitting at a table in the far corner; three men talking in low voices. She knew Creasy, of course, and owed her present happiness to him. She had also met Frank Miller, an Australian ex-mercenary who had worked with Creasy in Africa and Asia. He looked like the antithesis of a mercenary. He was in his mid-forties, completely bald with a big body and a small head; his face was slightly cherubic. She had met Maxie and Miller at the same time, on Maxie's last job, when the two of them had been spectacularly successful in protecting a prominent American senator from a Mafia kidnap gang. Creasy had hired them for that job. She had also met the other man very briefly on the same job. His name was Rene Callard, an ex-legionnaire and mercenary who had also worked with Creasy for many years. He looked more like a mercenary: tall and lean with a tanned, lined, scarred face. But he had a ready smile which took away his air of menace. She turned to look at Maxie again. He was watching the three men through lowered eyes. He felt her gaze on him and quickly picked up another glass and polished it thoroughly.

She smiled and ruffled his hair and asked, 'Were you ... are you as tough as them?'

He smiled a little sheepishly.

'I guess so. Well, at least as tough as Frank and Rene. I wouldn't rate myself alongside Creasy.'

Curiously, she asked, 'Would you rate anyone alongside him?'

He thought only for a moment and then answered, 'Yes, his best friend, Guido Arellio. You've heard us talk about him. He also promised his wife that he'd never fight or kill again from the day they married.'

She nodded thoughtfully. 'You told me about it. ... but there is a difference. She died about seven years ago, didn't she?'

'Yes, about then.'

'In that case,' Nicole said, 'under the same circumstances, she could not let him break his promise. I can let you break yours.' He started to say something but she touched his arm, and very quietly said, 'Listen, Maxie. I was a whore when I met you. You knew that and you didn't care. You showed me more love in the first few days than I had known all my life. It was that love that cleansed all the sin I had in me. When I went to your bed I felt like a virgin. You took in my sister and treated her like your own. I love you now as much or more than during those first days in Florida.' She smiled at the memory, and then her face turned serious as she went on. 'I think I'm an intelligent woman. I want to keep that love and if it means risking seeing you back in that world then I will take the risk.' She gestured at the table and said firmly, 'Now go and sit with your friends. You're dying of curiosity.' She smiled. 'And so am I. I'll bring over coffee and Cognacs in a few minutes.'

The three men looked up as Maxie hooked a chair over and sat down.

He said, 'Nicole sent me over. I'm released from my promise, so whatever it is, I'm available if you need me.'

Creasy turned and looked at Nicole behind the bar. He saw her almost imperceptible nod. Then she moved towards the kitchen.

She brought coffees and Cognacs on a tray and put it on the table.

Creasy thanked her and said, 'Why don't you join us, Nicole, and hear what it's all about?'

She looked at Frank and Rene; they both nodded. She went to the bar to collect her Armagnac, and Creasy pulled up a chair. Half an hour later she turned to Maxie and said in a tight voice, 'I don't just release you from your promise. If you don't help them find and kill those bastards I won't sleep easy. I was lucky. I only ever worked for Blondie, and you know how well she treated me and all her girls. But I've seen the result of what those bastards do. They're not fit to live.'

Maxie shrugged and looked at Creasy. 'I guess I have no choice now.'

Rene grinned and said, 'It will be like old times. I've spent the last six months playing nanny to a Swedish industrialist ... about as interesting as watching paint dry. If he ever gets kidnapped whoever does it will send him home within a couple of days. Hell! They'll even pay his family to come and pick him up!'

They all laughed and then Creasy said soberly to Nicole, 'Thanks. We all feel better having Maxie along. We always did make a good team.'

'Who else is in the team?' she asked.

'Blondie, of course,' he answered. 'She'll handle communications up here. Guido will do the same in Naples, but I won't get him directly involved.' He thought for a moment and said, 'Then there's a Danish policeman called Jens Jensen. He was involved at the very beginning and is desperately keen to keep that involvement.'

'Is he good?' Maxie asked.

Creasy shrugged. 'He's intelligent and experienced, tough and streetwise, a bit above average ... but not in our league.'

'How many are there in your league ... in the whole world, I mean?' Nicole asked with a slight smile.

The American answered. 'On our side of the fence, maybe less than fifty. On the other side, a few hundred.'

The others nodded in thoughtful agreement and then Rene asked Creasy, 'Might this Dane be something of a liability? Is one of us going to have to watch his back?'

Creasy drained the last of his coffee and shook his head.

'No. There's a Frenchman who watches his back. He was a body-guard to Leclerc in Marseille. You all know about Leclerc.'

'Then he's good,' Maxie remarked. 'Leclerc doesn't hire bums. How will you use the Dane?'

'As a tangent,' Creasy answered. 'After all, he is a cop who works in the Danish Missing Persons Bureau; he can open doors. He's also motivated and has at least another month of unpaid leave. I can get that extended if necessary.'

'What about Michael?' Maxie asked.

Creasy thought for a moment and then said, 'I told you about the girl, Juliet. I spoke to Michael a few hours ago on the phone. She's making a good recovery, both physically and mentally.'

Nicole was looking at him curiously. Only she noticed that his voice had softened as he talked about the girl.

Creasy went on. 'In a week or so she can go to stay with friends and Michael will join us. By that time we should know whether Satta and his sidekick Bellu have got more information on this guy Jean Lucca Donati.' He looked at his watch. 'I'm catching the three a.m. flight back to Milan. I have a meeting with Satta at ten o'clock in the morning.' He gestured at Frank and Rene. 'I'd like you guys to base yourself at Guido's *pensione*, starting from the day after tomorrow. Leclerc's sending some machinery to Guido. Hand-guns, grenades and SMGs. He's also sending a similar package to Milan.' He gestured at Maxie. 'I'll phone you tomorrow night. Depending on what information I get from Satta, I'll need you in either Milan or Naples.'

'What about the Dane?' Maxie asked.

'He's flying down to Milan tomorrow, and The Owl is coming in from Marseille. They'll meet me at my hotel there.' He pushed back his chair and stood up. They all did the same, and Nicole watched as they went through the ritual that never ceased to intrigue her when such men greeted each other or made their farewells. One by one, they put their left hands behind the other's neck and kissed them hard on the right cheek, very close to the mouth.

THIRTY-ONE

They swam twenty-five lengths of the pool. Michael kept his pace down so as to swim alongside her. When they stopped she was gasping for breath, but she got the words out. 'I can do another ten lengths.'

He pulled himself out of the pool, reached for his towel and grinned down at her.

'Do another five but no more.'

He towelled himself dry, watching her thin shape slide through the water. She was wearing a bright red one-piece swimsuit they had bought the day before, during a great shopping spree in Rabat. It was an hour after dawn. They had taken up a routine of rising early and going to bed early. After breakfast they would take the jeep and he would show her more of the island. Then they would have a big lunch at the Oleander in Xaghra. She liked the local dishes and she liked Mario, the owner, who treated her as a grown-up rather than a child. After lunch they would swim again, but this time in the sea, from the rocks at Qala Point. They would sunbathe for an hour or two. She always took a notebook with her and he would teach her Maltese. It had only been a few days, but he knew that within a matter of weeks she would be able to communicate in the language.

'If my passport says I'm Maltese,' she had said, 'then I'm going to speak the language.'

'Your passport says you are Maltese,' he had answered. 'But don't ever forget that you're a Gozitan.'

'Is there a difference?'

'There is. The Maltese think that Gozitans are the peasants of the islands, but we have a saying over here: it only takes one Gozitan to put three Maltese in his pocket.'

She had laughed and said, 'Then I'm definitely a Gozitan!'

She finished her last length and collapsed, gasping, over the edge of the pool.

He reached a hand down and pulled her up and asked, 'What do you want for breakfast?'

Her small chest was heaving, but her eyes lit up at the thought of food. 'Scrambled eggs, bacon, sausages, mushrooms and grilled tomatoes ... oh, and lots of toast ... and fresh orange juice.'

He walked to the kitchen shaking his head and heard her call out behind him.

'I'll make dinner!'

She came into the kitchen ten minutes later. She was wearing denim shorts and a white 'Smugglers Cave' T-shirt. Another restaurant that she liked, especially for its pizzas. Her hair was pulled back into a ponytail and her face was taking on a tan. She wrinkled her nose in anticipation.

He turned back to the stove and said over his shoulder, 'In about a week I want you to go and stay with Laura and Paul.'

'Why?'

'I'll be leaving.'

'Where are you going?'

'I don't know yet. Somewhere in Italy. I have to join Creasy.'

She sat at the table and asked, 'How long will you be away?'

'I don't know. It could be days or weeks or even longer.'

He turned to look at her, expecting to see petulance on her face. There was none. She was simply nodding in understanding.

She looked up at him and asked, 'Can't I stay here?'

He slid the food onto her plate, took it over, put it in front of her and said, 'If you stay here alone, Creasy and I will worry about you. We have enough to worry about.'

Again she nodded and, before starting to eat, said, 'On the day I move in with Laura and Paul I will make them promise only to speak to me in Maltese. When you get back I will be a Gozitan.' She looked up and said seriously, 'And I'll have three Maltese in each pocket.'

He grinned and went to get his own breakfast.

THIRTY-TWO

Creasy dozed on the flight. He disliked flying, not out of fear, but because he felt that such journeys held no interest. They stuck you into a tube and delivered you to a different place, a different culture and often a different climate. It was like being mailed in a package. He much preferred trains and ships, and would always use them when he had the time. Due to the usual air traffic controllers' go-slow over Italy, they had left Brussels an hour late, and that also irritated him.

He was not in a good mood when they touched down in Milan, but since he only had an overnight bag he was spared the wait for customs.

He quickly found a taxi and, as he ducked into it, said, 'The Excelsior Hotel ... near the railway station.'

The driver cursed under his breath. Anyone staying in that fleapit near the station would not leave a centime of a tip. Italian taxi drivers can be loquacious, but this one remained silent at least during the early part of the forty-minute journey. After twenty minutes Creasy leaned back and closed his eyes and dozed again. The city of Milan had no beauty to keep him awake. Had he not dozed he would have noted the sudden interest in the taxi driver's eyes as he looked at Creasy in the rearview mirror. Five minutes later Creasy was woken by the driver's voice.

'Are you staying long in Milan?'

Creasy's eyes opened and he shook his head to clear it.

'Just a couple of days.'

'Business or pleasure?'

'Just to look up an old friend.' The tone of his voice was curt enough to indicate that he was not looking for conversation, but the driver was persistent.

'Are you from Naples?'

'No. But I spent some years there.'

The taxi driver nodded. 'I can tell it from your accent. It's not a city I like myself. Neither a taxi driver nor anyone else is safe on the streets.'

Creasy grunted non-committally. The driver seemed to take the hint, and they completed the journey in silence.

The driver did get a tip. A thousand lire note. He looked at it and then at the back of the man who was walking into the shabby hotel entrance. The driver engaged the gears, drove around the corner and reached for his mobile phone. Almost every taxi driver in Milan and many other Italian cities is an informer of one kind or another. It's a general sideline and the masters are sometimes the police, sometimes drug pushers, sometimes a pimp and occasionally a local Mafia *capo*. This taxi driver was linked to Gino Abrata, one of the two *capos* who ran Milan.

Within two minutes Abrata was on the line, even though it was only seven o'clock in the morning. Five minutes later Gino Abrata was on the phone to Paolo Grazzini, the sole *capo* of Rome.

'Yes, he's sure. He swears to it . . . Yes, I know he's supposed to be dead. Of course I know he's supposed to be dead! I saw his bloody funeral on television . . . No, the taxi driver had never seen him before face to face, but he'd seen that face on television and then full size in the newspapers six years ago. It's a face you don't forget. Also the taxi driver says he speaks fluent Italian with a Neapolitan accent . . . that also fits. My guy's reliable . . . I'll have a couple of my men round there within half an hour . . . OK . . . OK, I'll send half a dozen of my best guys . . . Yes, sure, how could I forget? Sure I'll call you the minute I see that face myself.'

THIRTY-THREE

Michael was reading *One Hundred Years of Solitude*. At first he found it heavy going, but Creasy had pushed him to read it, telling him that it was one of the great works of the century. He was sitting in the shade of a rock at Qala Point. Occasionally he glanced over to look at Juliet, who lay on her stomach in the sun. She was studying her Maltese language book, sometimes calling out for a clarification.

After an hour they both went to cool off in the sea and then sat in the shade. He took out a can of beer for himself from the cool box and a Coke for her.

They sat in companionable silence for a while and then she said, 'I want to talk about it.' She was gazing across the flat, dark blue sea to the island of Comino. He stared at her.

Very quietly, she continued, 'About what happened to me in Marseille. I'm better now, physically. All the good food, the sun and the sea have made me better ... I'm starting to put on weight and I feel stronger every day.' She turned to him and then said almost defiantly, 'But I cannot sleep well at night, and sometimes I have nightmares and sweat a lot ... I think it's all in my mind and I think I have to talk about it to you.'

Creasy had discussed this possibility with Michael, and so he answered, 'Juliet, there are people who are experienced in this kind of thing. Specially trained doctors and social workers. What's happening to you is a delayed reaction. It's quite normal. Sometimes people who have been through such a terrible experience need weeks, months or even years to get over it. It depends on their character and on their background. The horror for you started when your step father began abusing you. You should talk to an expert and go back to that time. There's a very good one in Malta, a woman, trained in England.'

The girl shook her head emphatically. 'I don't need a psychiatrist, Michael. I just need to talk to somebody I trust. It has to be you or Creasy, and you both might be away for a long time, so it has to be you. Can we do it now and then forget about it?'

He drank some beer and then said, 'Go ahead.'

She talked for half an hour. She cried twice and each time he put an arm around her shoulders and waited until she had controlled her tears. At the end of it he was both thoughtful and puzzled.

'So your stepfather never actually raped you?'

'No ... he never put his thing inside me. He just stroked me and made me use my hands on it ... maybe it was worse that way. Also he beat me. He liked to do that.'

He nodded and said, 'Maybe that's all your mother would let him do.'

She shook her head.

'She would have let him do anything. You see, it's why I ran away. He kept telling me that he would do it on my fourteenth birthday ...' she looked up at him, her eyes filled with tears. 'He told me it would be a special birthday present ...'

Michael was silent. His mind was far away in Germany, and he was thinking that when this was all over he would make a journey there. He would give a certain man his last ever birthday present. A present of eternal damnation. He brought his mind back to the present. 'And the same thing happened with those bastards in Marseille?'

Her voice was almost inaudible. 'Yes, they made me use my hands ... and my mouth. They brought a woman in to show me how to use my mouth ... she was a very beautiful woman with long blonde hair and they used to watch her while she did things to me ... sometimes there were three or four of them ... afterwards, they would make me use my mouth.'

She started to cry again and Michael pulled her close and held her head against his shoulder. It was a warm day but his body and mind were totally cold. He thought of the beautiful, blonde woman and said, 'Juliet, I don't know if it will help, but I killed the woman who did that to you.'

She looked up and pulled herself away from him.

'You killed her ... yourself? When ... how ...?'

He told her in detail about the cellar under the villa in Marseille. He told her how Denise Defors had panicked and run for the steps and how he had shot her first in the back and then in the head.

He saw the fierce fascination in the girl's eyes and she asked, 'And the man she was with, the handsome man? The one who always wore shoes made from a snake or a lizard or something?'

Michael nodded. 'Creasy killed him. He tied him to a crooked policeman who had a bomb strapped to his back. The bomb was detonated and blew them both into pieces.' Again he saw the satisfaction in her eyes. 'Does it help?' he asked quietly.

'Yes,' she answered. 'You killed her and Creasy killed him ... It's just like I took a warm shower.'

She could see the slight puzzlement in his eyes. 'What is it?' she asked.

He spread his hands. 'Well ... I can understand that animal of a stepfather waiting for a few months in anticipation, but I can't understand those bastards in Marseille waiting. They certainly didn't wait with that poor Danish girl.' A thought struck him. 'Juliet ... were you ... are you ... a virgin?'

'Yes,' she said solemnly. 'They even had that old woman there check it out ... she seemed to know about those things ... she put a finger inside me and said, "Oui ... c'est là ...!" I speak French quite well because I went to an international school.'

'That's it then,' he said. 'They were probably keeping you a virgin to sell you to the highest bidder. Beautiful virgins around fourteen or fifteen years old fetch a huge price in the Middle East or the Far East.'

She shook her head.

'I think it was something else.'

'Like what?'

'I'm not sure,' she answered. 'But it was something they said. The woman was there and the man with the snake shoes. There was another man. Of course they spoke French but they didn't know I understood most of it. Snakeshoes was polite to the other man ... he must have been important. He wanted me but Snakeshoes said no, I was a virgin. The man became very excited and pushed Snakeshoes, but still he refused. Then the man said, "Of course you can get a fortune for a young virgin like that." Then the woman laughed, the one you killed, and said, "We get more than a fortune for a virgin. We get a bigger fortune for her virginity, her youth ... and her life ... all together." Then Snakeshoes told her to shut up.'

Michael was still puzzled. 'Virginity, youth and life ...' He shrugged and stood up. 'Let's go. I'll make a barbecue tonight.'

They drove in silence until they had passed through Rabat. Then she said, 'Michael, tonight I think I will sleep.'

He glanced at her and smiled.

'You will sleep. After a big meal and two or three glasses of good red wine you'll sleep like a baby.'

At the house he carried the cool box into the kitchen just as the phone rang. She had gone to her bedroom to shower and change. He slid the cool box under the sink and picked up the phone. It was Guido from Naples. He told Michael that Creasy had disappeared that morning. He had arranged to meet Colonel Satta at ten a.m. but had not turned up or phoned. Satta had checked with the airport and learned that Creasy had arrived on an Alitalia flight from Brussels at seven a.m. Satta had then checked with the hotel and been told that Creasy had checked in around eight a.m. but had left the hotel half an hour later. He had not returned. His overnight bag was in his room. Meanwhile the Dane, Jens Jensen, had arrived and was at the hotel, together with a Frenchman whom Guido knew only as The Owl. Michael responded that maybe Creasy had established a link to 'The Blue Ring' which he had to follow up without having time to contact Satta. Guido's voice was dismissive.

'You know Creasy well, Michael, but I know him better. He would have left word somehow.'

'You think he's been "snatched"?'

'I think it's ninety per cent sure.'

'"The Blue Ring"?'

'Maybe. Maybe not ... He has plenty of enemies in Italy. Satta has got his people on to it, and I'm leaving for Milan within the hour. I got word to Maxie and he'll be flying in with Miller and Callard. I tried to get you earlier but you must have been out, so I booked you on an Alitalia flight at eight tonight. The ticket will be at the Alitalia desk at the airport.'

Michael looked at his watch and said, 'I'll be there.'

Half an hour later he was driving Juliet to the Schembri farmhouse. He had been pleased by her response to the news and at his having to leave immediately. First she had wanted to go with him; maybe she could help in some way, but she had seen the look on his face. So she had packed her bag and begged him to keep her informed.

At the farmhouse Laura welcomed her warmly, and pointed upstairs to Creasy's old bedroom. She told her to unpack. Juliet hugged Michael goodbye and obediently picked up her bag and went into the house.

Laura stood with Michael next to the jeep. He saw the concern in her eyes and simply said, 'We have a good team assembling in Milan, a very good team.'

Nothing else needed to be said. As she hugged him, Laura whispered, 'Good luck' and turned away.

THIRTY-FOUR

'I did you a favour,' Creasy said.

Across the table, Gino Abrata snorted in derision.

'A favour!' He looked up at the two bodyguards standing behind Creasy. They both held submachine-guns, cocked and pointed at the American's back, even though his arms and legs were bound tightly to the heavy chair. One of them sneered, but the other never took his narrowed eyes from the back of the head of the man in front of him. He was a careful and cautious bodyguard and he had heard all the stories about the man known as Creasy. His eyes flickered very briefly to his boss' face. It was a fat face above a short fat neck which itself was above an elegant suit. Gino Abrata was known for his good taste in food, clothing and maliciousness.

He snorted again, 'What favour did you ever do me?'

Creasy shrugged painfully; the right side of his face was swollen and blood had dried from a cut on his forehead. He said, 'Six years ago I made you the most important *capo* in Milan.'

'You what!'

'Sure. Cast your mind back ... if you have one.'

Abrata lifted a finger and one of the bodyguards took two paces forward and with carefully calculated force smashed the butt of his submachine-gun into Creasy's back, just below his neck. Creasy made no sound and his eyes never left Abrata's face.

'Yes, I have a mind,' the Italian said. 'And right now I'm using it to work out the most painful way to kill you. What fucking favour are you talking about?'

Creasy moved his shoulder slightly but no expression of pain showed on his face. 'Six years ago,' he said, 'you were the junior *capo* in this city, under Fossella. I killed Fossella. Do you remember?'

At this Abrata smiled. It made his face even more ugly.

'Sure, I remember. You stuck a bomb up his ass and splattered him against the ceiling.'

Creasy nodded. 'I also killed his top lieutenants, which gave you a free hand to become the top *capo* here.'

Abrata sneered at him and leaned forward. 'I would have become a top *capo* anyway.'

Creasy shook his head.

'I doubt it. Fossella was smarter than you and he attracted better people.'

'If he was so smart,' Abrata answered, 'then how did he let one man working alone snatch him and stick a bomb up his ass? It would never have happened to me.'

He saw the slight smile on the American's lips, and then heard him say quietly, 'I had no argument with you, only with Fossella and his bosses in Rome and Palermo. If I had an argument with you then be sure you would not be sitting here now.' He gestured behind him with his head, then leaned forward and said, 'But I tell you, Abrata, if one of your monkeys hits me again we shall have an argument.'

The room was very quiet and seemed to be colder. For a long time Abrata looked into the American's heavy-lidded eyes, then up to the eyes of his bodyguards. When he spoke his voice carried a measure of disdain. 'So you have nerve ... we all know that. You sit trussed up like a turkey with machine-guns at your back and you offer threats. You are threatening the man who is deciding not when to kill you but how to kill you.'

The small smile touched the American's lips again. He said, 'Let me paint the picture. You positively identified me two hours ago. No doubt the first thing you did was to phone Paolo Grazzini in Rome. I'm sure that's the first thing you ever do when faced with a big decision. If you acted alone on something like this, Grazzini would come up here and smack your bottom. No ... I can be sure that Grazzini told you to keep me alive and in a physical condition to be able to answer his questions when he arrives either tonight or tomorrow morning.' Creasy looked into the Italian's eyes and saw the truth of his words reflected in them.

Abrata tried to bluster.

'No one gives Gino Abrata orders ... no one.'

'Sure.'

Abrata stood up, walked around the table and took the SMG from one of the bodyguards. He placed the muzzle against Creasy's left ear and repeated, 'No one gives Gino Abrata orders.'

Creasy sighed and said, 'So pull the trigger, asshole.'

Seconds passed and then Abrata said lightly, 'In the *Cosa Nostra* we co-operate. It is true that Paolo Grazzini now sits on the council. Of course I will co-operate with him and he with me. Certainly, I informed him of the fish I had caught. Since he has a special interest in you ... Conti was his brother-in-law, and you brutally killed Conti. It is reasonable that I let him talk to you before I take pleasure in killing you.'

Creasy turned his head, pushing the muzzle of the SMG away from his ear. He looked up at Abrata. 'Of course that's reasonable. It's also reasonable that you ask one of your monkeys to bring me a glass of cold water or, better still, a glass of good red wine. I'm looking forward to talking to Grazzini ... after all he owes me the same favour as you do. Six years ago Conti used to treat him like an office boy, even if he was married to his sister.'

Again there was a long silence, then Abrata nodded to one of the bodyguards who left the room.

Creasy stretched his shoulders and said, 'Also I have to take a leak.'

Abrata sat down again. 'Then pee in your pants. You're not getting out of that chair until Grazzini gets here ... and when you get out of it you won't be worrying about taking a leak.'

THIRTY-FIVE

Early autumn rain lashed across the darkness of Milan airport as Michael walked through customs. He could hear it on the high-tech roof. It was in keeping with his mood.

That mood lightened when he saw Guido at the back of the welcoming crowd. They embraced and Guido led the way through the concourse to the parking area. As they approached the black Lancia the back doors opened and they slid inside. Maxie MacDonald was at the wheel. Frank Miller sat next to him. They pulled out into the traffic.

Over his shoulder, Maxie said, 'Rain and shit, but hello, Michael.' He gestured with his right hand. 'This is Frank Miller. You've heard about him.' Frank turned his head and in the dim light Michael saw the almost cherubic face.

Miller said, 'Good to finally meet you.'

'Likewise.' Michael turned to Guido and said, 'Fill me in.'

Guido was hunched up in the corner of the car. He spoke rapidly and concisely. 'Creasy is almost certainly held by the Mafia ... We think by the major *capo* here, Gino Abrata. He must have been recognised, and of course the Mafia never forgets a vendetta.'

Michael's voice was terse. 'What do we have?'

Guido told him, 'Creasy has strong connections in this city, particularly with a Colonel Satta of the *carabinieri* ... You will have heard of him. Satta has learned that Creasy left his hotel about half an hour after he arrived from Brussels. About two blocks away there was a commotion. Six men were involved. Two in a large black limousine and four on the pavement. A single shot was fired into the air and then Creasy was bundled into the limousine. Eye-witnesses here are reticent, but it was almost certainly Creasy. That was this morning, and since then we have more information, which is being updated by the hour. It's better that we wait until we get to our base and Satta will bring us all completely up to date.'

'Who do we have here?' Michael asked.

Guido gestured at the front seats. 'Well, we have Maxie and Frank; we also have Rene Callard, the Dane, Jens Jensen, a French guy called The Owl, Satta, of course, his number two, Bellu, and one of Satta's undercover men, known only as The Ghost.'

Michael murmured, 'So within our team we have three Italian policemen ... I'm suspicious of any policeman.'

Guido shook his head. 'You can trust those three and the rest of our team. Trust nobody else.'

It was a small house in a nondescript suburb of Milan. An old woman opened the door, looked them over carefully and ushered them in. The lounge was crowded. Michael knew Jens and The Owl. Guido introduced him to Callard, Bellu, The Ghost and Satta, saying, 'You know the rest.' It was half an hour to midnight.

Michael embraced them all. Chairs had been pulled around a table. The man called The Ghost was sitting at a small, sophisticated radio console, speaking into a microphone. As Michael sat down, the others ignored him; they were deep in discussion. Bellu was talking.

'It's certainly Abrata ... all his "soldiers" are off the street. We know he has two main boltholes on the outskirts of the city. Creasy will be held in one of them. We think the one to the north, which is on high ground and easily defended.'

Rene Callard asked, 'When will we know which one?'

'Within the hour,' Bellu answered. 'But we have to be careful.' He glanced at Michael. 'Unfortunately, like every other institution in Italy, the *carabinieri* is infiltrated by the Mafia. We have to work only with those few that we can trust ... and they are very few.'

Satta grimaced, nodded his head and confirmed, 'We can count them on the fingers of one hand.'

Maxie said, 'The machinery has arrived from Marseille. We're well-equipped. Once we know the location, we can blast our way in.'

Satta shook his head.

'By the time you finish blasting your way in, Creasy will have a bullet in his head. Let's think about it. Let's think carefully.' He gestured at Guido. 'Our friend here was once Mafia and understands how they work.' He tapped his chest and then gestured at Bellu. 'Together we spent five years fighting the Mafia. We know the structure, and we know how they think. Tell them, Bellu.' The short, round-faced Italian gave them a thumbnail sketch of the situation.

'Creasy once waged a one-man war against the major Mafia family ... around six years ago. He set them back about ten years. The current situation is that Gino Abrata is the chief of two *capos* in Milan. His nominal boss in the hierarchy is Paolo Grazzini from Rome. We know that Grazzini had a meeting late this evening in Rome with a visiting *capo* from Detroit. We know they had dinner in the Ristorante Adessio, and just after midnight Grazzini left in his limousine, followed by another car full of bodyguards, and took the autostrada to Milan. He hates travelling by plane or train. He will arrive at approximately five-thirty a.m. Until that time we know that Creasy will be kept alive. Both Abrata and Grazzini will be very puzzled, because for the last six years they thought that Creasy was in a grave in Naples. They will suspect that he is again waging war against the Mafia. They will torture him to find out how and why.' He looked around the room at all the others. 'We know that Creasy will tell them nothing. We know he will hold on for many hours ... My guess is at least twenty-four ... After that they will kill him painfully, and will leave his body publicly, as an example of vengeance, and a sign not to mess with the Mafia.' He looked at his watch. 'We have about thirty hours.'

Maxie stood up and started walking around the table. He was agitated. 'Thirty hours is plenty of time. Once we know the location for sure we mount an operation. We throw up a diversion ... and Frank, Rene and I hit the place.'

Satta shook his head.

'The obvious answer would be for the *carabinieri* to seal off the location and go in with our anti-terrorist unit. There are two things against this: firstly, with the corruption in our unit, they would have at least an hour's warning. Secondly, we would need a magistrate's approval to mount such an operation, and that would take many hours. We would first have to find an honest magistrate or judge, and most of those have been killed.' He shrugged eloquently. 'That is our situation.'

Then Rene Callard stood up and spoke in his heavily accented English. 'We need nobody except ourselves. We have done this before. Creasy is our man. Give us the location. We'll get him out.'

Michael had been looking at the table in front of him. Now he lifted his head, looked at Satta and said, 'I need some more information. Does Abrata have family?'

Satta looked at Bellu, who provided the information.

'Abrata's parents are both dead. He has no children. His brother and sister live in New York. His wife is estranged and living in Bologna, shacked up with a minor *capo*.' He gave Michael a wry smile. 'You have no route there.'

Michael asked, 'And Grazzini?'

Bellu shrugged.

'A wife and countless mistresses. He has no emotional ties except to his mother.'

'Where is his mother?'

For the first time, Satta's lips twisted into a thin smile. He was catching the drift and supplied the answer. 'Grazzini's mother is called Graziella. She lives in a small town twenty miles north of Rome called Bracciano Lago. She is aged and very religious. She prays every day in church for the soul of her son ... I would say that her prayers are futile.'

Michael looked at The Ghost and said, 'It's going to be a long night. Can we get something to drink and maybe some pasta?'

The Ghost stood up, went to the door and shouted down the stairs. 'Bring us some food and drink, you old bag! Don't you know an army marches on its stomach?'

In a manner unknown to them all, the group of hard, experienced men found themselves deferring to the youngest of them all. Michael pointed first to Guido. 'I want you to return immediately to Naples. You have no part in what is to come, except to act as a communicator between us all.' He pointed to Maxie. 'We will not try to storm their bolthole.' He pointed at Bellu. 'Before dawn tomorrow I have to be in Bracciano Lago. Frank, Rene and The Owl will be with me. We will take Grazzini's mother and trade her for Creasy.' He pointed to Satta. 'Colonel, by dawn tomorrow I need a wheelchair and a priest's outfit –' he pointed at Jens Jensen – 'to fit that Dane.' He pointed to The Ghost. 'Since you know the terrain, you will lead Maxie to the closest point to their bolthole and wait for instructions, in case we fuck up in Bracciano Lago. If that happens you will not go in. Maxie will go.' He stood up and started pacing, deep in thought. He pointed again at Satta. 'We need voice communication, not just between ourselves, but also direct to The Ghost and Maxie. Can that be arranged within the next couple of hours?'

Satta nodded. He had a smile on his face. He was sitting in a room surrounded by some of the most dangerous human beings he had ever met in his dangerous life, and he was observing a young man, almost a boy, dominate them. It appealed to his sense of irony. 'What else do you need?' he asked.

Michael stopped pacing.

'Apart from The Ghost, who I assume is clean, I need you to keep the *carabinieri* right out of this, for reasons you understand. I need two unmarked vehicles here in Milan for The Ghost and Maxie, and two more in Rome for myself and the back-up team. I need a hole in Rome. I assume we can use this place as a base here in Milan. I also need to charter a plane to get my team to Rome in three hours. It should be a private charter and not connected with the *carabinieri*. Can do?'

Satta nodded as the door opened and the old woman came in, carrying a tray piled with bottles of wine, glasses, a huge saucepan of pasta and plates. She looked at The Ghost. Old eyes in an old face, but a smile which held affection.

'If you ever call me an old bag again, I'll take you to bed and prove that you're wrong.'

The Ghost, a handsome man in his early thirties, looked at her, nodded and crossed himself.

As they ate and drank Michael refined his plan.

THIRTY-SIX

A single spotlight from a far corner lit him. The two bodyguards
were behind, in darkness. They had been changed every two
hours. They had been told that even though he was bound and
immobile, never to relax their vigilance. They had been told that he
was 'death on a cold night'. His chin was slumped onto his chest. He
was practising what he had learned many years ago; he was half-
asleep and yet his brain was awake. He had long ago ceased to
reproach himself about his negligence. Of course he should have been
more careful. Of course he should not have used the same hotel twice.
Of course he should have been watching for a waiting car by the
kerb. Of course he should have seen and recognised the lurking men
for what they were. But that was history. He remembered with irony
his lecture to Michael back in Marseille. His mistake was as bad. He
thought about Michael. He knew that by now he would be in Italy,
looking for him. He knew that Michael would have a team that
would be the dream of every leader. He wondered how Michael
would handle that team.

His thoughts then turned to Grazzini. He knew about Grazzini.
He was more northern Mafia and not like the animals from Calabria
and Sicily, who had long ago given up every vestige of honour in the
pursuit of drug dollars. Grazzini was relatively young. He was certainly ruthless, but he kept the code of separating business from
family. Would Michael understand that? If not, would Guido or Satta
be able to explain it to him?

As he sat in pain the feeling washed over him; a feeling that Michael
would take control. A feeling that the hard and experienced men
around him would follow Michael. They would see in Michael a
window on himself.

His thoughts turned to the child-woman in Gozo and a pain went through him. She now had a brother, but above all she needed a father. His thoughts again turned to Grazzini. He knew that Grazzini dealt in drugs, protection, corruption and ostensibly legitimate construction and trade. He did not deal in women. He knew that Grazzini hated his guts and that his death by Grazzini's hand would be a huge coup for the Rome *capo*. He knew how he would deal with Grazzini.

THIRTY-SEVEN

Michael just held on to the edge. It was a mental edge. He knew that by the force of his personality, and by his filial association to Creasy, he had managed to dominate a group of vastly experienced hard men. He also knew that his one major exploit would be known to those men. An exploit that had directed a sniper's bullet precisely into the shoulder of a terrorist from a distance of five hundred metres. An exploit made more significant by the fact that when he had pulled the trigger Creasy had been lying alongside him with the same sniper's rifle and had, in that category, deferred to Michael's skills. He knew that in the eyes of the likes of Maxie, Miller, Callard, Satta, and even Guido, he had cut his number. And yet he was not quite twenty years old and the mental burden was heavy. He balanced it with the hatred for the men who were holding his father.

The Lear jet swept down to the runway. It was raining lightly, but the forecast was that it would be a cool, sunny day. It was four o'clock in the morning. The small airport was fifteen miles east of the city and handled most of the smaller internal charter flights. Michael had been assured that there would be a minimum of bureaucracy. The small jet followed the flashing light of a guide car, which finally pulled to a stop next to a floodlit hangar. A large stretch limousine pulled up alongside. Michael led the way down the steps, and within a minute they had unloaded their personal bags and those which contained the machinery.

An hour later they were in the safe house on the northern outskirts of Rome. It was another nondescript house in a nondescript suburb. The door was opened by another old lady who showed no surprise at the arrival of five strangers at that time of the morning.

The priest's clothing had been delivered, together with the wheel-chair and a detailed map of the town of Bracciano Lago. There were also road-maps showing alternative routes from Bracciano to the safe house. They sat around the kitchen table. The old woman prepared a pot of coffee, and Michael went through the details of the plan once more.

When he finished, Miller said, 'It's good and simple, but one thing bothers me.' He gestured at the Dane. 'You're putting Jens in the front line. He doesn't have that much experience. Why not me or Rene or even The Owl?'

Michael shook his head and smiled.

'For some reason Jens does look like a priest ... a slightly over-fed one. We know for sure there will be one bodyguard and it's possible there may be more. We have a description of that bodyguard, and we know that he usually hangs around outside the church while the old woman is inside. Frank, you will have to be alongside him when she comes out. Rene will be waiting in one of the cars to pick you up, after I make the "snatch". It's better if you don't have to kill him, but do so if necessary.'

Rene interjected, 'I guess it's almost certain that Frank will have to kill him. After all, he's supposed to be guarding Grazzini's mother. If he lets her get snatched he's dead anyway.'

'It's possible,' Michael said. 'But he's been her regular bodyguard for a long time ... a couple of years. She's not really regarded as a target, so he won't be on his toes. Frank might be able to slug him.'

'I'll play it by ear,' Miller said.

Michael turned to The Owl and said, 'You'll be driving the other car, ready to collect myself and Jens and the old woman.' He made a general gesture at all of them. 'We only take hand-guns which are easy to conceal if there are any random police road-blocks on the way to Bracciano.'

For the first time The Owl spoke. 'What if there are road-blocks on the way back?'

'We shoot our way through,' Michael answered tersely. 'Sure, if we had more time and people, we could plan it more elaborately and have a safe house closer by.' He shrugged and looked at his watch. 'But we don't have more time. We have to rely on surprise and then speed. The traffic both there and back will be fairly heavy. The police will be reluctant to set up road-blocks.' He reached down and unzipped the bag at his feet, took out the transceivers and handed them out. They tested them and then Michael pushed the buttons to connect himself with Maxie. Maxie's voice was slightly distorted but audible enough.

Michael said softly into the microphone, 'We are moving in about an hour. Be in position by nine o'clock and check in.'

Maxie's voice came back, 'Will do ... Good luck.'

THIRTY-EIGHT

Grazzini spoke conversationally. He was speaking to Abrata but his words were directed at Creasy.

'Eighteen hours,' he said. 'That's the longest I've ever known. He was a Frenchman from the "Union Course". We caught him about three years ago, trying to pull off an art theft in Rome ... on my territory, the bastard. I decided to make an example of him. I had two of my best men work on him. The kind of guys who would make the Pope renounce his faith in half an hour. Eighteen hours ... He surprised me and my guys.' He turned to look at the bound Creasy. 'You will not be that stupid, will you? You know what the end result will be.'

Creasy yawned, then leaned forward slightly and said, 'Grazzini, I have no argument with you. I am not in Italy to have any arguments with you or your people. I was minding my own business when this clown had me grabbed on the street. Unless he lets me go immediately he will die regretting it ... and since you are his boss, you will do the same.'

Grazzini smiled.

'You are in no position to make threats or talk about arguments.' His voice became angry. 'You killed my brother-in-law and one of my cousins.'

'Who was your cousin?'

'His name was Vico Di Marco. He was a bodyguard of my brother-in-law. He was a "soldier". You fried him along with my brother-in-law and two other "soldiers" in that Cadillac in Rome.'

Creasy nodded at the memory.

'Then he died doing his duty, trying to protect his boss. It was nothing personal. I was just the "instrument".'

Grazzini snorted in anger.

160

'We do not like "instruments". We never forget those who make war on us. I will have revenge. But first you talk.'

Creasy stretched his shoulders and asked quietly, 'What do you want to talk about?'

'I want to know why you are in Italy. What is your purpose, who are you with and where is your base, both in Italy, and outside Italy?'

The Italians received a great shock, as Creasy responded, 'That's no problem. Apart from my base outside.'

Grazzini and Abrata glanced at each other in surprise.

Creasy's voice went on, 'But, Grazzini, I only talk to you. The others have to leave.'

Immediately, Abrata said, 'Forget it.'

Creasy kept looking at Grazzini. A long silence and then Grazzini said, 'Gino, give me a few minutes with him ... I would be grateful.' He spoke as if to an equal asking a favour, but the order was implied.

At first, anger filled Abrata's eyes, then they cleared and he said, 'You realise that it's a trick. He is cunning, this one. Let us not forget how cunning. Let us not forget the lives we lost to the bastard.'

Grazzini nodded.

'You are right, of course, and believe me, Gino, I will never forget. But a few minutes before he dies could be useful.'

Another silence, and then Abrata slowly stood up and nodded at the two bodyguards behind Creasy. They left with their submachine-guns.

Abrata said, 'Are you armed?'

'No,' Grazzini answered. 'I rarely carry guns these days.'

Abrata reached under his jacket and pulled out a pistol. He flicked off the safety and put the gun on the table in front of Grazzini, saying, 'He's tied up tight ... but be careful.'

Grazzini smiled slightly and said, 'My friend, I have lived so long because I am very careful. I intend to die in bed at a great age ... I will call you.'

Abrata gave Creasy a last look which promised a future retribution. Then he left the room.

THIRTY-NINE

'There's no doubt about it. She's a man's girl and she is going to be a man's woman.'

Laura was looking out through the kitchen window and down at the fields below. Her daughter-in-law, Maria, was standing beside her. Paul was digging up a field with a rotovator. Juliet was following him like a little puppy. The noise of the rotovator made conversation between them difficult, but Laura could faintly hear his raised voice. He was telling Juliet what he was doing and why. He reached the last corner of the field, cut out the rotovator, sat on a low wall and pulled out a flask from his canvas bag. The girl sat beside him and they shared a glass of cool wine.

'You're right,' Maria agreed. 'It's only been a day and a night but already she can twist Paul and Joey round her finger. I wonder if she can do the same with Creasy.'

Laura thought about that and then nodded.

'Yes, she will. Creasy will see in her his lost daughter grown up ... but she will not be able to twist Michael any way at all ... Michael will be the stern elder brother, and he will get mad with Creasy for being soft with her ... It will make a good triangle for a family.'

'That's if Creasy ever gets back,' Maria said. 'If it's true the Mafia have him, they will take revenge.'

'He's lived a long time,' Laura said. 'Lived through bad times ... mostly alone. Now he has Michael, and right now Michael is looking for him. Michael will bring him home ... and that too will be good.'

On the wall below them, Juliet was asking questions.

'How long have you had this farm?'

Paul glanced at her and smiled. 'My family has farmed this land for generations.' He pointed at a field of almost ripe tomatoes. 'Of course it's crazy, I work about twelve or fourteen hours a day, and when I sell those tomatoes in the market next week I will get about fifteen lire for them. If I cost in the fertiliser and insecticides I used, plus my labour at one pound an hour, I would be losing money.'

'So why do you do it?'

'It's in my blood,' he explained. 'It's in the blood of all Gozitans. When I hold that fifteen lire in my hand it will feel like free money ... And there is something else. All the vegetables and fruit we eat on our table are grown in our fields. All the chickens and eggs, rabbits and ducks are reared on this farm. It is hard to explain the satisfaction that gives. If all the shops were to close tomorrow my family would not go hungry.' He lifted the beaker of wine, took a sip and handed it to her. 'And would not go thirsty either ... We have a spring for water and we have vines for wine.'

She took a sip and smiled up at him. 'Very good wine. I think I know how you feel.'

He nodded. 'Maybe you do ... Even though you're a child you have been through much trouble. In all our history, over thousands of years, we have also gone through much trouble. Always being invaded, sold into slavery and used by outsiders. I can remember the last war ... all the shops were shut then. I was just a child.' He gestured at his small fields. 'But I worked on the farm with my father and my uncle, and our family did not go hungry. What food we had left over we sent to Malta, where the people were hungry.'

'So you are a happy man?' she asked.

He took back the beaker of wine and drank a little more while he thought over his answer.

'In some ways I am happy. I have a wonderful and strong wife, a son to be proud of, a daughter-in-law whom I love and who will give me grandchildren. I have Creasy, who for me and Laura is a combination of son, brother and father. I also have Michael who now is another son.' He put a gnarled brown hand on her head, patted it lightly and said, 'And now it seems I have another daughter. That is good, but for you it is difficult, because you have to replace the two daughters I lost ... and they were wonderful daughters.'

She was looking up at the farmhouse above her. She saw Laura and Maria sitting on the patio. Very quietly she said, 'I know all about Nadia and Julia ... Michael told me. I can never replace them. I can never take away that pain ...' She turned to look at him. 'But I can love you and Laura and Joey and Maria. I can promise nothing except that.'

He stood up, brushing the dust of the wall from his backside. He moved to the rotovator. 'Let's do one more field, and then I have to go over to a friend who has some problems with his wine press.'

'Can I go with you?'

'Why not?'

FORTY

The car pulled up in front of the church at two minutes to nine. Michael watched from his wheelchair a hundred metres away across the square. He held a book on his blanketed knees. Jens stood behind him, garbed in the black of a priest. Both of them wore hearing aids.

It was a black car, an old but perfectly maintained Lancia. The driver got out and opened the rear door. An old woman emerged. The driver tried to help her but, imperiously, she waved him away. With the help of a white stick she hobbled up the shallow steps to the entrance. An old priest was waiting for her. He took her by the arm and guided her through the door. The driver climbed back into the car, drove it across the square and parked it beside a small café. Within a minute he was drinking a *cappuccino* and biting into a brioche.

Michael glanced around the square, then lifted the book and spoke quietly at it.

'Just one,' he said. 'The usual one. Do you see him?'

Miller's voice came into the hearing aid. 'We see him.'

'About thirty minutes,' Michael said. 'My priest will take me for a walk.' He looked up at Jens and nodded. The Dane reverently pushed the wheelchair across the cobbled square to the café.

FORTY-ONE

Creasy tossed the three words across the table, watching the Italian's face closely for any reaction.

'"The Blue Ring".'

At first there was no reaction. Grazzini's dark eyes simply looked puzzled. Slowly he repeated the words as a question. '"The Blue Ring"?'

Creasy said nothing, just watched him. Grazzini repeated the words.

'"The Blue Ring"?' Almost imperceptibly, he nodded. 'I have heard something ... vague rumours ... over many years ... I doubt that it exists.'

Creasy's voice was flat and direct. '"The Blue Ring" does exist. It is my reason for being in Italy.'

It had immediately become a poker game. Each of the two players trying to fathom out the cards that the other one held. Creasy remained silent.

Finally Grazzini spoke. 'If they do exist, they have nothing to do with the *Cosa Nostra*.'

Both of Creasy's hands and feet were now numb. He tried to move his fingers and felt nothing. He stretched his shoulders and said, 'I know that. If I thought they had anything to do with the *Cosa Nostra* I would not be tied up here. I would be in Rome, talking to you – and you are the one who would be tied down.'

Grazzini shrugged dismissively.

'What do you know about "The Blue Ring"?'

'I will tell you,' Creasy answered. 'But first I will tell you what I know about Paolo Grazzini.'

The Italian smiled sardonically and waved a hand in invitation.

Creasy leaned forward as far as he could and spoke in a matter of fact voice. 'Paolo Grazzini was a small time "soldier" in Rome until he married the sister of Conti, the chief *capo* of Rome and northern Italy. That marriage fuelled his career, and he became an important lieutenant although Conti never treated him with the respect he thought he was due.'

Grazzini shrugged, the sardonic smile still on his lips. Creasy went on.

'About six years ago, Gino Fossella, the head *capo* in Milan, and nominally under the control of Conti, kidnapped a child very close to me and in doing so wounded me, almost to my death. Later the girl died. I killed Fossella and his lieutenants. I was angry. Angry enough to go to the very top. So I blew away Conti and all his lieutenants except you.'

'I know all this,' Grazzini said impatiently.

'You know it but there are things you don't understand. I'm explaining to you now. I went on to kill Cantarella in Palermo and all of his top lieutenants. After that I faked my death.'

Grazzini nodded. 'With the help of your good friend, Colonel Satta.'

'That's immaterial. With the death of Cantarella my vengeance was settled. I have nothing against you personally, or the *Cosa Nostra* in general.'

The Italian smiled coldly again.

'It takes two to stop a vendetta. You disturbed us. You will pay for it. This time your death will not be fake ... believe me.'

Creasy smiled. An open smile. He said, 'You are not talking to somebody who is ignorant of this matter. In the past six years things have changed. You rose to the top in Rome and in the north, but you can never control Naples, Calabria or Sicily. There are now two *Cosa Nostre* in Italy. One to the south of Rome and one to the north. In the north you are trying to become civilised, trying to become at least partly respectable. In time, maybe you'll succeed ... but not with the likes of Abrata. He represents the last generation.'

Grazzini was feigning indifference, but Creasy could see the interest in his eyes. He went on.

'Paolo Grazzini is a different breed. Yes, he deals in drugs, or lets his minions do so, and then takes his cut. You deal in coercion and protection, but mostly you deal in corruption in collusion with politicians and big businessmen.' His voice went quiet, almost reflective. 'But you do not deal in women; you have no hand in prostitution. When you order killings it is only among yourselves ... unlike the animals in the south and in Sicily. You do not wage war on civilians. You do not kill women or use them.'

There was a silence and then Grazzini spoke one word. 'So?'

Creasy shrugged.

'So you tell me what you know about "The Blue Ring" which is a stain on the honour of *Cosa Nostra*.'

There was another silence, and Creasy waited, knowing that the Italian's reaction was going to be crucial. The reaction came.

'Why is it a stain?'

Creasy knew that he had crossed the first bridge.

'It is a stain on *Cosa Nostra*, and you personally, because you let such filth operate in your territory.'

The Italian became angry, and Creasy knew that he had crossed the second bridge.

'What the hell do you mean?' Grazzini snarled. 'They are only a rumour, just a name in the dark. There are always rumours. I doubt they exist.'

Very emphatically Creasy said, 'They do exist. They exist in your territory and in others. I am going to find them and wipe them out.'

'Why?'

'I hate them.'

'Why?'

'I have seen their work.'

'What is their work?'

'They buy and sell young women. They abuse them even beyond an imagination like yours. They abuse their bodies and their minds.'

Grazzini was nodding.

'I have heard this ... But is that your business?'

'There is a reason why I have made it my business.'

'What is that reason?'

Creasy enunciated each word very carefully. 'Because when they abuse these girls ... even children ... they take pleasure from it. The pleasure is more important than the profit.'

For several seconds Grazzini looked at the top of the table, then abruptly he stood up and turned away and moved across the room. There was a picture on the wall. A still-life of a bowl of fruit. He stood looking at it. Creasy knew that he had crossed the next bridge.

FORTY-TWO

She hit Michael hard across the face with the white stick screaming, *'Vaffanculo!'* at him. He reeled away from her, almost dropping his pistol, then came back quickly as she took another swipe. He grabbed the stick and pulled her towards him and got an arm around her waist. She bit his shoulder and her false teeth came out. He turned and ran down the steps clutching her under his arm. He saw the old Mercedes pulling up beneath him, with The Owl at the wheel. His wheelchair was bouncing across the cobbles. Jens was running towards the car, his robes flapping. Halfway across the square Michael saw the bodyguard crumpled up, with Miller standing over him. He saw the Australian pistol-whip the bodyguard once more and then run for the corner. Jens had pulled open the back door of the Mercedes. Michael bundled her in and dived after her. The Dane leapt into the front seat and The Owl hit the accelerator. There were screams and shouts above the squealing of the tyres and then they were gone. It had taken no more than twenty seconds.

FORTY-THREE

'But we have a vendetta.' Grazzini was still looking at the painting. 'You killed members of my family.'

Creasy's voice was harsh. 'I killed your brother-in-law, whom I think you hated. I killed your cousin who was a "soldier" and who died in a battle. I did not kill your sister ... she remarried four years ago and gave birth to a daughter to whom you are a godfather. Conti treated your sister like shit ... and you know it.'

Grazzini turned, moved back to his seat and sat down. For the first time his face showed a trace of emotion. 'There is a vendetta,' he stated flatly. 'Only your death can end that.'

Creasy looked at the Italian steadily for a few seconds and then spoke. 'Let me tell you of a terrible shame. A stain on any society. About eight years ago, in a village in the mountains of Calabria, a vendetta ended. That vendetta had lasted for thirty years, during which more than twenty men of two families had been murdered. That vendetta lasted so long that nobody could remember why it started. At the end there was only one male member of one of the families left alive. In the wonderful code of such vendettas a boy becomes a man when he is sixteen years old, and then becomes eligible to kill or be killed. That boy was fifteen years old when his mother and sisters informed him that on his sixteenth birthday he must take his father's gun and avenge the death of his father, brothers, uncles and cousins. He decided that he wanted no part of a vendetta. His mother and sisters were ashamed of his attitude. The local priest knew of the story and informed the press. The story became known throughout Italy and the world.'

Grazzini was nodding, his face sombre.

Creasy went on, 'Many families in Italy offered to take the boy in. Of course the police offered protection. The boy refused all offers.

On the night before his sixteenth birthday his mother and sisters left the house, after spitting on him. They left the doors open. One minute after midnight men from the other family came with their guns and shot him at the table where he sat. His mother and his sisters refused to attend his funeral ... Was that vengeance? Is that what you seek with me?'

Grazzini looked at the pistol in front of him. He picked it up and then slowly replaced it. Quietly he said, 'You know our system. I have to maintain my authority.'

Creasy laughed softly.

'If you have to show how strong you are by putting a bullet into the brains of a bound man, your authority is already lost.'

Grazzini was silent and then the door burst open and Abrata was calling urgently. Grazzini hurried from the room. A minute later he was back, his face suffused with rage. He grabbed at the gun and pointed it at Creasy's head. His chest was heaving and his words came out as a snarl.

'Vendetta! You talk of vendetta! You snatched my mother! My mother, you bastard!'

Creasy shouted back at him. 'I've been tied to this chair for the last twenty-four hours!'

'Your people, then!' He reached forward and put the muzzle of the gun between Creasy's eyes.

Creasy drew a breath and then said quietly, 'If it was my people and you pull that trigger then your mother is dead.'

The Italian was breathing deeply. From behind him Abrata said, 'Kill the bastard.'

'It's not *your* mother,' Creasy said loudly, and then in a quieter voice he said to Grazzini, 'When and where?'

Grazzini withdrew the gun a few inches. 'Outside the church of her home town. Fifteen minutes ago.'

Creasy closed his eyes in thought, then he motioned with his head to the chair. 'Sit down and wait. If it was my people they will phone here within fifteen or twenty minutes. Have a phone on the table.'

Tension filled the room like an unseen presence. Abrata spoke again. 'They will try to trade her for him.'

'Never,' Grazzini snarled. 'He will never leave this room alive.'

'It's possible,' Creasy conceded. 'But fifteen or twenty minutes will make no difference. I don't make war on innocent women. Not even on the mother of a *capo*.'

Another silence, then Grazzini turned and said, 'Get a phone extension in here. The phone should have a loudspeaker.'

The call came eighteen minutes later. Grazzini picked up the phone and listened. By now he was back under control, but the gun was still in his hand, and pointed at Creasy's head. Finally, the Italian put his hand over the mouthpiece and said, 'He says he's your son and that he has my mother . . . I didn't know you had a son.'

'Until a minute ago, I didn't know you had a mother . . . Let me speak to him.'

Behind Grazzini, Abrata rolled his eyes and said, 'The bastard's crazy.'

'Why don't you shut your mouth,' Creasy told him. 'She's not your mother.'

Grazzini wrestled with the two parts of his brain, then he held the phone to Creasy's ear and punched a button on the console.

'Michael?' Creasy asked.

His son's voice came into the room. 'Yes, are you all right?'

'Yes. Are you holding Grazzini's mother?'

'Yes.'

'Let her go immediately.'

The console was silent for at least twenty seconds. Finally, Michael's puzzled voice came through. 'Did you say that because they have a gun to your head? If so, tell them I have a gun to her head.'

'Michael. It's important that you do exactly what I tell you. Release her immediately and have her driven to Grazzini's home in Rome. She is to be harmed in no way. Tell her to phone Grazzini at this number as soon as she is at his home. I assume you have some of our friends with you. You are all to go to the man you know as my brother and to wait for my call there.'

They heard the click of the phone through the loudspeaker. Very slowly, Grazzini replaced his own receiver.

Into the silence Abrata said, 'It's a trick. Why would he do that?'

Creasy was looking at Grazzini. He said softly, 'A man like that would never understand. I told you . . . I don't make war on women.'

FORTY-FOUR

Colonel Satta came into the room. It was not a typical room in a typical hospital, but rather like the suite of a luxury hotel. Only the orthopaedic bed and the stands for the drips betrayed its medical purpose. Also the severely attractive nurse, although her uniform could have been designed by Valentino.

She was taking Creasy's blood pressure. She checked the dial, nodded in satisfaction and said, 'Now all you need is a good sleep.' She gave Satta a stern look. 'Which means that your visitor must leave in fifteen minutes.'

Creasy reached out his bandaged hand and touched her on the wrist and asked, 'What is your name?'

'Gianna,' she answered.

He smiled at her; a very tired smile.

'Gianna, I may have to talk to Colonel Satta for some time. Would you please bring us a bottle of good Barolo and two glasses.'

'Make it three,' Satta said. 'Bellu will be here in ten minutes.'

The nurse sighed in exasperation. 'Well, you will have to explain to Doctor Sylvestri. He has predicted a possible delayed shock reaction.'

Satta smiled at Creasy who smiled back. The Colonel turned to the nurse and said, 'The only shock he'll get is if you don't bring that wine within five minutes.'

She shook her head and bustled out. Satta pulled a chair up close to the bed.

'I talked to Guido. I didn't go into details. I told him you were fine and will be travelling to Naples tomorrow. Meanwhile he's heard from Michael, who followed your orders up to a point.'

Ominously, Creasy said, 'Up to a point?'

'Yes. And I think he's right. He's on his way to Naples with the entire team except for Maxie.'

'Where is Maxie?'

'Maxie is not a million miles from here. Don't ask me where because I don't know, but I guess somewhere in the grounds of this little hospital ... Michael thinks like you.'

Creasy nodded thoughtfully.

'It's stupid and unnecessary ... But knowing Maxie is somewhere close watching my back makes me feel good.'

Satta grinned.

'Like I told you: Michael thinks like you.'

Creasy looked down at his bandaged right hand.

'That doctor Sylvestri got it exactly right. It wasn't the finger that did the damage. It was being bound so tightly for all those hours that almost gave me gangrene. In a few more hours I'd have lost all my fingers and all my toes.' He shrugged and half smiled. 'I hadn't realised, because you lose all feeling. At first there's pain, but then the pain goes away and you don't know that those parts of your body are dying.'

There was a tap on the door, and Bellu entered, carrying a briefcase. He pulled up a chair on the other side of the bed, put the briefcase down, then leaned over and kissed Creasy on both cheeks. Creasy put his good arm around his neck, pulled him close and hugged him. It had been six years since they had last met. Bellu sat down, picked up his briefcase, put it on his knees and opened it. He took out a slim file and looked at Creasy who said, 'Tell me.'

Bellu opened the file and read from the police report: '"At ten thirty-two in the morning Signora Grazzini emerged from the church in Bracciano Lago. At the foot of the steps a young man was waiting in a wheelchair under the supervision of a priest. Witnesses testified that the priest was of medium height, blond-haired and slightly plump. Signora Grazzini's bodyguard, one Filippo Cossa, was moving towards her car. At that moment the young man in the wheelchair tossed aside his blanket and leapt up, holding a pistol. Cossa immediately ran across the square towards her, but was cut off by another man, also holding a pistol. He wore a dark sweater and dark trousers and a black beret. Cossa did not have time to draw his weapon before he was struck down. Signora Grazzini struck out at the young man with her stick, but he grabbed her round the waist and carried her down to a Mercedes which had pulled up. He threw her in the back and went in after her. The priest went into the front seat, and the car pulled away at speed. Some ten seconds later a second car pulled into the square next to Cossa. The latter's assailant jumped into the passenger seat and that car also pulled away at speed. It is estimated that it took twenty-five minutes to establish police road-blocks on all exit roads out of Bracciano. The prognosis is that this was a highly professional kidnapping."'

Bellu closed the file, looked first at Satta, then at Creasy, who said, 'It sure as hell was!'

Satta shrugged. 'Like father like son ... but he had a hell of a team with him. With those boys the president of the country would not have been safe.' He looked at Creasy. 'From the timescale, Michael would have used the mobile phone to call Grazzini. We know that an hour later Michael delivered Signora Grazzini to her son's home in Rome ... Now tell us, Creasy. Why did he do that, and what happened next?'

Creasy looked at his bandaged left hand and answered, 'Of course Grazzini wanted to kill me immediately, and he was being urged on by that little prick, Abrata. You have to understand that Grazzini had a major problem. On the one hand, we had built up something of a rapport. But when Michael snatched his mother it was necessary that he showed his ruthlessness and his machismo. He was then thrown out of balance when I ordered Michael to let his mother go and deliver her to his home.'

Bellu was enthralled. He asked, 'You gave those instructions while you were still bound to that chair?'

Creasy nodded. 'Yes ... it was a very calculated risk.'

Full of curiosity, Satta asked, 'In return for letting his mother go without condition, he cut off your finger?'

Creasy's mind went back to those moments in that room. The moments when his life was precisely on the line. He saw it as though he had wound back a video and was watching it again.

Grazzini was totally confused. If it was a trick he did not understand it.

Creasy said, 'Wait for the call from your mother. If she's the character I think she is, she will not tell you lies because my son is holding a gun to her head ... I suggest you wait alone.'

Grazzini paced the room several times, and then snapped at Abrata, 'Leave us alone!'

Reluctantly, Abrata left the room, saying over his shoulder, 'Don't trust him. I'll be right outside.' He closed the door behind him.

They waited in total silence. Grazzini paced the room. Occasionally he stopped and looked at the painting on the wall as though it contained the meaning of life itself. Creasy watched him and every so often glanced down at his bound right arm. The call came twenty minutes later. The loudspeaker was still switched on, and Creasy was able to follow the conversation. Grazzini's mother was angry.

'What the hell is happening?'

'Where are you?'

'I'm at your apartment.'

'Are you alone?'

'Maria is here.'

'Are you all right?'

Her voice came through the loudspeaker in pained, truculent tones. 'All right? ... I hear mass. I say a prayer for the sins of my children ... I put five thousand lire into the poor-box, and then some young kid grabs me outside God's church, throws me into a car, smothers me with a blanket and drives me away!'

'And then what happened?'

'Then he talks on the phone, which I cannot understand. Then he drives me home, kisses me on both cheeks and hands me over to Maria ... Paolo, what the hell are you doing? I told you, the day you got involved with that animal Conti, that you would end in the hands of the devil ... How can my son come to this? ... All my prayers ... All the candles I've burned in all the churches ... You know that young man had a priest with him ... a priest! ... What are you doing now with priests who kidnap old ladies?'

Creasy couldn't help but smile.

Grazzini grimaced at him and punched the button to turn off the loudspeaker. Into the telephone he said, 'Mama ... put Maria on the phone.' The *capo* spoke a few words to his maid and then cradled the phone. He looked at Creasy for a long time and then asked, 'Why?'

Creasy shrugged. 'I told you ... I don't make war on women.'

Grazzini shook his head in puzzlement.

'I don't understand. You are now totally in my power ...' Realisation came over him. 'You knew that if you kept my mother, I could never have let you go. You also knew that if I killed you, your son would have killed my mother. It was a stand-off.'

Creasy nodded. He was still half-smiling, occasionally glancing at his right hand. 'Yes it was. Now there is no stand-off ... But now you have a problem.'

'What problem?'

'Well ... being the kind of man you are ... in a strange way, a man of honour, you have to let me go ... But if you let me go, you will lose your machismo with the little idiots who look up to you.' With his head he gestured towards the door and the unseen Abrata. 'The little idiots who give you power ... You cannot afford to lose your machismo, which is your power, because if you do, one night the little idiot will blow your brains out.'

Grazzini looked at him steadily, acknowledging nothing and admitting nothing.

Creasy told him what to do. 'Go to the door and tell the idiot Abrata to bring a sharp knife from the kitchen. It should be a serrated knife.'

Grazzini's eyes narrowed in puzzlement.

'Do it,' Creasy urged.

Seconds passed and then Grazzini stood up and went to the door. He came back three minutes later, holding a knife. He closed the door and walked over to Creasy.

'Is it sharp?' Creasy asked.

Grazzini ran his thumb over the blade and nodded.

Creasy said softly, 'Look at the little finger of my left hand.'

Grazzini leaned over and looked. The whole hand was white. There was only half of a little finger.

'The rest was shot off,' Creasy said. 'A long time ago. It's amazing how little a man has to use his little finger ... except sometimes to pick his nose.' He looked up at the *capo* and then said, 'Cut off the little finger of my right hand at the second joint.'

The *capo* looked at him uncomprehending.

'It's a good way out,' Creasy said casually. 'You cut it off without anaesthetic. I will give a very comprehensive and realistic scream. Do you have a clean handkerchief?'

Grazzini had a numb look on his face.

'Do you have a clean handkerchief?' Creasy repeated.

The *capo* nodded and pulled a cream silk handkerchief from his top jacket pocket. Creasy nodded approvingly.

'After you've cut it off wrap it round the stump. At that point I faint.' He smiled again. 'It will be very effective. You take the finger out and give it to Abrata, and tell him to have it embalmed and set in crystal and have it sent down to your home in Rome as a gift to your mother.... He will understand that kind of thing. Then you have them send me back to my hotel.'

Grazzini looked at the knife and then at the little finger.

177

Satta and Bellu were silent, looking at the bandaged right hand.

'It hardly hurt,' Creasy said. 'My hand was totally anaesthetised anyway ... But Grazzini was no surgeon.' He smiled at Satta. 'Your brother could give him lessons ... I screamed very effectively and then fainted.' He reached with his good hand to the bedside table and picked up the bloodied silk handkerchief. 'I lost half a useless finger and gained a lovely handkerchief.'

FORTY-FIVE

The Initiate was called forward. Under the black cowl his face was dark and thin; a long jutting chin, beneath a straight narrow mouth. His eyes were also dark, within deep sockets. Those eyes showed trepidation. They flickered from side to side and the man hesitated.

He was called forward again. For a moment he looked at the black altar. The centrepiece was a black inverted cross about two metres high. Behind it stood a huge black candle in an ebony holder. Six smaller black candles were arranged on either side of the inverted cross: thirteen in all. In front of the cross lay a long silver-bladed knife with a black horn handle. On the left of the altar was the figure of a rearing, stuffed goat, its mouth pulled back to reveal white teeth in a hideous grin. On the right side of the altar was a pure white cockerel, tethered by its feet with black silk cord. Next to it was a white human skull.

The high priestess moved from the left-hand side to stand in front of the inverted cross. She was dressed in maroon robes topped by a black cowl.

She called his name again and the Initiate moved forward on legs that no longer took orders from his brain. He climbed three steps and stood one step below her. He looked up into her white-powdered face. Her lipstick was black, as were the horns of a goat painted on to her forehead above her mascaraed eyes. She reached forward and placed the flat of her hand on his head and intoned the words: 'Do you renounce God?'

Without thought, he spoke. 'I renounce God in any form.'

She lifted her eyes and looked at the assembled congregation, all dressed in black gowns. Beyond them was a long table laden with food and wine. The congregation numbering thirteen spoke in unison. 'He renounces God.'

The high priestess withdrew her hand, turned to the altar and picked up the silver-bladed knife. With her back to the Initiate and the congregation, she raised it high above her head. The congregation repeated in hushed whispers, 'He renounces God.'

The high priestess moved along the altar to the cockerel, grasped it at the base of its neck and, with a practised slash of the knife, cut off its head. She then cut through the black bindings, laid down the knife, grasped the twitching body and inverted it over the skull squeezing it as the blood dripped down. After a minute she turned and flung the carcass at the congregation. There were screams of anticipation as they scrabbled for it on their hands and knees.

The high priestess picked up the head of the cockerel and dropped it into the cavity of the skull together with its blood. Then with her left hand she reached down and lifted the hem of her robe. With her right hand she picked up the skull, held it between her straddled legs and urinated into it.

The Initiate stood as still as a slab of granite, looking only at the inverted cross.

The high priestess dropped her gown and, holding the skull reverently in both hands, moved back in front of the Initiate. She held out the skull to him. Very slowly, he reached out his hands, took it from her, brought it to his mouth and drank.

The congregation whispered again. 'He renounces God.'

The Initiate pulled back the cowl of his robe. It revealed a young face, no more than thirty years old. Dark, long hair parted in the middle. The high priestess took the skull from him and poured the remaining contents over his head. She then placed the skull back on the altar and in one movement slipped off her gown. She was naked. Her body was white and plump. Immediately, the Initiate and the rest of the congregation also disrobed. The congregation comprised seven women and six men. Their ages ranged from the early twenties to the late fifties.

They all moved to the banqueting table and for the next half hour gorged themselves with rich food and fine wine. Then the orgy began and continued until dawn.

As the sun rose two men emerged from the remote villa, and stood looking down the valley towards the small village five kilometres away. They could see the tower of the church and heard the chimes as the bells rang to summon the faithful.

The men were in their mid-fifties. They were dressed in well-cut, sober business suits. One of the men was short, thin and sallow. The other was tall and muscular. His face was ebony black and he was totally bald.

The small one turned to the other and said, 'It went well.'

The black man nodded. 'Very well ... It has taken a year to bring him to that. He will never forget that night.'

'I agree,' the first man answered. 'But still, within a month he must attend a full mass with a genuine sacrifice.'

The second man shrugged. 'It will not be easy. We had a good prospective candidate, but she was lost in that fiasco in Marseille.'

'Yes,' the first man said grimly. 'Lost, together with our deposit of twenty thousand dollars. We must have a replacement.'

The second man said, 'At the moment the only ones available are from Asia or Africa.'

The first man shook his head and said quietly but emphatically, 'No! She must be fair-skinned and younger than puberty. We must pay as much as necessary. Perhaps we can persuade Gamel to bring forward the Albanian project. After all, he already has the premises, and the cover is well in place.'

The big man raised his black head and looked towards the southeast and slowly nodded. 'Yes. I will visit Tunis and confer with him. It will be much easier to find such a one in Albania, while that country is in such chaos. Also I must report to him fully on the disquieting events that have happened in the last few days. It has been many years since enquiries have been made.'

'You think it is serious?' the small man asked. 'Do you think there may be some connection with what happened in Marseille?'

The tall black man shook his head. 'I think it has nothing to do with Marseille. That was probably just a gang war. But I'm not happy that we heard of two enquiries being made from such different sources ... No matter ... I have already taken action.' He gestured at the villa behind them. 'Our Initiate inherited a vast fortune last year. He will part with it in time, but only if he continues to slide ever deeper. The Goat must have its sacrifice.'

FORTY-SIX

Laura took Juliet shopping in the village of Nadur. First they went to the baker and bought four crusty round loaves, hot out of the wood-burning oven. Juliet asked her how to say bread in Maltese, and repeated it several times until Laura was satisfied. Then they went to the butcher and Laura had to teach her words for all the different kinds of meat. The usual crowd of black-clad old ladies were in the butcher's shop, as much to have their morning gossip as to buy meat. Laura had to explain that Juliet was newly arrived and had been adopted by *Uomo* as a sister for Michael. The old ladies nodded in approval. Some of them had up to fifteen children of their own and definitely approved of large families, even if they were adopted. They went on to the grocer's and Juliet's lessons in Maltese continued.

On the way back to the car they passed a newly opened boutique, and stopped to admire the dresses in the window. On an impulse, Laura took Juliet's hand and led her into the shop, saying, 'It's Joey and Maria's second wedding anniversary on Saturday. It will be a big party and you can't go in those jeans.'

She bought her a bright red dress, which Juliet thought was a bit loud, but she didn't object because of Laura's obvious enthusiasm. The owner of the boutique thought the dress was a bit large and offered to take it in, but Laura, practical as ever, pointed out that Juliet was rapidly putting on weight and would soon grow into it. Instead she bought her a wide black leather belt to keep it tight. Then, naturally, Juliet had to have some shoes to go with it, so they went off to the shoe shop.

Michael had given his sister a hundred and fifty Maltese pounds before leaving, but Laura would not let Juliet pay for anything.

'You always insist on doing the washing up and helping with the cleaning,' she admonished. 'So this is my present for you.'

Back at the farmhouse, Juliet helped her make lunch, which was always the biggest meal of the day. First a thick vegetable soup, which Laura explained was called Widow's Soup because, with such an abundance of vegetables in Gozo, it was both cheap and filling. Then she made a pork casserole with lots of vegetables. She made enough for about ten people, explaining that it kept well and you never knew how many people might turn up for a meal. The dish was called *kawlata* and happened to be one of Paul's favourites. He came in from the fields exactly at twelve o'clock, having been working for six straight hours. Juliet watched as he ate a huge bowl of soup followed by an even bigger bowl of *kawlata*. During the meal he demolished a whole loaf of bread and drank a bottle of his own wine.

The phone rang as the table was being cleared. It was Creasy. He spoke a few words to Laura, and then she called an excited Juliet to the phone.

He spoke to her for a long time, first assuring her that both he and Michael were well. She asked where they were, but he only replied that they were 'somewhere in Italy' and might be away for a few more weeks, but would try to make at least a quick visit to Gozo. He then told her that, starting next week, she would have to go to school.

'I don't want to go to school.'

'You have to,' he answered gruffly.

'I don't speak the language yet,' she said petulantly. 'It will take me at least another month or more, so I would be wasting my time at school.'

She heard his soft laugh.

'That's not a problem. There's a school in Kercem which is run by nuns. They teach in English. I already spoke to Laura about it; she will arrange it.'

Juliet gave Laura a baleful look. Laura smiled back at her sweetly.

On the phone Creasy said, 'You'll meet children of your own age, and make friends.'

'I already have friends.'

'Like who?'

'Well ... like Laura and Paul, and Joey and Maria ... and the old fisherman Loretto who brings Paul fish and drinks all his wine.'

'You're going to school,' Creasy said firmly. 'I don't want a stupid daughter and Michael doesn't want a stupid sister ... When I get back I'll buy you a bicycle.'

'A bicycle!' she answered excitedly.

'Don't bribe her,' Laura shouted from across the room.

Meekly, Juliet said into the phone, 'OK, Creasy. I'll go to school. But it has to be a red bicycle to go with my new dress.' She explained about the party and chatted on for another few minutes. Later, helping Laura with the washing up in the kitchen, she said wistfully, 'I never had a bicycle ... I don't know how to ride one.'

'I'll teach you,' Laura said with a smile, and then sternly went on, 'Don't think you can get around me like you get around Creasy and Paul. What a girl like you needs is a strong woman around to keep her head level.'

'I'm sure you're right,' Juliet answered, thinking about the red dress and the black leather belt and the matching shoes.

FORTY-SEVEN

The Dane had often attended strategy meetings and seminars run by the police force in Copenhagen. It was his nature normally to keep his counsel at such meetings, unless even a very senior officer made a stupid remark which related to his own expertise. But Jens Jensen had never participated in the kind of meeting which was now in progress.

First of all, he had never been to a meeting at which the food had been so spectacular. They sat at a large oval table on the terrace of the Pensione Splendide. The sweep of the lights of Naples was below them and the huge bay beyond. The meal had been expertly served by a gruff old man who looked as though he should have retired years ago. Jens looked around at the participants and yet again had the schizophrenic feeling that, on the one hand, he was totally out of place in such a group, and on the other, that he was somehow part of it. He was sitting at the centre of the table. Creasy sat opposite. On one side of Creasy was Michael and on the other side was Maxie. At the right-hand end of the table sat Guido and on the left-hand sat Colonel Satta. The others were Massimo Bellu, The Ghost, Frank Miller, Rene Callard, Pietro and, on Jens' left, The Owl. With the exception of himself, Satta and Bellu, he doubted whether a harder bunch of men had ever been grouped together. He knew that even the young Pietro, who was Guido's semi-adopted son, had clawed his way up from sleeping on the streets as a thirteen-year-old to being a very hard young man of twenty-two.

The dinner was delicious. Of course they had *antipasti* to start, and that was followed by *pasta della frutta di mare*. The main course was *cernia al forno* cooked with white wine and olive oil. As *contorni* to the *cernia*, they had *patate lesse* and *piselli al finocchio*. For dessert the old man served *charlotte di fragole*.

Jens glanced again at Creasy's right hand and the bandage around the stub of the little finger. Once again he felt goose bumps at how Creasy had lost that finger, and once again his mind was almost numb at the reason he had done so. He tried to put himself in the same position, trying to face down a Mafia *don* while strapped helplessly to a chair. Not just face him down, but enlist him to a cause.

The conversation had been both light-hearted and serious. Light-hearted when he himself had drily recounted the kidnapping of Grazzini's old mother. How she had whacked Michael across the face with her stick. Michael had grinned ruefully and rubbed his bruised cheekbone. He then told how the old woman had taught him a whole new dictionary of swear words and how, when they had let her go into the safe arms of Grazzini's maid, Maria, she had gone through the door not cursing her abductors but calling on God to give her son some brains for a change.

The conversation had become serious when Michael had stated flatly that Creasy could no longer move around Italy openly. There were other Mafia families who bore a death grudge, and next time Creasy might not be so lucky. Jens had expected Creasy to take umbrage, but he had taken the implied criticism in silence, merely nodding his head and then saying, 'In future I'll be more careful.'

Jens had remembered the stupidity of Michael and himself, in being so easily snatched in Marseille and Creasy's subsequent spectacular rescue. He felt that between Creasy and Michael matters were now even. Then he felt something else: Creasy dominated this group of men. Not by what he said, but by his presence, which radiated a strange aura. Everybody around the table had above average intelligence; some, like Colonel Satta, had extreme intelligence. The likes of Miller, Callard, Guido, Michael and The Owl were unquestionably physically hard and experienced men. But none had quite that same aura as Creasy. In time, the Dane guessed that Michael would attain it; perhaps as Creasy moved into old age and Michael moved into the prime of his life. That was quite a few years away.

He turned to glance at The Owl on his left. The old man had just served dessert and The Owl was tucking into the *charlotte di fragole* with relish. It was not strange that The Owl was sitting next to him. Somehow, since that long car journey up to Copenhagen, he had never seemed to be more than a few yards away. An ever present shadow. Jens had discovered that The Owl was a strange man. During their conversations he had admitted to killing several people. He had admitted spending most of his life as a criminal until he had gone to work for the arms dealer Leclerc, as a bodyguard. He had no family and, apart from the pistol and the throwing knife he always carried, he was never far away from the small, sophisticated compact disc player and its padded earphones. Jens had been surprised to learn that The Owl's passion in life was classical music and, in particular, the chamber music of Schubert, the operas of Mozart and the symphonies of Beethoven. On that long drive to Copenhagen the earphones had hardly ever left his head.

The serious discussion had taken place over the main course. Creasy had informed the gathering that Grazzini had indeed heard rumours of 'The Blue Ring' and at this moment was trying to find out if those rumours had substance. In future, Grazzini would be known by the code name 'Papa'. Creasy had smiled wryly when he passed on this piece of information and added, 'I suggested it . . . he liked it.'

Bellu informed them that suspicion had fallen on two men: an Italian in Milan called Jean Lucca Donati and a Nubian Egyptian called Anwar Hussein who lived outside Naples. There was a tenuous link between them which he was following up. In the meantime, their names had been passed on to Papa, who was also using his own network to check them out.

Creasy had then gone on to say that it was necessary that their group distance itself from the *carabinieri* forthwith. He had not been apologetic, but had simply said to Colonel Satta, 'It's better that way. You don't want to be implicated or seem to be implicated in what is, after all, an illegal operation on your territory. Similarly, we must be careful not to be associated with the authorities. However, whatever information Massimo can unearth and pass on to us via Guido will be much appreciated.'

Both Satta and Bellu had nodded. The Ghost looked a little disappointed. He was obviously enjoying himself.

Jens had to examine his own position carefully. He was a policeman and he was involved in an illegal situation on foreign soil. He had already taken part in a violent kidnapping, and now was part of a group which was actively planning mayhem and murder. He thought about it for several minutes, and made his decision as the old man served the strong black coffee. He looked across the table at Creasy.

'I need to go back to Denmark.'

Those around the table went silent as Creasy nodded. 'We understand, Jens. Now that the Mafia is involved this is not for you. We appreciate your help very much and wish you well. If at any time we can return it, you know where to find us.' He glanced at Michael. 'Please be sure that Jens has no financial deficit.'

Before Michael could respond, Jens spoke out. 'Hold your horses. I said I *need* to get back to Denmark. It's my daughter's birthday the day after tomorrow. I'll return the day after that.' He glared at Creasy and then at the others around the table. 'No one is throwing me out. I was in this from the start and I'll be here at the end.' He made a gesture. 'OK, maybe I'm not as tough as some of you guys ... or as ruthless ... but maybe I can contribute something which you need.' He pointed at Satta and then at Bellu. 'You've just distanced your-selves from the only detectives here. I understand the reason. But now you understand this ... There will be fighting and there will be pure detective work. I am trained for that. You need a proper operational headquarters which links all of you together; the left hand needs to know what the right hand is doing. There should be proper planning and organisation. It's no good just charging into battle. Michael did that in Marseille and Creasy did it in Milan.' He was addressing the whole table now. 'OK, I know Creasy's a brilliant and experienced leader, and when the actual battle starts he'll need no help from me or anyone else ... But before that some detective work will be necessary ...' He ended defiantly, 'I am a detective ... and I do have a motive ... finding these people is my job.'

Creasy was silent. Both Satta and Bellu slowly nodded their heads. The Owl had a small smile on his face. Satta broke the silence.

'Jens is right. By training and intuition, good detectives have special minds. They see things that other, even more intelligent people, don't see. Occasionally they see the wood not just the trees. You'll be getting information from Massimo and possibly from your new friend Papa. That information has to be correlated and cross-referenced and then passed out in a concise manner. I think Jens is a good detective and will be useful.' That statement, together with the distant chimes of the doorbell, ended the discussion.

Pietro immediately went inside to the *pensione*. The old man poured more coffee. Pietro was back in two minutes. He carried a blue envelope. He handed it to Creasy saying, 'Two men in a black Lancia. They had that look about them. One of them gave me this and said it was for *Uomo*.'

Creasy opened the envelope and took out a single sheet of paper. He read the words, looked up and said, 'It's from Papa.' He glanced back at the paper and read out: ' "The rumours have substance. But there is more to it than just the white slave trade. Much more. It goes as far as the Middle East and North Africa, maybe Tunisia. It will take a few days to get more information. I will be in touch. Papa."'

He folded the paper and tucked it into his pocket, and then looked thoughtfully at the Dane.

'OK then, Jens, go to your daughter's birthday and give her a kiss from all of us. Then return here.' He looked at Michael. 'I want you to go to Brussels and arrange for Corkscrew Two to meet you there. We need to establish our own holes in Milan and Rome and possibly Tunisia. They should be equipped as usual. Like we had them in Syria on the last job.' He looked at Maxie. 'In the meantime, Maxie, you may as well go with him and see your family.' He looked at Miller and Callard. 'Take three or four days off and then liaise with Jens here.' He looked at The Owl. 'Will you go back to Marseille for a few days? Do you have family there?'

The Owl shook his head and glanced at the Dane. 'No, if it's all right with Jens, I'll go to Copenhagen with him. I like that city.'

Jens nodded in agreement.

Creasy beckoned to the waiter and spoke a few words in his ear. The old man nodded and went away. He returned a few minutes later with an equally old woman. She was plump, dressed all in black, her grey hair pulled back into a bun. Creasy rose as she approached and embraced her, then introduced her to the others as Ornella, the cook. With the exception of Guido and Pietro, they all immediately stood up and applauded her. She glowed with pride and bustled away.

'What will you do?' Michael asked Creasy.

Creasy shrugged. 'I'll spend a few days in Gozo.'

FORTY-EIGHT

Jens Jensen and The Owl drove north to Copenhagen in the same BMW.

'It's sort of become a company car,' Creasy had explained that morning. 'Leclerc won't take it back, so it's yours. Papers will be forwarded later on.'

Jens enjoyed driving long distances, listening to pop music on the various FM stations as they passed through Italy without stopping. The Owl sat in the passenger seat with his compact disc player on his lap and the padded earphones over his ears. He was not a large man and had managed to curl up in the comfortable seat. Occasionally he pulled one earphone away from his head to hear what Jens was listening to. He would grunt in derision and push the earphones firmly back into place. Apart from that there was little conversation. Jens was aiming for a small hotel just over the Swiss border. They would spend the night there, have a good dinner and press on to Copenhagen early in the morning. The Owl had insisted that on the way they stop at a Swiss gift shop so that he could buy Lisa a cuckoo clock for her birthday. It was then that Jens realised The Owl was going to become a family friend.

On the same morning Miller and Callard had taken an early hydrofoil to Capri. They planned to stay in a decent hotel and act as a couple of tourists and pick up a couple of girls.

'Just stay out of sight and let me do the work,' Callard had said sternly. 'If they see your ugly face they run a mile.' Miller had smiled complacently. In spite of his features he had never had problems with the opposite sex. The two men were old friends and companions in war, and were looking forward to good food, autumn sun and perhaps a little physical relaxation. On the hydrofoil they briefly discussed the operation and the rest of the team. They decided that it was well-balanced. As mercenaries they had often fought in different countries with the good and the bad. One weak link in a team could be a disaster. They could find no weakness in this team. Maxie, of course, they had known for many years. They had not met Michael before, but they knew he had been trained by Creasy and that in spite of his youth he had already been under fire and come through. They liked The Owl because he had the quiet confidence about him which comes from experience and professionalism. They had noted how he had already attached himself to the Dane. This was not uncommon within their milieu; men under extreme danger and hardship often bond together in couples. The most obvious example that they knew of had been Creasy and Guido, who had been together since their early days in the Foreign Legion and had gone on to fight side by side through the mercenary wars of Africa. It was a pity that Guido had retired. They knew him as the most lethal exponent of a machine-gun in any army in any country. But they understood his promise to his dead wife. Neither of them had ever married, but they shared a very old-fashioned respect for women and wedlock. They liked the Dane too, and had no qualms about him being on the team.

Michael and Maxie flew to Brussels via Rome. At Rome airport Michael phoned Corkscrew Two, and arranged to meet him in Brussels the next evening. On the flight from Rome, Michael explained his personal motivation for smashing 'The Blue Ring'. Maxie had not heard the full story of Michael's early life. He listened in silence and warmed to the young man who was more than slightly emotionally involved with his sister-in-law.

Creasy took the overnight ferry to Malta. He enjoyed travelling by sea, and even though the ferry was not normally comfortable, the captain was known to Guido and a pleasant cabin had been arranged for him on the upper deck. But for most of the night he stood at the stern, watching the foaming wake and wondering what he would find back in Gozo.

He found Juliet. He got to the house on the hill at about noon. She was in the kitchen preparing lunch. He smelled the aroma of rabbit stew cooked in wine and garlic. She kissed him briskly on the cheek and ushered him away to take a shower.

Fifteen minutes later he was sitting by the pool, drinking a cool lager. He had gone into the kitchen to try to help, but she had shooed him out, telling him that Laura had dropped her off early in the morning and she had spent the whole time cooking him lunch and that he was not to interfere. It had only taken him some seconds to realise that the young and shattered child that he had found in that room in Marseille had, within a very short time, rearranged her mental state to fit in with her rearranged life. It was a silent lunch. She served it with aplomb. He recognised the recipe. He had eaten Laura's rabbit stew many times; it was indistinguishable. During the meal she kept glancing at the gift-wrapped package on the table next to his elbow. She also glanced occasionally at the bandage on his hand. Apart from asking about Michael, there were no other questions.

After the rabbit she served thin slices of melon with ice cream, and finally large *espresso* coffees made with the Neapolitan coffee he had brought with him. At last he pushed the package across the table and, like every child, she opened it excitedly. Inside were two brightly coloured silk sarongs.

'I always sleep in them,' he said. 'So does Michael. It's a habit I picked up in the East.'

She fingered the fine silk and smiled at him mischievously. 'I also sleep in them,' she said. 'I found a drawerful in your bedroom.'

He raised an eyebrow. 'So you've been snooping around.'

'Oh yes,' she admitted. 'I've been through everything. I even found your safe and worked out the combination lock.'

He grinned at her and said, 'You're a little liar. Michael showed it to you.'

Abruptly, she pointed to his hand and asked, 'What happened?'

He lifted his hand and looked at it and slowly unwrapped the bandage and pulled away the dressing.

She looked at the stump of the little finger and repeated, 'What happened?'

Very quietly he told her the story, the whole story.

That night he reciprocated. He cooked one of his famous barbecues; portions of steak, chicken, local sausage and Lampuki fish. He also cooked the sauces he had learned in Africa: the hot piri-piri from Mozambique, the thick bean sauce from Rhodesia and the green chilli sauce from the Congo. He was wearing one of his sarongs tied around the waist. She came out wearing one of her new sarongs, tied above her small breasts.

They talked as adults and he explained to her as much as he could about his life. She felt very much an adult. She had many questions and, after a hesitant start, asked them openly and directly. He answered all of them even though some caused him pain. Especially when he talked of his dead wife and child, and of the dead girl called Pinta.

'It that why you brought me here?' she asked. 'Because you wanted to replace Pinta and your daughter?'

He thought about that carefully and then shook his head.

'I brought you here because you had nowhere to go. At least as I saw it. If I had sent you to an institution or even home to your mother it would have been a death sentence.' His voice went quieter and lower and for the first time she had a glimpse of what lay under the armour that surrounded his feelings.

'I cannot tell you how many children I have seen dead or dying. In war it is always the same. It was like that in Africa, in Asia, in Vietnam, Cambodia and Laos and all the rest. You see it now in Somalia, the Sudan, Mozambique, and everywhere there's a bunch of so-called patriots and nationalists, politicians and statesmen convincing themselves they're doing the best thing for their people. The average person sees it now because it comes into their homes through their television screens. But it has always been like that ... children, bombed, shot, napalmed ... and starved.'

It had grown dark. Abruptly he stood up and went to switch on the pool lights. When he returned she could see that his quiet outburst had disturbed him. Nothing showed on his face but she could feel the disturbance in him. She had the intuition to say nothing. They sat for many minutes in silence, looking out over the lights of the villages below. Finally she stood up and cleared the table.

After the journey and the traumas of the day before he was tired. He kissed her on the cheek, promised to take her fishing in the morning, and went to bed.

She sat for another hour by the pool. There was a little wine left in the bottle. She filled her glass and slowly sipped it. She knew that she had seen a glimmer of Creasy's real character. She had wanted to react to it but in her youth did not know how. She tried to remember her dead father. She could see his features and his smile, but most of her feelings had been cauterised by the brutality she had gone through. Her instincts told her that she must reach out to Creasy. She did not know how to. She went to bed.

It was about two in the morning when Creasy heard the soft tap on his bedroom door. He was instantly awake. He heard her voice calling his name, then the door opened. He switched on the bedroom light.

She was wearing the same sarong. He saw the tears on her cheeks and abruptly sat up.

'What is it?'

'I'm sorry … mostly it's all right now. Mostly I can sleep … but sometimes I have bad dreams.'

He patted the bed beside him and she moved forward and sat down. He put an arm around her and pulled her close and with his other hand gently brushed her hair.

'Can I stay with you?' she said. 'Just for a little.'

'Of course.'

He pulled a pillow across and she lay down.

He woke at dawn with the feeling of something warm against his back. She was snuggled up to him, her arms around his big chest. She was asleep. Gently he moved her hands and tucked her up with a couple more pillows. Then he rose to make breakfast.

FORTY-NINE

Fear is always relative. A spider can strike terror into the heart of some people; others make pets of them. Fear can be dulled by ignorance or experience.

Fear is one of mankind's greatest weapons. And none was more aware of this than Paolo Grazzini. He had often felt it himself in his younger days. He knew its effect and had witnessed its effect on others. He sat looking at the elderly man across his desk. He had not expected to see fear in those eyes. Torquinio Trento had been in the *Cosa Nostra* since he was a boy. His father and three uncles had died in prison during the thirties, under Mussolini's merciless crackdown. They had operated in the semi-civilised world of Calabria. At the age of seventeen, Trento had emigrated north to stay with a distant cousin in Naples and had naturally been initiated into the life of his father and forefathers. He had never risen very high. His first *capo* had been wiped out in the inter-gang rivalry that had erupted after the war. He had moved further north to Milan, always managing to escape the internal genocide of the *Cosa Nostra*. He was a survivor, never rising high up the ladder, but always keeping his nose just out of trouble. Life had shown him much and he was generally immune to the shocks of life and death.

For the past few days Grazzini had been talking to many of the old ones of his 'family' and others. He had made it a kind of exercise in public relations; calling them into his office and chatting about their families, if they had one, and their problems, both financial and personal. He had enjoyed the exercise, feeling more like the chairman of a public corporation than a criminal *capo*.

He had seen about fifteen of the old ones so far and, towards the end of each interview, had enquired what they knew of an organisation called 'The Blue Ring'. In each case up to now he had received a blank stare and a shrug of the shoulders. He had begun to doubt the very existence of 'The Blue Ring', until he had dropped the name to Torquinio Trento. The old man's head had jerked up and for an instant Grazzini had seen the fear deep in his eyes.

' "The Blue Ring",' Grazzini repeated.

The old man's eyes had glazed over, then the fear in them reappeared. He glanced nervously to left and right of the opulent office, as if expecting to see some spectre come out of the panelled walls. Grazzini waited patiently. Finally the old one asked in a tremulous voice, 'What do you want of me, *Don* Grazzini? I am an old man who only sits in the sun and waits for death.'

Grazzini smiled at him.

'Torquinio Trento, before you retired you worked for my brother-in-law, God rest his soul, and before that for his father. Were they not good to you?'

Very carefully, Trento nodded.

'Of course. They were my family ... I was their child.'

'You are still their family,' Grazzini said. 'Even though they have passed.'

'What do you want of me?'

'I want what you know of "The Blue Ring".'

Again the old man's eyes darted around the room. He moved uncomfortably on the comfortable chair. Again Grazzini waited patiently, until the old man began to speak in a coarse whisper.

'They are not of us, those people. They have nothing to do with us.'

'I know that. Who are they?'

The old man whispered on as though talking to himself. 'Compared to them we are saints. Even the bad among us are saints. Their evil has no measure. Even to think about them is dangerous.'

Grazzini leaned forward, fascinated and asked, 'Why?'

The old man's head jerked up as though he was coming out of a reverie. His eyes focused on Grazzini and his voice firmed up. '*Don* Grazzini, I urge you not to even ask about such people. Your brother-in-law's father may have died because he once asked.'

Startled, Grazzini said, 'He died of cancer.'

Trento nodded slowly, took a handkerchief from his breast pocket and wiped his forehead and cheeks. He tucked away the handkerchief, looked down at the desk and whispered, 'That is what they say. But I know he had contact with those people. His cancer came suddenly. He was only a young man of forty-three. Within a month of being healthy and strong as an ox he was a dead skeleton.'

'What are you saying?'

The old man shrugged. 'I am saying he had contact with those people.'

Harshly, Grazzini said, 'Are you telling me that they gave him cancer?'

'I am telling you only that they have powers ... powers that they can use as weapons, more than we know how.'

Grazzini remembered he was talking to a man who had grown up in the mountains of southern Calabria and was imbued with its suspicions and superstitions. 'Apart from such powers, what else do they do?'

'They deal in flesh.'

'Flesh?'

The old man nodded. 'It is what I have heard. That is all I have heard.'

Grazzini sensed that he would learn no more from the old man. Courteously, he thanked him and sent him away. For fifteen minutes the *capo* sat silently. Then he phoned his brother-in-law's mother who, if he remembered, would be in her late eighties.

Massimo Bellu looked at his computer screen. For the last hour he had been tracing the lineage of Jean Lucca Donati and he had made an interesting discovery, although he doubted that it could have anything to do with the purpose in hand. But when a brain like Massimo Bellu's started to interface with a complex computer with almost unlimited information access it became something like pure mental excercise. He had discovered that Jean Lucca Donati's father had been a very senior official in the Italian Fascist Party. In fact, he had risen so high as to become a personal aide to Mussolini himself. He had been killed by partisans in the last days of the war. Bellu decided to conduct a similar exercise on the forefathers of Anwar Hussein. And again came up with an interesting fact. The Nubian Egyptian's father had been a senior official in the Cairo court of King Farouk and had been exiled with him and had died in 1952 in the south of France under mysterious circumstances.

Under Satta's orders, Bellu already had a surveillance team on both men. Although the teams were highly experienced, both men had vanished two days before and only resurfaced in their respective offices in Milan and Naples that very morning.

FIFTY

She had a face wrinkled like an old apple and a brain as sharp as a new razorblade.

Grazzini had not seen his late brother-in-law's mother since the funeral. He felt guilty about this, and opened the conversation by apologising for his busy schedule. She gave him a slightly sarcastic look through her thick spectacles, but she had been mollified by the large bouquet of red and white roses which had accompanied his visit. Old ladies, especially Italian old ladies, never lose their vanity.

Grazzini approached the subject carefully. They chatted about the weather and the vascillation of politicians, the rising cost of living and the declining value of morals. Eventually she asked about the purpose of his visit. He sat in a chair too low and soft for comfort, with his knees almost up to his chin. The room was heavily over-furnished in a style much beloved by those who shunned modern values. Dark and heavy furniture with dark and thick curtains, the gloom only relieved by the light from the vast chandelier hanging in the centre of the ceiling.

'*Signora* Conti,' he said formally. 'I have come to ask your advice.'

The bouquet of roses had been arranged by her maid in a large Chinese vase on a table by her side. She leaned towards it, cupped one of the roses in her bony hand and inhaled its aroma.

'You surprise me,' she said, looking first at the rose and then at Grazzini. 'Why would such a great *capo* come to an old lady for advice? I suspect that you come to me for information more than advice.'

Grazzini coughed uncomfortably at hearing this truth, then he plunged on. 'This morning I was talking to one of the old ones.'

'Which one?'

'Torquinio Trento.'

Her eyes studied him through the thick spectacles. She nodded. 'Yes, I remember him ... a nice young man.'

Grazzini smiled.

'Yes indeed. He remembers you well. He asked me to send you his respects.'

'What of Torquinio Trento?'

Grazzini plunged further.

'He seems to think that your husband's death may have been connected with an organisation known as "The Blue Ring".'

She stared at him for a long time and then said, 'My husband died of cancer.'

'I know that, *Signora*. But what makes me curious is why the mention of "The Blue Ring" brought fear into the eyes of the old one.'

Under her crocheted black shawl the old woman's thin shoulders shrugged. 'Torquinio Trento is from Calabria ... the asshole of Calabria.' The obscenity shocked Grazzini. She noted the shock and she smiled. 'Yes, we call them the fearful ones ... but they only fear what they do not understand. They fear the unknown.'

'What is the unknown?'

Her laugh was reedy and without mirth.

'They fear black in the night. They fear mystery which the priests cannot explain. They fear the curse of the evil ... although I never met anyone from southern Calabria who was not evil in himself.'

Grazzini sighed inwardly and tried to bring the conversation back to reality.

'Do you know anything yourself of "The Blue Ring"?'

She tapped sharply on the table beside her and instantly the door opened. Her maid came in, a woman almost as old as herself. She gestured with her hand. The maid crossed the room to an old sideboard and poured two glasses of an amber liquid from an unmarked bottle. She gave one to Grazzini and placed the other beside her mistress. The old lady was beginning to enjoy the visit.

Grazzini sniffed at the glass.

'Very old Cognac,' she said. 'A dying old *capo* left me a dozen cases.' She smiled. 'He did not know that the bullet he was dying from was fired by my husband.'

Grazzini lifted the glass and said, 'I drink to the memory of your husband ... a great man.' He took a sip and savoured the silky taste, then tried to redirect the conversation. 'Do you know anything of "The Blue Ring", *Signora*?'

'Very little,' she answered. 'Rumours first started in the early thirties when the Fascists were coming to power.'

'What rumours, *Signora*?'

'Rumours that there was a connection with the Fascists. It was when Mussolini was trying to crush *Cosa Nostra*. My father was in prison twice ... for nothing, you understand.'

'I have heard about it. What about "The Blue Ring"?'

'My father told me that they supplied drugs and women to the Fascists ... to the top Fascists ... even to Mussolini himself. He liked women, that old goat. You have to understand, *Signor*, that when the Fascists made war on the *Cosa Nostra* they had no one to supply them with drugs and women.'

Grazzini leaned forward. 'How do you know this?'

'My father told me. When he came out of prison the second time he only lived for a few months. He died of poison.'

'Are you sure? I heard he died of a heart attack.'

'He died of poison,' she said firmly. 'He died slowly from poison they gave him in prison ... poison that I am told was supplied by "The Blue Ring".'

Grazzini sat back in his uncomfortable chair, looking at the old woman from between his knees. 'Did your husband know about this?' he asked.

She nodded. 'I made the mistake of telling him. At first he thought it was just a woman's suspicion. But he started to make enquiries about "The Blue Ring".'

A long silence and then Grazzini said, 'And he died of cancer.'

'Yes,' she said. 'Six months later.'

'Do you think they had anything to do with it? The old one does.'

She shrugged again.

'I believe in poison. I know nothing about cancer.'

Grazzini pulled himself more upright. His knees were beginning to ache. He glanced at his watch. 'How would I find out more about this "Blue Ring", if it still exists?'

'You would ask a priest.'

He almost spilled the last of the Cognac from his glass.

'A priest!'

She smiled again; thin and mean.

'Yes, a priest. But a special one. Do you not have good connections with the Vatican? It was always so during the time of my father and my husband and my son.'

Now Grazzini smiled, also without mirth.

'Yes, of course. We maintain very good connections ... especially on the financial side. It is very necessary.'

She nodded in approval.

'Then use those good connections to arrange a talk with a priest who devotes his time to Satanism.'

'What would a priest know about Satanism?'

She laughed.

'Everything. Don't you think that the most important thing in any conflict is to know your enemy?'

FIFTY-ONE

'Will you teach me what you taught Michael?'

Creasy turned to look at her. He had been dreading the question, knowing that it was coming. They were walking along the cliffs of Ta Cenc. It was late morning and a warm breeze was blowing from North Africa. 'It's a different situation,' he said.

'Why?'

'In the first place, you're a girl.'

'And in the second place?'

He sighed. 'Listen, Juliet, I adopted Michael for a purpose. You know all about it.'

'Yes,' she stated. 'I know all about it. And when you adopted him you never thought you would come to love him like a son or that he would love you like a father.'

'That's true,' he admitted. 'But that's the way it worked out.'

They walked on several paces and then her voice hit him between the eyes. 'You adopted me because of the guilt you felt for all those dead and dying children, which you did nothing about.'

He stopped and turned to look at her on the dusty path. His voice was angry. 'I could do nothing about them.'

She had stopped a few paces ahead.

'I know, but that doesn't mean you didn't feel guilty. Creasy, last night you told me always to be honest with you and that you would always be honest to me. You also told me to be the same with Michael. I'm trying to be honest. I woke up this morning knowing I had a father and a brother, but not knowing how to be a daughter or a sister.'

'I don't understand.'

She flung a hand out to embrace the island.

'I have a home ... a beautiful home ... I feel safe. Yes, I am going

202

to go to school on Monday and study hard and learn the language and be obedient. I'll grow up to be a woman you and Michael can be proud of. But I've been thinking all morning ... in a few days you will go away and join Michael and chase those evil men. I know I have to stay here with Laura and Paul. I like them, but it's not easy to stay here while you're away, doing what you are going to do.'

'You're thirteen years old, dammit!'

She smiled, turned and continued walking. He found himself hurrying after her.

'Don't make it harder for us, Juliet,' he said.

'I'm not going to,' she answered. 'I just want you to promise me that when you and Michael get back you will train me, so that in future I'll be able to defend myself.' She stopped again, turned and said very seriously, 'It's important to me, Creasy. I never want to be helpless again.' He had continued walking and she followed, her voice loud. 'Don't you understand? It's important to me!'

He took her hand and they walked on together. He was deep in thought; she had the wisdom to remain silent. Eventually he turned to look down at her.

'Yes, I understand. We will train you to defend yourself. But I'm not going to turn you into some Modesty Blaise.'

'Who's she?'

'A fictional character. Very young and beautiful. She goes around the world with her faithful sidekick, dealing out destruction and justice to all villains.'

'Isn't that what you do?'

He laughed out loud. 'No, I just deal out vengeance. I don't like people hurting me or mine.'

'So why "The Blue Ring"?'

'Because you are one of mine. It has nothing to do with guilt.'

FIFTY-TWO

This time Creasy took precautions. As he came through customs at Rome's Leonardo Da Vinci airport he was wearing a black moustache to match his newly-dyed short black hair. He also wore thick-rimmed spectacles with plain glass. After putting his small bag into an overnight locker he walked through to the taxi rank carrying a black leather briefcase. He was wearing a dark blue suit, a cream shirt and a maroon tie. He looked like any of the many business-men flocking into any large city for an overnight stay. To the taxi driver he gave his destination as Porta Cavalleggeri at The Vatican City.

Rome was not a city he enjoyed, even in early autumn. It always seemed to be too frenetic and its inhabitants unfriendly. The call had come the night before from Guido. Could he meet Papa the next day for lunch at the restaurant L'Eau Vive in Rome? Guido was to call Papa back within an hour. The Rome flight the next morning had been fully booked but Creasy had phoned George Zammit, who had pulled his weight and arranged a seat. He had confirmed this to Guido, who told him that he was to use the name Henry Gould and ask for a Mr Galli.

Creasy had heard of the restaurant L'Eau Vive. It was apparently run by a female religious order and catered mainly to clerics and their friends from the Vatican. He wondered what the likes of Paolo Grazzini was doing there.

During the forty-five minute trip he reviewed the situation. He had spent three good days in Gozo with Juliet and established a rapport with her, which pleased him. It had not taken him long to understand the depth of her intelligence which she used, in part, to get around him. He wondered if she did the same with Michael.

Guido had also told him that Jens had phoned, and that he and

The Owl were leaving Copenhagen the next morning and would be back in Rome within forty-eight hours. Michael had also checked in from Brussels and had started the ball rolling with Corkscrew Two. He and Maxie were waiting for Creasy's call before flying back. I'll bet, Creasy had thought. No doubt Michael wanted to stay close to the charms of Lucette as long as possible. Guido also had the phone number of the hotel in Capri where Frank and Rene were staying. They could be back in Rome within a few hours of his call.

The taxi pulled up outside the Porta Cavalleggeri. Creasy paid the driver with a reasonable tip, waited until he had pulled away out of sight and then strolled to his left. Fifteen minutes later he ducked down a narrow alley and found the small sign of the restaurant. He pushed in through the door and was immediately surprised; it was not how he had imagined. It was rather like a simple café with checked tablecloths. Most of the customers appeared to be low-budget tourists. In one corner was a bust of the Virgin Mary. But the waitresses were different. They were all very tall, wearing long gowns made from what seemed to be batik cloth; they were all beautiful, and they were all black. He looked around for Grazzini but he was nowhere to be seen.

A small middle-aged woman dressed in white approached him. 'I am Sister Maria,' she said. 'Can I help you?'

'I am Henry Gould. Mr Galli is expecting me.'

'Ah, yes. Please follow me.'

He followed her trim figure through the restaurant to the back, where she pulled aside a heavy green curtain. Beyond it was a large mahogany door. She tapped on it, opened it and ushered Creasy through.

This room was very different. It was richly furnished. In the centre was a round table with a white damask tablecloth and napkins, and antique silverwear with a beautiful gold and silver candle stick. Above it was a crystal chandelier which looked priceless. Three high-backed chairs were arranged around the table. In one of them sat Paolo Grazzini. In the other sat a priest in his early thirties. He wore thick spectacles, and he studied Creasy with an air of deep concentration, as though he were looking at a rare painting which had just been rediscovered. The door closed behind Creasy as both men stood up. Grazzini made the introductions.

'Henry Gould ... Father De Sanctis.'

They all sat down. Creasy placed his briefcase on the thick carpet beside him, at the same time pressing a small button on the handle.

The tape recorder inside would keep a complete record of the conversation.

Grazzini gestured at a small side-table which held several covered dishes. 'I ordered a simple buffet, so we could talk undisturbed.'

Next to the dishes were several decanters, glasses and a bottle of red wine. Grazzini stood up and moved to the table, asking 'What would you like for an aperitif? I recommend the Scotch – it's forty-year-old Macallan.'

Both the priest and Creasy nodded in agreement. Grazzini poured the drinks, brought them over and sat down.

'Perhaps you had better explain,' Creasy said.

Grazzini was looking pleased with himself. He gestured towards the priest. 'I told Father De Sanctis of our little problem concerning "The Blue Ring".' He smiled slightly at the hard look he received from Creasy. 'I will give you the background to Father De Sanctis. As you may know, the Vatican maintains a formidable intelligence unit ... some say it's the envy of the CIA or Mossad.'

The priest shrugged.

Grazzini went on. 'Of course, since the end of the Cold War and the religious liberation behind the old Iron Curtain it is no longer such an essential unit of the Vatican. However, within that unit there is a special department which concentrates on Satanism and black magic.'

Creasy saw the almost imperceptible nod which Grazzini sent him across the table. He went along accordingly. 'That's very interesting. I know that Satanism in various forms still exists in isolated cases, but I hardly think that the Vatican needs to be so concerned.'

For the first time the priest smiled. It changed his face. The severity dropped away and he looked almost boyish.

'You will be surprised, Mr Gould. Certainly my department is much smaller than it used to be in the Middle Ages and even up until the last century, but we still have to be very active, not only in South America, the Caribbean and Africa, but also here in very civilised Europe.' He gestured at the buffet table. 'Shall we eat while I explain?'

FIFTY-THREE

'I still find it hard to believe,' Creasy said, 'that Grazzini could simply summon up a Vatican specialist, just like that.'

Guido's laugh was ironic. 'You should know better. The links between the Mafia and the Vatican go back a very long way. Especially on the financial side. It wasn't so many years ago that the Vatican bank laundered hundreds of millions of dollars-worth of Mafia drug money.'

'I know that,' Creasy answered, 'but since then I thought they'd distanced themselves.'

Guido shook his head.

'They have not and they will not. Power always seeks out power.'

It was eleven o'clock at night. Creasy had caught a late afternoon flight from Rome. They were sitting on the terrace and had just finished a light meal. The other regular diners had all departed.

'That priest, De Sanctis. He's a Jesuit,' Creasy said.

Guido smiled again and nodded.

'The clever ones always are.'

'And he was young ... no more than thirty-five. Young to know so much.'

'Tell me,' Guido said with barely-concealed curiosity. 'What does he know?'

Silently Creasy collected his thoughts and then smiled at the recollection. 'Before he told me anything he asked to see the contents of my briefcase. It was embarrassing. I had a tape recorder in it. Nothing else, just the bloody tape recorder.'

Guido grinned.

'What happened?'

Creasy shook his head at the memory.

'First he admired it. Naturally it was state of the art, only about three inches by two, but it can pick up a conversation from twenty metres away. Then the damned priest gave me a long story about how short of funds his unit was, and how useful such a device would be for him in his work ... Naturally, I donated the bloody thing.'

Smiling, Guido said, 'Never underestimate the church.'

'Never again!' Creasy answered with feeling.

He went on to relate what he had learned from the priest. At first, he had to listen to a long lecture about Satanism and its antecedents. These of course went back beyond Christianity and flourished in tribal communities all over the world. The priest had explained some of the psychology behind it and its uses. At this point he explained that, apart from his other qualifications, Father De Sanctis had a master's degree in psychology. Creasy had also had to listen to several theories relating to the mixture of good and evil which existed amongst all mankind, and the constant on-going battle between them. At this stage the priest had given a dissertation about exorcism and how the church still had specialist exorcists who were kept busy. He himself had spent three years doing that work. It was only over coffee and Cognac that the priest had talked about Satanism and black magic in the modern age. At Creasy's suggestion he had confined himself to Europe and its links with peripheral regions. There were several sects stretching from Scandinavia to the Mediterranean; some were linked, others operated independently. They had their roots in medieval times and still used some of the same rites and rituals. Apologetically, De Sanctis had explained that some of these sects were led by renegade priests and other clerics, some of whom covered themselves by also practising the true faith. He described a typical black mass with the attendant feasting, blasphemous prayers, animal sacrifices, the drinking of obnoxious substances, initiations of new members and finally sexual orgies of unbelievable perversions. Animals always played a major part, sometimes in the form of head-dresses worn by participants and sometimes as objects of worship. Very often these sects took their names from a species of animal. The priests and high priests or priestesses held enormous psychological power over the sect's members, who only progressed up the hierarchy with their blessings. Often money was involved, because many such members came from wealthy backgrounds. More importantly, in order to improve himself within the sect, a member had to commit ever more bestial and obscene acts until his very soul was lost forever.

At this point Guido had crossed himself and muttered. 'I have heard of such things. But how does it involve "The Blue Ring"?'

'In a very simple but obvious way,' Creasy said.

The priest had explained how certain ruthless and charismatic individuals, very often charismatic priests who had broken away from their true calling, entered and manipulated some sects or even created them for their own egos or simply for material ends. The priest had pointed out the similarities between other modern cults, particularly in the west coast of the USA. Cults with charismatic, even hypnotic leaders, which pretended a spurious religion, for instance the Moonies, Scientology and a variety of eastern gurus. With a wan smile, the priest had said, 'There really is no limit to human gullibility.'

'He knows about "The Blue Ring",' Creasy stated. 'Perhaps he did not tell me all he knows. It has been in existence for about eighty years. It has or had connections with a bastard offshoot of Coptic Christianity and has particular roots in Egypt.'

The priest had stated that, as far as their records showed, 'The Blue Ring' had also had early connections with a French group called 'The Daughters of the Goat'. The French authorities had supposedly smashed that ring in 1934, but there had been no arrests because its members included high-ranking establishment figures. Both religious and political coercion had been involved. In Italy 'The Blue Ring' had enjoyed protection in the nineteen-thirties from certain Fascist luminaries.

The Vatican intelligence unit had thought that 'The Blue Ring' had died out during the war. But rumours had surfaced in the late fifties that it was still in existence, although in a different form. Rumours pointing to the suspicion that it engaged in extortion, blackmail and an extreme form of forced prostitution. These rumours were given substance during the investigation of the so-called Masonic Lodge P2. Several oblique references were made to it in seized papers and during interrogation of some of their members. By now Guido was totally fascinated.

'In that case,' he asked, 'why did the Italian authorities do nothing about it?'

Creasy smiled grimly.

'That's exactly what I'm going to ask our friend Satta.'

FIFTY-FOUR

Creasy did not have to ask the question. A phone call came from Satta at dawn. He was flying down to Naples on the eight a.m. plane and it was important that Creasy meet him at the airport.

They had *cappuccini* and brioches in the coffee shop. There was latent anger in the Colonel's eyes.

'I'm thinking of taking early retirement,' he said bitterly.

'What happened?'

Satta looked around the almost deserted room, leant forward and said, 'Just before I left for home yesterday I was called into the office of a very senior general of the *carabinieri*. He should have been put out to grass years ago, but the man has strong political connections right across the party spectrum. He wanted to know why my assistant, Bellu, had put a twenty-four hour watch on two men, namely Jean Lucca Donati and Anwar Hussein. It was a surprise, because I did not anticipate that anyone higher up would know about it. But that's the *carabinieri* for you!'

'So what was your reaction?'

The Italian spread his hands eloquently.

'First I controlled my anger. Then I told the old fart that I was following up a lead involving political corruption. He questioned me about it but obviously I could give him no answers. He became angry and gave me two orders: first, I was to withdraw all surveillance from those two individuals; second, I was to give him a written report on why I had instigated the investigation.'

'Can you do the second?' Creasy asked.

Satta smiled grimly.

'Oh, yes. It will be a very short report and will simply mention a suspicion about a couple of the good General's friends. But I've had to call off the surveillance because we have to use a special department for that, and now the General will be monitoring it.'

Creasy took a sip of his coffee. He said, 'I think I know why your General acted that way.' He recounted his lunch at L'Eau Vive with Grazzini and the priest.

As he listened, Satta's face was sombre. Very quietly he said, 'My friend, you're up against something deeper than you or I had realised. I have to tell you that last night Paolo Grazzini was shot to death leaving a Rome restaurant. Two bullets in the heart from a parked car.'

'A gang war?' Creasy asked.

Satta shook his head.

'I think not. There is no reason for it within the organisation. But Grazzini was not the only *mafioso* to die yesterday. There was another. He was retired, but he used to work for Grazzini's clan. His name was Torquinio Trento.' The Italian's voice went even quieter. 'He was fished out of the river Tiber. He had been tortured ... an inverted cross had been carved into his forehead by a sharp knife. His genitals were missing.'

FIFTY-FIVE

'It's a different ballgame,' Creasy stated. 'They're not just a bunch of evil bastards who trade in women – these people go to the very bottom. Not only can they stop a high-level *carabinieri* enquiry, it also seems they can take out a top Mafia *capo* on his own territory.'

The whole team was assembled around the same oval table on the terrace of the Pensione Splendide. For twenty minutes Creasy had briefed them on what had happened in the past few days while they had been taking a break. He now felt it necessary to open the door for anyone who, in the light of these new circumstances, wished to gracefully retire.

He started with Guido, reminding him of his promise given to his dead wife never to kill again. He strongly suggested that in future the team's base should be elsewhere. Guido smiled and shook his head.

'I never promised Julia not to defend myself or my friends. She would not have wanted that. At the moment I only have four guests in the *pensione*: an old German couple who are leaving in the morning and two British backpackers who are not sure when they are leaving. I'll find them alternative accommodation tomorrow. This will be your base.'

Creasy glanced at Pietro, who immediately realised the implication behind the look. Angrily he said, 'I made no promise to anybody. I guard the base with Guido.'

Next, Creasy turned to the Dane. He said, 'Jens, this whole thing has gone over the top. It is not just dangerous, it's like walking on very thin ice with hot boots. I'm assuming that "The Blue Ring" think they have cut off all sources of enquiry. I'm assuming that they don't know about us. I could be wrong.'

'I think you're right,' Jens answered. 'Unless Grazzini told either the old man Trento about you, or if he told the priest ... It seems unlikely.'

'But it's still extra dangerous,' Creasy insisted. 'You have to think of your wife and child and the fact that you're a policeman, not a "soldier".'

The Dane inclined his head in understanding and then stated, 'That last night in Copenhagen I talked to Birgitte. I deliberately exaggerated the danger. She urged me to go on. She understands how important it is to me. As for being a policeman ... well ... having lost Satta and Bellu, I'm the only policeman you've got left.' He smiled. 'I stay.'

Creasy looked at The Owl, who said in a tone to preclude argument, 'I also stay.' Before Creasy could say anything to the others he got his answer. Maxie glanced at Miller and Callard and received their slight nods. He said to Creasy, 'Stop wasting your breath. Let's look to the future.'

Michael spoke for the first time. 'We have our targets: Donati and Hussein. We need to have a little talk with one or the other ... or both.'

Creasy said, 'There is something else ... Before Satta had to pull off the surveillance, they followed Hussein to the airport here. He flew to Rome and got a connecting flight to Tunis. That was two days ago.' He looked at the Dane and said with a smile, 'OK, Mister Detective. Why don't you sum it up for us?'

The Dane smiled back reached behind him for his briefcase and took out a lined, yellow legal pad and a gold Parker pen. He placed the pad carefully in front of him, uncapped the pen and said with a smile, 'A gift from the grateful parents of a girl I once found and returned ... Don't think I can afford such things on my salary.' He smiled again. 'There will be enough eyebrows raised in Copenhagen when certain people see me driving around in a BMW.'

He looked down at the pad. 'Let's start from the beginning.' He glanced at the young man beside him. 'Michael first heard about "The Blue Ring" from his dying mother. He contacted Blondie who put him on to me. He more or less hired me to go with him to Marseille where we screwed up and got caught by what now appears to be an arm's-length supplier to one sector of "The Blue Ring". Creasy pulled us out of it and, by so doing, gained a daughter. He put together this team and in due course got caught himself and lost a finger.' He glanced at Creasy's right hand. 'It seems that the loss may have been worthwhile. It gave us an insight into what we are facing. Let us immediately discount or at least put into perspective the Satanism aspect of the whole affair. Of course it exists ... I know of examples in Scandinavia. But what we learned from the priest De Sanctis indicates that the hierarchy of "The Blue Ring" use it for their own purposes rather than out of belief. It is a clever but not uncommon phenomenon. They built their powerbase during the Fascist era. They were not alone in this: Hitler and his henchmen used a similar tactic in creating myths about the SS and binding them with mystical oaths and the rest of the paraphernalia.' He wrote a word on the yellow pad. Michael leaned across slightly and read it: 'Paraphernalia'. Michael chuckled. The Dane gave him a narrow look and continued.

'We can assume that there are two profit centres for "The Blue Ring". One is the white slave trade, and the other is coercion and blackmail by enticing wealthy individuals into their cult.' He wrote another word on his pad: 'Motivation'. He looked around the table and said, 'Their motivation is money and power. They go hand in hand, but with such people power is usually more important ... In my opinion our strategy should be in some way aimed at both the power and the money.'

'How?' Michael asked.

Jens shrugged and said, 'I'm a detective more than a strategist.' He gestured at Creasy. 'I leave that to the expert.'

Creasy's eyes were narrowed in thought. He looked up at the Dane and then at the rest of them. He said, 'We have to assume that they do not know who we are. They may suspect that somebody's coming at them, but I think after all these years of virtual immunity they will be arrogant in their powers. We have to attack them from behind.'

'How?' Guido asked.

Creasy smiled.

'We have to infiltrate "The Blue Ring". Someone has to study Satanism in all its aspects and then ... join them.'

There was a pregnant silence around the table.

Miller broke it by asking, 'Who the hell is going to infiltrate that bag of snakes?'

Creasy was looking at his son.

FIFTY-SIX

For Michael it was a totally different world.

Satta took him first to his tailor. An elderly, elegant man who surveyed Michael with an air of slight distaste. He circled him twice, examining him from head to toe. Then he spoke rapidly in Italian to Satta, who smiled and said, 'Signor Casseli tells me that he has handled worse cases. You will need at least six suits, a dozen shirts, two dozen silk ties, ten pairs of shoes and, of course, elegant underwear for any eventuality!'

Michael smiled as Signor Casseli took his measurements. He had arrived in Rome the night before, and been met at the airport by Colonel Satta, who had explained the situation on the way to his apartment.

He only had two weeks in which to be introduced to that level of Roman society in which he might find the kind of people who would be associated with 'The Blue Ring'; those people would be on the fringe of Roman society. Michael's cover was that he was the illegitimate son of a fabulously wealthy Arab potentate, and could not be part of the normal family circle. He had been sent to a top school in England and was now spending six months in Italy to improve his cultural and social background before going on to Harvard University.

This cover had been arranged on the telephone between Creasy and Satta. Afterwards, Creasy had phoned Senator Jim Grainger in Denver to arrange the necessary details to protect the cover. Grainger had chuckled at the request and told Creasy to have no fears. If anyone checked Michael's background they would discover that the name of Adnan bin Assad was indeed enrolled to start the spring semester, studying political science at Harvard University. From his own funds Jim Grainger would deposit ten million US dollars in an account for Adnan bin Assad with the Banco di Roma. The money would be transferred from a bank in the United Emirates. The manager of that bank would call the manager of the Banco di Roma and impress upon him the importance of Adnan bin Assad, and indicate that further funds would always be available for the young man.

'It's a fortune,' Michael had muttered when Satta told him the amount.

The Colonel had smiled and said, 'Not in this day and age, but impressive enough to attract the sharks. Rome is like a small village when it comes to financial matters. As you move into social circles it will quickly become known that you are an heir to a vast fortune. I will rent you a Ferrari and install you in a luxury apartment close to the Spanish Steps, complete with a cook and a butler.' Satta had smiled. 'The butler will be well-known to you.'

'I don't know any butlers,' Michael had remarked.

'You do now ... It's Rene Callard.'

'Rene?'

Satta grinned. 'Yes. It works very well, and is not unusual here in Rome. Rene will be more than just a butler ... a sort of general factotum ... butler, chauffeur and bodyguard.'

'Bodyguard?'

'Yes,' Satta replied emphatically. 'As I said, it's quite normal here in Rome with its history of kidnappings. An extremely wealthy young man studying here would be provided with such a man. He might have the title of butler or driver, but in reality his main job is bodyguard. Rene fits the picture perfectly. First of all, he is a genuine bodyguard, who happens to be registered with an agency in Italy which supplies such people. He is a linguist with very passable Italian. He is elegant, yet discreet and, because of his background, knows how to move in social circles, mix cocktails, serve canapés and be trusted not to pinch a hostess's bottom.' The Colonel had sighed. 'I could use such a man myself ... However, there is another very important factor: because Rene is registered in Italy with an agency, he is also registered with the police. Therefore he can be licensed to carry a gun.'

'That could be useful,' Michael had said thoughtfully.

'Definitely,' Satta had agreed. 'Now, listen carefully. You will be invited to a party and that will lead to invitations to other parties. You will meet beautiful women and invite them for dinner at the best restaurants. You will buy them expensive presents. You will indicate that you are interested in investing some of your vast wealth in the entertainments business, particularly films.' He had glanced at Michael and smiled. 'You will have to obviously be susceptible to feminine charms . . . which of course you are. Enjoy yourself, Michael, but never drop your guard. Always remember that you speak English with an English accent because you were schooled there. Your Arabic carries a slight Lebanese accent because your tutor in early life was from there. You must appear to drink to excess but, of course, not do so. Some of the people you meet will try to borrow money from you. Lend it to them in moderate amounts. Never ask them for an IOU. The word will quickly get around that you are a chicken ready to be plucked.'

Michael had smiled at the thought and wondered about the women he would meet.

FIFTY-SEVEN

At first the interview was tense. Anwar Hussein had arrived in Tunis during the early afternoon. He took a taxi to the Hilton Hotel and had several short business meetings. At seven in the evening he was picked up by a black Mercedes and driven ten miles to a secluded villa.

He had been kept waiting half an hour which was not a good sign. Finally, he had been ushered into the presence of the supreme puppeteer and high priest of 'The Blue Ring'.

At first glance, Gamel Houdris looked precisely like a successful and fastidious businessman. He was seated behind a wide mahogany desk inlaid with intricate patterns of ebony and mother of pearl. He was bone-thin and his dark suit hung from him as though he was a wire coathanger. Black eyes were sunk into deep hollows above prominent cheekbones. His skin was smooth and sallow and his thin hair jet-black.

He did not rise when Hussein entered the room, nor even look up. He simply waved a hand at a chair in front of the desk and carried on reading from the slim file in front of him. Hussein sat down and waited. His face was the colour of the ebony on the desk but it was sheened with a slight sweat.

At last, Gamel Houdris took a gold Cross pen from his inside jacket pocket, made several notes on the report and then looked up and studied his visitor.

'I don't like it,' he said. His voice was thin and high-pitched, and carried the menace of a high velocity bullet. 'It has been so many years since anyone enquired about our activities and suddenly from two different directions, within a space of days, we hear talk out of the Mafia and of enquiries emanating from the *carabinieri*.'

'It may just have been coincidence,' Hussein said. 'The old man Trento knew nothing. He died under torture without saying a word, but we know he went to see the *capo* Grazzini two days earlier. He would not disclose the conversation. As a precaution we eliminated Grazzini, to make it look like a gang killing. If he was interested in us then that interest died with him ... And he was the senior *capo* in central and north Italy.'

'That was your first mistake,' Houdris said flatly. 'You should have kidnapped Grazzini and made him talk.'

Hussein shrugged nervously.

'We considered it. But kidnapping a *capo* of such seniority is not easy. We concluded that to kill him was sufficient.'

Houdris leaned forward.

'On such a matter I should have been informed.'

'Of course,' Hussein agreed, 'and as you know we tried; but you had gone incognito for forty-eight hours. We felt we had to make a decision quickly.'

For the first time Houdris' voice softened slightly.

'In fact, I was in Albania,' he said. 'I was conducting a mass, the first for "The Blue Ring" in that country ... but not the last.' He smiled slightly at the memory and said, 'Great poverty and a sudden loss of total power is a potent mixture.'

Hussein ventured a question. 'May I ask how the orphanage is coming on?'

Houdris waved a hand and said airily, 'Rapidly. But we must move with caution. The staff are above suspicion but the paperwork must be clear as well.' He smiled. 'The first inmates will start arriving within a few days. I estimate there will eventually be between forty and fifty, with a turnover of up to twenty a month. We can start milking that at the rate of two a month very shortly ... But let us come back to the matter in hand. We need to find out who is behind the enquiries emanating from the *carabinieri*.' He tapped his pen against the file. 'The active officer was a Major Massimo Bellu. His superior was a Colonel Mario Satta.'

Hussein nodded.

'That's as high as it goes, according to our informant, who you know is very senior indeed ... so senior that he was able to cut off the enquiries immediately.'

'That's not the point,' Houdris said sharply. 'I doubt that this Colonel Satta was acting on his own. Maybe he was being used by Italian intelligence.'

Hussein shook his head. 'I doubt it, Gamel. We also have our sources in that direction.'

Houdris said, 'You are probably right, but who can be sure within such a corrupt organisation as Italian intelligence? It may have been from someone outside. We must find out who.' He thought for almost a minute, studied the file again and then asked, 'Do you think the death of this man, Boutin, in Marseille had anything to do with it?'

Again Hussein shook his head.

'Very doubtful. Donati had a solid cut-out. Donati is very experienced.'

Thoughtfully, Houdris said, 'It was a pity. That girl was perfect for our purposes ... completely untraceable. Do we have any idea what happened to her?'

'We do not,' Hussein said sorrowfully. 'She simply vanished.'

Houdris leant forward and pressed a button on his desk. Immediately, a door opened and a white-robed servant appeared, carrying a copper tray. He served them coffee and sweetmeats. They did not stop talking in his presence; simply because he was deaf and dumb, as were all the servants in the villa. When Houdris summoned them he pressed a button which illuminated a different coloured light, depending on the servant required.

'We need a replacement quickly,' Hussein remarked. 'Our initiate is ready, and we cannot delay too long. At the moment he is fervent, but that diminishes with time.'

Houdris nodded in agreement.

'It must be within three weeks. I will try to get one from the orphanage. But she must be young and beautiful, and I have not yet seen any of the first intake ... If that fails we have to risk kidnapping one from the streets of Naples or further south ... That would mean dyeing her hair blonde.' His eyes narrowed in pleasure at the thought. He looked at the huge ebony man in front of him and murmured, 'But a fair skin and real blonde hair is always the best.' He took a sip of coffee and changed the subject. 'The first priority is to find out who instigated these enquiries. I doubt if it was simply a result of Colonel Mario Satta's personal curiosity. Perhaps we should find a way to have a little talk with the Colonel or, easier still, his assistant Major Bellu?'

FIFTY-EIGHT

They were both young with elegant dresses and beautiful faces, but a close look into their eyes showed the same depth of experience, ambition and calculation. One of them was blonde and blue-eyed, the other was a brunette with green eyes. Apart from their colouring, their faces and bodies were more or less interchangeable. They watched Michael from across the wide room in the manner of carnivores inspecting their dinner.

'Sensational!' the blonde murmured.

'Near perfect,' the brunette agreed. 'And he's the real thing, not like the hangers-on that sneak their way into these parties. The watch is genuine Patek Philippe, the opal ring's genuine too, and the suit is definitely from Casseli. You're looking at a minimum of a hundred thousand dollars on the hoof.' Although speaking Italian, such women always related wealth to dollars.

An elderly man who had been eavesdropping on their conversation moved up behind them with a smile. He was dressed in a new silk dinner jacket but his ravaged face would never match its elegance, even with the help of a dozen plastic surgeons. His thin mouth curled into a smile as he said, 'That's quite a catch, *signorine*. Giorgio tells me that he opened an account two days ago with the Banco di Roma. His initial deposit was ten million dollars.'

They turned to face him, their eyes suddenly hungry.

'He's a friend of Giorgio's?' the blonde asked.

The old man shook his head. 'No, just a recent acquaintance.'

'Then how does he know?'

The old man smiled again; he was enjoying himself. 'In this town Giorgio knows everything.'

'What else does he know?' the brunette asked.

The old man's information came out like a well-rehearsed litany.

'His name is Adnan bin Assad. He is twenty-two years old, reputedly the illegitimate son of a very wealthy Arab. Apparently, his mother was from England, which is where he was educated. He is spending six months in Rome on cultural matters and to improve his Italian and perhaps make some investments. He has rented a luxury apartment near the Spanish Steps, complete with butler and cook ... He drives a Ferrari Dino.'

Silently the two young women turned and gazed across the room. Michael was in earnest conversation with an elderly woman dripping in diamonds. She was a well-known Roman hostess who liked to sprinkle her parties of elderly roués with beautiful young people. It had been very easy for Satta to arrange an invitation through one of his mother's legendary connections. It had also been very simple to plant the details and authenticity of Michael's new persona. He had chosen the party well. Of some fifty guests, there was a smattering of film and television personalities, other media people, fringe aristocrats, a dress designer, a slightly suspect banker and several of the young and beautiful people.

Their hostess was slowly moving Michael around the room, making introductions and stroking his elbow as she did so. The two young women waited impatiently. They watched as he chatted to an up and coming television executive and a jaded actor; both the producer and the actor gave him their cards.

The two young women held their breath as the hostess moved him on to meet an actress whom they knew to be of at least forty-five hard years, even though with the help of imaginative surgery, superb make-up and a red pouting mouth she looked no more than thirty-five.

'Don't worry,' the old man whispered from behind them. 'The rumour is that he likes younger flesh.'

Michael left just after midnight, with the blonde and with the brunette.

FIFTY-NINE

While Michael slid into Roman society, Creasy made his dispositions. Jens and The Owl were to man the headquarters at the Pensione Splendide. Maxie MacDonald and Frank Miller went to Milan to keep a watch on Jean Lucca Donati; Creasy would do the same in Naples on Anwar Hussein.

Jens had set up a small office in a room of the *pensione*, complete with fax and telex machines and his sophisticated lap-top Compaq computer. Creasy had been impressed with his organisation and thoroughness. Within forty-eight hours Jens had gathered every scrap of information that had come from all their sources. Creasy watched the small screen of the Compaq as the Dane collated everything they knew.

Creasy phoned Gozo regularly and learned that Juliet had settled well into her school. Laura had been amazed by the speed with which the child was learning Maltese. The nuns at the school had pronounced her intelligent and wise beyond her years. However, Laura cautioned that Juliet had become often silent and preoccupied, and frequently asked about Creasy and Michael. Creasy understood that the girl was becoming frustrated, missing the two men who had become such a part of her life, both of whom she knew were in extreme danger, and because she could do nothing to help. He thought of phoning her every day but then changed his mind. If circumstances meant that he could not make contact she would worry. Instead he would write to her frequently, and urge Michael to do the same, even if only a few lines. A brief letter could be more satisfying than a long phone call.

He sat looking at the phone. He could almost see her face and he realised how much he missed her.

SIXTY

The nun watched the car wind up the dusty road. She stood in front of the long, low building which, until three months ago, had been a derelict storage depot for an agricultural commune.

Sister Assunta was on assignment from the Augustine order in Malta. The order had a long history of missionary and teaching work and, in truth, Sister Assunta had become slightly bored at the home convent. She had done five years' missionary work in Kenya which she had found both fascinating and fulfilling. But she had been back in Malta for the past three years, and although it had been good to be home, she had felt restless in recent months. When the Mother Superior had summoned her two months ago and given her this duty she had felt no apprehension, even though Albania was in turmoil and the assignment could be dangerous.

At first it had been dangerous but also exhilarating. During the early weeks she had often heard gunfire from the direction of Tiranë, twenty miles to the south. Several times armed groups, some in uniform and some in ragged clothing, had passed by the would-be orphanage. But they had not bothered the nuns, simply begged for food and then passed on. Now it was quiet and Sister Assunta was able to enjoy the peace and the view of the surrounding wooded countryside. Such a green contrast from the stark brown, limestone bareness of her native country.

There were five nuns in all to run the orphanage. She was the only Maltese and the Superior. The others consisted of a robust Irish lady of indeterminate age and three young Italian nuns. This was no problem for Sister Assunta, because she spoke both English and Italian fluently.

The orphanage had been set up through the help of several charities, the main one being a private international organisation based in

Rome. In Malta her Mother Superior had told her that, strangely enough, it was funded by several wealthy individuals who preferred, in the main, to remain anonymous. However, she knew that the approaching car contained one of the major benefactors, who was coming to inspect progress. Sister Assunta and her staff had managed in a very short time to get the basic facilities of the orphanage organised and had already received the first intake of girls, whose ages ranged from four to thirteen. Within the context of her instructions all those girls had come as orphans, not from broken families or as stray children. All of her girls had been given up at birth, or found abandoned.

The car pulled up in front of her. The driver was an Albanian whom she knew. Sitting in the back seat was a man. His face was dark and thin. For a second something flashed through her mind. She had a sense of *déjà vu*, as though she had seen that face many years before. She shook the thought from her head. The man emerged. She looked him up and down, full of a curiosity which was fuelled by the fact that he had an Arab name. He was dressed in a dark finely-cut suit. An extremely thin man with a dark sunken face and a sharply beaked nose. She wondered why an Arab would be financing a Catholic charity.

Being of a curious and direct nature, Sister Assunta asked that question during lunch, after they had inspected the internal construction work. During the tour she had been impressed by his interest and insight. The orphanage would be employing six lay Albanian women to work under her direction. His first question had been whether she herself could speak the language. She had explained that she already had a working knowledge, thanks to a crash course, and that within a few weeks she would be proficient. He had then asked whether she and the other nuns had comfortable quarters for themselves. She had smiled and said, 'Enough for our needs.' He had smiled back and told her how he respected the dedication of herself and her fellow nuns.

So came her first question when they sat down to a simple lunch. The question was prompted very much by his obvious kindness and interest in the children. Among them had been a young twelve-year-old girl, the only child of parents who had both been machine-gunned during the first night of the uprising. Her name was Katrin and she had blonde hair, a pale face and the eyes of an angel.

He had held that face in his hands, kissed her gently on the cheek, turned to Sister Assunta and said in a low voice, 'We must find this child a home where the flower of her character will blossom in a way to fill both our hearts.'

So she had asked, 'You are not of the faith?'

He shook his head. 'I am not of your faith, Sister.'

'Islam?' he asked.

Again he shook his head and his mouth formed its thin smile.

'I have my own faith. It has no direct bearing on any established religion.'

They were sitting at a round table in the newly constructed dining room; the other four sisters had joined them. The lay workers ate at a separate table. All the nuns listened intently as he went on, 'Of course I believe in a supreme being. Any man who does not is a fool. I cannot define my supreme being in any usual way. I have searched through all major religions and many minor ones and while I agree with some aspects of all of them, I cannot accept the whole.'

The first course had been a *minestrone*. Abruptly Sister Assunta put down her spoon and asked, 'You are a Mason?'

He laughed and shook his head.

'Please be reassured, Sister. I am no such thing ... far from it.'

Sister Simona asked, 'If you are not of our faith, why do you support the work of our order here?'

He turned to the Italian nun and explained. 'My organisation supports much good work. Over the years we have discovered that such work must be carried out in the field by people who have a vocation. It is not necessary to be religious to have such a vocation.' He smiled and gestured at them all. 'But we have discovered that it is easier to find such people within the religious orders. Of course we also support the Arabic Red Crescent and several interdenominational charities. We asked the Augustine order to help on this project because of the proximity of its Maltese branch to Albania, and because over the past months they have gained experience in this ravaged country.'

Sister Assunta asked another question. 'The parameters for this orphanage were very clear. It was only to be for girls between the ages of four and fourteen. Why was that?'

He shrugged disarmingly.

'Naturally, we are very careful as to where we place our limited funds. In giving to charity it is essential that every cent counts. Our research showed that here in Albania charities had already moved quickly to alleviate the suffering of the very very young. On the other hand, my own thinking is that any girl over the age of fourteen is already an adult and is better able to fend for herself. Hence our parameters.'

Sister Assunta was about to ask another question when he interrupted with one of his own.

'Now that you have the first intake, are you ready for a full house within the next two weeks?'

She nodded firmly.

'Yes. We are just waiting for delivery of more beds, linen and basic medical supplies. They have been promised for Friday.'

He nodded in satisfaction.

'Good. As you know, we will try to settle most of our orphans with Italian families. Italy is close and the logistics are simple. You also know that we have set up an office in Bari to handle the adoptions. That office is already in place and you'll be receiving a visit from its director within a few days. Our policy and philosophy is based on much international research. We do not believe that children should remain for too long in an orphanage, because very quickly it becomes a permanent home and therefore the wrench of adoption is all the greater. Consequently, we would like to view this orphanage as more of a transit home; and our office in Bari is planning accordingly. Hopefully our first adoptions can take place within the next one or two weeks.' He turned again to Sister Assunta and said sternly, 'And so, Sister, it is important that neither you nor your fellow sisters nor the lay workers become emotionally attached to these girls ... I know it is difficult not to become surrogate mothers, especially as many of them will have suffered both mentally and physically. However, with your experience I'm sure you agree with me.'

Sister Assunta nodded.

'Yes, of course, difficult ... but I agree with you. It can be painful to us ... But the faster good homes can be found for these girls the better. It also means that we can help so many more. And there are so many out there who need help.'

'Yes,' he murmured quietly. 'So many.'

Sister Assunta felt comfortable with the knowledge that the benefactor of her orphanage was both intelligent and perceptive. But she could not shake the thought from her mind that somewhere and at some time, she had seen his face before.

SIXTY-ONE

Michael kept the scream under his breath. He reached out and grabbed her hand. She hissed at him and the fingernails of her other hand slashed down his back. He groped behind him and caught her wrist, pulled both her arms up above her head, pressing them hard against the pillow. She writhed under him, slamming her pelvis into his. She opened her eyes and he could see her orgasm in them, the pupils dilating. Her white teeth were clenched behind red lips. One wet wrist slipped from his grasp and again she raked his back. This time he grunted in pain, and slapped her hard across the face. She grinned up at him, and he felt himself coming.

Michael almost screamed again as Rene applied the antiseptic to his back.

'Some woman,' the Belgian commented. 'Was it worth it?'

Michael was sitting on a stool in the vast bathroom off the sumptuous bedroom. Rene was sitting on the toilet seat behind him, applying the medication. The woman had left half an hour before.

'I had no choice,' Michael muttered. 'I've been to half a dozen parties and our little party here tonight was the culmination. That woman Gina is the key to what we're looking for.'

Rene grinned and used more antiseptic.

'The things that a man must do in the line of duty ... I'm proud of you, Michael.'

The young man grunted with pain and said, 'I have just learned that sometimes in life you have to take the pain with the pleasure.'

It had been eight days since Michael's arrival in Rome. Hedonistic days. He had once seen an old film called *La Dolce Vita* and assumed that it was exaggerated. He now knew the opposite. The first party had led him on to others. He was the season's new find. Everybody

228

wanted him at their parties and soirées. Every man wanted his ear; almost every woman wanted his body. He had moved through it all, watching and listening and occasionally making comments to selected people to indicate that, much as he was enjoying himself, he would enjoy something more bizarre and exciting. He had smoked hash and snorted coke and popped pills, indulged in one full-blown orgy, in which he had acquitted himself with great style and energy; and had finally narrowed down his new acquaintances to a group of five. He had invited these five to a party at his own apartment that night, together with another two dozen to fill out the numbers.

During the past days Rene had been invaluable. He would have made a brilliant actor; he played his part as Michael's Man Friday to perfection. So much so that several of Michael's new acquaintances had surreptitiously offered Rene a job after Michael's eventual departure from Rome. Of course, everybody knew that Rene's job included that of bodyguard. This simply added to Michael's glamour.

The party that night had been an unqualified success. The cook had prepared a cold buffet that would have done justice to the finest restaurant. The champagne was vintage and the drugs of designer status. The woman, Gina Forelli, had naturally arrived late. Michael had never met her, but had been induced to do so by one of his new-found friends, Giorgio Cosselli, who lived life very much in the fast track. He had dined with Giorgio two nights earlier at Sans Souci. They had been alone, and over coffee and liqueurs Michael had agreed to lend Giorgio fifty million lire as seed money for a new night-club venture he had in mind. He knew he would never see the money again, but he also knew that Giorgio knew more about the dark side of Roman society than anyone. During dinner Michael had let slip that he had heard Rome was an interesting place for those who were curious in the occult. Giorgio was a man in his mid-forties who lived the life of a bloodsucker. He was the black sheep of a black family, and his greatest pleasure in life was flirting with danger and the unknown. He had been drawn to Michael like a leaf to a whirl-pool, and as he swirled around in ever decreasing circles, mesmerised by the undoubted scope of the young man's wealth and naïvety, he gushed forth information.

After dinner they had walked the few blocks to Jackie O's disco and stood at the bar drinking negronis. Giorgio had pointed her out on the dance-floor. She was tall and almost too thin. Long shimmering black dress, long shimmering black hair, black eyes, red mouth and white face.

'Gina Forelli,' Giorgio had whispered. 'She is the one to lead you where you want to go. But be careful, my friend. If there is a witch in Rome, it is she.' He gave Michael a thumbnail sketch. Gina Forelli was approximately thirty years old, the granddaughter of a Fascist general who had been close to Mussolini. Her mother had been a semi-famous actress in the fifties who had died of a drug overdose. As far as he knew, Gina had never worked. Her first husband had been the third son of a wealthy industrialist who had died in an alcoholic car crash. Some said it was deliberate after catching his wife in bed with three men. Her second husband had been a wealthy businessman twenty years her senior. He had died in bed. The police had found half a dozen broken phials of amyl nitrite on the bedroom floor. Apparently his heart had not been able to stand up to the combination of Gina and the drug. By rights she should have been a wealthy woman but, apart from her other passions, she had a fatal attraction to gambling, and after the death of each husband had blown away her money in Monte Carlo.

'Her nickname is "Zero",' Giorgio had explained with a smile.

'Why is that?'

'Because too many zeros come up in her life. Especially on the roulette table.'

'What does she do now?' Michael had asked.

Giorgio had smiled again. 'She opens the door to what you are looking for.'

'Introduce me,' Michael had said.

Giorgio had shaken his head. 'It would not be a good idea in this place.'

'How do I meet her?'

'Let's go,' Giorgio had answered. 'I'll tell you outside.'

The entrance to Jackie O's is a long, canopied walkway. They had strolled to the end, near to the street. It was dark there. Giorgio stopped and Michael turned to look at him.

The Italian said, 'Michael, this deal we talked about at dinner ... Can't fail ... Of course you will be a fifty per cent partner. You are young but you must know that such deals have to be closed quickly. How fast can you transfer the fifty mill. to my account?'

Michael had looked at him and even in the gloom could see the anticipation and anxiety in his eyes. Very quietly he asked, 'Would US dollars be all right?'

'Of course ... even better!'

Michael reached into the inside pocket of his jacket and pulled out a wad of notes held together by a thick elastic band. Very quickly and expertly he counted off forty-eight of the notes and pulled them from the band. He held them out and Giorgio stared at Michael, his mouth slightly open.

'They're thousand-dollar bills,' Michael said lightly. 'I haven't checked the exchange rate but it should be about right.'

Very slowly Giorgio reached out and took the notes. He did not count them. As he tucked them into his back pocket he muttered, 'Of course I'll send you a receipt ... and a contract. My lawyer is to be trusted.'

Michael had shaken his head.

'Send me nothing, Giorgio. It is better that nothing is written down.'

Giorgio had seen the white of Michael's teeth as he smiled. He had smiled back and said, 'I will make sure that Zero attends your party.'

She had entered the apartment late and alone. Rene had been briefed. He took her name and led her through the room to Michael. She was wearing only a tight black leotard under a short wool ivory-coloured skirt. Her black hair was piled high on her head. She wore plain gold rings on all her fingers and a plain gold necklace. No earrings. Michael had noticed that the colour of her skin exactly matched the colour of her skirt. He had felt his heart beating; not out of fear but from anticipation.

Rene had presented her and then asked, 'Champagne?'

She had shaken her head.

'Do you know what a bullshot is?'

Rene had inclined his head. 'Of course, Signora. Do you want it half and half?'

She had studied Rene's face for a moment. 'No. Make it one-third bull and two-thirds shot.'

Michael had been puzzled. 'What have you just ordered?' he asked.

She smiled. Her teeth were also ivory and quite small. She flicked a pink tongue across them. Her voice was very low and he had to lean forward to hear her above the noise.

'A bullshot is half beef consommé and half vodka; usually in equal amounts. I asked your butler to go heavy on the vodka.' She inclined her head slightly to one side and studied him, and in her husky voice said, 'It's true what they say.'

'What do they say?'

'They say that Adonis is in town ... Why did Adonis invite me to his party?'

For the first time since getting off the plane in Rome Michael felt lost. The realisation washed over him that he was only nineteen years old. In reality the sum total of his knowledge boiled down to weapons and martial skills. The reality was that he had killed people who had tried to kill him and had rarely felt fear. Suddenly he felt fear. It only lasted a moment and then it was washed away by a sense of exhilaration. He had hoped he had kept the fear concealed.

'I'm told they call you Zero.'

She smiled again. 'Giorgio talks too much. What else did he tell you?'

'That you are dangerous.'

Her smile widened. 'Is that why you invited me?'

'Absolutely.'

She lifted her head and laughed. Like her voice, it was husky. Rene moved through the crowd with her drink on a silver tray. She took the glass and drank and nodded her approval. Rene gestured at the laden buffet table. She shook her head and raised the glass. 'This and those that follow will be my dinner.' Still looking at Rene, she asked, 'When will the other guests be leaving?'

Slightly startled, Rene had glanced at Michael who merely smiled, glanced at his Patek Philippe, nodded to Rene and said, 'Usher them out in about an hour.'

In the bathroom Michael stood up, stretched and grimaced slightly in pain. Rene also stood up, still smiling.

'What's the next step?' he asked.

Michael turned and said, 'The next step is tomorrow night. I'm having dinner with her, alone. Afterwards she's taking me out to a place in the country.'

'Just another orgy?' Rene asked.

Michael shook his head. 'That's what I asked her ... she said, "No, it will be more than that".' Michael noticed the flicker of concern on Rene's face. 'I'll be fine. And there's no other way, except to take a few risks.'

'Any idea where the party's going to be?' Rene asked.

Michael shook his head. 'No, but she told me it's only half an hour's drive from here, so I guess it's on the outskirts of the city. Don't worry, Rene. So far I'm above suspicion. The real danger will come later.'

SIXTY-TWO

Creasy eased his left leg and winced slightly in the darkness. Definitely the first twinges of arthritis. He cursed silently. He had never bothered about the years creeping along, but lately he had begun to feel his bones, especially when he had to sit totally still in the open for hours on end. He had been sitting on this knoll for the last four hours, watching the villa about a kilometre below him.

Guido had obtained high grade aerial photographs of the location, and when he had arrived, Creasy knew that there was a high steel-mesh fence surrounding the villa at a radius of about eight hundred metres. He had pulled a Trilux night-sight from one of the voluminous pockets of his black leather jacket, and quickly picked out the high steel poles of the fence. He assumed that it was connected to a sophisticated alarm system and would probably be electrified. He decided that Anwar Hussein had skimped on the cost of that fence. He should have run it up and behind the knoll. From where he sat, Creasy had a good view of the entrance to the villa. At his position, any half-decent sniper could pick off anyone going in or coming out.

By the time he had arrived there were two cars parked near the entrance. Four more arrived during the next half hour. In all, they disgorged six men and four women. As they passed under the light above the entrance, Creasy noted that they were all dressed formally. It must be a dinner party; Italian society preferred to dine late.

The villa itself was a white two-storeyed building with a red tiled roof. The only lights showing were on the ground floor. He faintly heard the sound of classical music. They were probably dining on the open terrace on the far side of the villa. There was no way he could get around the other side to catch a decent view. The night was cool and he felt the twinge in his left leg again.

He wondered what Michael was doing. The last message had been a phone call from Rene that morning. He had simply said that Michael was progressing and to expect results within a few days. Creasy felt his impatience mounting. He did not like taking a subsidiary part while Michael was in the forefront. He clamped down on his impatience. There had been no other way. Michael was the logical choice to infiltrate 'The Blue Ring'. Creasy tried to picture what he was doing at that moment, and a twinge of envy pushed away all shreds of impatience. He guessed that at this time of night Michael was probably with some beautiful young Roman socialite, either in bed with her or heading that way. Ruefully Creasy tried to remember how long it was since he had been with a woman. He decided that it had been too long.

In Milan Maxie MacDonald and Frank Miller were engaged in the same kind of work. They were sitting near the window of an apartment on a corner of a side-street off the Corso Buenos Aires, watching Donati's apartment on the fourth floor of a building two hundred metres away. They sat behind two tripods; Maxie's held a pair of powerful binoculars and Frank's a Nikon camera with a telephoto lens.

The building they watched was small and old, containing only six luxury apartments. For the past two hours Frank had been photographing everybody who went in and came out. So far there had been only four. The work was boring but they were used to it, both having served their time as bodyguards and in military intelligence.

Frank burped and glanced apologetically at Maxie, who grinned. That evening Maxie had made a huge pot of *spaghetti al vongole*. They both reeked of garlic.

A long black limousine pulled up at the entrance of the apartment building. A uniformed chauffeur emerged and opened the rear door. Maxie refocused the binoculars and watched the tall, grey-haired man in a dark overcoat move towards the door. He heard the hum and the clicks of the Nikon's motor-drive.

Frank burped again and said, 'It must have been the Chianti.'

Creasy watched the first of the guests emerge from the villa. The distance was too great and the light not strong enough to distinguish their features, but he saw that they all shook hands with the tall, bald-headed black man, who must be the host, Hussein. After the second car had left, Creasy decided to follow the third. He slipped back down the knoll through the underbrush to the rented black Fiat which was tucked away in the trees off a side-road.

Ten minutes later he saw the lights of the car sweep by. It was a pale blue Lancia. He waited a few seconds, pulled out after it and followed it the fifteen kilometres into Naples. The Lancia pulled up outside a mansion on the Via San Marco. The gates of the mansion rolled open and the car drove in. Creasy drove slowly past the mansion and made a mental note of the registration number and the address.

It was after three o'clock in the morning when he got back to the Pensione Splendide. They were all still up playing poker. No one looked up as he approached. They were engrossed in their cards and there was a big pile of notes in the pot. Slowly Creasy walked around the table, looking at the hands. Jens had a pair of queens and a pair of tens; Pietro held a full house, jacks on eights; The Owl had a hearts flush; Guido held a running flush in spades.

First Jens folded with an incomprehensible curse in Danish. Pietro held on for two more rounds and then tossed in his cards. The Owl and Guido looked at each other. In an irreverent moment Creasy thought that Guido looked like a pussy-cat. Finally The Owl called him and with an apologetic smile Guido laid his cards on the table. The Owl swore in French as Guido raked in the pot.

He looked up at Creasy, smiled and said, 'You guys can stay as long as you like. I'm making more money than looking after a bunch of tourists ... and the work's easier.'

Creasy grinned and dropped a slip of paper in front of him.

'That's the registration number of a blue Lancia and the number of a large house in the Via San Marco. Can you check them out in the morning?'

Guido picked up the paper, looked at it and nodded, then gestured at the table and said, 'Do you want to sit in?'

Creasy grinned and shook his head.

'I'd rather jump into a furnace.'

SIXTY-THREE

Juliet was subdued over dinner. Laura noticed that she did not eat with her usual, single-minded concentration. Since she had first arrived, the child had eaten as though it was a duty and a mission, and indeed she had filled out and grown remarkably quickly.

It was a Saturday night and Joey and Maria had come for dinner. At first Juliet had been light-hearted and relaxed, but during the early evening they had talked a lot about Guido and the many times he had visited Gozo both before and after Julia's death. Every year he had sent money, explaining that it was just a device to reduce his taxes in Italy. But they had known differently. They were by no means poor people, but they lived simple lives. They had used the money to build a guest wing onto the farmhouse and Guido used to stay there on his yearly holidays. Creasy had also stayed there on the two occasions he had come to Gozo to recover from his wounds. It was where Juliet now stayed. They had also talked about the Pensione Splendide in Naples which Guido had run with Julia and which he now ran with Pietro. Juliet knew that the *pensione* was now Creasy and Michael's base. Because of the girl's mood, Laura soon changed the subject.

After dinner the girl helped her wash up, and then said that she had a headache and asked to be excused. She kissed them all good-night, went up to the guest suite and sat on the wide bed. It was a beautiful room, made from ancient stones and constructed in the old manner with high arches. She thought of Creasy in that room, and suddenly she could see his face vividly. The clipped, grey hair, the mahogany cheeks and the scars. Quietly she started to cry. She stopped as soon as she heard the soft tap on the door and Laura's voice calling her name. Wiping an arm across her face, she called, 'Come in.'

Laura opened the door and looked at her. Then she crossed the room and sat down beside her, putting an arm around her.

'I know you miss them,' she said. 'We should have thought about that and not talked so much.'

Juliet shook her head.

'No ... it's all right. It's not so much that I miss them. Well of course I do ... but I know what they're doing, and I worry. It's not so bad at school because I have to concentrate; but later I think about it ... perhaps too much.'

'It's natural,' Laura said in a matter of fact voice. 'Of course you miss them. But you must not worry too much, Juliet. They are survivors, those two ... believe me. Is there anything we can do? Maybe we should be more active. Tomorrow's Sunday, and Joey's going fishing with some friends for Lampuki. Would you like to go with them?'

Juliet shook her head and then smiled.

'No ... I know they would take me, but I also know they don't like to take girls fishing. They think it brings bad luck.'

Laura nodded. 'Yes, it's true. We are blessed with a bunch of very superstitious men on this island. Is there something else you'd like to do?'

'Yes. Do you think I could go up to the house for the day? I could swim in the pool, and perhaps take a picnic.'

'You want to be there alone?'

'Yes. Do you mind?'

Laura smiled. 'Of course not. I understand. Paul will drive you up after mass, and I'll pick you up in the evening.'

It was just after ten in the morning when Juliet turned the large key in the huge garden gate. She waved to Paul who waved back and drove away.

She walked across the patio to the pool and stood looking down at it for a moment. Then she raised her eyes and looked out across the vista of rolling hills, villages and the sea and islands beyond. She felt immediately at peace.

She went to the kitchen and put her cold lunch into the fridge and changed into her swimsuit. It was a warm autumn day. She swam twenty lengths of the pool, then dried herself, pulled a book from her bag and lay on a lounger in the sun. For the next hour she studied the book which contained lessons in Maltese. Afterwards she remembered something and went into Michael's bedroom. Next to his bed was a portable Sony cassette player and a selection of tapes. She flicked through them and picked out some disco music.

Ten minutes later the music was echoing around the pool area, and she was dancing under the trellis. Michael had promised that when he came back he would take her down to the disco and dance with her. She was determined not to let him down. She danced for about an hour, changing the music and trying out new steps. Then she went into the kitchen and brought out her lunch and unpacked it on the table. Laura had prepared it and there was enough for three strong, grown men. Slabs of smoked ham, a portion of Lampuki pie, boiled eggs, local sausage, a cold potato salad, tomatoes, cucumber and, of course, a loaf of crusty bread.

On an impulse she jumped up and went into the cave. After her ordeal there, Michael had restocked it with Creasy's large collection of wine. He had explained the different types to her, pointing out the labels of the particularly good ones. She searched down the rows until she found it: a bottle of Margaux. Before she closed the door to the cave she stood there, looking and remembering. A great welling of love for Michael went through her. She found a corkscrew in the kitchen and a long-stemmed glass, and carried them out to the table under the trellis. An hour later she was very full of food and slightly dizzy. She noticed that the bottle was half-empty and giggled to herself.

She spent the next hour prowling around the old house. First she went up the stairs to Creasy's study. She marvelled at the rows and rows of books, and pulled a few down to look at them, some old, some new, novels, reference books and many biographies and auto-biographies. She wondered if he had read them all. There were cupboards full of magazines and drawers full of highly-detailed maps. In a small annex there was an IBM computer and a fax machine and several padlocked metal filing cabinets. Then she wandered through the lounge with its great stone fireplace, comfortable chairs and old mahogany bar in the corner. She went back into Michael's bedroom and smiled at all the posters on the walls, mostly of rock groups and a few semi-erotic women. Finally she ended up in Creasy's bedroom. There were two large windows; one looked out along the ridge towards Zebbug, and the other had a small balcony outside and a view of the rest of Gozo. She was feeling very light-headed. She turned and looked at the bed again and the wall behind it. Her eyes rose to the top right-hand corner of one of the great slabs of stone that made up the thick wall. She remembered.

She walked around the bed to the stone and pushed the heel of her hand against the top right-hand corner. Silently it swung open to reveal the gun-metal grey of the door of the safe. She closed her eyes in thought and remembered again. She reached up and dialled the numbers: 83 ... 02 ... 91. From the middle shelf she pulled down several files. She knew that they contained details of many people, some friends, some enemies. For the next two hours she sat on the bed, reading through them; then she replaced them. She sat thinking and then made her decision. Beneath the bottom shelf was a metal drawer. She pulled it out and looked inside and saw the tightly wrapped bundles of notes. She counted out five million Italian lire and two thousand US dollars. She then located the envelope which contained her new passport and extracted it. She closed the safe, repositioned the stone, went to the kitchen and found the telephone directory.

Laura arrived just after six o'clock. She opened the gate and found the girl asleep on the lounger by the pool. She was dressed in jeans and a T-shirt, her bag beside her. For a long while she stood, looking down at the girl. Her face was completely at rest. Laura called out her name and saw her eyes open and the sudden panic in them; but as soon as the girl recognised her she smiled.

'Did you have a good day?' Laura asked.

'Wonderful,' Juliet answered with a smile. 'Can I do it again?'

'Of course.'

SIXTY-FOUR

Colonel Satta shuffled through the 8 x 10 photographs. He was sitting with Maxie MacDonald and Frank Miller in a discreet banquette of an elegant restaurant in Milan. He came to the last photograph, stiffened and then swore quietly. He swore for about half a minute while he looked at the photograph.

'Who is he?' Maxie asked.

Bitterly Satta answered, 'General Emilio Gandolfo ... May he roast in hell.' Maxie and Frank waited patiently while the Italian distastefully perused the photograph again. Then he explained. 'Gandolfo is one of my superiors in the *carabinieri*. Like others of his rank, he has Fascist antecedents. He was the man who ordered me to stop the investigation into Jean Lucca Donati and Anwar Hussein.'

Frank leaned forward and said, 'It's not definite that he went to Donati's apartment. There are five others in that building.'

Satta shrugged and smiled wryly.

'If I were a betting man, and I am, I would lay a thousand to one that he went to Donati's apartment.'

'Does he have much power?' Maxie asked.

Satta's face turned grim.

'Unfortunately, yes. He is powerfully connected, politically, socially, and within the military and intelligence.'

Frank had been making notes on a pad. He ripped off the page, stood up and said, 'I'll go to a phone box and pass this on to Jens.'

'What do you want to eat?' Maxie asked. 'I'll order for you.'

'Ah, just a plate of *spaghetti*,' the Australian answered. 'Just bung a little brown sauce on top.'

Satta rolled his eyes and Maxie chuckled.

Guido got back to the *pensione* just after six in the evening. He found

Creasy, Jens and The Owl in the small bar, drinking negronis. Pietro was behind the bar. Guido nodded and received his usual glass of Chivas Regal and soda. He pulled a slip of paper from his pocket and slid it in front of Creasy saying, 'That's the owner of the light blue Lancia and the house on Via San Marco.'

Creasy looked down and read the name 'Franco Delors.'

'What do you know about him?' Creasy asked.

'Personally, nothing,' Guido answered. 'But as you know I have friends in the police here, and connections into the Mafia. Franco Delors is an interesting character. Born of an Italian mother and a French father. He settled in Naples about twelve years ago. Shortly afterwards he was indicted for his part in a paedophile ring. Somehow he got off with a suspended sentence. Thereafter, according to my sources, he turned to God and took up good works. His record had been squeaky clean ever since, and he is considered a paragon of virtue. He sits on the board of several charities and is much involved in helping to settle the influx of refugees coming into Italy from the turmoil in Eastern Europe ... particularly Albania.'

'Anything else?' Creasy asked.

Guido shook his head.

'I'm still digging, and something may come in later.'

Jens reached forward, picked up the slip of paper and moved to the door, saying, 'I'll put this onto the computer, together with the information we got from Frank on General Gandolfo.' As he reached the door Guido's voice stopped him.

'Oh, there was one other thing. Apparently one of the charitable organisations that Delors heads up has recently opened an office in Bari to help find homes for Albanian orphans.'

'Bari?' Jens asked.

'Yes,' Guido answered. 'It's the closest Italian port to Albania ... Apparently he spends much time there.'

SIXTY-FIVE

Some people live inside and enjoy their own minds. They are content within a structured mental environment, and uncomfortable outside of that structure. Such people usually have physical or mental drawbacks; sometimes real and sometimes imagined.

Massimo Bellu was such a man. He considered himself unattractive to the opposite sex. He was short and somewhat plump, no matter how much he dieted. His hair was lank and not quite black enough to be interesting, no matter what expensive shampoos and conditioners he used. He would always recall the comment of a hairdresser who had contemplated his hair when he was nine years old. His mother had taken him there and waited expectantly. The hairdresser had been an attractive young woman. She had circled him three times and then stated, 'We either shave it all off and try to make him look like Kojak, or we do the best with it.'

His mother had become angry. Massimo had become sad. He had retreated into his intellect, which, even at that age, had been considerable. At school he had been the butt of scorn from his contemporaries. Unco-ordinated at sports, unskilled in social mores, unsuccessful with girls. His only anchor had been his mind, and he withdrew into it.

It had taken him through school and by a scholarship into the University of Rome to study Social Science. From there he had gone into the most cerebral department of the *carabinieri* to specialise in social trends, including the analysis of the criminal mind. Within a few years he had found himself working with Colonel Mario Satta as a backroom boy, supplying analysis relating to the phenomenon of the Mafia. As he looked back on his life only two people had profoundly affected it: one was Colonel Satta and the other was Creasy. Within the distortions of Italian society and social structure, they were the only two people who held any value for him.

He lived in a small studio apartment in Trastevere. Apart from his narrow bed, the tiny bathroom and the even smaller kitchenette, the whole apartment was filled, wall to wall, with books, and in one corner his computer, which lately had become the centre of his life. He had long ago given up the hope of being a social lion. He occasionally basked in the reflected light of Satta's glamour; and he always enjoyed that, but for him, that was enough. On this night he was in communion with his computer. Sometimes he felt he was attached to it by some umbilical cord.

They came for him just after eleven o'clock. A soft tap on the door. He thought at first that it must be his upstairs neighbour, an elderly widower, retired from the civil service, who often came down to borrow a cup of sugar but who, in reality, wanted a chat to relieve his boredom. Bellu had long decided that the old man must have accumulated several thousand kilos of sugar. One day the ceiling would collapse, and he would die smothered in the stuff. He closed down the computer, hitting the keys which coded its information. Then he opened the door. It was not the old man. It was two young men, darkly-dressed and holding pistols.

They allowed him to put on an overcoat before taking him away. His intelligence told him that he was going to die. They did not blindfold him; that was the first sign. Over the years his nose had developed an instinct for the Mafia. They were not Mafia; that was the second sign. They conducted themselves as though they were above and far beyond civic authority; that was the third sign.

His destination was a cellar in Focene. He did not struggle as they bundled him out of the car and down the steps. He felt no foreboding, only a sense of inevitability. They strapped him to a chair in front of a table and waited. He asked no questions. Ten minutes passed and then the door opened to admit Jean Lucca Donati. Bellu recognised him from the photographs in his files. Donati sat down across the table, pulled out a pen from his inside pocket and a small notebook. He laid them in front of him, looked at Bellu and said, 'You have been making enquiries about me and also about a man called Anwar Hussein. Why?'

'It is my job,' Bellu answered.

Donati shook his head.

'It was not your job. No doubt you took instructions from Colonel Satta but it was also not his job. From where or whom did those instructions emanate?'

Bellu shrugged. He dropped his voice and said, 'I know who you are and what you represent. You are the filth on this earth. You will learn nothing from me.'

They spent four hours torturing him. He sat bloodied and physically broken. His fingernails had been torn out slowly, as had four of his teeth. His nose and both cheekbones had been smashed. His testicles crushed. But Massimo Bellu was not there in his body. His whole being had retreated into his mind. At the end, he had smiled sickeningly into the frustrated face of Donati, sending the message that such methods would achieve nothing.

Donati received the message and understood it clearly. He was a patient man. He issued instructions to one of the young men, who left the cellar. Donati and the other young man unstrapped Bellu's broken body, lifted it up and laid it on the table. He had neither the strength nor the inclination to struggle.

The young man came back after a few minutes, carrying a small briefcase. He laid it on the table next to Bellu's head and opened it. Donati hovered alongside like a vulture. From inside the briefcase the young man picked up a syringe.

Donati nodded and said to him, 'Twenty milligrams ... no more. Be very careful. Too little is not enough, too much can be fatal.' He looked down at Bellu's ravaged face. His voice was cruelly soft. 'So your body can take anything. Now we try your mind. In moments from now you will feel no pain ... only bliss. I am giving you pure Valium. Not the dosage that neurotic, socialite ladies take to ease their imaginary traumas, but enough to make your brain go on a journey you could never imagine. I regret that you may never return from that journey.'

Through the pain Bellu felt the slight prick of a needle. It took only a few seconds. He found himself playing again as a child, playing in the fields behind his grandfather's house in Tuscany. He saw the face of Mariella, his young cousin, laughing at him and teasing him maliciously. He saw the face of his mother scolding him because he had smacked Mariella. Through clouds of blue and green he heard the soft voice.

'Who sent you to spy on "The Blue Ring"?'

For the next forty minutes Donati learned much about Bellu's childhood. He learned about his frustrations, his fears and his ambitions. He learned that twenty milligrams of Valium was not enough. With a sense of trepidation he instructed the young man to

244

inject ten more milligrams. After that he learned about Bellu's masculine love for two men, but somehow, in spite of the miasma in his mind, Bellu was unable to speak their names.

'Where are they from?' Donati hissed in frustration.

Bellu's mangled mouth had twisted into a smile. 'One is from Rome,' he said.

'And the other? Where is the other from?'

Donati heard a word from the smashed mouth and leaned closer. 'Where? From where?' he asked insistently.

'From a stone house on a stone hill,' Bellu said, with what sounded like a giggle.

Donati glanced up at the two young men who were also listening intently. They leaned forward.

'Where is it?' Donati asked. 'Where is the house on the hill?'

They all heard the word.

'Gozo ... of course. Gozo.' And then Bellu's chest heaved and he gurgled in his throat and died.

SIXTY-SIX

There was only Bellu's sister and Satta and a priest. Others from the office had wanted to come to the funeral, but Satta had discouraged them.

The coffin was lowered into the grave; the priest said a prayer. Bellu's sister threw some earth on the coffin, and then she and the priest left. The grave-diggers would come later to fill in the hole in the ground and erect the simple headstone.

A cold wind swept across the cemetery, dropping late leaves from the gaunt trees. Satta remained, wrapped up in his dark overcoat and silk scarf, sitting on a nearby headstone. He sat for more than an hour, looking down at the grass in front of him. He was not a man to analyse grief or fate. He just sat there, looking at the grass and slowly letting the rage build up inside him. He had no children, and aspects of love had never really entered his life; but at this moment he knew that the mutilated corpse lying in the open grave in front of him represented the kernel of any real love he had ever known. He realised that Massimo Bellu had been more than a son or brother or friend or a lover. It was the very discretion and isolation of Bellu that he had loved. Above all, he knew that Bellu had loved him, Mario Satta, and perhaps little else.

The cold went through his overcoat, through his flesh and into his bones. Finally he looked up and saw a man standing on the other side of the open grave. He was dressed in jeans, a denim jacket and a black polo-neck shirt. His hair was short and steel-grey. He was looking down into the grave.

Satta stood up and slowly walked around the grave. The man lifted his head and his arms and pulled Satta against his chest. For the first time in his adult life, Satta wept. The man held him for a long time and then spoke quietly.

'Tomorrow morning you will resign from the *carabinieri*. I will send Maxie and Frank to you. We will take General Emilio Gandolfo and chart his path to hell. On that path we will find the rest of them and send them to the same place.' Creasy looked down at the grave again and his voice became colder than the wind. 'When you get tired, when you get cold, when you get totally dispirited, see in your mind the face of Bellu ... See the compassion in his eyes, and the kindness and the strength of the love he felt for you. And I see the same eyes and the same love ... Then realise what you and I have to do to satisfy his memory.'

SIXTY-SEVEN

They made a telephone conference call. The link was between Jean Lucca Donati in Milan, Anwar Hussein in Naples and Gamel Houdris in Tunis.

Donati explained what they had learned from Massimo Bellu. Just a place ... Gozo. He had spoken the name into the telephone, not expecting any reaction. He himself had never heard of the place. As it happened, neither had Anwar Hussein, but Gamel Houdris recognised it immediately.

'It's a small island,' he said. 'Part of the Maltese archipelago.'

'So what do we do?' Hussein asked.

'We send someone down immediately to check it out,' Houdris answered.

'Who do we send?' Donati asked.

'You send The Link ... Franco Delors. He's the best we have, and he's in Naples. Today is Tuesday. Tomorrow there's a ferry from Naples to Malta. Make sure he's on it. Then he gets the ferry over to Gozo and sniffs around.'

The conference went into abeyance for half a minute. Then Donati said, 'I will instruct him to be ultra-careful. Meanwhile, we have to move quickly to the final indoctrination of our Initiate. I would say within a week or so ... We're talking about fifty million US dollars minimum. It's a ripe fruit which must not fall off the tree. It has to be plucked. We need the subject for the sacrifice.'

Houdris said, 'I think I have her. As you know, a few days ago I was in Albania at our new orphanage. There is a prime candidate on hand. Franco Delors has arranged the necessary adoption papers. We will move her to Bari within the next few days, after Delors gets back from Gozo. Her name is Katrin. She is pre-puberty. Twelve years

248

old, blonde and very beautiful. Arrange the mass for the following Sunday.'

There was a contented silence.

SIXTY-EIGHT

Michael decided to abandon logic. He let his instincts take over. He knew he had to dominate the woman beneath him. It was a crucial moment. He realised that she wanted to be dominated, needed to submit. With that submission, the doors would open. Within his understanding of lovemaking, and within his character, he had always been gentle with women in bed. That gentleness had always satisfied them and himself. But on this occasion he knew that gentleness would be like a feather wafted in a storm.

He took her wrists in one hand and twisted her onto her stomach. She struggled, but he gripped the back of her neck with his other hand and forced her face into the pillow. She cursed in Italian and her body twisted under him. He let her use her strength, allowing her to roll onto her back. She tried to bite his shoulder, and he smacked her sharply on her cheek. She jerked a leg between his legs but he was waiting for it and her knee bounced off his thigh. A second later he had twisted her again onto her front, slid an arm under her thighs and pulled her bottom up. His penis was already wet from her juices. He rammed it into her bottom and she suddenly became very quiescent. It took only a few seconds more. They came together.

Instinct again took over. He pulled himself away and, without a word, padded into the bathroom. He took a small hand-towel and held it under the hot tap, then rinsed it out. She was lying on her front against the pillow, totally still. Gently now, he turned her over and wiped the sweat and residual make-up from her face, deciding that she looked more beautiful without it. Then he gently wiped her genitals, tossed the towel onto the floor, lay down beside her and waited.

'You have an understanding,' she murmured, 'about women like me ... How can it be in one so young?'

He smiled and answered, 'I was only young before I met you. I have lived a thousand days these last two nights.'

She laughed with pleasure, thinking that she now controlled him.

It took two brandies and many soft, whimpering kisses before she made her move. She made the move encompassed in the thought that, having given him the most secret part of her body, she now controlled his mind. She played on his ego.

'No one has ever done that to me before. In a terrible way it makes me your slave. What more do you want of me?'

He smiled in his mind.

'I want you to take me to the very depths. You are my door to that ... and my guide. I want to see more than the joke of the other night. I want to go to the limit.'

She thought for a moment, balancing the risks against the benefits, and then she murmured, 'It's possible ... And I think you have the strength to see it. But it will take much persuasion, and for me it will be very risky ... When I talk about risk, I talk about death.'

'What does the risk cost?' he asked.

Seconds ticked by, then she slid a hand down his chest, across his penis and onto his scrotum. She smiled in the semi-darkness and answered, 'Fifty thousand dollars could compensate for the risk.'

SIXTY-NINE

Creasy needed to talk. It was something very rare in his life; he had nearly always been able to commune with himself. He considered unburdening his thoughts a kind of weakness. He sat at a place which was one of his most favourite spots, the terrace of the Pensione Splendide, late at night. A half-full bottle of Johnnie Walker Black Label in front of him and, beyond him, the lights of the bay; and beyond the lights the darkness of the sea.

He felt a strong sense of *déjà vu*. It was as though he had been there six years before with the same bottle, the same lights, and the same darkness. After that night he had gone away and killed many people. He felt he was poised in time at that same moment.

Of course, Guido was the one he should have talked to. Guido from the long past. Guido his closest friend. Guido, the mirror to his own mind. But Guido was fast asleep in bed, probably smiling at all the lire he had won at that night's poker game.

He heard the door open behind him and a figure came out some metres away and walked to the edge of the terrace and looked out at the view. There was only a sliver of a moon but Creasy recognised the Dane. He himself had not been noticed.

Five silent minutes passed, and then Creasy called softly, 'Do Danes drink whisky?'

He saw Jens' head jerk up in surprise and turn. Then his voice came equally softly. 'On a night like this, Danes drink anything ... Even hemlock.'

Creasy smiled in the semi-darkness.

'Come and sit with me and tell me what makes the world go round.'

The Dane moved out of the darkness, pulled up a chair and sat down.

They sipped quietly for a few minutes, then Creasy said, 'You told me and the others why you are here. You explained about your job and your vocation and the acceptance of your wife. But you have never really told me why you are here.'

The Dane refilled his glass and spoke as though the words came from his toes and through his feet and up his legs, and then passed through his thorax and onto his lips. 'To understand why I'm here, you would have to understand the psyche of the Northern people. We do not do things by logic. If I looked at this whole situation logically I would not just run back to Copenhagen, I would keep going till I got to the North Pole, and then I would start looking for a spaceship to take me to the moon.'

Creasy chuckled. 'So why? Tell me why.'

The Dane swirled the liquid in his glass as he thought, then he said, lightly, but with emphasis, 'Oh, around a thousand years ago my ancestors pushed out frail boats, jumped into them and went off to conquer their known worlds. Perhaps I don't look exactly like a Viking, but I feel like one. I know that at this moment I live in total danger. I am surrounded by killers and I am pursued by killers ... It concentrates my mind like never before. My heart beats faster than ever before ... And I like it.'

Creasy chuckled again and then said, 'But you still have not answered my question.'

Another silence and then the Dane said, 'I am here because of three people. First, Michael; he walked into my life and into my house and jerked me away to Marseille. This kid almost young enough to be my son. Second, while I was in shit up to my neck, you arrived and dealt out death all around me. Third, I saw the face and the eyes of a child in hell, and watched you and Michael extract her from that hell and give her a life ... Why should I not be here?'

Below them in the bay a large cruise liner was moving out to sea. It was dressed like a Christmas tree. Over many minutes they watched its lights seemingly drift to the horizon, and then the Dane asked his question.

'Why are you here? And why is it possible that you attract to you men of such diversity, who would literally die for you?'

Creasy's answer was immediate. 'Because they know that I would die for them. That is the measure of leadership.'

The Dane digested that and then remarked, 'Obviously there is more than that.'

'Yes,' Creasy answered firmly. 'And thank God there is more than that. They're not just here because of me – that would never be enough for the likes of Maxie, Rene, Frank, or you, or Michael, or Guido, or Satta, or Pietro, or any other human being who can combine decency with a brain. They are here because they are angry to their guts. So what now, my Viking?'

The Dane could see the last glimmer of light in the horizon.

'What have you done about Gozo? It's possible that Bellu talked before he died?'

'I have made phone calls,' Creasy answered. 'Within twenty-four hours, five men of the calibre of Maxie, Rene and Frank will be arriving on Gozo. They will protect those whom I love. It's only a precaution, because I doubt that Bellu talked before he died. The pathologist reports that first he was physically tortured to the extreme. Obviously he did not talk then, because they later gave him a massive dose of pure Valium in an effort to warp his mind. He may have talked under the influence but it would have been disjointed at best. He must have died soon after.'

The Dane was curious to probe into Creasy's mind; the very idea fascinated him. 'What was your reaction to Bellu's death? How do you put it on your balance sheet of morality? Do the means justify the end?'

Creasy pushed his empty glass away from him and his soft voice was angry. Not at the Dane, not at himself, but at the twists and bends, bumps and holes of his entire life. 'Bellu's death shattered my friend Satta. That affects me more than the death itself.' He leaned forward in the semi-darkness and gripped the Dane's arm. 'I tell you, I have seen enough death to make me feel I walk always on bones. There is nothing new. When the flesh is gone the bones look the same. I don't care about death. I cannot see Bellu's face any more. A face is a face, and a bone is a bone. The faces pass by in the night. A friend on a ridge who has a face one second and a mass of blood and bones the next. A face of a child once bright with life and a second later black with napalm. Faces that turn into rows of coffins or bodybags. Open graves and white headstones ... Can you understand that?'

The Dane shook his head.

'Of course I cannot ... And Creasy, I think you indulge yourself. You sound like steel on this quiet night. But I do not see or feel the steel ... I sit with a man who knows more love than he understands. More love than he recognises. More love than he wants to accept. If you want my serious opinion, I think you're full of bullshit.'

Creasy laughed softly.

'So I have a wise Viking ... So what do we do now?'

Jens pulled himself straight in his chair, and his voice changed tone.

'Everything is speeding up,' he said. 'About now, Satta, Maxie and Frank are moving in on that prick General Gandolfo. Much will come of that. In the meantime, Michael is poised to penetrate "The Blue Ring" from inside. We now know the main characters. We know their philosophy and the parameters of their operation. No doubt in the next day or so you will move. The only thing missing from our knowledge is the name of the man behind it all ... The spider at the centre of the web ... There must be a spider ... In all such things there is a spider. I feel that very soon we will know who that spider is. While your team burns down the web ... you will kill the spider.'

The horizon was now totally black; the Christmas tree had passed over it. They both looked at the blackness, and then the Dane said, almost in a whisper, 'I have a sure feeling you will kill that spider. Then I will go home and be a husband, a father ... and a good policeman.'

SEVENTY

On that same night two children started their separate journeys.

In Gozo, Juliet yawned deeply as she helped Laura with the washing up. Laura glanced at her and smiled.

'It's the sea-air,' she said. 'It makes for a good sleep.'

It was a Saturday evening and early that morning Juliet had gone fishing with Joey and his friends. In spite of their superstitions they had caught ten boxes of Lampuki, and Juliet had caught more than her share. The men had paid her the ultimate compliment as they unloaded the catch at the jetty beneath Gleneagles.

'Come again,' they had called. 'Any time.'

In the bar Tony had treated her with unreserved respect, giving her a glass of his own wine.

'You are a fisherman,' he had said proudly.

'Fisherwoman,' she had corrected him.

Solemnly he had shaken his head. 'No, on this island you are now a fisherman, even if you put on a skirt and wear lipstick.'

She had suddenly felt very grown up.

Now, as she wiped the last of the plates, and stacked them in the cupboard, she said to Laura, 'It's Sunday tomorrow ... Can I sleep late?'

'Of course,' Laura answered. 'Sleep as late as you want, but don't forget we're having lunch at Joey's. Maria is making Lampuki pie and she prepares it almost as well as I do.'

In her bedroom, Juliet carefully counted out the money again and packed it away, together with her passport, into her purse. She selected the clothes she would need, put them into the canvas bag and put her purse on top. Then she sat on her bed patiently and waited, knowing that within the hour the rest of the house would be asleep.

She knew she would have to slip out very quietly. The dogs would not be a problem, because on the last two nights she had done a couple of trial runs, going out into the courtyard after midnight. The dogs were Tal-Fenecks, a breed almost exclusive to Malta; hunting dogs, famous for their ability to catch rabbits on the steepest slopes. On each occasion they had slipped up to her silently, sniffing and recognising her smell and whining with pleasure as she had patted them. But the bloody cockerel was a problem. It roosted fifty metres away in an old carob tree and announced any sound to the entire world. So she decided to slip out the front door and work her way down a narrow path to the seashore and then around the coast to the harbour.

First she wrote a note to Laura and Paul, telling them not to worry. She explained that she wanted to be with her father and brother, no matter what the danger. By the time they found the note she would be in Rome. She had booked her flight by phone from the house on the hill. She would catch the early four o'clock ferry to Malta; catch a bus to Valetta and then another bus to the airport, arriving in plenty of time to get the seven o'clock flight to Rome, arriving there at eight-twenty. Then she would catch a plane or a train down to Naples. She had the address of the Pensione Splendide. She knew that Creasy and Michael would be angry, but she had decided she was more than a child; she would handle their anger. At least she could cook for them and help around the *pensione*. She would be part of it.

She slipped out of the house just after two in the morning, her bag slung over her shoulder. The cockerel heard nothing, but she had not gone a hundred metres before two shapes loomed up behind her. She stopped and patted them and felt their cold muzzles poking at her face.

'Go home,' she whispered fiercely.

She might have been talking to the rocks around her. They followed her down the path to the shore and then around the coast to the small harbour, as though they were fellow conspirators.

The overnight ferry from Naples docked in the Grand Harbour of Valetta at three a.m. Franco Delors passed swiftly through customs and immigration, hailed a taxi and asked the driver, 'Can you get to Cirkewwa in time to catch the five o'clock ferry to Gozo?'

'No problem,' the driver said cheerfully. 'Just hold on to your seat.'

Juliet bought a ticket and walked onto the ferry together with a host of farmers and fishermen taking their produce and catches to the early Malta markets.

Half an hour later the ferry warped into Cirkewwa. She was one of the first off. As she went down the ramp a man walked past her onto the ferry. He glanced at her and carried on walking, but ten metres on he stopped abruptly, turned and watched her hurry towards the waiting green bus. He stood there for several seconds as the other passengers streamed past him. Then he followed her. He saw her get on to the bus. A taxi had pulled up and disgorged several tourists, their eyes bleary from lack of sleep. The bus was pulling away.

Franco Delors grabbed the taxi driver and asked him, 'Where is that bus going?'

'Valetta,' came the reply.

'Follow it,' Delors said, climbing into the back seat.

At the airport Juliet bought her pre-booked ticket at the Alitalia counter. Delors hovered in the background. She then went to the cafeteria and drank tea and ate toast and marmalade. In the meantime Delors had also purchased a ticket to Rome and made a phone call to Jean Lucca Donati.

'Yes, it is her ... I have no doubts. She was coming off the ferry as I was going on ... I followed her to the airport ... I'm booked on the same flight ... Have some people at Fiumicino. No, she did not recognise me ... she was zonked out on heroin the only time she saw me in Marseille ... No, I am not mistaken. She has the face of an angel. I would not forget it ... Of course. The flight gets in at eight-twenty. I'll be right behind her. Have your people in front.'

Katrin had no surname, as befits an orphan. Even that name had been given to her arbitrarily; with the trauma of watching her parents shot she could not remember her given name. But she had adjusted well to the orphanage. So well that she had been selected by Sister Assunta to be the first of her charges to be given up to adoption.

Sister Assunta herself had prepared the child, washing her long, blonde hair and dressing her in the new jeans and T-shirt which had been part of a large donation of clothes from Malta. She had talked to her reassuringly, telling her that she was going for the first time in her life on a boat trip to a wonderful new country called Italy, where she would meet her new parents. She would have a new home and much love and go to a good school and one day would come back to visit Sister Assunta and the other nuns and bring them lots of good Italian chocolate.

Katrin had laughed and promised to return.

SEVENTY-ONE

On Sundays Joey and Maria allowed themselves the unusual luxury of sleeping late. They would get up about nine-thirty instead of six o'clock, eat a light breakfast, attend the eleven o'clock mass and then go on to Joey's parents for a late lunch.

On this Sunday, however, Joey got up grumbling at six-thirty, because they had some English tourist friends who were catching the seven o'clock ferry on their way home. Joey felt he should wave them goodbye. He left a sleeping Maria, climbed into the Land-Rover and free-wheeled most of the way down to the harbour.

Having done his duty, he walked across the concourse to the Pit Stop snack bar and ordered a *cappuccino* from his friend Jason.

He had just taken the first sip, when Jason said, 'That girl staying with your parents . . .'

'What about her?' Joey said, immediately alert.

'Well, she went to Malta early this morning.'

Joey's head snapped up. 'What the hell are you talking about?'

'I'm sure it was her,' Jason replied. 'I was just opening up and saw her walk past to catch the four o'clock ferry. She was carrying a bag. I probably wouldn't have noticed, but she had your two Tal-Fenecks with her.' He laughed. 'They wanted to go on the ferry with her and she had to shoo them off. I watched them head back up the hill after the ferry left.'

For a moment Joey stood at the bar looking down at his cup, then he asked urgently, 'Are you sure it was her, Jason?'

The young man nodded.

'I'm sure, Joey. I only saw her once, but it was enough . . . The kind of girl you keep in mind for three or four years later . . . She's going to be a beauty.'

259

The next moment Joey was heading through the open door and running for his Land-Rover.

Laura was up and bustling around the kitchen. She looked up, startled, as Joey ran in.

'What are you doing up so early?'

'Never mind. Where's Juliet?'

'Fast asleep. She wanted a lie-in this morning. Why?'

'I was just down at the ferry,' he gasped. 'Jason at the Pit Stop told me he saw her catch the four o'clock ferry. The dogs were with her.'

'The dogs are here,' she said, puzzled.

'Yes, of course. They came back after she'd gone ... Let's look.'

They hurried up the outside steps to the guest wing. Laura tried the door. It was locked. She banged on it and shouted, 'Juliet!' several times. There was no answer, and Joey elbowed her aside, squatted down and looked through the keyhole.

'There's no key,' he said. 'She must have locked it from the outside.'

Paul came up the steps, his hair ruffled and his eyes sleepy.

'What the hell's going on?'

Joey explained while Laura ran down to the kitchen for the spare key.

The bed was neatly made. There was a note on the bedside table.

Laura picked it up and read the words out loud. ' "Please don't worry. I have been very happy here with you but I feel so nervous about Creasy and Michael and so useless just waiting. Maybe there is something I can do there. I know where they are and by the time you read this I will be in Italy. I have some money and I will be able to take care of myself. Love, Juliet".'

They looked at each other, and Joey said, 'Where on earth would she find money?'

'Up at the house,' Laura snapped. 'She was up there all day last Sunday. Creasy kept a lot of money there in the wall-safe in his bedroom. He or Michael must have shown her how to open it.'

Paul looked at his watch. It was seven-fifteen.

'She must have been going for the seven o'clock flight to Rome,' he said. 'Sometimes it's late. Maybe we can stop her.'

They all ran down to the kitchen and the ever practical Laura took charge. She phoned George Zammit at home and got his wife, who informed her that he had just left for police headquarters. Being a senior superintendent in an increasingly modernised police force, Laura was talking to him within a minute on his mobile phone. She was clear and concise. George simply told her to hang up and wait. He would call her back.

The three Schembris sat in the kitchen, looking at the phone. It rang two minutes later. Yes, the immigration computer showed that one Juliet Creasy had caught the Alitalia flight to Rome. It was scheduled for seven a.m. but had taken off at seven-fourteen. Its ETA Rome was eight thirty-eight. Laura looked at her watch. The plane would land in exactly one hour and three minutes.

'I can call Rome,' George said, 'and have the police waiting for her and put her back on the next flight.'

Laura thought for only a few seconds.

'No,' she said. 'Creasy's in Naples with Guido. I'll phone him now and see what he wants to do. I'll get back to you in a few minutes.'

SEVENTY-TWO

Creasy heard the phone ring as he was having breakfast. He heard Guido's faint voice answering in the kitchen. A few moments later the voice rose.

'Creasy. Get in here. It's Laura ... An emergency!'

Creasy listened to Laura's controlled words, then said, 'Wait!' He cupped the mouthpiece and rapidly explained the situation to Guido. They both glanced at their watches.

'Just about an hour,' Guido said. 'Add another twenty to thirty minutes for immigration and customs. Are you going to have George Zammit phone his counterpart in Rome?'

Creasy shook his head.

'No, let's keep the police out of this. The question is whether she left for the reasons she mentioned in her note or whether there's something else behind it.'

'Like what?'

Creasy shrugged.

'Who knows, maybe Bellu did talk under the influence of that Valium. Maybe they've already targeted Gozo. Maybe that's what's behind it. My people don't arrive in Gozo until this afternoon.'

Guido said sceptically, 'But the information is that she walked onto the ferry alone. It doesn't sound like a "snatch".'

'True,' Creasy agreed. 'But they could be waiting for her at Rome airport. She's only a child. Maybe she was led into this somehow.'

Guido glanced at his watch again.

'Anyway, Michael's in Rome with Rene, and Maxie and Frank arrived there last night.'

Creasy also glanced at his watch.

'I don't want to involve Michael. He's very close now, and I must do nothing to compromise his cover. I'll send Maxie and Frank. Rene

262

can cover them from the background. What's Michael's number?'

Jens was standing at the kitchen door. He had been listening to the last part of the conversation. He plucked the number from his photographic brain and called it out. Both men turned in surprise, and then Creasy was making the call.

Michael was fast asleep, but he came awake in seconds. He listened quietly without asking any questions, then he too looked at his watch and said, 'I'll get on to it. Rene is here, and Maxie and Frank will be at the hotel nearby. They weren't due to meet Satta until eleven. I'll plan the operation and get back to you.'

SEVENTY-THREE

She had been too excited to eat the plastic breakfast from the plastic tray. The plane was half-empty and she had a row of three seats to herself. She drank the good coffee and a stewardess refilled her cup, sat on the edge of the seat and chatted to her for a few minutes. She leaned across and pointed out of the window. It was a clear morning and Juliet could see the green fields and the rising Appenine mountains.

'Have you been to Rome before?' the stewardess asked.

'No, it's my first time in Italy.'

'Is someone meeting you?'

'No, I'm catching the twelve o'clock train to Naples. Is the railway station near the airport?'

The stewardess smiled.

'No, it's at least an hour's drive into the city, but direct buses leave every half hour from the airport, non-stop to the station ... Or are you rich enough to take a taxi?'

Juliet smiled and shook her head.

'No, I'll catch the bus.'

The stewardess stood up, brushing down her skirt. She said, 'Then, after you come out of customs turn left and go about a hundred metres. You'll see the transport desk where you can buy a ticket. The bus waits just outside. Be careful in Naples, young lady ... it's a dangerous city.'

Juliet smiled again.

'Don't worry. My father and brother are there.'

Franco Delors followed her through immigration and then through the green lane of customs, saying a silent prayer that he would not be picked out for a spot check. He had sat at the rear of the plane and was confident that she had not noticed him, either during the flight, or in the arrivals hall.

They both walked unchecked through customs and he slowed down and scanned the waiting crowd. The girl had stopped. She was not looking for anyone in the crowd, but was peering to her left. Delors spotted his man leaning against the Avis car hire counter. They exchanged looks and Delors nodded at the girl. She had started moving, walking slowly down the concourse. Delors felt a stab of elation at the realisation that there was no one to meet her. He quickened his pace and came up alongside her. Her canvas bag was slung over her right shoulder.

'Hello,' he said cheerfully. 'Didn't I see you on the plane from Malta?'

She looked up at him.

'Yes, I was on that flight ... but I didn't see you.'

He smiled engagingly.

'I was sitting at the back behind you. Are you staying in Rome?'

She shook her head.

'No, I'm going to the railway station. I'm just going to catch the bus.'

'Well, I can save you some money,' he said. 'I'm also going to the railway station. A friend is meeting me ... he's over there. We're going by car and there's plenty of room for you.'

She glanced at the man moving towards them. He was young, tall and dark-faced. His eyes were fixed on her intently. They had reached the ticket counter when she felt a sudden prickling of danger. Her mind went back over the weeks to the last time a stranger had talked to her, and to what had followed.

'No, thank you. I'll catch the bus.'

'Such a waste of money,' Delors said. 'And the bus takes much longer.' His hand moved to lift the bag from her shoulder. She gripped the strap tightly and shook her head vigorously.

'No! I'll take the bus.'

Suddenly there was another man beside them. He was middle-aged and bald with a round face and a square body. 'Hello, Juliet,' he said. 'Sorry I'm late ... the damn traffic.' He spoke perfect English but with an accent she had never heard before.

The bald man turned to Delors and said, 'No problem, mate, she's coming with me.'

Delors saw the puzzled look on the girl's face and quickly grabbed her elbow.

'Do you know this man?' he asked. 'You have to be careful here.'

Then everything was happening at great speed. The bald, square man took two short paces and his right fist slammed into Delors' belly. With an anguished grunt, Delors released Juliet's elbow and swung his right arm. His fist whistled over the bald man's head and she heard a sound like a wet towel hitting a tiled floor. Delors went down backwards. Someone began shouting, then the bald man had an arm round her waist, plucking her off her feet. She drew a breath to scream but then heard his harsh voice against her ear, 'Creasy sent me. Be quiet and run.'

Her feet hit the ground and his hand gripped hers, pulling her towards the entrance. To her right she saw the tall, dark-faced man running towards them, his hand reaching under his jacket. Then suddenly he too was sent sprawling to the floor from a blow behind. In all the speed and confusion she recognised the face of the man who had delivered the blow. She recognised it from a photograph in one of the files she had studied from Creasy's safe. She remembered the name printed under the face: 'Maxie MacDonald'. One of the good ones. She kept running as she saw Maxie pull out a pistol, his eyes darting around the concourse. Then they were outside and a black car was pulling up with the back, nearside door open. She felt herself lifted and tossed into it, then her breath was punched out as a body landed on top of her. She heard the door slam, then the squeal of tyres, and a voice above her saying urgently, 'Stay down, Juliet. Stay down. We are friends from Creasy.'

She had no choice but to stay down. The bald-headed man was lying right across her; she smelt garlic on his breath. She heard another voice from the front passenger seat saying, 'All clear. We change cars in about a minute.'

The weight lifted off her and she struggled into a sitting position. Maxie MacDonald was sitting beside the driver, the gun still in his hand. He was looking through the rear window. His eyes flickered towards her and he said, 'I'm Maxie MacDonald.' He gestured with the pistol towards the man beside her. 'That's Frank Miller ... The driver's Rene Callard. We are friends of Creasy and Michael.'

She collected herself and murmured, 'I know your names ... What happened?'

'Wait,' Maxie said. 'I'll explain later.'

They skidded to a stop next to another black car parked in a lay-by. Within seconds they had transferred to the other car and two minutes later had pulled off the autostrada onto a side-road.

Maxie slipped the pistol back under his jacket and said to Rene, 'It'll take them twenty minutes to put up road-blocks. We'll be long gone.'

'What happened?' Juliet repeated apprehensively.

Beside her, Frank Miller said, 'What happened was that you were stupid. You're going to have one angry father and one angry brother. I expect – and I hope – that they'll smack your bottom.'

She turned to look into his stern eyes. 'What's your accent?' she said.

'Australian,' he answered aggressively.

She nodded as if that explained it.

SEVENTY-FOUR

The child Katrin was excited. She had never seen the sea before. She had never seen a ship. Now she saw the sea – and a ship – big and white. She laughed in simple delight and Sister Assunta and Sister Simona laughed with her.

Katrin carried a plastic bag with her sole belongings: a change of underwear, two pairs of socks, a pink dress, two T-shirts and another pair of jeans. Plus a large toilet bag containing a bar of soap, a nail brush, a tube of toothpaste and a toothbrush.

The immigration officials checked the papers carefully. Of course they were in order. Everything perfect; signed and notarised. Sister Simona was to accompany Katrin to Bari and hand her over to the director of the charity and her new parents and, in doing so, establish a link for the future.

The white ship sailed away with Katrin clutching her plastic bag, and Sister Simona, young, determined and nervous. Sister Assunta turned away, climbed into the car and was driven back to the orphanage. She should have felt a sense of satisfaction, but in the past days there had been a shadow in the back of her mind. A chisel chipping away at a segment of her memory. An itch in a place she could not scratch. It had started with the visit of the benefactor. She had appreciated his kindness and his logic. She had looked at his face and into his eyes and listened to his quiet, persuasive voice and had decided that a closely defined religion such as her own did not exclude goodness in others who held different beliefs.

The very fact that Gamel Houdris was not of her faith generated her respect. He gave his wealth across religious boundaries. In her mind she saw his face again as she climbed out of the car in front of the orphanage. She saw the thin features and the dark eyes and she should have recalled the soft persuasive voice. But instead she felt a cold irrational prickling of her skin.

It was dark and late, but she decided to go through the dormitory. There were two night candles burning, casting dim flickering shadows across the long ceiling.

The children were asleep, except for one. At the far end of the room she heard a soft whimpering. She moved quietly between the beds towards the sound. It was the child, Hanya. She had arrived that morning from Tiranë. Five years old and thought to be simple-minded. But the simplicity had come from trauma, and Sister Assunta knew that love and security would heal the trauma.

She sat quietly on the bed and picked up the child and pulled her to her ample bosom. The child sobbed against her, adrift in a flickering world. The nun stroked her dark hair and crooned soft words. The sobbing abated and then stopped, and the child sighed and the rhythm of her breathing settled into sleep.

The nun held her into the night, wondering yet again if a child conceived in her own womb would not have been more perfect. As she laid Hanya's head back on the pillow and tucked the blankets around the small body, Sister Assunta decided, yet again, that her womb would have been limited to a volume of love unacceptable to the expanse of her heart. It was why she was a nun.

She moved back between the beds. All was quiet. She felt at peace. The first of her charges was on her way to a real home. The others would follow. She felt infinitely tired, but had found solace in the thought that in the morning she herself would be travelling back to Malta and to the womb of her own convent for two brief but consoling weeks of rest. She would tend the garden and pretend to watch the lemons grow on the numerous trees in the rolling garden and be at peace until she returned to ply her vocation.

Her room was small and her bed narrow. She undressed and washed her face in the cold water in the metal basin. She brushed her teeth and then wrapped herself in one of her incongruously bright *kikus* that had been a parting present from her congregation in northern Kenya. It seemed a lifetime away.

She had always slept well – be it on an earthen floor or a straw palliasse or a narrow metal bed. But on this night she could not sleep. She moved and turned on the thin mattress. Images came into her mind and went as quickly. She saw the wide eyes of the child, Katrin, as she gripped the hand of Sister Simona, gazing up at the white ship. She saw the eyes of the other children as they were delivered into her care from the back of an open truck. She saw the love and care in the eyes of her fellow nuns as they received those children.

As the dawn cast a sprinkling of light on the ceiling of her small room, she suddenly saw the eyes of Gamel Houdris looking out at her from the back seat of that black car.

The last vestige of sleep left her as that image lanced into her brain and triggered a long-ago memory. She pulled away the blankets and rolled her feet to the cold stone floor. Her skin became damp and cold as her mind sent messages to her body. From the past, she saw again the bundle at her feet. Saw the car pulling hastily away. Saw the pale face and the stricken eyes of the young woman and beyond that face, another. Darker, masculine. Eyes as black and cold as frozen ebony. It had been twenty years ago, but the image was unmistakable.

SEVENTY-FIVE

They waited for two hours in the car park of the roadside café. Maxie went in to fetch coffees and pastry. Juliet slept with her head on Frank's lap.

The men had the patience of long practice. The patience of watching and listening and knowing that danger is always as close as the width of a wafer. There was little talk as they drank and ate the cakes, and anyone not within their circle would have found what talk then was incomprehensible.

'The big one tonight,' Frank remarked.

'Just a puff of wind,' Rene commented.

'It pole-axed Satta,' Maxie added.

'He's a one, that one,' Frank stated.

'Coming through the hedge backwards,' Rene observed.

'But with his hair on his head,' Maxie added through a mouthful of cake.

Frank chuckled.

'What the hell are we doing? I haven't had so much fun in a yonk of years.'

'How's Michael tracking things?' Maxie asked Rene.

The Belgian grinned.

'He's ploughing a furrow accompanied by sighs, groans and sometimes screams. That kid walks on the edge ... I love the bastard!'

The BMW crept alongside. They were looking into The Owl's glasses.

Frank reached down and, with thumbs and forefinger, closed Juliet's nostrils. She opened her mouth and then her eyes. The Australian bent down and kissed her on the forehead, smiled and said, 'You leave these three uncles and go to a couple more. Say hello to your dad and Guido and Pietro. ... *Ciao*, kid.'

She sat up and rubbed her eyes and looked through the window at the BMW.

'Who are they?' she asked.

'Friends,' Maxie said from the front seat. 'You know one of them. You go to Naples now.'

Frank reached across her and opened the door. She felt the cool air. She leaned over the front seat and kissed Maxie on the cheek and then Rene. She picked up her canvas bag from the floor, reached out a hand and touched her fingers against Frank's lips, smiled and said, 'Don't worry, mate ... I think your accent's lovely.'

They watched her slip into the BMW and watched it pull away. Rene turned on the ignition and they headed back towards Rome.

'Some kid,' Frank said from the back seat.

'Definitely,' Maxie agreed. 'It took her about ten seconds to turn you into a whimpering pussy-cat.'

'Miaow,' Rene added.

Frank curled up in the back seat and muttered, 'Guys like you make an Aussie throw a technicolour spit.'

Rene glanced at Maxie with a raised eyebrow. Maxie smiled and explained, 'We make him vomit.'

SEVENTY-SIX

The black one came first. He was very large.

Laura opened the door, sighed and said, 'Creasy sent you.'

The black face split into a white smile.

'Sure thing, Ma'am. And I'm told you make the meanest rabbit stew north of the Equator.' He was carrying a black Samsonite suitcase. She opened the door wide and gestured, and he walked through. He put down his suitcase and studied the interior of the large and old room and sighed contentedly. 'How old is it, Ma'am?'

'This room? About four hundred years, but of course there are newer extensions. Can I get you tea or coffee, or a glass of wine?'

He smiled at her again and said, 'Coffee would be fine, Ma'am. I'm sorry to say that I drink quite a lot of it.'

She moved into the kitchen, asking over her shoulder, 'Are you American?'

'Yes, Ma'am. From Memphis, Tennessee. Though the fact is I've been out of the States for many years.'

He had followed her to the door of the kitchen. She turned and said, 'All this "Ma'am" business is going to be too much. My name is Laura. My husband is called Paul.'

He ducked his head in acknowledgement. 'Pleased to meet you, Laura. My name is Tom ... Sawyer.'

She smiled, and he smiled back.

'Well, actually my real first name is Horatio, but somehow ever since I was a kid I've been called Tom.'

She filled the large coffee-pot to the top and gestured to a seat. 'How many are you going to be?'

He sat down and the cane chair creaked ominously. 'By tonight we'll be five,' he answered.

The alarm showed on her face. 'Are you all going to be staying here?'

He laughed and shook his head.

'No, Laura, there'll only be me here. Another will be staying with your son Joey and his wife down the valley. The other three will be kind of roamin' around.'

'Roaming where?' she asked curiously.

He waved a hand airily at the window. 'Oh, out there, Laura. You know kinda just roamin' around, takin' in the scenery.'

She laughed and sat down across the kitchen-table from him. 'Tom, this is a small island. If you have three hard-looking strangers roamin' around, as you put it, then the locals are going to start to talk.'

He shook his head.

'No problem Ma'am ... Laura. We all have a good cover.'

'What's that?'

He smiled.

'We're all dedicated bird-watchers.'

She threw back her head and laughed at the ceiling and then said to him seriously, 'There aren't too many birds on Gozo any more, thanks to our dedicated hunters. They shoot anything that moves.'

He shrugged and said seriously, 'Like I said, we're dedicated. It just makes it more of a challenge.'

'What about at night?' she asked. 'Will you all be roamin' around at night?'

'Sure thing.'

'Looking for birds?'

His white grin came again. 'Looking for owls, Laura ... me and the boys are real keen on spottin' owls.'

She shook her head in amusement. The coffee was perking. She stood up and poured him a large mug and a smaller one for herself. 'Milk and sugar?' she asked.

'No thanks. I take it just as it comes ... as black as me.'

He took a sip and nodded in appreciation just as the phone rang. She picked it up and had a brief conversation with Joey. It ended by her saying, 'No, mine's an American ... as black as the coffee I just gave him.'

She laughed at Joey's answer, put the phone down and said, 'My son tells me a Chinese man just arrived on his doorstep.'

'Vietnamese,' Tom corrected. 'Do Huang ... we call him Dodo.'

'A Vietnamese bird-watcher?'

'Sure.'

274

'Where do the other three come from?'

'Two Brits and a South African ... Good men ... You and your family will be safe, Laura. We don't expect to be around too long. Just a matter of days. I'll try to be as unobtrusive as possible.'

She nodded thoughtfully and said. 'You'll stay in the guest wing, but of course take your meals with us, and, please, make yourself completely at home. I'll cook rabbit tomorrow. Tonight we're having roast baby lamb.' A thought struck her. 'By the way, what do I tell people? After all, we're not used to being visited by oversized black Americans.'

'I guess you just tell them that I'm a friend of Guido's ... Which happens to be true.'

'You know him well?'

'Very well.' Suddenly his face went serious. 'Ma'am ... Laura ... I also knew your daughter Julia. I visited with them a couple of times in Naples. She showed me a lot of kindness ... She was a very fine lady.'

There was a silence in the kitchen, and then Laura said, 'You are especially welcome, Tom Sawyer.'

SEVENTY-SEVEN

'Is he very mad at me?'

Jens took his eyes off the road for a second to glance at her. She was curled up on the seat beside him, her eyes radiating anxiety. The Owl sat in the back seat, the large earphones of his Discman clamped over his ears. Quite frequently he turned to look out the rear window. They would arrive in Naples in about twenty minutes.

'That's probably putting it mildly,' Jens said.

Defensively, she said, 'I don't see why . . . I only wanted to help. I mean, I can help with the cooking and cleaning and washing and everything at the *pensione* . . . I know how to do all those things.'

The Dane sighed and explained to her concisely, 'We're in the middle of a hazardous operation which is rapidly approaching a climax. Everybody involved is in danger. Some more than others. Everything had to be stopped in case they were on to you . . . and they were. The last time I saw you was in Marseille. You were lying on a bed in as bad a condition as I've ever seen any human being. If our team had been even five minutes late at the airport, you'd be heading back into that condition right now. Creasy had to send Frank and Maxie when they were already planning a very delicate operation. He had to pull Rene away from watching Michael's back at a time when Michael was extremely exposed. Me and The Owl had to leave our work at headquarters and rush north to take you over from the others . . . No doubt the people in Gozo who were looking after you have been worried sick and will still be worried sick until we get to the *pensione* and Creasy phones to tell them that you're safe. Yes, I guess Creasy is mad at you.'

She cried late into the night in a small room in the *pensione*. She did not cry because Creasy had shouted at her or been angry, because he had done neither. She cried because of the disappointment she had seen in his eyes when he had looked at her. She had immediately offered to go straight back to Gozo, but he had shaken his head and said, 'There's no way I can impose that responsibility back onto Laura and Paul. They've had enough tragedy in their lives.'

She had gone to her room refusing food, locked the door and thrown herself onto the bed, her heart close to breaking. Sleep eluded her, but after midnight she got up and started pacing the narrow room and formed a determination to be the first up in the morning and, come what may, to make herself useful.

SEVENTY-EIGHT

General Emilio Gandolfo was a hunter. The stalking of a bird or a stag or a wild boar was his greatest passion. He had hunted in Scotland, Rumania and Botswana; but he never changed his ritual of spending the last two weeks of September hunting for partridge in the hills with his close friend Julio Bareste, a right-wing lawyer with connections as impeccable as his own.

Every year on the fifteenth of September they would pack Gandolfo's Range Rover with a selection of food, wine, guns, and the most stylish hunting clothes available that season. They would kiss their wives goodbye and drive off to the isolated cabin in the mountains that they rented each year. Apart from the odd fellow-hunter they would see nobody. They would cook their own pasta, mix their own sauces and enjoy the supply of hams and cheeses and fine wines. They would rise at dawn and return at sunset. The evenings would be spent eating and drinking and fixing the world; which meant moving it sharply to the right. The rare interruptions came only via the mobile phone which Bareste brought with him and left at the cabin.

Colonel Satta was well aware of Gandolfo's annual habit. He discussed it at length with Maxie and Frank.

SEVENTY-NINE

Creasy had begun to feel akin to a general who sits in a command bunker while everyone in the field is preparing for battle. He had daily telephone reports from Rene or Michael. He spoke frequently to Laura in Gozo and to Tom Sawyer, and was quietly confident that no matter what 'The Blue Ring' was doing, the situation in Gozo was under control.

Juliet had surprised everybody by throwing herself into physical work at the *pensione*. She was up every morning at dawn, first cleaning the kitchen and then going on to the small dining room and, one by one, the guest rooms. She scrubbed the floors and washed the windows and polished the woodwork. At first the men had looked on with amusement, but as they had seen her determination they had viewed her with respect.

Slowly she had crept into their circle. They began to talk freely in front of her, discussing plans and dispositions. She watched and listened as Creasy used the phone to receive and give information, and to issue orders. To an outsider all would seem relaxed, but she could sense the tension building up, particularly in Guido and Pietro. She had mentioned this to Creasy when they were alone.

He had nodded and explained, 'Pietro has never been involved in such an operation. Not even on the edge. Guido on the other hand is very experienced, but has been retired for many years. He feels excitement rather than tension.'

The call from Satta came just before dinner. Creasy took it alone in his room.

Satta said, 'I decided not to resign.' He waited for Creasy's reaction but got nothing so he went on, 'To paraphrase Lyndon Johnson, I can be more effective inside the tent pissing out, than outside the tent pissing in ... After Gandolfo is out of the way I'll go after others of his type. I'm compiling a list in my mind.'

'It will be endless,' Creasy commented.

'Maybe, but chipping away at it will give me more satisfaction than sitting around looking at my feet.'

Creasy asked, 'How are you going to get the information out of Gandolfo without compromising yourself?'

The Italian explained about the General's hunting habits and the plan he had worked out with Maxie and Frank.

Creasy went through it in his mind, then asked, 'You're sure you can get those drugs?'

'Yes. I have the right contact, whom you know, and a cut-out between.'

'Is he sure they will work?'

'Yes, given Gandolfo's age and medical history.'

Creasy said, 'It sounds good, unless the General decides to return to Rome with his friend.'

'It's unlikely. If he does we have a back-up plan. We snatch them both on the road and then arrange a fatal accident later ... That's a dangerous road, especially at night.'

Creasy's mind was working through all the possibilities. He had much admiration for the subtleties of Satta's brain; and in Maxie and Frank he had total confidence. He asked, 'Who's going to toss that small bomb?'

'We had an argument about that,' Satta said. 'I was going to hire a small-time operator to do it, but Maxie and Frank objected. They considered it unwise to bring in anyone from outside.'

'They were right.'

'Yes, anyway. I suggested Rene but again was overruled. They said you wouldn't want the cover pulled off Michael at this late stage.'

'Again they're right,' Creasy said. 'Not because he's my son, but because he's now pivotal to the operation ... So who's going to do it?'

'I offered to do it, but the bastards just laughed ... So Frank's going to do it. He's going to use a small frag. grenade. It will cause quite a bang but do little damage.'

Creasy chuckled. 'OK. I guess Frank has a mite more experience than you. But how does it affect the time-scale?'

'No problem. Maxie and I will drive up to the mountains in the late afternoon. It takes about two hours. We'll keep the cabin under surveillance. Frank will toss his grenade at eight o'clock and drive on to us. I'll have a mobile phone, so will he. If Gandolfo decides to return to Rome with Bareste, then Maxie will set up a road-block at a predetermined spot. He will be wearing the uniform of a *carabinieri* captain. We'll be following the Range Rover down. Don't worry, Creasy. Maxie and Frank have it all worked out ... they seem to be enjoying themselves.'

'I'll bet they are,' Creasy said with a trace of frustration. 'It beats sitting here looking at a phone ... OK, Mario, keep in touch. Good luck.'

EIGHTY

Julio Bareste thought that his friend looked ridiculous wearing the deerstalker hat, but he did not say so. General Gandolfo was extremely sensitive about his taste in most things in life, and his choice of clothes, in particular. Both men wore tweeds, the plus-four trousers being tucked into calf-length tartan socks.

They felt themselves socially a cut above the hundreds of thousands of other Italian hunters, and this was reflected in their guns. Gandolfo carried a double-barrelled Holland and Holland twelve-bore shotgun, which had been a twenty-first birthday present from his father. For many years he had bragged about its increasing rarity and value, until ten years ago on a visit to London, Bareste had slipped into the discreet showroom of Purdey, the gunsmith's, and paid a massive deposit on their finest model. He had had to wait five years for it and would proudly tell anyone who would listen that he had to travel to London for two 'fittings' while it was being made.

The day had provided poor sport and they headed back to the cabin in the twilight. They only had four partridge in their leather shoulder-bags. But no matter. It was their first full day and the weather report for the next day was good. They had tossed a coin to decide who would prepare dinner, and Gandolfo had lost, which pleased him, because he prided himself on his cooking.

They reached the cabin just before darkness. It was small but comfortable: two bedrooms, a well-equipped kitchen, a compact dining room/lounge with a large, stone, open fireplace, and a spacious south-facing patio.

They changed out of their hunting clothes, took hot showers and put on warm, designer tracksuits. Gandolfo lit the fire while Bareste mixed negronis. There was no electricity in the cabin. Lighting, heating, the stove and fridge all ran on bottled gas. Bareste settled down in front of the crackling fire while Gandolfo bustled around in the kitchen.

The General had just placed a pot of pasta on the table when the mobile phone rang on the mantelpiece.

With a muttered curse, Bareste picked it up, pressed a button and barked, '*Pronto!*' His expression changed from irritation to alarm as he listened.

Gandolfo hurried to his side asking, 'What is it, Julio?'

Bareste held up a hand and asked into the phone, 'Are you all right? Yes ... Good ... Of course I have no idea ... Calm yourself ... Wait a moment.'

He turned to Gandolfo. 'About fifteen minutes ago a bomb was thrown at the front of my house.'

'God! Was anybody hurt?'

'No, only Carla was at home. Apparently, the front door was damaged, and a window blown in. Carla ran immediately to our son's house nearby. She is there now with our daughter-in-law, and the children. Paolo of course phoned the police and went straight to the house.'

The General assumed command. He took the phone and told Carla to phone back as soon as Paolo returned. Then he called *carabinieri* headquarters and issued a series of instructions. He then took Bareste by the arm and led him to the dining-table, saying, 'Of course we have to return, but eat first. The best people are now on the job. The Colonel who heads our bomb squad is handling it personally. He will call us from the site. Fortunately, no one is hurt.'

Bareste allowed himself to be seated. Gandolfo piled the pasta onto the plates and poured the wine. 'Any idea who might be behind it?' he asked.

Bareste shook his head.

'You know how it is with men like us – we make enemies. It's inevitable.'

'Anyway,' Gandolfo said firmly, 'whoever's behind it is going to be very sorry. Obviously they are unaware of our friendship. They will suffer for their ignorance.'

The two men ate in silence until the phone rang again. It was Bareste's son calling from the house. He told his father that it had been a small bomb or grenade. Very little damage. The place was swarming with police and *carabinieri*. There was a colonel next to him who wanted to speak to General Gandolfo.

Bareste handed over the phone and went back to his pasta while the General first listened, then asked questions, and then gave further orders. Bareste found himself feeling slightly sorry for the colonel. It was, after all, a fairly minor incident in a country where bombing and shooting were commonplace.

He said as much after he had spoken to his son again and told him he would be back in Rome within three hours. Gandolfo waved a fork dismissively.

'Of course it's getting special attention. That's what friends are for.' He glanced at his watch. 'We'll be on the road in half an hour.'

Bareste held up a hand. 'Now, listen. I'll go alone. There's no need for you to break your holiday ... God knows, you take so little time off! This is a small matter and you've done enough. Of course I have to go back ... Carla would get mad if I didn't. But I don't have to go for long ... one or two days at the most.' He gestured at the mobile phone. 'I'll leave that with you so you can keep in touch, but I refuse to let you spoil your holiday.'

Gandolfo pretended to insist for a couple of minutes, but his friend was firm.

'Anyway,' Bareste said, 'Carla was planning to visit her sister in Florence in a couple of days, so it's no problem. I'll be back on Wednesday at the latest ... Just leave a little sport for me.'

So it was agreed. Half an hour later they embraced beside the Range Rover and Bareste climbed in and drove off into the darkness. Gandolfo went back inside, washed the plates and pots and stacked them neatly. He decided to have Cognac beside the fire, but had only taken a couple of sips when he started yawning. The unaccustomed exercise and the mountain air had made him sleepy. He took the mobile phone from the mantelpiece, put it on the bedside table, changed into his silk pyjamas, and three minutes later was snoring contentedly.

EIGHTY-ONE

Michael rang just after ten o'clock.

At the Pensione Splendide they had finished dinner and were sitting at the small bar, drinking *espressi* and Stregas. Juliet had just gone to bed. Creasy took the call. It was brief. The black mass would take place on the coming Sunday night. Michael had no idea of the location, except it would be within an hour's drive of Rome. She was to pick him up. He would be alone and would be body-searched for any weapons or transmitters. He had agreed to give the woman half the money before and half the next day.

Creasy told him that they were formulating plans with several options, but they were still waiting to find out what Satta could get out of Gandolfo during the next few hours. He would call Michael in the morning.

Creasy hung up and said, 'It's vital we get some clue as to the venue. Otherwise we will have to follow Michael and the woman. They will be very cautious and so it will be difficult.'

Jens was sitting beside him. The Owl was at the table with his earphones on; he was not much interested in strategy. Guido was on the other side of the bar, polishing a glass.

He said, 'I wouldn't like to go into that situation without a gun or at least somebody good watching my back.'

Creasy shrugged and said, 'You wouldn't like it ... But you'd do it. I've seen you do enough crazy things in the past to get you certified.'

Guido smiled, winked at Jens, and said, 'Sure, we should have ended up in the funny house ... both of us.'

The Dane said seriously, 'I think you did. It's called the Pensione Splendide. What troubles me ... I'm also an inmate.' He smiled and gestured for another drink.

285

Half an hour and two Stregas later the phone rang again. It was Satta. He knew better than to talk details on a mobile phone, he simply said, 'So far so good. His friend left. Lights are out. The boys are going in now. I'll phone you when it's over and we're on the road.'

Creasy said, 'Location is everything. We have to have at least an idea of where it's going to happen ... It's going to be Sunday night.'

'Understood,' Satta responded.

Creasy heard a click and the connection was broken. He hung up, took a sip of his drink, glanced at his watch and said, 'Maxie and Frank are going in now. The other guy returned home as planned. Satta will phone back when he has something. Could be an hour or so.'

Guido reached behind him for the bottle of Strega.

EIGHTY-TWO

The General was a light sleeper but he heard nothing. The first thing to assail his senses was light; it penetrated his eyelids. He opened his eyes but they were blind in the light. He turned his head, his brain in confusion; coming out of sleep and not knowing where he was.

The light moved and he realised that it was the beam of a torch. He watched it flicker around the room; saw it light up the wooden walls. Abruptly he knew where he was. He was lying in bed in the cabin in the hills, and somebody was in the room. He pushed himself up in bed, his mind clearing. He remembered Bareste leaving. Maybe he had returned.

Hesitantly he called out, 'Julio ... is it you?'

The beam of light flickered back into his eyes and he had to close them again.

A voice said, 'No, it is not Julio. Be very still. I have a gun pointed at your head.'

Gandolfo turned his head away. He began gasping in air as fear gripped him.

'Who are you?' he gasped.

'Be still and be quiet,' came the sharp reply.

Gandolfo's mind began to work. Thieves. It was not unknown in these hills. There had been two robberies further south the year before.

'I am a General in the *carabinieri*,' he said angrily. 'You will not get away with this.'

'Be still,' the man repeated. He was speaking Italian with a very strange accent.

Gandolfo was trying to identify it when he sensed another man entering the room. There was more light but softer. The brightness left his eyes and he opened them. He saw two men, both dressed all in black. They were middle-aged. One was bald with a round face. He was holding a black, silenced pistol in one hand and a slim torch in the other. The pistol was pointed at Gandolfo's face. The other man was short and square with cropped black hair. Like his body, his face was square. In one hand he carried a gas lamp which Gandolfo recognised from the kitchen. In the other hand he held a canvas bag.

From their posture and the look on their faces, Gandolfo's instincts and experience told him that these two men were professionals. Strangely, this made him feel better.

'I have very little money up here,' he stated. 'And nothing else of value.'

At that moment he thought of his Holland and Holland shotgun which was worth a fortune. Then he realised that it was leaning against the wall, about a metre from his left hand. Instinctively he turned his head to look at it.

'Forget it,' the bald man said; then in English to the other man, he said cryptically, 'Let's get on with it.'

Startled at hearing the language, Gandolfo blurted out, 'Who the hell are you? What do you want?'

The square man moved closer to the bed. He put the lamp on the bedside table and the canvas bag on the floor. The bald man moved around the other side of the bed. The pistol was close, the fat silencer half a metre from the General's eyes, pointing exactly between them. Gandolfo squeezed backwards against the headboard, his fear increasing.

'We are just here to do a job,' the bald man said casually. 'Co-operate and you'll be all right ... otherwise you die. We don't care one way or the other.' He spoke as though he had arrived to fix the plumbing.

Gandolfo started to speak, but suddenly the pistol was only milli-metres from his forehead. He noticed that the hand holding it was steady and was clad in a black glove.

The voice hardened. 'Keep your mouth shut and do exactly as you're told.'

The General closed his mouth and swallowed hard. The pistol was withdrawn to about a metre.

The square man unzipped the bag and took out a plastic bag of cotton wool and a large roll of black masking tape. 'Put your wrists together,' he said in English.

Gandolfo hesitated and suddenly the pistol had moved forward again. Slowly the General brought his hands together. They were trembling slightly. The square man sat on the edge of the bed. He pulled a wad of cotton wool from the bag, reached forward and squeezed it between Gandolfo's wrists. The General watched in rigid fascination. Then the man took the roll of masking tape, pulled out a long length and wrapped it several times around the General's wrists. His arms and hands were now immobilised. The bald man stepped back, unscrewed the silencer and dropped it into a pocket of his black leather jacket. The pistol was slipped into a holster under his left shoulder. The square man pulled the sheet and blankets back, revealing the General's silk-clad body. From the canvas bag he pulled out several rolls of thick foam rubber. He worked quickly. First, he pulled Gandolfo's legs apart and wrapped several layers of foam rubber around the left one, from the thigh to the toes. He taped it firmly and then repeated the process with the right leg and then taped both legs together. He then did the same with both the General's arms from the wrists to the armpits. Gandolfo's fear was now tinged with a query. He started to ask a question but looked into the dark, cold eyes in the square face and shut his mouth.

Next, the man took a smaller strip of foam rubber, pulled the General's head forward and slipped it behind his neck. He taped the ends tight across the forehead just above the eyes. Finally, he connected the tape from the wrists to the tape around the ankles. The General was now totally immobilised.

The man stood back, surveyed his work and said to his companion, 'He looks like the Michelin man.'

The bald man nodded. 'Yeah ... all trussed up and ready for the oven.'

They walked out through the open door. Gandolfo heard the bald man's voice call, 'He's all yours. Shout if you need anything.'

Ten seconds passed in which Gandolfo tried to concentrate and calm himself. He had partially succeeded when a third man came through the door. He was also dressed in black, including his gloves. At first, in the dim light, Gandolfo did not recognise him, but as he pulled up a chair the face came into focus.

Gandolfo gasped and spoke his name, 'Satta! God, Satta ... What's happening?'

For a long time Satta looked into the man's eyes, then he leaned forward. His voice was very low, carried on the wind of hatred.

'You saw the pathologist's report on Bellu's body. You know exactly what inhuman things they did to him before they killed him ... It's probable that the same pathologist will examine your body. An autopsy is standard in the death of such a senior officer of the *carabinieri* ... But they will find no signs of torture ... not even the slightest bruise.' He gestured at the padding around Gandolfo's arms and legs and neck. 'No matter how much you struggle or resist, no pathologist will ever find a bruise on you.'

From his pocket Satta took a small plastic box. He opened it and showed the contents to the General: a small syringe, held in place by a thick elastic band. Next to it was a clear, plastic phial holding white pills. Satta explained. 'The pills are Amiodarone. Each of one thousand ccs. Taken orally, one will cause a massive and fatal heart attack. The drug in the syringe is Digoxin. It has the same effect but must be injected. Both drugs are untraceable. Anyway, there will be no suspicion. You had a mild heart attack six years ago and a bigger one three years later. You took eight months sick leave. You were advised to take early retirement but refused ... no doubt under pressure from your friends. Anyway, this time you will not have to make that choice. Obviously I prefer that you accept the pill, because a very skilled and diligent pathologist might just have a chance of detecting the puncture mark of a needle, even though it would be in an unlikely place.'

Gandolfo closed his eyes. His breathing rate increased. He heard Satta's voice again.

'You know how close Bellu was to me. You are cunning but you are stupid. Do you really think that what you did would go unanswered?'

Gandolfo opened his eyes and said, as though in pain, 'I had nothing to do with it.'

Satta's voice cracked back at him. 'You had everything to do with it! You fingered him, knowing what they would do ... your friends in "The Blue Ring" – Donati and Hussein and no doubt others. You have lived in evil, Gandolfo, and you will die this night. You will not be alone. Your friends will soon be joining you.'

The General was looking at the ceiling. Suddenly he turned his head, looked into Satta's eyes, and said, 'I had no choice ... even from the beginning. Their hold was like a vice. I had to think of my family ... let me go and I will help you.'

Satta leaned forward and spat in his face. 'You are living the last minutes of your life.'

He stood up and paced back and forth at the foot of the bed. In a cold, hard voice he explained Gandolfo's alternatives. He used the

Mafia code as a parallel. If a *mafioso* was discovered to be a turncoat he was given the choice of committing suicide or being killed. If he committed suicide his family were spared. If he resisted, his entire family faced death. In his early anti-Mafia years Satta had been surprised that so many jailed *mafiosi* cut their wrists. He had later learned that some had done so because they did not want those outside to even suspect that they might break the code of *Omertà*. He knew that Gandolfo understood that code; but he painted it in the clearest colours. Satta started pacing faster in his anger, up and down at the foot of the bed. Then he turned to look at the trussed-up General.

'Your wife died ten years ago and you hardly mourned her. In life you treated her like shit; and in death you hardly noticed her passing, so busy were you with your whores and mistresses. But she bore you three sons and a daughter. They all married and gifted you with nine grandchildren and a tenth due to your daughter next month.' He gestured towards the open door. 'Those men who trussed you up ... they are two of many, and they are pussy-cats compared to some of the others. Like me, their leader looked on Bellu as a blood relative ... Your children and grandchildren will not know they are coming ... they will visit your children and grandchildren like the plague.'

He stopped pacing and stood at the foot of the bed, looking down at the absurdly inflated man. Gandolfo was looking at the ceiling. Time passed and then he asked hoarsely, 'What don't you know?'

From his jacket pocket Satta took out a small notebook and a ballpoint pen. He sat down saying, 'From the beginning ... Your beginning. And to the end ... Beyond your end. First I want to know where the black mass will take place next Sunday.'

What could be seen of Gandolfo's face was the colour of unpolished ivory. Satta watched his lips form into a mirthless smile. His voice sounded already close to death.

'I will tell – and you will not believe me – but when I tell you everything ... then you will believe.'

EIGHTY-THREE

In Naples they played poker, but only for matchsticks. When Guido had won enough to supply every arsonist in Italy he quit in disgust and moved to the coffee machine; they had long ago given up drinking Strega.

Jens looked at Creasy with a pained expression. 'I thought that a winner at poker was not allowed to quit.'

Creasy smiled.

'True. Guido is very discourteous.'

Creasy's mind had not been on the game. It was far away in a cabin in the hills.

In Gozo, Tom Sawyer sat on the roof of the farmhouse, gazing across the Comino channel. He could see the lights of the fishing boats moving out through the darkness on their way to catch squid. He cleaned his submachine-gun and wondered how long this job would last. He hoped it would stretch out many days. He liked the people he was guarding; he liked the food and he liked the balmy air. Occasionally an owl would hoot softly from the distant darkness. Tom would smile. His guys were awake and doing their job.

In Rome, Michael and Rene played gin rummy, for money. Rene was well ahead. He laid down a full gin, grinned and said, 'Just as well you have all that money in the bank.'

Michael sighed and answered, 'I quit.' He looked at his watch, and then at the phone. His mind was also far away.

Satta came out of the bedroom holding his notebook. Frank was sitting at the table reading a hunting magazine. He looked up and then slowly rose.

'Are you all right?' he asked.

Satta's face was pale and drawn. He lifted the notebook and said harshly, 'As all right as anyone who has been immersed and almost suffocated in excrement.' He drew a breath and then exhaled slowly. He pointed with his thumb over his shoulder towards the open bedroom door and his voice filled with sarcasm. 'The good and honourable General has decided to take the pill.'

'Excellent!' Frank said heartily, as though hearing that a child had agreed to eat its spinach. 'Let's do it.'

Satta sat down at the table, tossed his notebook onto it and asked apologetically, 'Frank, do you mind doing it? I don't really understand ... putting that pill into his mouth should be one of the great moments of my life ... but ... I don't want to go back in there.'

The Australian nodded sombrely. He knew that sometimes words and revelations could carry as much impact as a high-velocity bullet.

'Sure,' he said. 'I'll call Maxie. Do you want me to make you a coffee first?'

Satta shook his head.

'No ... Thanks, Frank.' His eyes rested on a small table next to the fireplace. It held a selection of bottles. He stood up, went over and picked up a bottle of Cognac. Frank watched as he uncorked it, put it to his lips and held it there, letting the amber liquid pour down his throat. Then he choked and coughed, recorked the bottle, put it back on the table, turned and said, 'I just want to get the hell out of here.'

'No problem,' Frank said briskly. 'I'll call Maxie. You go and take a stroll. Get some fresh air and keep watch.'

He walked to the front door, opened it and whistled softly. An answering whistle came out of the darkness. Maxie loomed up. Quietly Frank explained the situation.

Maxie nodded, went up to the Italian, punched him lightly on the shoulder and said, 'Well done, Mario. We'll do the rest. Get some fresh air.'

Satta nodded numbly, and then suddenly embraced the man.

Maxie smiled at Frank over Satta's shoulder and then said with a light laugh, 'These Italians get real emotional.'

'Yeah ... It comes with their mother's milk.' The Australian answered.

Satta broke away with a curse at them both.

'Vaffanculo!' But it was said affectionately. He picked up his notebook and went out into the night.

The two men looked at each other. Maxie said, 'That's a tough guy who's seen a lot. Whatever happened in there really shook him up.'

'Yeah,' Frank agreed and looked towards the bedroom door. With a cynical smile he asked, 'Did you ever kill a general?'

The Rhodesian shook his head. 'No, I only got as high as a half-colonel ... Did you?'

Wistfully Frank answered, 'No, although one or two had me seriously tempted. Let's do it.'

Frank fetched a glass of water from the kitchen and then went through to the bedroom.

He watched them coming. He looked into their eyes and saw no mercy. He saw their eyes looking back at a dead man.

They eased him up to a sitting position. The box with the pills and the syringe was open on the bedside table next to the mobile phone. Maxie passed two pills over the bed to Frank and then held up the glass of water expectantly. Gandolfo's eyes were gazing into the distance.

Frank put his hand on the foam rubber behind Gandolfo's neck, gripped firmly and said lightly, 'Open wide. I'll put it far back on your tongue. Then my friend will put the glass to your lips and tilt it ... Take a good swallow.'

Gandolfo stared ahead. His mouth closed in a thin line. Frank's voice lost its lightness.

'Suit yourself. I'll just have to give you the needle. Then my friend and I head down to Rome and start looking for your bambinos. That suits us ... Extra money ... Good money.'

Gandolfo's eyes shifted and turned onto Frank's face. Seconds passed and then his mouth began to open. Then it shut. Then opened again. In a grating whisper, Gandolfo asked, 'Will it take long?'

'It's very quick,' Frank said.

'You won't feel a thing,' Maxie lied.

Slowly the mouth opened wider. The eyes closed.

'Wider,' Frank urged, leaning forward.

The mouth opened very wide.

Holding the pill between two fingers, Frank slipped it between the lips. His fingers came out and Maxie's hand came up with the glass. Gandolfo gulped twice, some of the water dribbling down his chin. Frank watched his Adam's apple move up and down twice. He gripped the neck harder and with his right hand squeezed the cheeks to open the mouth. He peered into it and nodded at Maxie. He eased the head onto the pillow and they both stepped back. Gandolfo lay there with his eyes closed. Maxie glanced at his watch.

The first spasm came after just ninety seconds. Gandolfo grunted in agony. Spasm followed spasm and he started to thrash about on the bed. His mouth opened and vomit spewed out. The two men watched silently, no strangers to death. Finally the body lay still. They both moved forward. Maxie pulled back the cotton wool and felt for the pulse at the wrist. Frank felt for it at the neck. After half a minute they looked up at each other and shook their heads.

Maxie said, '*Kufa*.' A Swahili word much used by mercenaries of the African era. It means 'dead' in a very positive way.

They cleaned up quickly, stripping the body of the foam rubber. The silk pajama jacket was stained with vomit. Frank rearranged the General's left arm on top of the bedside table as though he had been trying to reach for the mobile phone. Maxie packed the foam rubber, tape and box into the canvas bag, while in the kitchen Frank washed the glass, dried it and replaced it in the cupboard. He put the hunting magazine back on the rack.

Two hundred metres away Satta saw the lights of the cabin go out. He was holding a mobile phone. He punched in the numbers. A few seconds later he heard Creasy's voice.

'*Pronto?*'

'It's done,' Satta said. 'Perfectly to plan ... We have all we need. We'll be with you in a couple of hours ... *Ciao*.'

'*Ciao*.'

EIGHTY-FOUR

The ship from Albania docked in Bari just after midnight. It had been a rough crossing and both Katrin and Sister Simona had been seasick. So the approaching lights of the port and its shelter had assumed an added dimension of welcome.

They passed through immigration and customs with an ease that surprised Sister Simona, who was well acquainted with Italian bureaucracy. Even though their papers were completely in order, she had expected long delays because of Katrin's status as a foreign orphan. But as they took their places in the long queue a young immigration officer had passed down the line. He spotted Sister Simona in her white habit, introduced himself, took her large suitcase and Katrin's small bag and their papers, and ushered them smoothly through the maze of officialdom. Within minutes he was showing them into a room reserved for special immigrants. Katrin clutched the small posy of wild flowers she had picked that afternoon in the grounds of the orphanage. Like herself, they were much wilted from the journey.

There were three people waiting in the room: Franco Delors and a well-dressed, middle-aged couple. Delors came forward, his face beaming, and introduced himself. Sister Simona had been told he would be meeting them. He introduced the couple as *Signor* and *Signora* Maccetti: Katrin's new foster parents.

At first, the atmosphere in the room was naturally tense. Katrin spoke very little Italian, but as she looked at the couple, who were smiling at her nervously, she realised who they were. Shyly she walked towards them and held out the bedraggled flowers to the woman.

Signora Maccetti was a tall, stout woman. She beamed down at the child, stooped down and embraced her, crushing the flowers between them. Her husband was smiling and nodding his head.

Delors turned to Sister Simona with a broad smile and said, 'There has been a slight change of plan. They were supposed to pick her up from your Augustine convent here in Bari tomorrow.' He shrugged. 'But of course they were so impatient to see her . . . In fact, they would like to fly with her to Rome on the early flight and get her settled in as soon as possible.'

Sister Simona's face showed uncertainty. She watched as *Signor* Maccetti embraced Katrin, while his wife watched with a maternal smile.

Reassuringly, Delors said, 'I spoke to the Mother Superior here this afternoon. She said she would leave the decision to you.'

'I will talk to Katrin,' Sister Simona said. 'She is a sensible girl and will make her own choice.'

From a large handbag *Signora* Maccetti had taken a gift-wrapped parcel. She looked across at Sister Simona and said, 'Would you please tell Katrin that this is a small gift to welcome her to her new home.'

Sister Simona translated that into Albanian. Katrin looked at the parcel, smiled and held out her hand. She held the parcel and turned to look at the nun. Sister Simona smiled and nodded. Inside was a beautiful pink cashmere sweater with intricate multicoloured silk embroidery.

The child held its softness and exclaimed in delight, then threw her arms around the woman.

'I think it will be all right,' the nun said to Delors.

Sister Simona explained the change of plan to Katrin, who had immediately changed her grey, second-hand, donated sweater for the new one. She held her foster mother's hand as she listened. She smiled and nodded in agreement.

The nun hugged her and then said to the Maccettis, 'I'm taking ten days' holiday before returning to Albania. I'll be visiting my parents who live near Rome next week . . . I would like to pass by and see how she is settling in.'

'That would be wonderful,' *Signora* Maccetti said, 'but we had planned to leave on Sunday for Florida, to visit my brother who lives there. He has children of Katrin's age.'

Again, Delors noticed the uncertainty on the nun's face.

'It's a bit sudden,' she said. 'After all Katrin hardly speaks Italian, let alone English.'

Signora Maccetti laughed lightly.

'We have thought of that. My brother has engaged a maid of

Albanian descent who will live in. There will be no problem with the language ... We thought that the excitement of travel and the Florida sunshine would be good for her.' She patted the child's pale face. 'She needs sunshine and the sea, and children of her own age.'

The nun was mollified.

'When will you be back?' she asked.

'In a few weeks,' *Signor* Maccetti answered. 'Of course we will keep in close touch with *Signor* Delors. When you are next in Italy you must visit Katrin ... and be our guest.'

'You will be so welcome,' his wife added warmly.

And so Sister Simona stood beside the chauffeur-driven Mercedes and gave her charge a last hug, and watched her being driven away to a new life.

Delors gave the nun a lift to the convent. On the way he said cheerfully, 'Sister Assunta will be pleased that this first one went so well.'

'You know Sister Assunta?'

'Only by correspondence. I know of the wonderful work she is doing ... All of you, of course.'

'She is an angel,' the nun murmured, and then said absently, 'She left for Malta today.'

Delors glanced at her. 'She did?'

'Yes ... she has been working so hard. She needed a break. You know how it is.'

'Indeed, I do,' he agreed fervently. 'When will she get back?'

'She said a few days.'

Warmly, he said, 'Give her my respects when you see her.'

She turned and smiled at him. 'I will.'

EIGHTY-FIVE

The bays reflected the faith of the people, as much as the limpid blue of the Mediterranean Sea reflected the sun: St Julian's, St Thomas's, St George's and St Paul's, where the Apostle had been shipwrecked and then welcomed by the heathen Maltese; and in return for that welcome had brought the message of Christianity.

Sister Assunta sat on the north patio of the convent and looked out over the waters of St Paul's Bay. The water was not tranquil. High-powered speedboats, cruisers and sailing yachts criss-crossed the sea. The turbulence of the water reflected her own mental state. She had been subjected to an inquisition. The Mother Superior was of a character, chilled by experience, practicality and, therefore, cynicism. Sister Assunta's story of remembering a face through the window of a car twenty years ago had brought a raised eyebrow and a questioning tongue. The nun had stuck to her flimsy guns; insisted on her memory, until her Superior had nodded in dismissal.

A life given to devotion moves along a stony track, but occasionally it illuminates rare moments. Sister Assunta had one of these moments when she heard a quiet cough behind her and turned her head.

She recognised the priest. It was Father Manuel Zerafa, the priest who ran the orphanage in Gozo.

He pulled up a chair and sat silently next to her, looking out over the bay. Then, very diffidently, he said, 'Sister. Please tell me what you remember about that face in the car.'

Sister Assunta drew a breath as her heart was lifted. The Mother Superior had believed her.

EIGHTY-SIX

'There is a man. At this moment I assume he is contentedly asleep in a luxury villa in the hills of Tuscany. His name is Benito Massaro.' With that name, Colonel Mario Satta had the complete attention of his gathered friends.

It was dawn in Naples. They sat in the small dining room of the Pensione Splendide. A wet west wind splattered rain against the windows.

On the journey to Naples Satta had, at first, decided to give his information only to Creasy; but as they drove through the wetness he had glanced at Maxie at the wheel, and felt the presence of Frank behind him in the back seat. His thoughts had moved on to all the others who were taking part in what had become, for him, a personal nightmare. He had decided to take them all into his confidence.

Now they sat around the long table while Juliet dispensed coffee and brioches. They were all tired. Either from waiting, or from the tension of activity. It had only been necessary for them to look at the set seriousness of Satta's face to realise that what he was about to say would be profound. The name Benito Massaro confirmed it. For those who might not be fully conversant with the name, he elaborated.

'Benito Massaro was the real power behind the Masonic Lodge P2. Forget the other names which the newspapers dwell on; Benito Massaro is a general. Ten years ago he headed the committee which controlled and oversaw all of the security services of our country. He managed to draw into his Lodge an astonishing number of the most powerful people of Italy. He dispensed patronage on an immense scale. When P2 was discovered, his minions took the blame. He remained aloof.'

Satta surveyed the faces around the table and then came back to linger on the face of Creasy. He said quietly, 'I learned last night

300

from General Emilio Gandolfo something which caused me grief, humiliation, embarrassment and pain. As a man who has dedicated many years of his life attempting to find crime in my country, it will not be difficult to understand the shock I felt when I learned that Benito Massaro has not only retained his power in my sick country, but has continued to build on it.' He looked up again at Creasy and slowly at the others. His voice took on a shred of emotion. 'This may sound dramatic ... it is certainly ironic that the instruments to smash that power are sitting with me in this room. It is also ironic that only two of you, Guido and young Pietro, are Italian.'

No audience had ever been more rapt.

'There had been rumours,' Satta continued, 'that during the investigation of the Lodge P2, a list of over fifteen hundred names had been mysteriously lost. Those that had not been lost were frightening enough. The known names included nine hundred and sixty-two leading Italian figures. Among them four cabinet ministers, no less than thirty-eight parliamentary deputies and one hundred and ninety senior military and intelligence officers. Included were Michele Sindona, a leading banker connected to the Mafia, who was later mysteriously poisoned in prison. Roberto Calvi, head of the Banco Ambrosiano, known as God's Banker because he advised and was deeply involved with the Vatican bank. He was found hanging by the neck under Blackfriars Bridge in London in 1982 after his bank had somehow lost one and a half billion dollars.' Colonel Mario Satta sighed and said, 'What I discovered last night was that Benito Massaro has been able to form a new Lodge, which we may as well call P3 ... It threatens the very fabric of my country.'

The men around the table glanced at each other and Creasy asked the question in all of their minds. 'Mario. We understand about Benito Massaro. What does he have to do with us?'

Satta's abrupt laugh was chilling. He pointed at Creasy.

'What you and your son stumbled into represents a very slim chance for me to finally break and destroy Benito Massaro and his threat to my screwed-up country.'

EIGHTY-SEVEN

The rain had stopped and a watery sun lit up the sky. The others had returned to bed, but Guido and Creasy walked out onto the terrace, perhaps in an effort to clear their minds.

Guido said, 'If I had not known Satta these past six years and had come to appreciate his brain and integrity, I would have thought he was a lunatic.'

Creasy smiled.

'We have both lived long enough, and seen enough to know that he was telling the truth. Not just about Gandolfo or the rest of them, but also about his thesis that even as a senior officer in the *carabinieri* he's powerless to do anything about what he's learned.'

Guido grunted in exasperation.

'It's true,' he said. 'Who the hell can he trust? He has learned of four other generals senior to him in the *carabinieri* who are part of P3. He has learned that two cabinet ministers, not on the original P2 list, are members of P3 ...' He smiled wryly. 'He has also learned of a cardinal, two archbishops and five top judges. So who would he report to? How could he start an investigation? Without doubt Gandolfo told him the truth. A man who knows for certain that he is about to die, always tells the truth ... But such things are compartmentalised. Gandolfo knew only a part ... perhaps a small part.'

'That has to be true,' Creasy agreed. 'Let's examine the information in the light of our own operation and in the light of exactly what Gandolfo told Satta. First of all, Gandolfo had been blackmailed these past three decades by "The Blue Ring". Blackmailed on youthful, sexual and financial sins. He also knew that many powerful men had similarly been blackmailed. He made the connection between Massaro and "The Blue Ring", although Massaro perhaps used "The

Blue Ring" more than they used him. Gandolfo was certain that within "The Blue Ring" they have somewhere the missing list of P2 members – that alone would be worth millions.' He turned to look at Guido, gave him a tired smile and said, 'But let's simplify all this. Thank God, Satta has his own connections, both through his work and, strangely, through his mother. He cannot act unless presented with a *fait accompli*. Our smashing of "The Blue Ring" on Sunday night at their black mass will give him that *fait accompli*. His plan is good. He will have a team of junior *carabinieri* officers nearby; ostensibly about to raid the home of a suspected, corrupt industrialist. When we start the war against "The Blue Ring" on Sunday night, he will be the nearest senior law officer. He will be alerted. He will be the first on the scene with his team. We will be gone. He has the names of at least two honest judges who will have been vaguely pre-warned. They will be on the scene shortly afterwards. Nobody, not even the Prime Minister or the head of intelligence or the head of anything else will be able to stop Satta and those judges.'

Guido shook his head and laughed.

'What a country!' he said. 'I can hear a whirring sound . . . It must be Garibaldi spinning in his grave.'

Creasy also laughed.

'The biggest shock Garibaldi would have had was to learn that the De Muros were part of that whole sick scene. Didn't that aristocratic family help finance him in his crusade to unite Italy?'

'They did,' Guido agreed. 'And for the past hundred years they have been a pillar of Italian society. Now we learn that their progeny are under the influence of Massaro and, what's worse, "The Blue Ring". When Satta told us that the black mass on Sunday would take place in the De Muros' private chapel, presided over by a genuine Catholic bishop, I worried not for Satta's sanity, but for my own. Then I remembered that the De Muros are an offshoot of the Medici family . . . They had their own Pope some centuries ago and of course they poisoned opponents to pass the time.'

'It has to be true,' Creasy said grimly.

'It has to be,' Guido agreed. 'No one . . . not even a doomed general, could invent that.'

'We know the location,' Creasy said. 'We know the time. We know who will be there. What we do not know yet is whether Satta can convince his mother to plant that weapon for Michael in the De Muros' palazzo.'

EIGHTY-EIGHT

Tom Sawyer stretched his cramped limbs and watched the sun rise away to his left; it bathed the Comino channel red. He heard the hoot of an owl. He pulled up the binoculars and focused them on a clump of carob trees behind him and to the right.

He saw no owl, just the dark figure of a crouching man moving away from the trees. A few seconds later another dark figure replaced the first. Sawyer glanced at his watch in satisfaction. His men, as usual, were awake and on time. For him it was time to sleep. He stood up on the flat roof of the farmhouse, the binoculars dangling from his neck. Laura would be getting up ready to prepare breakfast.

As he came down the stone outer stairs, a battered old Ford clattered down the dusty track. It pulled up in the courtyard and a plump priest emerged.

He greeted Sawyer and asked, 'Has the bird-watcher spotted anything?'

Sawyer smiled and nodded.

'A couple of early kestrels looking for worms ... or maybe mice.'

The priest smiled knowingly and asked, 'Is Laura about?'

'She will be,' Sawyer answered. 'This house rises with the sun.'

Laura was up and in the kitchen. She greeted the priest warmly and introduced him to Sawyer as Father Manuel Zerafa. The priest's face had turned grim. He took Laura by the arm and led her away, talking urgently to her in Maltese. Sawyer heard the word *Uomo* mentioned. He helped himself to a mug of coffee.

Creasy took the call a few minutes later. Laura simply told him that Father Zefara had to talk to him urgently.

Creasy listened to Father Zerafa, interrupting only to ask, 'Is she sure?'

304

Five minutes later, Creasy was back on the terrace of the Pensione Splendide talking to Guido. His words dripped like acid in their anger.

'I know now who is the head of "The Blue Ring". He is an Arab. It seems that he is more than likely Michael's natural father.'

EIGHTY-NINE

In his entire life Colonel Mario Satta had never really confronted his mother. She was a lady who combined position, wealth, intelligence and pride, making a formidable character.

For the confrontation, he had summoned his elder brother, Professor Giovanni Satta, from his surgical duties at the Cardarelli Hospital in Naples to back him up at the family villa in Rome. It had taken an hour to brief Giovanni; but at the end of that hour his brother had been convinced, and together they went into the drawing room to talk to their mother.

Signora Sophia Satta was seventy-four years of age and had a mind that would have turned Machiavelli dark green with envy. It had been rumoured that just before the war Mussolini had made a pass at her during a state reception. She was a tall woman. She had patted his bald head and then reached down and, through his immaculately tailored uniform trousers, had felt his genitals, smiled and said, 'You are presumptuous both above and below the waist.'

The result was that the Satta family had spent the war in their country estate, rarely venturing to Rome.

She looked at her two sons as they sat opposite her. She tried to keep the affection and pride from her eyes. She had always castigated them for their choice of professions; but to her intimates she had always confided her pleasure.

Of course they knew this. But Colonel Mario Satta was worried that she would not believe or react to what he was about to tell her. In dealing with other people of the world he was seldom wrong, but in dealing with his mother he often made misjudgements.

She listened in total silence, glancing occasionally at her elder son, Giovanni. Mario's briefing took more than half an hour. At the end of it she merely nodded and said, 'I have to tell you that it is no secret to me that Emilio Gandolfo had been a puppet of everybody since the day he emerged from his mother's womb. I have to tell you that many of the people you mentioned were also born to be puppets. Your father died young, but the reason he attracted me and persuaded me to marry him was that he could never had been anybody's puppet.' She smiled fondly. 'Not even mine.'

Her sons smiled.

Giovanni said, 'Mama, I only vaguely remember our father. But one thing I do remember is that he never raised his voice to you.'

'He had other and better ways,' she said briskly. 'Now tell me, in all this terrible mess, what this old woman can do.'

Mario leaned forward and said, 'On Sunday night there is to be a black mass in the private chapel of the De Muros' villa. The black mass is to initiate Pino Calveccio into the ways of the devil. The mass is to be conducted by Bishop Caprese. Let me explain.'

His mother raised a hand.

'You do not have to explain. Pino Calveccio inherited a vast fortune from his corrupt father three years ago. During those three years he has tried everything from under-aged girls to drugs. Surely the bottom of his personal pit must be Satanism ... Bishop Caprese has been a degenerate since long before he took the cloth. His father was also a degenerate. You cannot surprise me with such information. What do you want me to do?'

'It is simple,' Mario said, 'but a little dangerous.'

She lifted her head and laughed.

'My boy, at my age, danger is almost as exciting as a perfect aphrodisiac ... What do you want of me?'

Mario glanced at his brother, who was looking slightly shocked. He looked back at his mother and said, 'I learned from Gandolfo the procedures at such events. The congregation will meet in the De Muro villa at approximately eleven p.m. Drinks and canapés will be served. At about half past eleven they will change into their robes. They will then proceed the three hundred metres to the private chapel in the grounds for the black mass. "The Blue Ring" will have a guard circling the grounds.' He paused for thought and then said, 'You have heard me talk before of my friend Creasy?'

She nodded. 'I have indeed ... He is a man I would like to meet. He is a man I would like to have met thirty years ago.'

Both sons smiled. Their father had died thirty-one years earlier.

Mario went on, 'You understand why I cannot possibly mount a *carabinieri* operation against that mass or those involved.'

'I understand perfectly,' she said. 'I assume your friend Creasy is going to do just that.'

Mario nodded. 'He has a very powerful team. What's more, his adopted son Michael has infiltrated "The Blue Ring" and will be attending the mass. Naturally, anyone entering the De Muro villa that night will be carefully searched. It is vital that when Michael moves from the villa to the chapel, he should be armed and carrying a tiny radio transmitter. Now let me tell you . . .'

His mother held up a hand.

'No, Mario, let me tell you. You want me to plant that weapon and a transmitter in the De Muro villa . . . No problem.'

Giovanni laughed.

'Mama, it's dangerous. Listen to Mario's plan.'

She smiled and shook her head.

'If I'm going to do it I will follow my own plan. There is no difficulty in my entering the De Muro villa. I will pass by tomorrow afternoon. Although they have a name, and a faded reputation, they will be honoured at my calling by. I will be welcomed for a coffee and a drink. I will bring some gossip to titillate their tiny minds. In spite of their family history they have become very provincial in the last hundred years or so.' She smiled again and winked. 'A visit from Sophia Satta would be far more important in their social calendar than a mere black mass.' She closed her eyes in thought. 'I'm trying to remember the layout of the villa. It has been some years since I was there. I recall that there is a dressing-room to the right of the main entrance. I presume that the congregation will change their clothes there.'

Mario Satta got her drift immediately. 'You will conceal the weapon and the transmitter in there.'

She gave him the kind of motherly look which conveyed the message, I hope one day you'll grow up. Then smiled to take away the sting and said, 'Mario, you will give me two guns and two transmitters. I will conceal them in two different locations, including the dressing-room. That gives Creasy's son two chances. I'll phone you tomorrow night and tell you the locations.'

Very quietly Mario Satta said, 'I'm grateful, Mama,' and started to rise.

She shook her head irritably. 'Sit down and listen to me, Mario, and you too, Giovanni. Do not give me this task and then forget me. What you learned from the *puta* Gandolfo is only part of it. You see me as an old woman, but I hear more and see more than you can imagine. When you go into that cess-pit it is only the beginning. Powerful people will try to cover up everything. Use my knowledge and my contacts. Which investigating judge will you use?'

Mario told her, and she nodded in satisfaction.

'He is honest and determined. His father died in the hands of the Mafia, his grandfather died at the hands of Mussolini. You chose well.' She leaned forward and her small bright eyes twinkled and she said, 'There are some things I command you to do.'

Again Mario glanced at his brother, who simply shrugged and smiled.

'What are they?' Mario asked.

'When all this is over, I wish to meet this friend of yours, Creasy. When you next talk to him you must give him an order from me ... When he enters that private chapel he should leave at least one of the senior members of "The Blue Ring" very much alive ... although perhaps wounded. That man will be the opener for you and your judge to open the can of filth.' Her voice hardened. 'The first thing Creasy or his son must do in that chapel is to kill the Bishop.'

'Why?' Mario asked.

Her voice carried an edge of exasperation. 'Learn, my son. Whatever you do, try to avoid embarrassing those you will need ... The Vatican.'

NINETY

The argument was heated, but there could only be one outcome. The team was moving out from the Pensione Splendide on its way to Rome. Maxie and Frank were travelling in one car. Jens was going with The Owl in the BMW. Creasy was following alone in the third car.

The first two cars had left; all the men embracing Guido, Pietro and Juliet, and giving them the ritualistic kiss. Guido had disappeared from the bar. Creasy gave Pietro a big hug and the kiss and then turned to Juliet.

He told her, 'As soon as it's over, Pietro will take you back to Gozo, to Laura and Paul. Michael and I will follow some days later.'

She clung on to him tightly and said, 'Don't worry about me. I will not be stupid again.'

He looked around for Guido, but when his friend appeared through the door, Creasy's face darkened. Guido was wearing faded old denim jeans, a denim shirt and a denim jacket. In his left hand he carried a large canvas bag. Creasy recognised that bag. It was very worn. In years past, Guido had carried it around from one war to another. Creasy firmly shook his head. 'No, Guido ... You made a promise.'

Guido also shook his head.

'You knew Julia and you know how she would feel now.' He looked down at the bag and said, 'My old SMG is in there ... Of course it's not the newest or even the most fashionable, but there's no time to familiarise myself with new weapons.'

Again Creasy said, 'No, Guido. I already have a good team.'

The Italian shook his head.

'Good but not perfect ... Now you have the perfect team.' He dropped the bag and turned to Pietro and gave him a hug and the kiss. 'Look after Juliet. You know where the money is. Tomorrow

310

night move into a suite on the top floor of the Regina Hotel. It's already booked. Take your gun with you and do not move from that suite until you hear from me.' He hugged Juliet and gave her a kiss, smiled and said, 'Don't worry, little one. Guido will look after your father and your brother.'

Juliet clung on to him. Over her head Guido looked at Creasy and said simply, 'I am an Italian.'

NINETY-ONE

They all looked up expectantly as Creasy walked into the lounge of the safe house in Rome. Their expressions changed to surprise as they saw Guido following him in, carrying his canvas bag.

Creasy said, 'We have another active member on the team.'

There was a shocked silence. And then Maxie and Frank grinned broadly as they stood up.

'Bloody bonzer!' Frank said. 'We were just going through the layout, and I pointed out that some real insurance would be a machine-gunner on the small hill to the east of the chapel.'

He turned to look at Maxie who said, 'The best in the world. I just stopped worrying about my back.'

Satta was looking at Guido. The look carried both a welcome and compassion. The look also carried a query. Guido gave him the same answer as he had given Creasy.

'I am an Italian.'

Satta moved forward, and the two Italians embraced.

It was the final planning and briefing. Rene had slipped away from the luxury apartment near the Spanish Steps with the news that Michael was completely ready and in good form. With a smile he said, 'Although slightly tired from his recent exertions.'

They all sat at the round table and looked down at the scale drawing of the De Muro villa and its grounds and private chapel. The Dane had a yellow, lined notebook in front of him, its pages covered in his spidery handwriting. He set the scene: 'I have crystallised all the information we have, both from Gandolfo, other sources and, of course, from Colonel Satta's intrepid mother.' He consulted his notes. 'First of all, Colonel Satta informed me that the police pathologist's report on General Gandolfo shows without doubt that he died from a heart attack ... and so there is no reason to think that "The Blue Ring" suspects any danger to their black mass. Secondly, Colonel Satta's mother has planted two pistols and two transmitters in the De Muro villa.' He pointed with his chin at the Belgian. 'Rene has been informed as to their exact location and will pass that information on to Michael. They are, of course, only coded transmitters, and the signal from Michael to attack will be three dots and a long beep. From Gandolfo we know that there will be at least a dozen guards in and around the grounds. Colonel Satta and his team will be three kilometres away and can expect to reach the chapel within a few minutes after receiving our signal.' He looked up at Creasy, gestured expansively at the plan in front of him and said, 'It's all yours, Boss.'

Creasy stretched his frame and then sat down. He was finally in his element. Guido pulled up a chair and sat beside him. For more than a minute Creasy studied the detailed drawing. The villa was set in the hills about five kilometres from lago di Bolsena. The grounds were heavily wooded and undulating.

He said, 'We have Trilux night-sights which the guards will not have. We will split into two teams. One team will infiltrate the grounds first. That team will comprise Maxie, Frank and Rene. They will identify the location of the guards and relay that information back to the second team, which will comprise myself, Guido and The Owl. It is necessary that we attack only after the mass has started and when the participants are totally involved in it ... in fact, just before the sacrifice. Michael will send the signal, and as we arrive, he will shoot the Bishop. My team will enter the chapel while Maxie's team stays outside, mopping up the guards.' He turned to look at Jens. 'You will be waiting a kilometre away in a twelve-seater mini-van. We will time your arrival at the chapel about one minute before Colonel Satta arrives with his team. We will position four cars a further three to four kilometres away from the scene and transfer to them, leaving the mini-van at that place. We'll go in with flares and stun grenades. I want a minimum of small-arms fire in the chapel. What killing has to be done, apart from the Bishop, I'll do.' He looked up at Satta. 'That will include Donati and Hussein. I'll wound Delors but keep him alive for you. He's the one who'll do the talking.'

Satta nodded in agreement, then asked, 'What about the rest of the congregation?'

After a moment's thought, Creasy said, 'I'll kill the Initiate. I'll leave the rest for you to talk to.'

Satta said, 'That suits me fine.'

NINETY-TWO

The child Katrin was giggling. It was something she had been doing most of the time, when not sleeping. It had nothing to do with natural happiness, but everything to do with the pills her new foster parents had been giving her at regular intervals. She saw the beautiful house and their smiling faces through a happy haze. Perhaps, she thought, her mental state was similar to that of all children of her age, who had escaped from a nightmare.

On the Sunday afternoon, when her new mother had told her they were going for a car ride to visit some friends in the country, she giggled happily.

NINETY-THREE

The doorbell rang at nine-thirty in the evening.

Rene answered it. Gina Forelli swept into the room, handing him a long maroon cape, and saying, 'One of your wonderful bull-shots, please, Rene.'

Michael was watching a football match on television. He stood up and they embraced.

'I'm feeling pleased with you,' she announced.

'Why?'

'Because you are the real thing,' she answered brightly.

'What are you talking about?'

She moved to the TV and switched it off. She was wearing a dark blue woollen, ankle-length skirt and a high-necked, blood-red cashmere sweater. He doubted that she was wearing anything underneath. She turned to look at him, her head slightly on one side, and then said huskily, 'You have to understand, Adnan. A lot of phoneys come to Rome. Some of them have money, and some only have clever tricks to pretend that they have money. In order for me to take you to this event tonight, it was necessary that some very important people checked you out completely. Believe me, they are the kind of people who have the connections and power to do that.'

With a tone of irritation, Michael said, 'And you – and they – were surprised to discover that I was genuine?'

'Not surprised,' she answered, 'just gratified. Of course I had heard rumours that you had transferred ten million dollars into your account here with the Banco di Roma ... I now know from which bank in the Middle East you transferred the money. I even know the name of the bank manager who made the transfer. I also know that a place is waiting for you at Harvard University when you leave Rome. I even know the names of your future professors.'

Michael forced himself to look impressed. He said, 'So maybe this little game tonight is going to be serious. Maybe it's not just a load of bullshit to separate me from fifty thousand dollars.'

Very seriously, she shook her head.

'It is certainly no game, Adnan. What you see tonight ... what you will be part of, is something so rare that it will live in your brain forever ... Perhaps you will never be the same again.'

Rene appeared with her drink and looked enquiringly at Michael, who shook his head. Rene left the room.

Gina asked, 'You are not drinking tonight, Adnan?'

'Not yet ... I will save it for later.'

She smiled.

'Yes. There will be plenty later ... There will be everything to sate your body and your brain ... Everything.'

He looked at his watch. 'When do we leave?'

'In about ten minutes,' she answered. 'But there are two things you have to do first.'

'Like what?'

She put down her glass and answered. 'Give me half the fifty thousand dollars ... and then strip naked.'

'What the hell are you playing at?'

She laughed and came close to him and kissed him almost chastely on the mouth.

'I have to give you a thorough body search. It has to be like that ... It will be pleasant more than painful.'

He smiled wryly and said, 'Of course I have no objection ... As for the money: I will give you the other half tomorrow after the event.'

She nodded seriously and said, 'I trust you. That's a little dangerous for me, because it might mean I'm falling in love with you.'

He gave her a doubtful look, reached into his inside pocket and pulled out an envelope. He handed it to her saying, 'There's twenty-five one thousand dollar bills.'

She did not count the money. She folded the envelope, lifted her sweater and tucked it into the waistband of her skirt.

'Strip,' she said with a grin.

It was the most careful search Michael could have imagined. She had obviously been very well briefed by a professional. She examined every item of his clothes meticulously, checking the seams and waistband of his trousers and even the buttons of his jacket. She felt every inch of the fabric of his suit and shirt and underwear. She checked

316

his shoes from every angle, banging the heels against a table and listening for an echo.

Michael and Creasy had discussed the possibility of concealing a tiny transmitter on some part of his body or clothes. He was relieved that they had decided not to take the risk.

Next she examined his body, first peering into his open mouth and checking there were no new fillings. Then her fingers probed into his ears. Finally she asked him to open his legs and bend over and touch his toes. He did so, knowing what was coming. He felt her finger enter his anus and probe around. She kissed the centre of his spine and said, 'Adnan, you are clean in every way.'

She drove the car, a Mercedes which Michael had not seen before. A small, dark man sat in the back seat. She did not bother to introduce him. Michael realised that there would be a gun at his back the whole way.

As soon as they left the centre of Rome she turned to him and said, 'We must blindfold you from here. You understand, of course.'

'Of course,' Michael answered.

He heard the man move behind him and then felt the black silk scarf slip over his eyes.

NINETY-FOUR

The sliver of moon was obscured by clouds. They stopped under a clump of trees about a kilometre from the villa. They were dressed identically: all in black, with high, rubber-soled boots. Blackened canvas army webbing and pouches covered their torsos. Knitted black skull-caps covered their hair; their faces had also been blackened.

Apart from The Owl they were all familiar and comfortable. The Owl was the only one who had never served in a disciplined army, but he had dropped into it easily, even cracking a rare joke as they had kitted up at the safe house. Jens had just smeared black ointment on his cheeks, forehead and chin. The Dane had stood back and surveyed his friend. The Owl looked the complete combat soldier from head to toe. Grenades clipped to the webbing on his chest, a hand-gun holstered at his hip, a submachine-gun hanging from his right shoulder, and pouches full of spare magazines; a Trilux nightsight was slung around his neck. Jens had nodded in satisfaction, but The Owl had said plaintively, 'Creasy won't let me take my Discman and headphones.'

It had taken the Dane a few seconds to realise he had just heard a joke.

Under the trees they all squatted on their haunches. Creasy pointed to Maxie and then in the direction of the villa. Soundlessly, Maxie slipped away into the darkness. He had been the obvious choice to recce the villa and the grounds. For five years he had served in the elite Selous Scouts of the Rhodesian army and could glide past a rogue elephant at ten paces without a qualm. Creasy lifted the flap of his watch and checked the illuminated dial. It was ten-fifteen. They had decided to move into final position only at the last moment.

Maxie returned at ten forty-five. He slid in between Creasy and Guido and whispered, 'I counted seven guards: four static and three mobile. They're all carrying SMGs. There could be more on the other side of the villa. The perimeter wall is dry-stone and about eight feet high. No wire or alarms on it. I went within two hundred metres of the villa and the chapel. No trip-wires, no dogs. People are arriving – seven of them while I was watching; three men and four women. There are no lights on between the villa and the chapel, although I noticed unlit external lamps between them and over both doors. There's a light from inside the chapel showing through a high window. It's a red light, but that could be caused by stained glass.'

Creasy leaned forward and looked at Guido. He saw the Italian's white teeth as he whispered, 'I don't like not knowing what's on the other side of the villa.'

'Nor me,' Creasy answered. Again he looked at his watch.

'We'll split into our two teams and move forward in twenty minutes. We should be in position before they start moving from the villa to the chapel. That will give Maxie time to get around behind the villa and see what's there.' He tapped Maxie lightly on the shoulder. 'After that come back to my position and let me know. We then have about twenty minutes to make any necessary change of plan.'

Three kilometres away Colonel Mario Satta sat in his command vehicle in a clearing about two hundred metres off a narrow side-road. There were six other vehicles lined up alongside: three jeeps with hard tops, another car and two black armoured personnel carriers, each holding twelve men. His second-in-command, Captain Brisci, sat beside him, tapping his knee impatiently.

'Why don't we move now, Colonel?' he asked. 'We know that Giardini is already home and probably having dinner with his wife.'

Satta glanced at him. Hoping yet again that he was as honest as his reputation and also as clever, he explained, 'In such matters, Captain, I sometimes deviate from the normal. Now it's possible that our friend Giardini has compromising papers at home. If we ring the doorbell while he's having dinner, he or his wife or his children or anyone else in the house may have time to conceal or destroy those documents. I prefer to wait until they have all gone to bed and are fast asleep. Then we break down the doors and before he's even properly awake we'll be in his study.'

'How will we know he's asleep?' the Captain asked.

Satta sighed. Maybe the man was not so intelligent after all. 'We have people watching the house from every direction,' he explained. 'They report that the only lights on are downstairs. When the lights downstairs go off and the lights upstairs go on we'll be informed through the radio. When the lights upstairs go off we can assume that the family is about to go to sleep. Half an hour later we burst in.'

The Captain was not so stupid. 'What happens,' he asked, 'if one of the lights upstairs stays on late into the night? Maybe one of the family is an insomniac . . . reading a book or watching a porno video?'

Satta smiled. 'In that case we wait until two o'clock in the morning and then go in anyway.' He glanced at his watch and then felt in his uniform pocket for the small black box that Creasy had given him. It should send out its beep within the next hour, and then *Signor* Giardini, his wife and family could enjoy an undisturbed night's sleep.

NINETY-FIVE

She led him by the hand. For a few steps he could feel and hear the crunch of fine gravel beneath his shoes.

'Four steps,' she said, gripping his hand tightly.

He found the first step and the others were easy. He felt a warmth as they passed through an open door. He heard the door close behind him.

'You can take it off,' she said.

He pulled off the black silk blindfold and blinked into the light. They were standing in the hallway of what he knew was a large villa. There was a thick carpet beneath their feet, chandeliers above and old portraits on the walls. There was an open door ahead; sounds of voices came from it.

She took his hand again, leading him forward and saying, 'No names will be used.' Her voice dropped to a whisper. 'You will be surprised . . . shocked to see a genuine bishop here. He'll conduct the mass.'

Michael would not be surprised or shocked. That afternoon he had studied several photographs of Bishop Caprese. He would certainly recognise the black goatee beard, the bushy eyebrows and the curly black hair.

As they walked down the corridor he noticed the door on his left. That would be the men's dressing-room. There was a staircase on his right. He knew that it would go up to the bedroom and a further dressing-room. They entered the room ahead. There were a dozen people there with champagne glasses in their hands. They all turned to look at the arriving couple. There were seven men and five women. Some of them nodded to Gina. All of their eyes appraised Michael carefully.

An elderly butler approached with full champagne glasses on a silver tray. They each took one. Michael sipped and openly gave back the appraisal. He was indeed surprised to notice that Bishop Caprese was wearing the purple gowns of his rank. He was taller than Michael had expected. Michael looked into his eyes and the thought crossed his mind that around midnight he would be placing a bullet between them. He could not fail to recognise the black, slightly sweating face of Anwar Hussein standing next to the other recognisable face of Jean Lucca Donati.

The men were all dressed in sober suits; the women in long dresses or long skirts and blouses. Two of the women were in their twenties and very attractive; another two were about ten years older and also attractive. Three of them were just passing middle-age; one of those retained an obvious beauty, but the others could not be helped, even with the plentiful application of make-up. Apart from the Bishop, Hussein and Donati, Michael did not recognise any of the women or the other two men, who were middle-aged and overweight.

He looked around him and said to Gina, 'It's a beautiful room, in what must be a beautiful house. Are the owners present?'

She smiled and shook her head.

'They go away for the weekends on such occasions.'

She took his hand and led him over to the Bishop saying, 'You just shake hands and make pleasant conversation. Ask no direct questions. In about twenty minutes we'll change and go to the chapel.'

He shook hands with the Bishop and again commented on the beautiful room. The Bishop nodded and pointed to a large landscape on the wall nearby.

'Not a Caravaggio,' he said with a smile, 'but very worthy all the same, and dating back a hundred years earlier.' The Bishop gave Gina a conspiratorial look and, dropping his voice a decibel, said, 'What a pleasure to see you again, my dear. Your beauty adds so much to these rare occasions.' He gestured at Michael. 'And your young companion also adds lustre to our gathering.'

Michael felt his skin creep as he recalled the description of what would normally happen after the mass; the orgy would be bisexual. He shook hands with the others. Donati's handshake was limp, but Hussein's grip was like a vice. Canapés were served by the butler. Michael looked about him and decided that he might well be at any boring cocktail party. He only focused on what was coming when Hussein loomed up beside him, took him by the elbow, and suggested they go and change. They all moved out of the room into the hall. The women turned left up the stairs. Gina gave him a reassuring look.

The men moved down the corridor and went through the door on the right. It was a very large room with damask walls, and furnished with brocade-covered settees. Half a dozen long black cowled robes with tasselled belts were laid out on one of the settees. On the floor was an assortment of black sandals. Michael looked across the room and with relief saw the two doors described to him by Rene. He knew that they were both bathrooms, and that he had to get into the right-hand one.

Without ceremony Donati and Hussein started taking off their clothes. The others followed. Michael knew that he had to go into the bathroom after he had put on his robe. Donati and Hussein stripped naked. Donati had a paunch, but Hussein's black body was rock hard. Hussein picked up one of the robes and held it up to Michael's shoulders.

'It will make a good fit,' he said with a smile. He bunched up the hem in both hands and lifted the gown over Michael's head. It fluttered down to the floor.

'It is a good fit,' Michael said with a smile. 'My tailor would approve.'

'Who is your tailor?' Donati asked.

Michael gave him a level look and answered, 'I was told not to ask, or answer, direct questions.'

Both Donati and Hussein nodded in approval. Michael realised that he had just passed a test. He found a pair of sandals that looked the right size, sat down and buckled them on.

As he rose he said, 'I must visit the bathroom ... I don't suppose there's one in the chapel.' With a smile at Hussein he remarked, 'I must confess to being slightly nervous.'

Hussein smiled back and gestured towards the two doors.

A catastrophe almost happened. One of the other men who was completely naked was also heading for the doors. Michael hurried after him and said, 'Which is which?'

The man shrugged and said, 'Since we're all men either one will do.'

Michael quickened his pace and arrived at the right-hand door. Inside was one of the largest bathrooms he had ever seen. A huge enamelled bath stood on four legs alongside one wall, an equally huge wash basin beside it. At the end was a toilet and next to it a bidet. On the right was the piece of furniture that Michael was praying he would see. A very tall white wardrobe, inlaid with a swirling, gold-leaf pattern. He wondered how Satta's elderly mother

323

had reached that high. Then he saw the flimsy chair standing beside it against the wall. He quickly pulled the chair out and stood on it. An ominous creak came from below his feet. He moved them to the outside of the chair, reached up his hand and felt along the top of the wardrobe. He literally sighed with relief when he felt the hard metal. He pulled down the gun and the two-inch-thick rubber bands and the small black metal box which housed the transmitter. Within ten seconds the rubber bands were around his waist, firmly holding the Colt 1911 and the transmitter in place. With another sigh Michael moved to the toilet and relieved himself.

NINETY-SIX

Creasy watched through his night-glasses; they turned the figures a dim yellow, making the procession even more obscenely evil. From their gait he could tell that the women led the way, dark and hooded. The men followed. With their cowls up he could not identify Michael, but suddenly he saw one of them at the back move an arm to the waist of his gown. Two seconds later the little black box in the canvas pouch at Creasy's waist beeped softly twice.

Guido was lying alongside him, also watching through his night-glasses. He gently thumped Creasy's shoulder and whispered, 'That brat of yours is armed and in communication.'

Creasy grunted and whispered back, 'My mood has improved by a thousand per cent. If we had to go in there cold, Michael would have been their first suspect. We have no idea if any of them are armed, but if so at least Michael has a fighting chance.'

He aimed his night-glasses at the rear corner of the villa. He was looking for Maxie who had been checking out the other side of the building. He saw nothing. He turned to look at Guido and, beyond him, The Owl. They both had their glasses trained in the same direction. They were about three hundred metres away.

'Do you see him?' Creasy whispered.

The Owl grunted back and said in his Marseille-accented French, 'I swear on the grave of my mother that nobody's come round that corner for the last ten minutes.'

Guido's voice held a trace of anxiety. 'I hope Maxie didn't walk into something unexpected.'

Creasy was about to say some reassuring words when a dull thud sounded beside him. It was Maxie, down on his stomach and breathing just a little heavily.

He said, 'Just one static guard, asleep on a stool in the doorway of the garage. I could have cut his throat.'

The Owl inched forward on his elbows and whispered across Guido and Creasy, 'Which way did you come back, Maxie?'

'The same way I went in,' Maxie answered. 'Around that corner.'

'Bullshit!' the Frenchman whispered. 'I had my glasses on that corner all the time. I never saw you go in and I never saw you come out.'

Creasy heard Maxie chuckle and then whisper to The Owl, 'Listen, pussy-cat, I could have come back here and taken off your trousers without you feeling a thing.'

'Enough,' Creasy whispered. 'That guard will be wide awake as soon as the first shot's fired. How will you cover him?'

Maxie chuckled again. 'I won't have to. I left him the old wake-up call.'

Creasy and Guido laughed softly. The Owl did not understand.

Guido explained, 'Maxie rigged up a frag. grenade. I guess about two feet in front of the guy. He would have pulled out the pin, let the lever click twice and tied it down with a string and a slip knot, and then looped the string round the guy's leg. When the bastard wakes up, and stands up, the slip knot unravels, the lever clicks one more time and we have one less guard to worry about.'

The Frenchman had only one word in his vocabulary. '*Merde!*'

'He won't have time for that,' Creasy said. He was watching the chapel through his glasses. The congregation had all gone inside. He turned to Maxie. 'Time to get back to your team. We know there's a back door to the chapel, leading into an ante-room. When we hit the place that back door has to be covered.'

'Rene will cover it,' Maxie said. 'Frank and myself will be stalking the mobile guards. The static guards are exactly that. There'll be so much confusion they'll remain static for at least ten seconds. We'll have time to get back to them.'

Creasy reassessed the deployment of his men. He stretched forward and said to The Owl, 'Go with Maxie.' He turned back to Maxie. 'Have him in a position to take out two of the statics; then it's a one on one situation for you and Frank. Guido and I will hit the chapel.'

Guido said, 'That means there's no one up here covering their backs.'

Before Creasy could answer Maxie intervened. 'There's no need,' he said. 'I've done a complete perimeter of the grounds. There's no one going to be shooting at us from behind ... not unless any of those guards get loose, and that's not likely.'

Guido nodded and studied the chapel again through his glasses. He turned to Creasy and whispered, 'It looks good ... So now we wait for Michael.'

'We do,' Creasy answered. 'I guess it takes about twenty minutes.'

Maxie slid away behind them, tapped The Owl on the shoulder and whispered, 'Follow me real close ... I don't want to lose you.'

NINETY-SEVEN

Gina Forelli glanced across the aisle at Michael's face. Light and shadow flickered across it from the candlelight. It was as though his face had been cast from iron. She assumed his rigidity came from fear or shock. She was wrong. His face was cast from a white-hot rage. He was looking at the centrepiece of the mass, an altar covered with a black silk cloth. On it lay the body of a supine child. Her long blonde hair had been beautifully braided to curl back over her ears. Her eyes were closed. Her perfectly shaped white body was strapped to the altar by black silk cords from her wrists and ankles.

At first he thought that he was looking at a corpse, but then he saw her small breasts rising and falling gently to the rhythm of her breath. Close to her head was an upright, golden knife with its tip impaled into a black block of cork. Long, flickering black candles were arranged in a semi-circle behind her. Bishop Caprese was standing on the far side of the altar. He had discarded his purple gown for a black robe. Above his beard, his mouth was set in a straight rigid line. Above his head, hanging from an unseen thread, was an inverted, black cross. On each side of the altar stood a black-gowned man and woman, whom Michael had not seen in the villa. He assumed that they were the spurious foster parents. On his knees in front of the altar was the Initiate.

Michael glanced around him and realised the skill of the organisation. The mood had been perfectly created. From hidden loudspeakers high up on the walls a Gregorian chant floated down, deep and rhythmic and hypnotic. There was incense in the air, no doubt wafted through the chapel from hidden fans. No film director could have surpassed the mood of that moment.

The thin line of the Bishop's mouth moved. In a strong baritone voice, he recited the Lord's Prayer backwards. The congregation chanted in unison.

Michael turned and looked behind him. At the back of the chapel was a long table, covered by a black cloth and laden with bowls of food. Fruit, almost overripe; huge mounds of grey caviar nestling in beds of ice; undercooked joints of ham, beef, lamb and game. Surrounding it all was a ring of jugs containing heavy red wine. There were no knives or forks or plates. Michael knew that after the sacrifice the frenzied congregation would strip naked and gorge themselves, using only their hands, letting the juices and blood run over their bodies ... before they mixed those bodies with each other.

To the left of the altar were three men. He recognised Donati and Hussein. He also recognised the third man from Rene's description passed on by Satta, which had been passed on by Gandolfo. The face under the cowl was dark, and the deep eyes were darker. He knew he was looking at Gamel Houdris, the supreme leader of 'The Blue Ring'. He saw the dark eyes looking back at him.

Abruptly Michael realised that this was not going to be a long ceremony. There was no need for minor animal sacrifices to wind up the anticipation of this congregation. He glanced around and was able to see some of their faces, dripping with sweat in the cool air, mouths slack, and eyes already half-glazed. Days, maybe weeks, of anticipation had turned them into starving animals whose gluttony for evil craved to be sated.

Again the Bishop was speaking and gesturing at the Initiate, and then gesturing at the poised knife. Michael could not understand the words but knew they were in Latin. At the same time he realised that he might have waited too long.

At once he discarded the carefully timed plan. He reached to his waist and felt the outline of the tiny transmitter. He pressed the button and sent out the code: three quick bleeps and one long one. The Initiate had risen to his feet. He stepped up in front of the altar and stood looking down at the naked child.

Michael's mind was ice-cold. It flicked along like a computer. He could almost see what was happening in the darkness outside: Creasy's team moving swiftly towards the chapel, Maxie's team moving to take out the guards, Jens revving the engine of the van a kilometre away, Satta hearing the beeps from his own receiver three kilometres away and ordering his men to move.

The Initiate had reached for the knife. He plucked it from the cork and with both hands held it high above the child's heart. The Bishop was intoning a prayer in Latin, no doubt backwards. His eyes were also fixed on the child's breasts. Michael glanced around at the congregation. All their eyes were transfixed on the altar. With his left hand he pulled up the hem of his gown past his knees and to his waist. With his right hand he reached across and pulled out the heavy Colt. The Initiate raised the golden knife higher.

Michael shot him in the back of the head. The unsilenced explosion echoed around the chapel. The Initiate was hammered forward over the child's body. Blood and brains sprayed the face of the black-clad bishop. Michael fired two shots into that face. Both hit the open mouth. Then there was confusion, screams. Michael twisted away from his pew and ran down the aisle to the back. He turned at the table and shouted in Italian the words he had practised.

'Stand still! Who moves dies.'

The teams had moved the instant that Michael's signal came over the airwaves. Maxie was only ten metres away from one of the mobile guards. A one-second burst from his SMG spun the man around and dropped him. Another mobile guard twenty metres away was shouting in panic. A two-second burst cut him down. In a blur of motion Maxie changed the magazine and ran in the direction of one of the static guards. Two hundred metres away Frank also opened fire with his SMG. He was in a fortunate position. The other two mobile guards had been lax; they had stopped for a whispered chat and the drag of a shielded and shared cigarette thirty metres from his crouched position. It was not shielded enough. He got them both with a full burst. Like Maxie, his magazine change was a work of high-speed art. He also turned towards the villa and his targeted static guard.

From the back of the villa they heard the *crump* of a grenade. That static guard had just heard his wake-up and goodbye call. Neither Maxie nor Frank had time to take care of the other static guards. The Owl did that. They heard three short bursts from his SMG, a single scream and then another burst.

Maxie crouched and looked at the chapel. The red light from the high window suddenly turned bright white. He knew that Creasy and Guido were inside. He ran towards the back of the chapel.

NINETY-EIGHT

Only Gamel Houdris got away. He combined the survival instincts of a snake, a fox and a hungry shark. When the front door of the chapel crashed open and the first flares blinded the room, he pulled his cowl further over his head and screamed at Donati and Hussein. 'The back door! Get to the back door!'

They could not see, but he pushed them towards it. Behind him he heard Delors scream in agony as a bullet smashed into his right knee. Once behind and below the altar their eyes functioned again. Donati opened the door and ran out, followed by Hussein. Houdris paused, watching and waiting. They had not gone five metres before Rene cut them down. Hussein did not die immediately. He scrambled to his feet, clutching his torn belly, and with the rage of a wounded bull charged his attacker. Another burst from Rene's SMG slammed him back and down. Houdris heard the click of the magazine being changed. In a crouch, he ran into the darkness and towards the distant trees.

From behind him he heard the stutter of the SMG. He threw himself to the ground. A bullet plucked at his robe and seared the skin at his waist. He rolled and kept rolling until he crashed into some low bushes. Bullets whiplashed over his head. He crawled into the trees. Minutes later he dragged himself to the top of the dry-stone wall. He looked back towards the villa and the chapel. External lights had come on now. He saw a black mini-van pull up and black-clad, armed men jumping into it, then he heard the scream of its tyres as the engine revved and it pulled away.

He waited, considering his options. He was dressed in the black robe and nothing else. Obviously the black-clad men had not been the law. He saw some of the congregation coming out of the chapel, walking around like zombies. He considered going back down but rapidly changed his mind as the headlights of several vehicles swept into view. He saw the two cars, the three jeeps and the two armoured personnel carriers. He saw the uniformed *carabinieri* spew out of the vehicles. He turned and jumped from the wall.

A westerly wind had blown away the clouds, and the thin curve of the moon cast little light onto the clearing in front of him. A black-clad man was standing there, five metres away. A man with a square, scarred face, cradling a submachine-gun.

Houdris leaned back against the stone wall. He recognised the man who had burst into the chapel and thrown the flares. The man moved slowly forward until he was standing a metre away. His voice was deep and carried a trace of an American accent.

'You die tonight. You can die making a joke with your past. You would not have died for the evil you have done tonight or the evil you have done these past twenty years. You die for the evil you did to a woman in Malta twenty years ago. You die for a woman who sat so often on a dry-stone wall to catch a glimpse of her son, whom you fathered and discarded.'

The mind of Gamel Houdris was trying to understand the words when the man tossed aside the submachine-gun, reached out with his square hands and slowly strangled the supreme leader of 'The Blue Ring'.

EPILOGUE

The girls had long gone home. Blondie was in her over-furnished suite of rooms, putting the last of her curlers into her hair. The doorbell rang. She cursed eloquently in three languages, glanced at her watch and went to her door. As she opened it she heard Raoul moving down the corridor. He was also cursing quietly. Whatever over-sexed drunk had arrived at four in the morning would get short shrift from him.

She stood on the upper landing and listened as Raoul opened the front door. She dimly heard voices. Raoul's voice was not angry. She put on her flowered nightdress and went down the stairs. The voices were now coming from the kitchen. Creasy was sitting at the kitchen table. In all her years she had never seen his eyes so tired. His whole body seemed bloodshot.

'Michael?' she asked.

'He's OK.'

'Go to bed, then. Tell me in the morning.'

He sighed and pushed himself wearily to his feet, managed to smile at her and said, 'Will you join me for breakfast?'

She smiled.

'I will prepare your breakfast and join you.'

It was like the old times. He looked down at his plate: six rashers of bacon, four fried eggs, hash brown potatoes, grilled tomatoes and grilled kidney.

He cleared the plate, drank two cups of coffee, looked at her and said, 'You want it from the beginning?'

'Of course.'

It took him the best part of an hour. She knew some of it, but only the early part. He took her through the entire story of 'The Blue

333

Ring', without a single interruption.

When he had finished she said, 'Of course I have read in the papers about that final black mass. It has titillated the whole of Europe. I was angry that it took you two weeks before you came to tell me all about it.' She began to ask her questions. 'How is Satta progressing?'

He lifted his head and said with a tired smile, 'Colonel Satta will soon be promoted to General Satta. It will not compensate for the permanent pain he feels for Bellu, but he has much to keep him occupied. He is cutting a swathe through entrenched Italian corruption. He has a new assistant called Captain Brisci. I hope in a way that it's like losing an old and faithful dog: the best therapy is to get a new puppy. Meanwhile Satta is closing in on Benito Massaro. That will be something to watch.'

'What about the child on the altar?'

Creasy sighed contentedly.

'Satta's mother, the venerable Sophia, has taken an interest. Her elder son Giovanni has been married for ten years and has yet to produce a child.' He shrugged. 'I think his mama will arrange something.'

Blondie nodded firmly, as though such an event was both practical and correct. 'I know Maxie has been home these ten days, but that's all I know.'

'Maxie is fine and well. I got slightly drunk with him in his bistro last night. But he cannot solve my problem, which is why I came to see you.'

With a wave of her arm she brushed that aside. 'What about Frank and Rene?'

'They're on holiday in Gozo, staying at my house and being spoiled rotten by Juliet. She has turned them into a couple of maudlin pussy-cats.'

'What about the Dane and The Owl?'

A twinkle came into Creasy's eye.

'They're in Copenhagen. Jens resigned from the police force. They've opened a private detective agency specialising in missing persons.'

She smiled.

'I like that policeman ... that ex-policeman. Tell him he's always welcome here, and his friend The Owl.'

'I will.'

'What about Michael?'

Creasy took a sip of his coffee and said, 'That's my problem.'

'You deserve a problem,' Blondie said severely. 'What is it?'

Creasy sighed.

'I strangled the man, Gamel Houdris. Michael does not know that Houdris was his natural father. My problem is that I do not know whether to tell him.'

Blondie shrugged dismissively.

'What's the difference? He must have hated the man anyway.'

'I would have thought so,' Creasy answered quietly. 'But I assumed that he hated his natural mother. I was wrong ... I almost lost Michael.'

The old woman patted her curled hair into place. It was a gesture she always employed while thinking deeply. 'Where's Michael now?' she asked.

'Not far from here. He's across the border in Germany, at a place called Wiesbaden.'

'Doing what?'

Creasy looked up from his mug and said flatly, 'Killing Juliet's stepfather.'

Blondie rolled her eyes to the ceiling and muttered, 'What a pair you are.' Her face became very serious. 'Creasy, I understand you and I understand Michael, who is your creation. I've lived a long time and seen much of life and death ... I worry that for you and Michael death has lost its real meaning ... I worry that you and Michael dispense death like a poker player deals cards.'

Creasy looked up at her and shook his head.

'Blondie, don't judge me and don't judge Michael. We react to what people do to us and to those we love.'

She sighed.

'Creasy, the trouble is I understand you, and I know what drives you, and I know what drives Michael ... But it doesn't make me sleep easy. I would wish to see a softer side to both of you.'

Creasy shrugged.

'Maybe one day we'll both find that softer side. I thought Michael would be here. He was supposed to do the job a couple of days ago.'

'You've heard nothing?' she asked.

He shook his head.

'I offered to go with him, but he wanted to do it alone.'

The doorbell rang. Two minutes later Michael came into the kitchen, looking troubled. He hugged Blondie and kissed her on both cheeks, then sat down opposite Creasy. Blondie moved to the stove and started cooking Michael a breakfast.

335

The young man looked across the table and said, 'I sort of fucked up.'

'Tell me.'

Michael was obviously embarrassed. 'I got a bomb from Corkscrew Two. I wired it up under the bastard's new BMW and sat three hundred metres away with the remote control. I sat there, relishing the moment when I would hit the button. I sat there thinking of Juliet and what that bastard had done to her. I thought about that bitch of her mother standing by and doing nothing. I thought of that BMW going up in a blinding flash.'

'So?'

Michael sat back in his chair, looked at the ceiling and said, 'I couldn't do it.'

'Why not?'

The young man leaned forward, cupped his face in his hands, looked at his adoptive father and said, 'While I sat there with that remote control in my hand I had this feeling that we had killed enough people lately. I found that vengeance had become a very cold meal.'

Creasy also leaned forward and said, 'I've heard that somewhere before. So you didn't press the button.'

Michael smiled. 'Oh, sure. I blew up that nice new BMW with no one in it. He'll have a hard time explaining that to the insurance company.'

They both laughed. Blondie watched them from the stove. She watched the laughter leave their faces.

She heard Creasy say very quietly, 'Michael . . . you know I strangled Gamel Houdris.'

'Of course I know.'

'You don't know that Gamel Houdris was the man who forced the woman on the wall to forsake you . . . He was your natural father.'

'Are you sure?'

'Yes.'

Michael leaned back in his chair and again looked at the ceiling. His breath came out with one exultant word. 'Halleluja!'